SO-BIN-949

INTERNATIONAL

Felipe Alfau

CHROMOS

VINTAGE INTERNATIONAL
VINTAGE BOOKS
A DIVISION OF RANDOM HOUSE, INC.
NEW YORK

FIRST VINTAGE INTERNATIONAL EDITION, JUNE 1991

Copyright © 1990 by Felipe Alfau

All rights reserved under International and Pan-American
Copyright Conventions. Published in the United States by
Vintage Books, a division of Random House, Inc., New York,
and distributed in Canada by Random House of Canada Limited,
Toronto. Originally published in hardcover by
Dalkey Archive Press, Illinois, in 1990.

Library of Congress Cataloging-in-Publication Data
Alfau, Felipe. 1902–
Chromos / Felipe Alfau.—1st Vintage international ed.
p.   cm.—(Vintage international)
ISBN 0-679-73443-0 (pbk.)
I. Title.
PS3501.L45C47   1991
813'.52—dc20   90-55672
CIP

Manufactured in the United States of America
10 9 8 7 6 5 4 3 2 1

"Una ella de algo más vaca que carnero..."
—Cervantes

CHROMOS

The moment one learns English, complications set in. Try as one may, one cannot elude this conclusion, one must inevitably come back to it. This applies to all persons, including those born to the language and, at times, even more so to Latins, including Spaniards. It manifests itself in an awareness of implications and intricacies to which one had never given a thought; it afflicts one with that officiousness of philosophy which, having no business of its own, gets in everybody's way and, in the case of Latins, they lose that racial characteristic of taking things for granted and leaving them to their own devices without inquiring into causes, motives or ends, to meddle indiscreetly into reasons which are none of one's affair and to become not only self-conscious, but conscious of other things which never gave a damn for one's existence.

In the words of my friend Don Pedro, of whom more later, this could never happen to a Spaniard who speaks only Spanish. We are more direct but, according to him, when we enter the English-speaking world, we find the most elementary things questioned, growing in complexity without bounds; we experience, see or hear about problems which either did not exist for us or were disposed of in what he calls that brachistological fashion of which we are masters: nervous breakdowns, social equality, marital maladjustment and beholding Oedipus in an unfavorable light, friendships with those women intellectualoids whom Don Pedro

7

has baptized perfect examples of feminine putritude, psycho-neuroses, anal hallucinations, etc., leading one gently but forcibly from a happy world of reflexes of which one was never aware, to a world of analytical reasoning of which one is continuously aware, which closes in like a vise of missionary tenacity and culminates in such a collapse of the simple as questioning the meaning of meaning.

According to Don Pedro, a Spaniard speaking English is indeed a most incongruous phenomenon and the acquisition of this other language, far from increasing his understanding of life, if this were possible, only renders it hopelessly muddled and obscure. He finds himself encumbered with too much equipment for what had been, after all, a process as plain as living and while perhaps becoming glib and searching if oblique and indirect, in discussing culturesque fads and interrelated topics of doubtful value even in the English market, he gradually loses his capacity to see and think straight until he emerges with all other English-speaking persons in complete incapacity to understand the obvious. It is disconcerting.

Dr. de los Rios does not agree with Don Pedro and suggests that complications generally set in whenever one learns anything, but I want to believe that this argument is churlish, eclectic and inconvenient to the purpose of my reasoning.

Rather I am inclined to side with Don Pedro who, being among other things an authority on tauromachia and therefore often expressing himself in such terms, announces that de los Rios belongs to that very castizo class of Spaniards who always neu-tralize the charge of extremism with a philosophical veronica and whose lemma should be: to tame the enraged bull of radicalism with the cool cape of tolerance.

But perhaps here one should abandon such considerations to say something about these two individuals.

Dr. José de los Rios was an old friend. I had known him since Spain where he had gained good fame as a general physician. Then he had begun to specialize in things of the nerves and the mind; he published several technical books that were very suc-cessful outside Spain; he lectured in various countries and was at present one of the leading neurologists in the world. It was as such that he had come to this country where we had resumed a friendship which to me, considering his eminent position in the world of science, was a source of great pride and an honor as undeserved as unquestioned. Through him I had met Don Pedro here, but the two of them seemed to have known each other for centuries.

Don Pedro Guzman O'Moore Algoracid was his very full name, at once sonorous, lofty and unconvincing. The Guzman part very Castilian, the other requires no explanation for the English reader and the last starkly Moorish. Of somber countenance and attire, with Mephistophelian suggestions of a clowning Dracula flashing out of the night in a Spanish cloak he favored, weather permitting, he boasted of pure unadulterated Irish and Moorish blood and ancestry which, according to his genealogical chemistry, made him the most castizo Spaniard.

Due to an accident in his youth interpreted as the agent which had changed the course of his life, he enjoyed a marked limp, thus justifying his other prop and inseparable companion: a formidable walking stick with all the disquieting protuberances of a shillelagh. I understood in a general way that in Spain he had been a very promising musician and possibly that the accident had had something to do with his abandoning all serious thoughts of music, but what I knew was that at present he was the best-known Spanish bandleader in these parts, often referred to as the Emperor of Latin American music and the Svengali of Swing. In the rendering of tangos, conducted like all his music, through justifiable affectation, with his shillelagh, he was peerless and he played them all with such an exaggerated rhythm that, in his own words, they all sounded like someone sawing a heavy log.

With a liberal education proudly shared between the University of Dublin and Salamanca's Colegio de Nobles Irlandeses, his multiple personality was at present divided into two main hemispheres: one, that of an eccentric and temperamental bandleader intended for his well-paying public; the other, that of a character of recondite and esoteric accomplishments, reserved for his Spanish friends. A familiar figure in those sections of New York referred to for expediency's sake as Broadway and Harlem and the widely scattered Spanish quarters in the city, such as Cherry and Columbia streets, radio announcers, commentators and feature writers, with blissful disregard for Castilian dignity, had shortened his name to Pete Guz, which had stuck and as such he was known to the American public and there was nothing anyone could do about it, though Dr. de los Rios had cleverly amalgamated his name and personality into the nickname of the Moor and this is what most of his Spanish friends always called him, with the exception of some who, because of his biting comments, referred to him as Don Pedro el Cruel. He was changeable and he was complicated and, in his manner of speaking, it would have been interesting to trace the wanderings of this complex variable over the subconscious plane and evaluate the integral of his real conclusions. To me, he was an absurd combination of a slightly daffy Irish-Moorish Don Quixote with sinister overtones of Beelzebub and the only Irishman I ever heard speak English with an Andalusian brogue.

He laid what to me appeared ridiculous claims to his past, but for that matter he always spoke of everything in the most fantastic manner. He told of remarkable exploits of his ancestors in Ireland and often told of a grandfather who had returned to Spain from Africa with a monumentally archaic and rusty key to reopen the house of his ancestors in Granada only to find that the lock had since been changed, whence he climbed in through an open window, and he also referred to the year 1492 as that fateful dark day when Spain had committed its two greatest strategical errors: the expulsion of the Moors and the discovery of the Americas. In the beginning I had taken all this phantasmagoria with reservations mixed with that suspiciousness which most Spaniards feel for one another when they meet outside of Spain which makes us think that any Spaniard claiming to be so must be an imposter, particularly if he claims to come from Madrid, to the point that we never believe that anyone comes from there, as if it were an empty city or a place which no one can ever leave. It seems that to be from Spain is quite a claim, but to come from Madrid is unbelievable. I have been doubted so much that now I say that I am a Latin American and save myself a good deal of trouble.

This is something that we frequently do when abroad, so that one has the strange situation of two Spaniards posing before each other as Latin Americans and both being surprised at their accent and suspecting that after all the parents of both were gallegos. I think this is very foolish and take this opportunity to advise all my countrymen who read this to carry their passports with them at all times and thus squelch any doubts as to their nationality and if they come from Madrid, to run to the nearest consulate and there have the fact stated in bold type.

However, Dr. de los Rios's attitude gradually conquered my misgivings. He who had always impressed me with his affable skepticism listened to the Moor's tales without batting an eye and with a manner that tended to lend credence to them and I began to think that perhaps the Moor was a true living legend and not something on the other side of the footlights.

They were very different, these two men, and they represented two fundamental types of Spaniards. It has been said many times that Cervantes portrayed the two main types of Spaniards with Don Quixote and Sancho Panza, but speaking in the manner of de los Rios, one ventures to believe that this is somewhat specious because one can find two such main types in any other country and they really divide humanity into two classes, which fact possibly constitutes their greatness, but in the case of these two contemporary men, the division was part of the national history and structure. It was ethnological and racial within the same country, one showing the Visigoth and the other the Moorish influences.

Yet these two different men shared one national characteristic: neither one showed even remotely his real age. Although I do not think they would much mind, I will not divulge it but will content myself with our classical and noncommittal saying: they were younger than God. They belonged to a class common in our country which is ageless and eons of time can only succeed in mummifying. Dr. de los Rios had not changed physically since I first met him, except for a few white hairs lost in his blond mane, mustache and goatee. Spiritually is another thing. While I remember him many years ago in Spain alive with an adventuresome scientific outlook and eager for risky and modern experimentalism often fired into whimsicalities by a tremendous imagination and moral courage that easily overcame medical conventionalities and politics, he had settled—not materially, mind you, but morally—into a cold realism which under a mist of indifference was vaster and relentless as destiny in its heuristic approach to all problems. As for the Moor, I believe he had been born with the same thick iron gray hair which he wore cut very short and brushed forward like the schoolboys of my childhood, or like that of an anachronic bootblack who had just offered to polish our shoes and got a tip from de los Rios for not doing it.

We were in Bryant Park and Dr. de los Rios spoke of his inability to allow anyone to polish his shoes and Don Pedro instantly seized on the subject to elaborate and generalize. Typical of the two men was that the virtuous implication which in Dr. de los Rios had become the modest description of an individual case of personal failing, grew with the Moor to transcendental proportions of social and national attitudes surging into patriotic boastfulness embodied in himself, even if done with careful indirectness. No matter what he spoke about, and that was many things, he sounded as if he were talking of himself. It seemed as though his personality and viewpoint approached a subject, elbowed their way into its midst and then exploded in vociferous and violent altercation, dispersing everything to remain there alone, with nothing to say, the enemy ignominiously routed in a battle which it had never fought.

From this it was but a step to his favorite subject of assault: an obsession with the position of the Spaniard in the world, with more assurance in Spain and with more complications in foreign lands—all right, in this country. His bad foot resting lightly on the bench where de los Rios and I sat, his shillelagh hovered above us like the sword of Damocles and he spoke down on us in a way all his own. It was intimate and kidding and disconcerting and it bounced along on hypnotic expressions and necromantic gestures, presenting the obvious as an incantation, his sentences disconnected and frequently unfinished, bifurcating, darting from one thing to another, like a school of herringbones which have not stopped swimming and the whole interrupted almost rhythmically by a stroke of laughter with a rising inflection ending in a protracted cough. He held and shook before us like a marionette his straw man: the "Americaniard."

This, a word of his own composition, he had begun originally to employ when referring to Spaniards in the Americas and at one time might have included Latin Americans, but he had gradually varied the meaning until at present it applied to Spaniards in New York and then by association even to other foreigners, especially of Latin origin, in the same circumstances. It implied a certain attitude and behavior of the emigrant, incapable of standing up under the pressure of a majority, and referred more to physical and spiritual deportment than to a condition. Knowing the Moor as I imagined I did, I don't think that it was flattering.

"He is a queer bird, the Americaniard; yes sir, very queer— while adaptability was a natural virtue, he overdoes it to the point of being chameleonic, but the expert eye can detect—and what an ape— His health never suffered when he was at home, but the moment he learns a little English, he begins to consult the directory for physicians and psychoanalysts. You ought to know . . .," he addressed the placid Dr. de los Rios, ". . . yes, he is quick to seize upon all types of unheard-of ailments to use them as so many alibis for his traditional laziness which he imagines, naively enough, to be reprehensible in his new surroundings, wants to be a regular guy, and in the end finds himself prostrate in the recumbent company of the conquering majority. He is a beaten individual with delusions of mediocrity whose defeat has gone to his head and he has no match when playing the ingratiating role of repentant foreigner— He is unique, this Americaniard. He learns to be good-naturedly patronizing toward animals, minorities and foreigners in general, provided they are not his countrymen; speaks of cooperation, and dispensing advice freely to anyone who wants it or not fills him with overflowing well-being and kindly superiority. His childhood having been nursed with wine, he nevertheless learns to backslap and shake hands at the slightest alcoholic provocation. He becomes a freethinker and a liberal, but eats fish on Fridays served with the excuse that it is fresher, and he quotes the Bible. I tell you—the pharisee. Trying to run away from himself, he is always running into mirrors and endeavoring to make the best of his imagined prison. Doesn't know what it's all about—"

He concentrated on me: "You should write a book about the Americaniards, somebody should, but you have not written for a long time—anyway you could not write anymore about your people in Spain—have been too long away, forgotten too much—don't know what it's all about and you could not write about Americans—don't know enough—impossible ever to understand another people. I could not understand them when I first came and every day I understand them less. We meet, we talk, but neither knows what it's all about—total confusion. My English was abominable when I arrived and every day I speak it worse—impossible; can't understand a damn thing."

I have it on good authority that his English was perfect, but he had nursed an invincible accent and an unassailable syntax. He continued: "To write about the Americans would be presumptuously impolite and besides the competition would be formidable both in quality and quantity. . . ." He waved at the public library, the proximity of which probably had something to do with the turn of the conversation, or rather monologue: "Why, between all the publishers, they put out so much that they could pump that whole structure full every year from top to bottom—yes, that should be out of the question. . . ."

I was about to interpolate something but he slapped the intention in midair. "Now, about the Americaniards, that is different. You should be an authority on the subject by now."

Dr. de los Rios raised a restraining hand: "Leave this fellow alone, you infidel Moor. He wants no trouble and has been making an honest living for a long time as it is. Don't tempt him."

"Of course, to the rescue, Dr. Jesucristo"; this was his established rejoinder for the nickname of the Moor. "To save a soul from a minor intellectual crime," he addressed me, "snatch yourself away from the sanctimonious hands. Don't let him rob you of eternal condemnation and besides what indeed more shrewdly appropriate, more shamelessly opportunistic in these good old days of the Latinamericanization of the United States? In this age of good-neighbor policy, which began in the days of the tango and then fortified with daiquiris, rum and Coca-Cola and tequila, cavorted through the rumba, the conga, to wind up with the crying jag of the ay, ay, ay?" He sang it and took a few dancing steps despite his bad leg, oblivious of the perplexity of passersby and his stick pointed to the former Sixth Avenue. Then he became sober and his criticism of the Americas more pointed.

Feeling well-stocked with demagogic ammunition of irresistible clichés, I thought of mentioning the tactlessness of such comments coming from one who had been so successful, at least financially, in both continents through the frequent tours with his band and was almost ready to use even the one about if you don't like it here why don't you go back..., which even Dr. de los Rios had pronounced unanswerable, but well I knew what his disarming answer would be: "We Spaniards reserve the patriarchal privilege to criticize, advise and even scold, by the divine right of the discoverer, the conqueror, and having staked first claim in lofty defiance of the patented rights of the Vikings with their winged helmets and immodest, though ruggedly exposed knees, which we, fully clothed, dressed formally, Christianly and uncomfortably, decline to take seriously." Furthermore, I knew that he would blast me with his remarks on the Indian and his past and present distribution over the Americas; quoting the well-known saying that one example is worth one hundred arguments, he would deluge me with one hundred devastating examples and I, not well versed on the subject, could never find an adequate rebuttal. He had gained such confidence that the last time I fell into the argumentative trap he simply squirted through his teeth the three words "the American Indian" and I gave up.

Unhindered by my unspoken objections he went on with his paradoxical theory of a country accused of imperialism and being invaded by a pacific penetration to the tune of popular torrid music, twice imported Afro-Antillean tempos and tropical concoctions, a fanciful parallel on a soporific smoke screen of narcotics blown ahead over the Orient to gently overcome resistance and render it droolingly happy in its surrender—the devil's own lullaby. All strange, transoceanic parallels indeed to be used as tracks on which to launch his theory of the Latinamericanization of the United States.

But is this the new conquest of the Americas, by the Americas and for the Americas? This mutual transcontinental, translinguistic, transracial osmosis? If so, it is a far cry from the conquistadores to these frightened hybrids, from those who knocked down the door of a new world, to those who knock at the door of a richer world, and the majority of which are lost in a subterraneal labyrinth, like slaves in a mine, to trade their machete for a dishrag, or if more fortunate, though less radical, to transform and adjust their guitar and castanets asymptotically to the afrodisiacuban rattle of the maracas. It is a far, heartrending cry from those Spaniards to these Americaniards.

And yet the Latinamericanization of the United States may be but a special case of its internationalization, as Dr. José de los Rios points out when he remarks that it is an even longer cry from Alexander, Phidias or Archimedes, to a modern Greek running a small shop in some obscure corner of New York, or from the proverbial Asiatic splendor to one of these Chinese laundries. No modern liner has the dignity of the *Pinta*, the *Niña* or the *Santa María*, but neither does the bullet have the dignity of the arrow, nor the airplane the dignity of the eagle. And even so, I insist that the objection is temporizing and disregards the main issue by generalizing a secondary, common characteristic. Unquestionably there is sadness in the final surrender and dissolution of any nationality that has come to less, which are most. Witness the mummies and other relics resting in museums of lands other than those where they lived. But what makes the case of the Spaniard especially sad and poignant is the obvious historical associations. I feel that this case must be considered very specially and that it has undeniable priority because after all they were the discoverers of this new world. This is what makes the irony so blatant and leads one to think even more soberly and with more melancholy, that one could have begun all this by parodying a famous speech by a famous North American, something like this:

"Twenty-score and many years ago, my forefathers came to

the Americas . . .," but the rest would be very different and I invite the reader to collaborate, to frame in his mind and consider carefully what might follow; the motives and the ends; one springing from idealism, risking—and perhaps succumbing to—disillusionment: ". . . whether that nation or any nation so conceived and so dedicated, can long endure"—the other running from fate or destiny and doomed to bitter realization.

We were walking east and at the corner of the public library turned and began to walk down the avenue. The Moor changed the subject abruptly by the simple expedient of taking up the new one and suggesting with enthusiasm that we go atop the Empire State Building. He praised the building, the view from its top, spoke like a barker, mentioning that it owed its existence to a great politician whom he admired greatly and considered so castizo that he should have been born in Madrid. He said it would give me perspective to write what he had suggested: "You will see the Americaniards scurrying about below—and many others, yes sir, many others." He said it very confidentially as one imparting the secret of the ages.

Dr. de los Rios stopped short: "Let's not and stop importuning this fellow. First you frighten him with your ghosts of complications that beset us in an English-speaking environment and now . . .," he turned to me: "Don't sell your soul to this devil. There is still time. Don't follow him." He saw me weaken, waver, ready to succumb under the hypnotic spell of the Moor who stood there shamelessly making passes, exorcisms and incantations, right in front of the library, and then Dr. de los Rios was magnanimous: "All right; go and sin no more. But I will not sanction this with my presence. In fact, since we left that bench I have been debating whether to go in there and look up one or two things, which I have been intending to do for some time." He turned suddenly and went up the steps of the library with extraordinary lightness and agility.

No sooner was he gone than the dark sleeve of the Moor closed over my shoulders like the cloak of Satan, propelling me along to my doom, and he renewed his assault. I was endeavoring to think up objections and I knew there were plenty, but I was confused.

Vaguely I thought that the task he proposed was well beyond my ability, that to choose representative characters from the imposing array of what he called the Americaniards and to put them on paper was as much above my head and meager stock of diligence as the building toward which we were walking, but I'd swear that the sly Moor was reading my mind. The master promoter of intellectual pranks was in full command.

"Don't worry about that. You do not have to use new ones. Use any old ones you may have about. In fact, you must have smuggled some already without the immigration authorities being the wiser —on paper. Know what I mean?" He held me at arm's length without interrupting our syncopated walk, "And I know where we can find them and you too know the place." I was dizzy and was sure that I was walking in my sleep and dreaming. The monotonous beating of the bare end of his shillelagh against the pavement must have been instrumental in the hypnosis. "We will go back there, but after dark. First we go up and look and wait, and then when night falls, we go down back there. The prophecies say that your little smug intellectual crime must be thus perpetrated, without attenuating circumstances, thus it will be lower, more revolting, more dastardly and—more fascinating." So help me, he actually hissed the last words loudly, with bestial mockery.

Never a match for him, I was lost. Staggering drunkenly under my opprobrium, I blubbered hopelessly, inaudibly: "Haven't got a typewriter," but I knew that all resistance was useless and this last gesture as pitiful as trying to save oneself from a conflagration by spitting on it.

"I'll get you one, if I have to get your own out of hock—" and on he swept me.

Entering the elevator had a quality of sepulchral irrevocability, of being walled alive, of the catafalque, and I knew that I was at his mercy, in his mental grip and certain that he was thinking through me, but that he must have found me a very crude tool. The momentary increase in weight in this minimum of space equated the sensation of motion to zero, or compensated it by creating the feeling of moving in opposite directions simultaneously. All the time that we were going up, we were falling with constant acceleration and this made one think of the misleading and pitiful attempts at propagandizing relativity. Then the slight pressure in the ears brought anticipation reflecting in the future, childhood reminiscences of Verne, Wells and Flammarion and when finally one emerged, it was like coming out of a long anesthetic, with a gasp and a vertigo at the explosion of the view which reached dangerously near the confines of pleasure.

Don Pedro ambled about and took his position here and there, frowning his contemplation almost truculently and when he stopped, hunched, holding his stick in both hands, he looked like a bird of prey, perched, poised, ready to dive, but then he only waved his arm downward like a readying dark wing and pointed in silence. Thus we stood and looked, never uttering a word, and then night began to arch and close over us like a dome from the East.

Manhattan looked like a quarry. The conglomeration of buildings seemed to point, to call and appeal and crowd about this leader for guidance, their sharp outlines reaching vainly, and with nightfall the quarry was a mine shining with gold that increased in profusion and brightness and gradually overflowed and ran in rivers to the hazy horizons. Under the crescent moon glowing like the lamp of Aladdin, one could not help thinking of it as the gold mine which has lured and swallowed so many, and the buildings continued to call and appeal temptingly and dangerously, until nothing but the lights could be seen. Down on the prism of the sidewalks, they were diffused reflection of livid dancing polarization, the streets spectral bands. This was the light fantastic on the sidewalks of New York and as each star appeared above, it found its reflection below, until the city had become a multiplying mirror of the sky.

And at last, to wake up from the dream or sink further into it, his fateful words: "Time to go."

If the building had become a medieval castle and he had descended clinging to the outside walls . . . but we went down by way of the elevator with the sinking sensation that often startles and makes one jump in bed when falling asleep.

Everything was foreordained and all inevitable. The old but

well-kept Hispano-Suiza that slid to a stop before us, quietly, dark and foreboding like a hearse. The uncanny timing, everything suggested Satanism and witchcraft, the dragnet of Lucifer.

No doubt his Cuban boy was at the wheel as usual and this was one reassuring contact with friendly reality. He was a simpático fellow in perennial good humor and with a well-developed incapacity to take anything seriously. Probably well-trained in his native and tough school of voodoo and the evil eye, he was hardened by his association with the Moor and could keep his equanimity under the most trying circumstances. But I could only guess that he was there because the dividing curtain was drawn and we might as well have been driven by a ghost. I ventured to suggest meekly that the place might have been torn down, but the Moor answered in cryptic jest that we were returning to the past by the fourth perpendicular and I would find everything as I had left it. Nothing more was said and the drive across town and then down the West Side was swift and deliberate with all the ephemeral finality of a blackout.

One block from our destination we got out and before I had time to look into the driver's compartment, the car drove away. We walked along the dark street and I tried to lag behind, to find one last desperate excuse, but the Moor took hold of my arm and marched me until we were in front of the old basement. Then came the blinding flash of hope:

"But the key. I am sure I don't have it."

"Seek and thou shall find; haa—"

Inserting one's hand in one's pocket and finding it empty is conceded to create the deepest consternation, but this was worse; the key was there and I was crushed.

"But suppose that someone has moved in since."

"Don't worry. It is empty all right." And I knew that he was right, that he was master and this was destiny, that there was no escape: "Go and get it over with. It won't take long."

"Aren't you coming in?"

"No. I'll wait for you out here and act as a lookout." The shameless conspiracy of it, the insulting confabulatory implication: "But give me a cigarette. I am all out of them." The crowning insult.

I gave him the cigarette and lighted it for him endeavoring to postpone things—the nadir of abjection—but then the conviction that I was dreaming decided me to sleep the thing through to certain awakening and calmly I inserted a key which I had never expected to use again. As I did this, the last hopeful and irrelevant memory of the Moor's ancestor returning to Granada ran through my mind, but the door opened easily and swung inward without a squeak.

The street outside had been dark enough, but the room was pitch-black. I still held the matches in my hand and lit one. There was no furniture, and as I advanced toward the far wall, I felt my shadow creeping and growing behind me and bending with the ceiling as if to pounce.

Ever since I had entered the former neighborhood and as we approached this house, the tense anticipation had been growing at a rate suggesting the law of the inverse square which I had often heard Don Pedro mention, and on entering the room, it exploded with the full force of memories that were overpowering as the present multiplied by their distance.

I looked around carefully, keeping my vigilant shadow unmolested behind and above me, like a cobra. The stains and cracks on the walls became those of bare stone, creating confusing and bizarre designs like those of a sarcophagus. Some old calendar chromos still clung to them: one showing a man with calañes and short jacket serenading a young lady with high comb and very black, mournful eyes at a window with bars and profusely surrounded by flowers; another was a chapel with a recumbent bullfighter dying on a couch with a beshawled woman, her head buried in his bloody chest and all around the austere, stoic, classical countenances of the loyal members of his cuadrilla and a tearful old lady staring her reproach at the altar and the eternal old priest withholding discreetly his understanding and faith and soothing blessing, but attentive to the duties of his office in performing the last rites; chromos that had once been brilliantly bursting with color and drama, but were now faded and desecrated by fly stains; chromos in disrepute.

The bookcase with its books was still at the far wall, the only piece of furniture left in that room once abandoned in the great divide of life. I reached for one of the books, felt the thick dust on it and pulled. A cockroach crawled over my hand and I let go of the book. It fell on the floor where it lay open and I fancied I saw more bugs run out of it in all directions. They ran up the walls, over and under the chromos which in the uncertain light of the match seemed to oscillate painfully, to grow dolefully animated and gather the deceptive depth of a reverie, reaching for the cracks, the shadows in the walls as if to pull them like a shroud over their shame, to resume their disturbed sleep, and as the walls seemed to recede, the shadows running through them like waves, merged with the pictures to form a confused tapestry depicting people and scenes that came to life, but more like things remembered or imagined, because the walls were no longer there.

"You must let me tell you about this family in Spain," Garcia said. "It is like a novel and for that matter, I am making one of it. It could only have happened in Spain."

I thought that many people are always saying that a thing could only happen in a certain place. Why? and I told him so.

He said that I had not heard the story yet, but he had told me several times about this family. "Well, possibly I have, but superficially. I would like to tell you more in detail and discuss the novel I expect to make out of it with you. I have all the data which I obtained from several people, but mostly from my mother. She knew them very intimately. Are you doing anything this afternoon?"

I had seen this coming for some time and I thought that I might as well get it over with. Garcia's persistent enthusiasm about belles lettres is more that of a Latin American than a Spaniard. We were at the café El Telescopio where we had lunched together and were now facing that vacuous panorama to which most of my countrymen are committed by traditional respectful consent and which extends indefinitely after every meal, connecting it effortlessly with the next. So, I reached for my bottle, took a good swallow and resigned myself to listen.

But first, and to ape Garcia, you must let me tell you about El Telescopio which, as he would contend, could only happen in New York.

23

I cannot remember the real name of the place, but it was a remarkable café. There were no wineglasses in sight at El Telescopio and everybody drank out of the bottle—a tradition that was started by a fantastic habitué, a certain Don Pedro, known to most of us as the Moor, considered an authority in anything typically Spanish. He had stated sententiously that the true Spaniard would drink manzanilla from cañitas, sherry from chatos, but regular wine only from the bottle, leaving the wineskin for picnics and ordinary wine, but glasses, never.

Now, I wouldn't put it past him to have made the whole thing up out of his own head, because this fellow could invent traditions out of thin air to suit his fancy or perhaps his lazy thirst as in this case. I have questioned other Spaniards on the subject and some have said that they had never given the matter a thought but that now that they thought of it. . . . Others have denied it flatly and called it a manifestation of distorted patriotism, Españolism, or plain nonsense and the matter stands there, but the result is that the thing caught and at El Telescopio all those Spaniards who insist on living in Spain wherever they are sat from morning to night drinking wine out of bottles and when they leaned back to drink, sighting their interlocutor along the label or squinting into the green depths to search for a last drop, they certainly looked like some tipsy astronomer aiming a wobbly telescope at the stars too distant to matter in one's condition of libating bliss. When they did this in the summer, sitting by the open windows or on the patio, the effect was perfect. Therefore the nickname of El Telescopio with which our same authority on the typical had baptized it.

This café was located on Cherry Street where there were others like it, although not quite as big, as popular or offering such a representative cross section of all classes of my people. It gathered laborers, businessmen in the import and export lines, nightclub entertainers in moments of repentance at their disloyal success, plain expatriates and even derelicts from the not-too-distant Bowery in extraordinary moments of self-respecting affluence, all of whom, no matter how different otherwise, had two things in common: their language and the phenomenal respect which every

Spaniard has for his food and his wine, and El Telescopio made good on both scores.

It had a large dining room that developed into an ample bar with two billiard tables and on the other side spread onto a yard with an awning for summer dining. But what made El Telescopio authentic is that it was not decorated in the so-called Spanish style. True, there were posters, some imported, advertising bull-fights in Madrid or Sevilla that couldn't do one any good here, and others domestic, advertising some Spanish film or play in some theater usually in Harlem—I mean, the one in Manhattan. It was in the yard that Garcia and I were sitting.

Through the open windows and door came the sound of voices in the bar punctuated by the knocking of the billiard balls, and there was also a radio turned to a Spanish program whose announcer for once did not have that punctiliously exasperating and forced intonation which is as tedious as an American putting on a British accent.

Oh yes, everything was quite Spanish; the setting just right to make one forget that one was in New York, and Garcia had that look in his eye and those papers in his hand. He regarded his semi-empty bottle, called for two more and then emptied what was left at one draft.

The thing was upon me:

A summer in the early 1870s, Mariano Sandoval came from Jauja to Madrid. He was accompanied by his wife Rosario and their two children, Fernando about ten and Julieta about five. They brought with them a lanky young man of eighteen or nineteen years of age, with faded clothes and complexion: Ledesma.

Señor Sandoval came to Madrid with as much resolution as transportation permitted in those days. That trip meant to him a great deal and Madrid should be, at least for that reason, the place to describe here. However, as the average reader may be considered somewhat acquainted with that capital, a word or two about Jauja will be more adequate at this point, so that the reader will form an idea of the place these people he has just met came from.

Jauja. Houses built on sloping grounds. There is a persistent recollection of buildings some three or four stories high in front, their sides invariably slashed diagonally by a hilly street and, in the back, roofs fading into the stormy ground.

Roofs projecting from the ground; treacherous roofs of Jauja. A man is likely to walk unnoticingly onto one of these roofs and then fall down and break his neck. Animals walk on them. One can often see the head of a burro looming about four stories above the street. In Jauja streets run above and below. Topography and dirt have done for Jauja what engineering and steel are trying to do for modern cities. Why should one worry and not be lazy in Jauja when things can be achieved without toil?

Walking onto those roofs of Jauja, one experiences the feeling of attaining height without the effort of rising, as if the world sank to look up at one, or walked resigned, indifferent, below.

Most disconcerting, almost demoralizing roofs. Such is one's memory of Jauja; a somber town and broken houses seeking their level on the slanting ground.

And it was from this city that Sandoval and his family came to Madrid so many years ago.

The purpose of Señor Sandoval's trip was to establish himself as a jeweler. He was not coming to Madrid in full ignorance as other people who come there from second-rate towns. He had weighed this step at length and had even discussed it with his wife.

Sandoval was well provided for Madrid. He had a nice frock coat, it was not the latest fashion, but it was immaculate and it became him. He had a good top hat and underneath that a great deal of cunning and common sense; this, overshadowed by much ambition.

In Jauja he had owned a small silversmith and junk shop where he developed a vague idea of what the jewelry business might be, a business which had always lured his commercially romantic mind with the glamour one naturally associates with it.

For that reason and dreaming of jewelry shops in large cities, Sandoval had never learned to respect his own little business and regarded it with contempt.

He was loath to waste time on it by bargaining over petty transactions, but as Spaniards are fond of bargaining even in Jauja, Sandoval would invariably say to a customer: "This merchandise is worth fifty centimes, you can have it for ten." And he insisted that in this way he had saved himself four long grueling arguments and made a five centimes clear profit.

Nevertheless the business had lost a great deal. Everything in the shop was in tumultuous disorder. It was almost impossible to find an object there.

People walked into the stores and asked for something and Sandoval after several vain attempts to locate the object told them to come around the next week, that he knew it was somewhere in there but that he could not find it.

The customer went away and never returned, and Don Mariano Sandoval filed another grudge against Jauja.

It was obvious that Don Mariano had no interest in the little shop, that he resented its pettiness and filth and that he considered himself and his family entitled to something better.

One day Sandoval was in his shop alone with young Ledesma, the boy who helped him and who was supposed to run errands, although he had not been given an opportunity to display his zeal.

Not one single sale had taken place that week and people had only come into the shop to talk, kill time and spit on the floor. This particular day it was raining and no one had come.

Young Ledesma was sitting by the window reading and Señor Sandoval walked up and down looking at the shelves with scorn and shaking his head before them in silent reproach.

He stopped before Ledesma: "Listen."

Ledesma closed the book and stood up.

"I don't mind your reading all you want as long as this lasts. Since there is nothing else to do, you may as well broaden your culture."

"Well, sir?"

"I don't feel like working here myself. Who the devil is going to undertake putting all this junk in order? The whole thing does not deserve it."

"..."

"You must have ambition; you read a great deal and people who read a great deal sometimes have much ambition. Undoubtedly you want to get somewhere in life, but this place does not give you an opportunity. No one can get anywhere sitting on this junk pile. Have you thought of that?"

Young Ledesma had not thought of that but now he did. He looked at his master and waited a few moments to make his answer true: "Yes sir, I have."

"Naturally! And I think that a young serious man like you would have a much better opportunity in a larger city, like for instance, Madrid."

Young Ledesma was following his master's thoughts closely. He knew now what the latter was driving at. The question came and it did not surprise him.

"Would you like to go to Madrid?" And Ledesma answered without hesitation: "Caramba, sir! I'd love it."

"Well then; I have decided to move to Madrid. I am going to sell all this out and establish myself in the capital in a real jewelry business and I thought that if you wanted and your father consents, I will take you along to help me run the business before taking some unknown person whom I might not trust with what I don't have."

"Sir, I'll work like a slave for you. I want to thank you. I will work for you like a burro, or like something that works very much, sir."

"You better had. I don't mind your reading here, as I said. The place does not deserve attention, but there you will have to work real hard and forget about books—these books anyway. After all, reading is not a very good occupation. It is well to read when one has nothing better to do, but life is not that bad."

"I will work hard, sir. I will slave for you. And I won't read another book. Why should I read about things if I am going to see them?"

"That's right, my boy, and remember that when you work for me, you are working for yourself."

Ledesma was to remember this many times in his life, but he did not know it then and his answer was candid: "I know that, sir, and thank you."

"Tonight you obtain your father's permission and we will be leaving as soon as I can get this off my hands."

When young Ledesma asked his father that night, his father was classic: "Go, go in peace. Señor Sandoval will take better care of you than I can. I won't be long here now. He is very kind to take you to Madrid. Thank him for me and go with my blessing."

After this speech, old man Ledesma should have died with his hand raised in the act of blessing to round up the scene, but he waited a few months instead.

Having resolved to move to Madrid, Sandoval could scarcely wait to sell the business and be on his way. He became irascible and hated the shop and all its contents. He was in a hurry to sell out, he could not even stand the town any longer. The obsession of a jewelry shop in Madrid pursued him day and night.

"You must not want things in such a hurry," said his wife Rosario one day. "It makes you suffer."

"Well, that is my temperament. I suppose I inherit it. Probably the children will inherit it too. One should get things when one wants them, provided one wants them enough; otherwise, by the time one gets them, one does not want them any longer."

Fortunately Don Mariano did not have to wait long. A man offered to buy his business.

Sandoval was so impatient that he did not even want to make an inventory of the shop. He simply took the man around and told him to look the store over, get an idea of its value and make a flat offer.

The man did so and his offer was entirely too flat and sounded ridiculous. Madame Sandoval was indignant, especially when she saw her husband ready to accept.

"This is literally throwing things away, Mariano. It is a crime. After all, this is worth something. We have lived on it."

"Yes, and how we have lived! If you call that living. That is why I hate it so."

"You are insane with impatience now and behaving like a fool. You don't care what happens as long as you go to Madrid."

Señor Sandoval became suddenly aware of the presence of the man who had made the offer and this angered him. He saw it only as one more unpleasant experience he owed to the hateful shop and wanted more than ever to rid himself of it.

"You keep out of this. It is my business and I need no advice."

"It is your business because my father left it to you. If you had built it up yourself you wouldn't treat it this way."

"And who do you think I am doing this for? Is it not for you and the children? Am I not taking you to Madrid to see if I can give you and them the things this will never give you?"

"I don't see what that has to do with not getting what you are entitled to."

"And what has that to do with our going to Madrid?" He had already reached the point of irrationality.

"It has a great deal to do with it. We will have more money to take us there."

"Well, don't you mind about that. We'll get there all right. I am not going to waste any more time bargaining for a few dirty centimes. I am not that poor yet."

And the deal was closed and later Sandoval told his wife confidentially that she had nearly spoiled a good deal with her talk, that the man had given more than the shop was worth and that the poor fellow did not know what he was in for. His object attained, Don Mariano was in excellent humor.

The trip of the Sandovals to Madrid was fundamentally like the trip is today, except a little slower, a little less comfortable.

Garcia looked up from his papers: "What do you think of it so far?"

Although his question did not startle me, I had been listening in a desultory manner, allowing other thoughts to wander in and out, as well as the music from the radio and other noises and disconnected phrases from the café, and I had formed no particular thought. The waiter had already brought the two fresh bottles ordered by Garcia and I had taken some swallows out of mine thinking of the pleasant alternation of wine and cigarette tastes and, as I say, I was not prepared for him, but feeling contented and as yet uninvolved, I waved expansively: "Go ahead."

In Madrid Sandoval left his Casa de Huespedes every morning accompanied by Ledesma and toured the city and looked around. They both kept this up for about a month. They visited every jewelry shop and, although there was much for them to admire, they never made an utterance of surprise. Sandoval took notes and passed them to Ledesma who looked them over like a very serious man and pocketed them in his bulging coat.

Every evening upon their return, they were eagerly questioned by his wife and Julieta, but Sandoval always answered laconically: "Everything is going fine. Don't worry."

"But our money is also going!"

"Everything is going fine."

And one morning Sandoval and Ledesma left the house as usual and went straight to a store that was for rent on the corner of the Street of Arenal and the Puerta del Sol.

Sandoval asked of the owner the price and without further hesitation, having learned it, took out the money and began to count it.

The owner was not in the habit of closing a deal in such an easy manner. He felt that at least a bit of bargaining was a requisite of every transaction and consequently became several things in succession: first, perplexed, then embarrassed, after that suspicious and at last almost indignant.

Was this man trying to boast of his wealth? Or had he made a mistake when naming the price?

He assumed an insulted air and repeated the price to make sure.

"Yes, I heard you," said Sandoval, "and here is the money."

This was too much. Why should this man be in such a hurry to close the deal? People were never in a hurry, especially in such circumstances. Undoubtedly this man had discovered some hidden value in the little store.

"But, do you mean that the price suits you, like that?"

"Naturally! Otherwise I wouldn't rent the store."

"But just like that? Without any talk?"

"Why not? I see no reason for any more talk. You name a price, it suits me and I pay it. Is there anything unusual in that?"

"Of course—I mean—I could let you have it cheaper if you insist."

"But I haven't insisted on anything. Did you not give me the right price?" Sandoval was now pressing the man. He had a haughty disposition that showed itself in matters of money. The poor man was plainly embarrassed. The situation had caught him unawares and his mind was in a turmoil.

"Well, sir; you know how it is. I like you people and would be pleased to have you for tenants—that is, it would be an honor to me, and since you are doing me this honor, I might as well let you have it cheaper."

Don Mariano was beginning to enjoy the situation: "But this is not a question of honor, my dear man. It is purely a business matter."

"Then, sir, if you insist on paying the price . . ."

"Certainly. I never bargain, do you understand? Never! I always pay the price."

"But in this hurry . . .," he murmured, already a broken man without spirit, "there is plenty of time."

"No. You are mistaken, there is very little time."

Sandoval rented the store which was small but very well appointed and he also rented the floor above for his family.

In the short time Sandoval had been in Madrid, he had taken the measure of the capital and had discovered that general quality which some people call metropolitan good taste. The opening of his shop was therefore a subdued affair, partly for the above reason and partly because he could not afford much advertising.

Sandoval had faced the problem of buying stock, of getting jewels for the jewelry shop. After the initial expenses, renting the place and the floor above and buying furniture, he had very little left. The day the doors were opened to the public, there was a plain sign outside which read Joyeria La Estrella. In the window there were half a dozen knives, forks and spoons very finely made and the best to be had. Inside the store the shelves and counter were curtained in velvet: "So that the public will think that the treasures are hidden there," as Sandoval told Ledesma that memorable day.

In later years he used to say jokingly: "I was an early pioneer of the Anti-display Curiosity-arousing League which has invaded these modern days of fake merchandising."

"But how did you manage without stock?" some friend would ask him. "Suppose someone came in to buy something that was neither knives nor forks?"

"I sold them spoons."

"But supposing still that they wanted something else?"

"I sold some things on samples and then got the stuff on credit. In other cases I would say that a particular thing had to be made in France. You know the allure France still has for Spaniards who buy in Spain. I did a number of things to pull me out of every difficult situation. I gathered prestige and then a friend lent me money to buy some private stock. After that the business sailed beautifully and . . . here I am."

"Here you are and all your plans worked out."

"Yes, mine and Ledesma's. I got the jewelry shop in Madrid and made a success of it, but this wouldn't have been possible without Ledesma. That fellow has literally slaved for me."

"Everything worked out exactly as planned."

The rise and fall of the Sandoval family was a thing which people in Madrid commented about for a long time.

After the Sandovals came to Madrid, they rose steadily and rapidly. They owned a good business in town. Despite their wealth, however, the aristocracy of the town had closed its doors to them. They were obviously newly rich, at least the older generation, and behaved as such publicly.

At the present moment, money has more weight in Spain and it could conceivably pave the road to a higher social level. Not then, though, when the Sandoval family rose.

Unfortunately, as society grew more lax, disgrace closed upon the Sandovals whose fall was as steady and fast as its rise. Misfortune persecuted them mercilessly and for many years it was like a siege. As many people in Madrid say, it seemed as if a curse hung upon the family.

According to many, the Sandovals did everything in their power to precipitate misfortune. Of course people in Madrid contribute their own theories to every gossip which trails along the town, but several of them knew the family closely enough to discover the authentic facts.

It was known to everybody that the Sandovals were boastful and ostentatious, that incompetence in the younger generation annihilated the business, that discord reigned among them, that, as they would say now, neuroses ran in every member of the family, but as they said then, they were all crazy in the head.

There were many things said about the Sandovals. Things spoken too loudly to be believed and things spoken too softly to be understood. But through that struggle against misfortune and against themselves, the stronger walked quietly upon the road which leads to peaceful rest; the others scattered wildly in that sad stampede of the weaklings toward oblivion.

Doña Rosario had once said almost prophetically: "The place where people are brought up has a decided influence upon their lives, it charts their existence which acquires in time almost the same shape that their place of origin and early development presents."

And Ledesma had answered cautiously: "One should never generalize. In that case everybody who has been brought up in the same place would have exactly the same kind of life to live," and she persisted: "They usually do."

Ledesma granted politely but not convinced: "Perhaps."

However, the life of the Sandovals ran very much in the same style of the city they came from, Jauja and its characteristic sloping ground, if that is what Doña Rosario meant. It was accidented inasmuch as it rose and then descended, but the temperament of the Sandovals always ran true to form. It always traveled in a straight line and only the accidents of life met it occasionally. Sometimes it seemed as if the depths rose to the plane of their existence.

That family was broken like the houses of Jauja, their path was accidented, their temperament straight as if it found, by thus continuing, its restful level on the slanting ground.

Had it not happened in this age, it would have very well formed a legend. However, the happenings are too recent and only constitute gossip, but considering that the gossip of today forms the legend of tomorrow, one may assume that this story will accumulate with time a certain degree of significance worth recording.

Garcia looked at me over the page he was reading and which I noticed with relief was the last: "I expect to write the facts exactly as I learned them and only change the names and places slightly in order to avoid the accusation of libel and also to spare some people any embarrassment." He resumed his reading:

At this time of true narratives, biographies and earnest confessions, when many people seem convinced that even if truth is not stranger than fiction, it leaves more to the imagination, it is well to risk this deficient account of unreliable data, too short and incomplete to be considered the biography of a family or even to satisfy this general thirst for supposed truth. But as things when written have an inevitable tendency to wrap themselves in the unfitting garments of secondhand literature, this will probably turn out to be but a grotesque parody of what once was truth.

He began to stack up his papers and pocket them: "Well?"

"Oh, it is fine, fine—the only thing: to come all the way to New York to write a novel about a family in Spain. . . ."

"I did not come here to write it, you ought to know that. I am here and I happened to think of writing it. That's all."

"But who is going to read it? Unless it is for your own satisfaction or records. . . ."

"I am not thinking of publishing it in Spanish here. I have in mind one or two publishing houses in Latin America, or perhaps even Spain, although I would rather—but what I was really thinking is that you might help me with the English translation. I will show you some other parts I have already written out, even if they still need a little polishing."

"Well, I don't know about that. My English is not so good. I think that an American. . . ."

"Now, come, it would not be the same thing. You come over to my place one of these nights and I will show you what I have written."

"All right. We'll see."

The seats were getting hard and in spite of all the wine, or maybe because of it, I was growing a bit chilly and this was summer. It seems that with a man away from his native land the weather is like the coffee, either too hot or too cold. We both stretched.

"Let's go in and watch the billiards."

"It is getting late," I said, "and I will have to be going. I am having dinner with Dr. de los Rios."

"Come in for a while anyway and let us finish these in the barroom."

Bottles in hand we went through the dining room which was empty at this time of day and into the barroom with the billiard tables.

The bartender was leaning on the bar following the progress of the game, his chin firmly planted on the heel of his hand, yet his head bobbing up and down. He was chewing gum. When he saw us he came immediately to attention, but Garcia waved him at ease and he resumed his acquiescent pose with relish. The men playing were mostly Basque and laborers, probably factory workers, one could see from their good clothes. At one table they were playing plain billiards with three balls, and at the other, some Spanish version of the game with a dish in the middle of the table which had some coins in it.

One of them had finished a good run. He shrugged off the last miss generously and walking to a table by the windows reached for his bottle. It was empty and he called for another.

The bartender did not bother to disturb the barmaid who was perched on a stool reading a tabloid paper. Instead he reached ponderously behind and sent a bottle across the room at the man. He did not throw it holding it by the neck, but against the palm of his hand as a football player might throw a pass, and it sailed beautifully, smoothly and true. Whether it is in a free-for-all with intentions of mayhem, or simply as a friendly serve as in this case, this is the approved Spanish fashion of propelling a bottle and the only one that will yield consistent good results.

The man caught it in his left hand and with the same flowing motion, set it on the table. He tucked the cue under his arm and uncorked the bottle himself. Then he began to drink with long, thirsty swallows, the bottle pointing at the ceiling, his neck going like that of a gobbler. Most extraordinary drinking capacity and technique: El Telescopio in its glory.

His opponent, a swarthy, heavy-set man with sharp features and a sharp mustache, was squinting at the balls on the table, figuring his shot, a cigarette delicately held not in his lips but between his teeth. He poised his cue, concentrated and then, as if he had eyes on the back of his neck, he said as he struck the ball, to the barmaid: "Que piernas, Nescacha, que piernas. . .!"

The girl looked up from her paper and hastily pulled her skirt over her knees: "You attend to your game. If your wife ever hears you. . . ."

A couple of kids looked in through a window and one of them called at his father to come home for supper.

It was getting late and I spoke to Garcia: "I'll have to be going. . . ."

Garcia did not hear me. He seemed transfixed and, although his eyes were on the billard table, I knew that he was not following the game. He was looking beyond. He had been transported to the past and I knew what he was remembering.

I said "so long" as a formality and left Garcia there, staring into space and looking into time.

Vacation time is the time to do as one likes but the two kids did not know what they liked to do. Maybe they wanted to do nothing but they were too young to know that and so they wandered aimlessly through the quiet of the village and Vizcaitia was very quiet that afternoon. Little Garcia, the one with the soulful eyes, took out a top and spun it. Then he picked it up as it died out. The other kid produced a sling and lazily slung a pebble against a distant tree. The pebble banked and struck the tree but he was already looking in another direction and pocketing the sling. They walked on through the afternoon toward the village park. The two kids had all the time in the world to play and they never had to go back to school and therefore they were happy to walk like that.

When they entered the park, everything was cool and tranquil under the oak and chestnut trees with their trunks submerged in pools of shadow with floating patches of sunlight. The kids heard on the other side of the park the irregular crack of the pelota against the frontón. Little Garcia borrowed the sling from the other kid, slung another pebble high and far over the treetops and he watched it go and saw it shine like a gem in the sun against the blue sky. They approached the handball court and continued to hear the crack of leather-covered ball against granite wall and this made them walk faster.

The two kids never tired of the handball game. Besides there were always a few ball players drinking in the tavern of the Gorriti who also owned the frontón and it was good to listen to their talk about the game as the kids admired the players very much. Perhaps they would be allowed to play ball at one end of the frontón against the side wall. If the Nescacha said so, they would be allowed to play. They liked the Nescacha and she was their friend. She waited on the customers of the Gorriti and she always gave the two kids wine and anis biscuits to dip and she also gave them balls to play. Once she even had the Gorriti himself make a ball exactly like the big regulation ones, but smaller for the two kids. She was nice, la Nescacha.

When they arrived at the tavern, there were several men in there. The Gorriti was sitting in his chair against the wall, but he was always there anyway. He was fat, with a big stomach and his face was purple red. He sat there all day with a very small boina on top of his head and a porrón of chacolí next to him on the floor and he had to lean over laboriously to reach it. The kids liked the way he drank out of the porrón. He held it high and the red stream dropped straight into his open mouth and into his big storehouse and his throat did not move and he did not even say "Ahhh!" like other people when they finish drinking and did not have to wipe his mouth because the chacolí never touched his lips. He sat like that all day and he looked like a wineskin propped up in the chair against the wall, and he was a regular wineskin, this Gorriti. He did not speak much but when he spoke it sounded very final, except sometimes when it sounded as if he did not speak to anyone in particular. Sometimes one could see him sewing the leather cover on a ball. During the right season the porrón held cizarra instead of chacolí.

There was the Nescacha sitting at a table with Begoña. She had very red hair and the upper half of her face and arms was laden with freckles and she had vivid green eyes, but her mouth was fresh and she showed strong white teeth when she smiled or laughed and this she did often. She was very young still, probably fifteen or sixteen years only, but she was very womanly, with fine broad hips and shoulders and full round breasts. Begoña was a professional ball player and a great one too, everybody said. The kids admired Begoña and his very easy and graceful style of playing. They tried to imitate him when they played ball holding their arm poised after striking but when little Garcia did it, he looked as if he were endeavoring to express some difficult idea and when the other kid did it, he looked as if he were thumbing his nose and the two kids were as different as that, but they never could get the gestures of Begoña just right. He intrigued the kids, this Begoña. He drank all the time like the Gorriti, but he drank out of a regular bottle. He had massive shoulders and a thick neck. He looked congested and had steel gray eyes that were always bloodshot and also a black mustache with ends turned up. He looked like a good bull of lidia.

What made Begoña more important than the others was that he had been in the army and had fought in Morocco for which he could show decorations and he had also traveled to America, to Cuba, to play the handball there, but now he had come to roost in his native Vizcaitia and he picked up some extra money here and there in the neighboring towns, particularly in Bilbao, playing ball. He never spoke about himself, however, and all the women liked him so well that once the kids heard the Gorriti speak to him like this:

"One of these days some husband will kill you. Maybe your wife will kill you."

Begoña shrugged his wide shoulders: "And what can one do? That is life."

"Yes, so it is," and the Gorriti said no more and he went back to his porrón of cizarra because this was during the season of the cizarra.

Gorriti meant that when Begoña returned from Cuba he married la Euscarra who owned the house and the heredad behind the frontón and she had many gold and silver coins in a chest and had given the key to Begoña after their marriage so he did not have to play the pelota if he did not feel like it, although he still played now and then, and la Euscarra was a very jealous woman who was always quarreling with Begoña and making trouble for him and she had so violent a temper that when they quarreled she tried to strike him, but he held her and said in his gruff voice:

"Sometimes I wish you were a man. You wouldn't do this then."

This was strange because Begoña looked cruel and if he was standing around when the kids played ball and the ball bounced his way, he always struck it hard against the wall and sent it far and then laughed when the kids had to chase it across the park and sometimes he hit it way over the wall of the frontón and onto his wife's heredad and the kids had to go up the stairs on the side of the park behind the public school building and walk all the way around and past the old tree of Vizcaitia on Santa Clara, to the other side of the court, and when they looked for the ball in the heredad, la Euscarra hollered at them. But Begoña was a great ball player and he had traveled and fought in Morocco and everybody liked and respected him and the kids were proud that he even hit their ball.

Lanky Chapelo was also in the tavern leaning against a wall and talking across the room to the Gorriti. His boina was on the back of his head and a lock of blond hair hung down in front and his mustache was also blond and hung but turned gently at the ends, not sharp like Begoña's. He was the clown of the handball court and a very uneven player, but when he had one of his good days, no one could match him, everybody said. He was gay and easygoing, this Chapelo, with his fine blue eyes. He was talking to el Gorriti in Spanish and el Gorriti answered little and in Vascuence. They all could speak Vascuence and el Gorriti could also speak Spanish, but they always spoke Spanish and el Gorriti was the only one around who spoke Vascuence most of the time.

The kids only knew by sight the other three men sitting at the table next to the window.

La Nescacha looked up at the kids and said "hello," being their close friend, and the kids said "hello," but none of the men noticed them except Chapelo and he smiled their way and they smiled back. Chapelo sometimes played ball with them and acted like a clown, falling down or striking the ball under his leg or backhand like. Then el Gorriti called la Nescacha.

"This porrón is empty, Nescacha."

She got up and walked on her new patent leather high-heeled shoes. She always had new shoes on with very high heels since la Nescacha liked to be all dressed up with fine clothes and she wore rings in her ears and on her fingers and also bracelets, but she never wore stockings with her fine shoes as the kids could tell by seeing the coppery fuzz on her muscular legs.

La Nescacha took the empty porrón behind the counter and from the small room in the back, she brought out another covered with fresh moisture but before she could lay it on the floor beside her master, el Gorriti took it from her and began to drink and the kids watched him closely. Then la Nescacha filled two glasses with wine and took some biscuits from the shelf and gave them to the kids.

They said "thanks" and she patted their heads and the kids stood outside the door watching the ball game that was in progress. It was not an important game because the Gorriti was sitting inside. If the game was good and Begoña or Chapelo or any of his boys, as the Gorriti called the better players, were out there, he always sat outside in his chair and watched with his porrón beside him. Therefore this was not a good game and the porrón and the Gorriti were inside.

And then the kids saw the woman coming through the park and across the clearing in front of the tavern with people following behind. She was talking loudly and stepping so hard that she raised dust when she crossed the dried clearing where the sun beat. The kids entered the tavern again and then stood to one side of the door to let her pass, but she stopped right at the door. She was la Euscarra, a swarthy and powerfully built woman.

Begoña had one arm around la Nescacha when he saw his wife. He did not remove his arm, though. He only said: "What do you want, woman?"

She shouted in a loud masculine voice that sounded like a man almost: "I want to see your guts in the sun, bad man. I knew you were here carrying on with this girl and I come to tell you that you cannot do that to me," and she went on like that to insult him using very abusive and bad language.

La Nescacha disengaged herself from Begoña's arm and, walking around the table, stood before la Euscarra very serene: "Why do you tell him, if you want to tell me? I know you have been talking behind my back. If you have anything against me, tell me."

"You stay out of this," la Euscarra said. "I am talking to my man now."

The other one said: "Yes, you talk to him because you don't dare talk to me like that. He is a real man and can do nothing. Why do you come here? If you have a quarrel with me, let's have it over with."

The kids saw la Euscarra pale under her sunburned skin.

"You are only a fresh girl and you ought to be ashamed to run around with men twice your age. You are not even a woman and you should not try to compete with grown-ups or you will learn a good lesson."

La Nescacha was very furious then and she said: "I am more of a woman than you will ever be and it will not be you who will teach me any lesson. I run around with him and what are you going to do about it?" And then the two women insulted each other and used vile language.

El Gorriti talked from his chair in the back of the room: "Don't bring your quarrels here, women." But then Chapelo, who was spinning his boina on a finger, said that it was better for the men to stay out of women's troubles and let them fight it out themselves and he also made a joke which made everybody laugh except the kids who did not understand it. Begoña looked unconcerned with a cigarette between his sharp teeth and his face without expression. La Euscarra yelled at him:

"Come home with me, man without conscience. You sit and drink while I work all day in the heredad and I will murder you yet. I am not a woman to play with."

Begoña removed the cigarette from between his teeth. He pointed the wet end at his wife and he told her: "I am tired of you and I stay. You do what you want. I have heard you many times and others have also heard you say that you were going to kill la Nescacha. Well, she is right in front of you now and I don't see you do anything." La Euscarra looked very embarrassed, and he finished: "What are you waiting for?"

And then la Nescacha, hands on swaying hips, closed in on the bigger woman. She had courage, la Nescacha. Her well set-off body was almost rubbing against her rival's and there was insulting challenge in every curve of it.

"You are going to kill me?" she laughed aloud and impudently up into la Euscarra's face. "You don't have what a woman should have to kill. Get out of here now."

Everybody looked on with great suspense. A crowd of people had collected before the door of the tavern attracted by the loud voices because they all wanted to see the fight between the two women. The kids were still holding their glasses of wine and had forgotten about them. They were afraid for la Nescacha, because they liked her and the other woman always hollered at them when they walked in her heredad after their ball. La Euscarra was not hollering anymore now, though. She was mumbling:

"I won't go until he comes, and besides I don't have to go if I don't want to, as anybody has a right to come in here because this is a tavern." She was talking stupidly and everybody began to think she was talking this way because she was afraid of la Nescacha, which was very surprising because she was bigger and looked stronger and then she had said she was going to kill la Nescacha. The ball game had stopped also and everything and the day was very quiet and silent so that the kids could hear very plainly the voice of la Nescacha:

"Then I will make you go like this," and she struck la Euscarra hard across the face with her open hand. La Euscarra stepped back and uttered a little cry and the bright blood that trickled from her nose made her face look muddy gray. Then she began to holler:

"I will kill her if nobody holds me," and she looked all around. "She has struck me and I will kill her as certain as my name is la Euscarra." But nobody held her and she had to fight now, but she only said those things and did nothing and for that reason someone said:

"What happened, Euscarra; did you leave your courage at home?" But the word used was not "courage" but another one which the kids knew to be very vulgar indeed and then la Nescacha struck her face again.

Howling like a wolf, la Euscarra lunged at the girl, trying to claw at her hair and scratch her, but la Nescacha was too quick for her, because she knew all the tricks, and she caught la Euscarra by the face so she could not see well and drove her against the counter, pulling her back by the hair, and began to pound her mercilessly with her fist and la Euscarra screamed with every blow. La Euscarra tried to escape and retaliate, but that young woman knew how to fight and had her cornered and helpless, and then la Nescacha fell upon her and began to pour vicious blows with both fists upon her face and they sounded very ugly and la Euscarra howled shamelessly until it was fearful to hear and to see. Everybody yelled and little Garcia watched with eyes wide open and the other kid joined in the general pandemonium and both kids forgot about the wineglasses in their shaking hands. Then several people said that la Euscarra had enough.

Begoña stood up and said: "She has had enough now," and he pulled la Nescacha who was saying: "Who is the better woman now?" and he patted her because she had won.

La Euscarra sank to her knees covering her face, her hair all hanging down and she dragged herself that way to the door like a beaten dog who is very much ashamed of his beating and the blood dripped on the floor as she went, but when she was outside the door she stood up reeling so she made a frightful sight in the bright sun because her face was all covered with blood as was the front of her working dress and some of her hair hung over her face. She cried: "Maybe you can whip me this way," and she choked moving her hands like one who is fighting, "but not like this," and then she moved one hand like someone stabbing with a knife and she stood like that looking at her husband long and then with a moan she staggered away, the people making way for her.

Everybody talked about the fight and they were surprised because la Nescacha was younger and smaller and she had thrashed the other woman so easily and they all said that she was a great fighter since she had so much courage and then the Gorriti said that fear made people weak. He said:

"When one is afraid, one loses one's strength," and he lifted his porrón and drank without saying another word and Begoña must have congratulated la Nescacha also because she answered:

"One does what one can" and "I had to defend myself," which sounded very funny because she had done all the attacking. After that she went over where the kids stood and she caressed their faces very lovingly as she liked them so much: "I did not mean to frighten you chavales. Finish your wine and you will feel better." Then she noticed blood on her hands and she walked behind the counter and poured wine in a cooking basin and rinsed her hands in it.

"You see?" she said to Begoña, "I cut my hand on her teeth," and Begoña went over to the counter and helped her dry her hands and he kissed the hand she had cut like a very romantic gentleman so that the Nescacha looked very happy and deep into his eyes, with worship. Begoña pointed at one of her rings:

"That ring cut into your finger." He had a cigarette again between his teeth and he lifted one eyebrow and smiled with one side of his face in that way of his that the kids tried to imitate, he being such a famous ball player. "It must have cut more into her face."

"Next time I will take the rings off," the kids heard her whisper, but el Gorriti also heard her because he said:

"You expect to fight all the time? Then don't fight in my tavern, because I don't want women's troubles in my tavern and there are wide fields all around to do your fighting and if you stayed away from married men, you could keep your rings on." He lifted his porrón again and this time he drank longer since he had talked so much longer than usual.

The people who came attracted by the fight had dispersed and the men who were playing ball went back to their game and only a few people remained outside the tavern and three women in a group who walked looking at the tavern and moving their heads in the direction la Euscarra had gone as they were probably talking about her quarrel with the Nescacha. Then they all looked again where la Euscarra had gone and talked excitedly and the kids looked also and they saw la Euscarra who was coming back. Her face was still bloody and her hair hanging and streaming behind her because she was walking fast. When she arrived she stood in front of the door of the tavern and began to yell again. The kids noticed she had a knife in her hand. She shouted very loud for everyone to hear:

"I will kill the two of you as you stand there, you accursed ones," and she opened the knife that was very large at that and had many springs that made it squeak loudly as she opened it, saying to la Nescacha: "You get a knife and come out here."

La Nescacha walked very calmly toward her.

"Don't lose yourself, Nescacha," the Gorriti warned. "Nothing is worth dying for." But la Euscarra only took a step back and said between her teeth: "I will kill you," and Begoña looked very unconcerned as if all this had nothing to do with him and were very boring and he drank what was left of the wine in his bottle.

La Nescacha said: "She does not have the guts to use the knife." She did not say "guts" but another word which the kids knew was much lower and they were surprised because they had never heard la Nescacha use language like she had used that day, and she continued to approach la Euscarra who stood with her knife in her hand. She had such courage, this Nescacha, and she said: "I don't need a knife for you. I told you that you don't have what you should to face a woman," and with that she twisted the knife from la Euscarra's hand and slapped her twice again. La Euscarra let out a curse and ran away sobbing and the people who had gathered again to watch began to laugh very much, which was also due to their relief as they had all feared that perhaps la Euscarra would really stab the younger girl. So the kids also laughed and even Begoña smiled a little more on the side of his mouth, but his smile was sad as usual.

Then the kids decided to follow la Euscarra and as they crossed the door the other kid saw the knife still lying on the threshold and he picked it up.

Little Garcia said: "That is for the two of us like everything else," and the other kid said that yes, that he knew.

When they passed the three women who were still standing there talking before the tavern, they heard some of their conversation which was like this:

"What happened to her is the worst thing that can happen to a woman, I think."

The other one said: "That is so, but she made trouble for him all the time, but now she won't anymore."

And the third one said then: "She gave him the key to her money chest anyway and that redheaded girl is a bitch," and then the kids heard no more of the conversation because they walked on and were too far to hear it.

They saw la Euscarra at the other end of the park reaching the stairs behind the public school building that was closed and empty since this was summertime. They saw her walk up the stairs slow and bent as if she were carrying a heavy load and they thought that maybe she was going home, so they followed knowing that they had nothing to do and that it was long before supper yet. They crossed the park that was quiet and with very few people and shot through with the aslant sun all the way to its farthest corners and sliced by long shadows like those of the two kids as they walked by, who judging by this should be very grown-up and tall men, but then shadows can grow faster than people and things. The kids heard again the crack of the ball against the frontón and saw the crowns of trees all aglow and golden green against the sky that was even bluer than before, this being late afternoon, and everything was peaceful.

The kids went up the stairs also and they walked along Santa Clara overlooking the park below, like a pond of sunny leaves. There were also trees in that part of town, bigger trees even. One of them stood leafless and branchless inside a large glass case, right where it was born and had flourished and died. It was the old tree of Vizcaitia looking through the dusty glass panes of its case at its son, a very large and leafy tree like the others, a short distance away.

That was something, that old tree, and the two kids were always impressed when they came upon it because it was hundreds and hundreds of years old and once upon a time the important men of the province sat under it to take some kind of an oath. The other kid said that any one of the other big trees around that spot might have been the old tree of Vizcaitia if the important men of the province had sat under it and taken their oath many hundreds of years ago, but little Garcia had told him that they probably chose that one because it was the largest then and gave more shade and the others must have been only saplings at the time and so it was considered like something holy by everybody, because the older a thing is, the holier it grows and for this it was the old tree of Vizcaitia and stood in a glass case for everyone to see and respect.

But the kids were not thinking of this as they were watching la Euscarra who was sitting on the edge of a horse trough. She was crying yet for the reason that this was the worst thing that could happen to a woman and she was washing the blood off her face that was all cut and puffed very badly and then she began to fix her hair too. The kids stood there looking at her and the other kid held the knife behind his back because maybe she would want it again. La Euscarra saw them and said to them:

"What are you standing there for? What do you want? What are you staring at?" But she did not holler at them as she always did when they went into her heredad. She talked as if she were choking. So she cried again and told them: "Go away and leave me in peace." But the kids did not go away as they were no longer afraid and they wanted to see a woman who had had the worst thing happen to her. So they stood there for a while until they saw Begoña coming along.

Begoña did not notice the kids, because he never did, but when he passed his wife he stopped watching her and she covered her face again and began to sob louder. He said nothing though, and only shrugged his wide shoulders. Then he took out a key from his pocket and dropped it on the ground at her feet, so when she saw this through her fingers, she cried even louder yet, but Begoña went on his way walking in that manner of his that the kids tried to imitate because it looked like a Cabo de Gastadores on parade and he went on to his house that was past the other end of the park. After a while, la Euscarra picked up the key and followed her husband.

The kids, having nothing more to do there, decided to go back to the tavern of the Gorriti but when they arrived, almost everybody had gone. Chapelo was still there eating percebes and joking with el Gorriti who did not answer because he was very busy sewing the wet leather cover on a ball and he had to be careful because this was a difficult job that must be done right and nobody else could make balls like el Gorriti.

La Nescacha was putting things in order and then she finished because she said that she was going home and therefore the kids went along with her because, although they had never found out where she lived, it was somewhere else and they still had time before supper for the walk. So the kids walked one on each side of la Nescacha and she had her hands on their shoulders. After a while she saw the other kid was carrying the knife and she said: "What have you there?"

And he said: "That is the knife la Euscarra brought to kill you with, but it belongs to me now."

"And to me also," added little Garcia, so the other kid said: "All right."

La Nescacha laughed, which sounded very pleasant and clear, everything being so quiet all around: "You give me that knife," she said, "and maybe I will have a collection soon with all these wives who want to kill me and they only talk behind my back and then do nothing because women are like that." She took the knife from the kid: "You chavales must not have a knife. When you grow up maybe you will have to fight and then you must do it like men, like me. You don't understand these things now, which are important things, but you will understand them when you are older," and she kept the knife.

But the kids understood and besides they did not mind because this was vacation time and this made them very happy and now they never had to go to school and they could play forever and the summertime went on and on. They understood better than the grown-ups because they were still that age when they could even understand eternity and they did not mind anyway because la Nescacha was their friend and she had so much courage and she also gave them anis biscuits with wine and balls to play with. She was a fine girl, la Nescacha.

After that, she said good night and "until we meet again," which would be the next day and they also said good night and went home for supper. It was dark already.

We were walking home this night, Garcia and I, after seeing a performance of the Spanish Theater and we were commenting about it.

Now, this Spanish Theater in New York, at least at the time of which I speak, was a living and dying monument to the tenacity of Spanish traditions. It had had countless starts under different managements and usually performed once a week on Saturdays or Sundays.

At present it was run by a very complex character, a Señor Olózaga who was also rumored to own El Telescopio Café, although I have never succeeded in tracking down these rumors.

Señor Olózaga was very vague in his dealings and spoke little of himself or his past. Everything about him was hearsay. I even doubt that he was Spanish, but one doubts so many things. . . . It was known that he had managed bullfighters in Spain and a couple of Spanish prizefighters in this country who had made out rather well for themselves and for him. He seemed to have a finger in every Spanish activity which might yield a dollar, but this last venture of the Spanish Theater appeared to be doomed to financial failure. Its artistic failure had been achieved since its inception. His wife, the Señora Olózaga, better known to the Spanish colony as Tia Mariquita, had a part in every play and it was said that he had taken over the Spanish Theater more as a means to indulge her weakness for the theater. She fancied herself quite the great actress, this Tia Mariquita, and she maintained to have played in Spain on the professional stage, before large audiences, who went delirious with applause and acclaim at her performances and every night turned the stage into a florist shop. She also affirmed that she had performed before the king and queen of Spain by royal command and before tumultuous South American audiences and she reeled off names of cities, like Madrid, Barcelona and Buenos Aires, all scenes of her triumphs, and also the names of famous actors and actresses, such as Morano, Valverde, Vico, Lamadrid and Guerrero and Mendosa, all of whom had considered her their dearest friend and greatest trouper ever. She did not keep her dates and places straight, though.

When I had first seen this Tia Mariquita in New York, some time before this, she still wore her hair dyed a bright red color and wore plenty of thick makeup and flamboyant clothes. All in all and for some reason, she had managed to look like a cross between a masquerader and a cockatoo. Now, however, she had finally let her hair go a dissolutory shade of white but the theater gave her a pretext for the heavy makeup which she applied like a mud pack and she had resigned herself to character parts which of course she claimed were the hardest to play and called for the truly fine histrionic points. It was not a matter of posturing prettily on the stage like an ingenue. This was real art.

The performance we had seen that night was really bad. I don't know why every time this theater presented a play it had to do it in that obviously stagey, artificial and stilted fashion of the end of the century. Perhaps it is a gesture of defiance and intended to assert and illustrate the changelessness of Spanish things. Also they played always the same old plays over and over again, which were even then quite old-fashioned and besides everyone knew by memory: early comedies and dramas by the Quintero brothers, Estremera, Vita Laza and others and the most daringly modern would be something by Benavente or Muñoz Seca, but they immediately made up for this by going classical with something of Calderón or Lope de Vega in all of which they were dismally inadequate. The audiences were also, with few exceptions, of the type that lives in the past, or as we say in Spanish, likes to stew in its own juice. Garcia was somewhat of this type. Strong inclination to relive the past and he is the one who had got the tickets and had persuaded me to accompany him.

The performance which had been given with impunity that night and which we had witnessed in impotent silence, had been one of *Don Juan Tenorio.* As every educated person knows, this is a great drama that has had many versions in as many languages and this being addressed to educated persons, I need not go into a description of it, but many scholars whose opinions carry a great deal of weight have classified it as one of the fundamental and basic dramas of our civilization. One can say without qualification that we saw that night the worst version of it and the contrast between the drama and its performance was something that would have tasked the equipment of the most eloquent assailant of human misdemeanor. But what tops all is that the Tia Mariquita, in order to build a better character part for herself, had changed whole sections of the play and contributed her own. She had carried her shameless irresponsibility and colossal gall to the point of collaborating in *Don Juan.* This was the limit.

The drama has to do with ghosts and as we Spaniards like so much to make puns, I had said something like this to Garcia: "If we were speaking English, I could say that the drama was not ghostly but ghastly, get it?"

And Garcia had answered that he got it all right but did not know what to do with it. So we left that behind us and kept walking. I had got even with him for the invitation.

This was a Saturday night and quite hot still. We talked of that and Garcia said that New York was the only city in the world where it got hotter at night in the summer than during the day and I reminded him that he only knew some cities in Spain and this one here, but he said that he felt certain anyway that it could not be as hot at night anywhere else in the world, but we did not mind too much, because I for one like the heat and everybody complains about the heat and humidity in New York and the Spaniards, who cannot complain about the heat because our country has some pretty hot places too, then complain about the humidity if only for the sake of complaining. But Garcia and I agreed that summer in New York is very good and could not understand why everybody wants to go to the country. It is the only time when one can loiter around in comfort in the city without one's nose and eyes running and one can walk about free to move without overcoats and mufflers. Even without a jacket.

And this is the way we were walking. We had removed our coats and loosened our neckties and walked on in freedom, unnoticed, unsung and uncondemned, something we could certainly never have gotten away with in Spain where everyone has to keep up appearances, and so we commented about this also and about the wonderful anonymity one enjoys in this city where no one knows or cares who you are, and most of the people we saw on our way had their coats off or no coats at all, even many young gallants who were walking their best girl home, and we went along talking like this because we had nothing much to talk about except the play we had seen and we did not want to talk about that.

Garcia suggested: "Let's keep going all the way to my place. I have a whole bottle of Fundador and anyway it is too hot to go to bed early. I want to show you what I have done with my story." He did not say anything about it being too hot for walking all that distance, but we both like to walk.

"You mean, the one about that Spanish family? You still working on that?"

"Naturally. You didn't think I was serious about it when I told you. I have already some chapters written out and some other parts somewhat worked out. I'll read you and tell you some."

I said that this was going to take too long but sounded lame. The Fundador was a good bait.

"Come on," he insisted: "After all, it is Saturday night and it is so hot . . ."

So I said all right and we kept going and we commented on how in Spain we are never as conscious of Saturdays as they are in this country, but we did not go into the reasons for that.

It was then that I bought the newspaper and looking through it, standing with Garcia under the street lamp, saw the headline on the second inside page. It was about some former Spanish millionaire who had died destitute in the Bowery. Garcia and I read the item. It explained that the man had been a familiar figure in that district although he did not mix much with the other men there, but usually sat in silence and if any of the men asked what he was doing, he would answer that he was waiting, but never said what he was waiting for and if they asked him what he was thinking, he only shook his head and said "Memories . . . memories." Whoever wrote the article had gone to the trouble of piecing his life together and had come up with the astonishing facts about his past wealth and influence on the financial world. His life had been a mixture of success and tragedy and then final dissolution. He had been found dead in a doorway, his eyes closed, his hands formed into fists at his sides, but despite this rebellious gesture, his face was serene. The whole item was written in the sentimental and tear-jerking style. I read it through and when I looked up at Garcia for a comment, I saw that he was looking away and seemingly absorbed in thought. So I went back to the paper and looked quickly through it until I came near the back and my favorite cartoon, which was the reason for buying the paper. I finished that and started walking again still laughing—that cartoon seldom fails me—when Garcia's attitude arrested me:

In the best theatrical tradition, a Hamlet incarnate, he declaimed in Latin: "Humbra fugit velox et sic fugens denotat horas."

I was nonplussed and inquired silently with shoulders reaching for my ears, with palms of hands turned to the heavens in an appeal for illumination.

"Yes," he continued: "that is the way I will begin my story about Julio Ramos."

"What story? what Ramos? what now?"

"The fellow we just read about in the paper, man. Haven't I told you? I knew him personally, that's why the shock at learning of his death so unexpectedly. I was with him not so long ago. . . ." His voice trailed off effectively and he was a picture of heartbroken desolation, then his voice, still talking to himself, came into resonant focus: "The most extraordinary experience I have had since I came to this country. I must write it down, because the most remarkable thing is that it is true."

I was not impressed. Garcia is given to exaggerations and to speaking carelessly and claiming that many things, including anecdotes which have been known for generations, have actually happened to him. Then when confronted with a challenge to his veracity, instead of yielding like a sensible fellow and admitting that he only presented it as his own experience to lend it more drama, he will insist on braving it out to the bitter end and sometimes creates very embarrassing situations. However, I did not know enough about this particular thing and waited.

"I tell you, the thing is incredible. It is a supernatural story and yet I have seen and spoken to the man, but of course, it would lend itself better to a moving picture because of the more flexible technique."

"A moving picture in Spanish?"

"I was thinking of that. I know one or two concerns in Latin America and have done a little work for them, but I would prefer to make it in English. It pays more, you know."

He was looking at me again in that way that suggested that I would wind up doing a lot of translating and perhaps a little collaborating too, although Garcia was quite impervious to suggestions, and I did not relish the thought. Translating being my business and means of livelihood, I am naturally disinclined to take on extra work, particularly of doubtful remuneration. Besides Garcia knows as much English as I do and is a professional writer which I am not. Maybe he likes to read to me and tell me stories.

But this one was a natural result of Garcia's spiritual equipment. The Lower East Side preyed on his mind. It worried him. He often spoke of its small and fast disappearing landmarks and said that they had the antiquity of day-before-yesterday as compared with a more convincing antiquity, that it was like the difference between a broken Roman lamp, which although useless for its original purpose still retained some artistic value, and a burned-out electric bulb or a rusty, discarded gas jet. Nevertheless that neighborhood fascinated him and he was considerably put out by the encroachment of modern urban developments which were obliterating it. We had often walked through the small, dingy streets and he always had a searching look during those walks as if trying to make out something and I suspect that he was trying to capture and savor a resemblance to his memories of Spain. It was his hobby, together with writing, to relive the past; but in the Lower East Side, it was more like rummaging among rubbish and I felt that we were but frustrated scavengers of memories.

He was certainly warming up to his story fast. It was a fantastic story about a fellow with a time-famished impatience, who would rather risk anything than wait, and how this had affected his life. Garcia declaimed again thoughtfully the Latin phrase.

It was the inscription which he had read upon the face of the discarded sundial while on his way to Julio Ramos. The dial lay upon the grass at the margin of the little cemetery for Spanish Jews in the New Bowery. Its position was such that the shadow of the indicator did not fall upon the dial but somewhere else where time, if it passed, was not marked.

Here Garcia shifted his point abruptly as if in afterthought to explain why he was on his way to Ramos. Even though he was making up this story to me face to face, he was employing second-rate literary tricks.

At the time he met this individual Garcia was working for the Sociedad Española de Socorro. Word was received that this fellow Ramos, a Spanish citizen living in New York, was in a very bad way both in health and finances and threatened the colony with the humiliation of becoming a public charge in a foreign land. To come forth to the aid of such cases, in the name of charity and patriotism and racial pride, was precisely the business of the Sociedad and Garcia was sent to investigate the case.

He found his man in a room in a dilapidated building on Cherry Street, a section abounding in the Spanish element, the man living in a condition of misery whose description would challenge and defeat the best that Garcia's prose and imagination had to give, and it was there that the remarkable tale was unfolded to Garcia, or so he insisted with wide-eyed, stubborn innocence.

"Imagine a young man living in one of those capitals of a province in Spain, Valencia I believe he told me, leading a life of monotonous poverty and frustration, deprived of the smallest pleasures so important in youth. Only his inconsequential job with a navigation company and his small room in a pension, with scarcely any money left over for the barest necessities, to frequent some café and, as they say, mingle with others."

I'll drop the quotation marks because I don't remember exactly Garcia's words.

One can imagine this young man, who is of course Ramos, burning with desire for all the sensuous pleasures and luxuries of an eventful and brilliant life while before him extends an endless, dismal vista of dreary privation. Then his feelings precipitate into abhorrence of his environment, which he blames for his fate, and perhaps because he works for a navigation company, his hopes combine with his feelings in an overpowering wish to escape and in those days, escape usually meant going to the Americas.

Then he begins the thankless, almost superhuman task of saving his pennies, of attaining his one goal which is to go to America at any cost. In his heart he knows it is hopeless but it gives his life a purpose, while at the same time it renders it more difficult, it makes his impecuniousness all the more acute. He grows haggard, anemic and desperate. Meanwhile his impatience is mounting, it grows into a frenzy, he cannot wait. At the rate he is saving, it would take a lifetime. One night he counts his savings and although knowing what to expect, the smallness of the amount is like a slap in the face. In a fever of rage at his own impotence, he hurls the few pesetas from him and staggers to the dresser and contemplates his aging face in the mirror. Impatience invading him like a hurricane, he shuts his eyes and pounds his fists. When he looks again he sees, where his reflection should be, a strange man who says:

"From now on you will do this many times. You will wish for something very much, you will shut your eyes in impatience and when you open them, the time will have passed and you will find yourself at the moment you wish for. You are impatient, Ramos. You want to attain things as soon as you desire them, without waiting, at any cost. I will give you the power to skip time at will, but I will not promise that you will get what you want. You will only get what is coming to you, but without waiting. Sometimes it may be good and sometimes bad. I will give you the power to remove from your path a section as long as you desire or is left of the road ahead. All you have to do is to shut your eyes and wish. Every supernatural power must have its ritual. But beware of turns in the road because you do not know what may be patiently waiting for you who do not want to wait."

This is a rather lengthy speech, but according to Garcia, young Ramos is spared by sinking to the floor where he lies unconscious, perhaps sleeping for the first time in many nights and this is a dead giveaway, as Garcia must have concocted at least part of the speech, but anyway, I will let him go on with his improvisation.

The next day he was sure that all had been but a hallucination, but still there was uneasiness. On his way home from work he went by way of the piers. There was a ship docked there and he could well visualize its itinerary: Barcelona, Valencia, Malaga, Cádiz and then the Atlantic to America, to New York. Unable to resist its attraction, he ascended the gangplank and went aboard. No one questioned his presence which was familiar from the many times he had come to deliver documents to this and other ships like it. He walked to the railing on the other side.

Standing there he imagined himself a passenger on his way to America. If he could only accelerate time, eliminate the long, almost hopeless wait that lay before him. The ship swayed ever so faintly. The motion would have been imperceptible to anyone, but the eager senses of Ramos detected it immediately, enlarged it to a time-conquering rolling motion over Atlantic waves. And suddenly his desire, his impatience burst upon him like a bombshell. Instinctively he closed his eyes as if to shut out his hateful present, he clenched his fists in threatening fury against his fortune and he wished, he wished as he had never wished before.

The sound of ships' sirens, of boat whistles, of hurried people and sharp voices, of words not spoken in Spanish, crowded in his ears and brought him to. Ramos opened his eyes and his knees sagged as his heart pulled him on its way down. The bay of New York was closing up on him.

Garcia waved his arms forward like an orchestra conductor. I looked in front and all I saw were our perspiring images reflected in the barroom mirror. This was the second thirst-quenching stop we had made to lay a foundation for the promised brandy at Garcia's. He had been so fired by his narrative that he had infected me and during the last part, leaning there against the bar, the impression had been as vivid as was the letdown now. We left there and walked on, Garcia still talking with the same enthusiasm. We made only one more stop with him pounding on the bar to drive his point home and reaffirm the veracity of his experience with the fellow Ramos and by the time we got to his place all the fight was out of me and he had his story or moving picture or whatever it was considerably well planned out.

Garcia went up to his rooms turning around to talk to me all the way up the stairs. He was quite winded when we reached his place. His lights were on. He never failed to leave his lights on, or have them turned on for him. Did not like to walk into a dark room.

We discarded our coats and I flopped on an easy chair by the open windows. Garcia moved to his desk, which was well littered with papers, a typewriter, and of all things an old slipper which I later learned he used to slap flies with. There was a sheet of paper inserted in the typewriter. He bent over to read it, then pulled it out and threw it crumpled into the wastebasket. It bounced to the floor to join other scraps of paper. The basket was overflowing already.

"What about that drink," I reminded him.

"Oh yes, the Fundador." He went to a chest at the far end of the room and returned with a bottle and two tumblers. He placed every-thing on a small table by my chair and also an open pack of cigarettes, and then he uncorked the bottle. Quite hospitable and also quite ensnaring—"said the spider to the fly"—I thought.

"Help yourself," he said, and I poured a couple of good ones and settled down.

"This is going to make us perspire more," I said as if I cared.

"The more one perspires, the less one feels the heat," Garcia philosophized absently and disregarding his drink went back to the desk and began fumbling again and stacking typewritten sheets: "Let me see, let me see." He shoved our coats over and sat on the daybed facing me:

"I have this part pretty well worked out. Of course, the whole story is old-fashioned and I would like to present it in some parts, especially this one," he waved the papers in his hand, "in a sort of old-fashioned —well stilted—if you know what I mean, to fit the period." He searched for the right word or explanation: "Cursi is what I mean. That is the word: cursi."

The word "cursi" is difficult to translate, its meaning almost impossible to convey with any other word, and the closest I can find to it in English is the word "corny." I told him that I knew what he meant and he went on:

"I am quite serious about your helping with the translation and if I convince you, I hope you will bear that in mind and try to create that cursi feeling in English."

I said that it was hard enough simply to express an idea clearly in English without attempting the fine points of style and shades of feeling, and then with modest, if true, self-appraisal, I added that he need not fear, because anything in which I collaborated in English was sure to turn out pretty corny anyway.

Garcia referred to his papers and settled more comfortably: "After what I read to you at El Telescopio as a sort of introduction, I may use this part to open the novel. I am not sure yet. Perhaps I might insert other material before. But listen to this now:"

Paco Serrano is a young man-about-town and has all the attributes that go with that title. He is very good-looking and dresses irreproachably. He does everything that is fashionable, or rather, everything he does becomes fashionable. Everybody knows him well in Madrid. His credit is ample and he has just enough honor.

Three or four duels (with a thin and becoming scar from one), many love affairs, and two acknowledged and generous mistresses complete his wardrobe.

Many things are said about Paco Serrano, among them that he is a natural son of the Count of X. and that his official father was an official cuckold.

According to many people, this official father never cared about the iregular life of his wife and profited handsomely by the generosity showered upon her and his official son by the Count of X.

Paco Serrano was excellently educated and never missed a luxury in life. His official father did not work, nor had he any known income, but nevertheless he lived with his wife and son in a luxurious mansion and went out in a carriage pulled by two horses with a coachman and a lackey.

It is told that he once said: "Horns are like teeth; they hurt when they come in, but after, they are good to eat with."

This sentence has been attributed to others, but after all there are so many people in the same situation and so many who would like to be in a similar one that it must have occurred to many.

Apparently the generosity of the Count of X. did not stop with the disappearance of Madame Serrano's youth, or perhaps he had provided indefinitely for her. This was the opinion of many who could not understand where Paco got the income that permitted him to lead the gay and brilliant existence he led.

Yet, all this is gossip. Who cares? Least of all Paco Serrano, who is tonight on his way to the theater and as a first-nighter is going to see the opening of a new musical revue.

The name of the revue is *La Gran Via* and it concerns the plans for the construction of a new avenue—which incidentally, has not been finished yet. Some of the streets through which it is expected to pass are represented by actors. There are the usual allusions to the political situation of those days.

Paco Serrano is reclining condescendingly in his chair. Although the play interests him more than the audience, he utterly disregards it to concentrate on the boxes and aim his opera glasses at the ladies. It is the fashion. Elegant Spaniards of the time go to the theater the first night and to church to the late High Mass, but only to see the ladies. In both places the performances are immaterial, even if they are confirmed lovers of the theater and devout Catholics.

A slender old dandy with a top hat at a rakish angle advances to the footlights with graceful steps. He is spinning a cane in his fingers and he begins to sing a waltz which has become internationally famous since that night:

"Caballero de gracia me llaman. . . ."

There were murmurs of approval. Paco Serrano felt eclipsed by a great actor on that memorable night and he turned languidly to inspect the scene. There stood the famous Joaquín Manini accepting the applause in a charming manner.

The performance went on. Something funny happened on the stage and the whole house roared with laughter and then above that roar, a unique laugh pierced the theater, a laugh like silver that for a moment seemed to steal and hold all the light and attention from the stage and music.

Paco turned around and three rows behind he beheld a stunning woman. She was what has been called afterwards a capital female. Slightly thick nostrils, generous lips, great somber slanting eyes, large and erect breasts. Serrano had had all this, but second hand and a brand-new good woman is quite extraordinary. Although she appeared to be very young, she had an air of maturity that made her very exciting. Her bosom was still heaving, her face flushed, her eyes moist from the recent outburst. She appeared like a wonderful flower after a rainstorm.

Paco looked at her long and impertinently, his eyes opaque, and he bit his lower lip. She noticed it and composed herself and then talked to a fat over-painted blonde sitting by her side.

Serrano felt almost sure that he had met this blonde sometime, somewhere in an amusement place that specialized in sex and he failed to connect both women. For the rest of the evening he continued to turn around and look at the beautiful woman until a vulgar lady who had looked exceedingly pleased with it realized that his eyes were focused past her when she said to her companion:

"In these theaters of Madrid they should place a big mirror at the back so that some people would not miss the entire performance. It seems that we have to see many faces we have not paid to see."

When the very successful performance was over, Serrano followed the dark woman and the blonde to the entrance of the theater. On the street he saw they were accompanied by a young man about his own age, whom he had not noticed before.

The young man placed them in a carriage waving at them familiarly. He then turned to a coupé that Serrano was summoning distractedly while still watching the other carriage recede. The two men did not notice each other and both said to the coachman at the same time:

"A La Gran Peña."

They turned to look at each other and laughed. Paco was worldly immediately: "Since we both belong to the same club, we may as well go there together. My name is Francisco Serrano."

They exchanged cards and shook hands. The other man said: "My name is Fernando Sandoval, at your service."

"I hope so," Paco thought and both entered the coupé.

Fernando Sandoval, who was quite lively, began a conversation immediately: "Fine performance tonight. How did you like it?"

Paco, who had not paid much attention to the stage, answered absently:

"I haven't the slightest idea," but Fernando Sandoval did not notice the answer and went on talking enthusiastically.

Paco was thinking of the connection this young man might have with the beautiful woman and also of how he had not been noticed looking at her. Of course a man in the company of a woman like that wouldn't notice anything else. But apparently Sandoval had followed the performance very closely by the detailed account he was giving of it. He sang, recited and jumped:

"Don't you think the brothers Mesejo were inimitable in the 'Jota de los Ratas'?" He sang:

> "Soy el rata primero
> y yo el segundo
> y yo el tercero . . ."

Paco thought that knowing a person like this, it did not matter whether one missed a whole performance. He brought a beautiful woman to distract people from the stage and then gave them a detailed account of the play. Fernando Sandoval was displaying an extraordinary memory for music he had heard for the first time:

"Let me see . . . let me see, how's it go . . . oh yes!" He gave a jump that startled Paco from his thoughts:

> "Cuando nos echa mano la policia
> estamos seguritos que es para un dia . . ."

Truly remarkable.

For a few moments Sandoval succeeded in turning Paco's thoughts from their course. The now well-known "Jota de los Ratas" born that night came vividly to his mind in contrast to the waltz "Caballero de Gracia," which he discovered he had subconsciously been singing in his mind. He had liked those two things in the performance and the Jota had particularly appealed to him. The gay, mocking music had all the vim and spark of Spanish roguery. It moved at a quick pace, it glorified the Ratas, the pickpockets of Madrid who guy all laws and amuse the public. In that dance of the pick-pockets lived the ever-seditious Spanish race. It was broad, fast, accurate, fearless, bold, indifferent, but underneath it concealed a torrent of melancholy, of cynical bitterness. It brought back the tradition of Gines de Pasamonte, scoffing Don Quixote's ideals; of Rinconete and Cortadillo aging prematurely in the poisoned shadow of the Patio de Monipodio; of the Lazarillo de Tormes, born with a wisdom which defies life and outwits age and experience. Listening to the "Jota de los Ratas," pompous and sad, brilliant, shady, straightforward and crooked, one could see the magnificent gallery of Spanish rogues parade in all its glory, pass by in all its wretchedness and fade away in all its sinful earnestness into that ever-thirsty, inevitable maelstrom of forgetfulness that keeps on swallowing every typical and worthwhile manifestation of Spanish life. Gone is Gines de Pasamonte, the man who most brutally disappointed the sublime madman in life, to whom the unique hidalgo owes his conclusion that "to do a good turn to a villain is like casting water into the sea." Gone are Rinconete and Cortadillo and with them the famous Patio, that worthy school of crookery, primitive laboratory of crime in which the masterful Monipodio presided with all the prestige and dignity of a man aged in depravity who has dedicated his life to the advancement of evil. Gone is the Lazarillo de Tormes, who led the blind through existence and therefore learned to rely on his own sight, who would have made old men lower their eyes for shame that he could see the rotten core of their souls, when after all his own soul was still pure. Gone are countless others, only a few pickpockets remain astray, but their spirit is the same in quality, their attitude the same. Listening to the "Jota de los Ratas" one felt that it was a last spark from a magnificent, extinguished cast, and it awakened something in the public, in this ever-seditious Spanish public who always is ready to aid the outlaw, to side with the Ratas, as a tacit reproach against the invasion of efficient morality, as a subconscious tribute to the great rogues who were.

The carriage bounced and Paco's thoughts settled down once more in the present. He thought the young man quite likable despite his overflowing stupidity. With such communicativeness, he soon would find out who the beautiful lady was.

They arrived at La Gran Peña and soon were surrounded by mutual friends.

"Hello, Serrano."

"Hello, boys."

"Hello, Sandoval. I didn't know you knew Serrano already."

"Who doesn't know Serrano?"

"Be careful, he is a real truhán."

"And what do you think of Sandoval, our new member?"

"Fine lad, my boys, fine lad. Excellent memory for music."

"Did you see *La Gran Vía?*"

"Yes, marvelous! A great success. Sandoval will tell you all about it."

"He should. I understand that he has helped to back it. Must know it by memory from rehearsals."

They sat at a gaming table and the noise subsided. Paco was distracted during the game but he played heavily through force of habit. Fernando

Sandoval imitated him. After a while Sandoval began to lose considerably and kept it up boastfully. He was drinking too and soon he and Paco were on familiar terms. When they left the table, Fernando, who had gambled beyond what he carried, handed Serrano a note:

"Never had such bad luck before. You played splendidly."

"You know the saying: He who is unfortunate in play is fortunate in love. There was a beautiful dark lady with you at the theater."

"Oh! That was my sister Julieta. The other one was my wife." Fernando laughed: "Which one did you like most?"

Paco was still holding the note in his hand and he began to smile: "That is a rather embarrassing question." The smile spread all over his face as he slowly tore up the piece of paper. He ended in a frank outburst of laughter and the small pieces rained from his hands to the floor. He was literally caressing Fernando with his eyes and his hand found his shoulder and pressed it in a friendly manner.

Sandoval was too drunk to be offended. He took the whole thing as only exaggerated graciousness from his new friend, who undoubtedly did not want to take his money the first time they had met. They left the place arm in arm. When they parted, Paco Serrano offered to meet Fernando Sandoval the next day for an aperitif.

When Julieta Sandoval was sixteen years old, she got a special maid for her personal use, a plumpish lively blonde called Trini, not much older than her mistress. She was the daughter of a washerwoman who had worked long for the Sandoval family.

This girl seemed to give an undue importance to the relations between men and women, an importance which nowadays would seem mild, but which at that time was excessive. She apparently thought of nothing else and considered it part of her duties to her mistress to act as a matchmaker and to encourage every young admirer whose florid missives she often brought in great secrecy.

Her duties as a maid were not sufficient to keep her very busy and consequently she had a great deal of time to herself which she employed reading strange things, standing on the balcony, or carrying on conversations on forbidden subjects with her mistress. . . .

At this point Garcia's story took a not entirely unexpected turn for the pornographic and I halted him. I don't want to project myself too much into this and am not averse to the grand classical ribaldry of a

Boccaccio or a Quevedo, but the uncalled-for and irrelevant pornography that mars like grease spots much of our literature at the turn of the century does not appear engaging and in Spain we have coined another word for it.

I told Garcia this and it precipitated an altercation. I said that this was not even pornography but what we call in Spain sicalipsis, which is not only unnecessary but reprehensible and not only discouraged but condemned and prosecuted by the postal and other authorities which maintain law and order and that I also objected to it on the grounds of literary integrity, because it was not of the essence in the story and I found its connection, if any, entirely too farfetched: "You have thrown that in only to shock the reader."

He protested heatedly that this was not the case, that the passage was not sicaliptic, but simply bold and real and that it showed more artistic integrity by not shrinking from facts no matter how objectionable and that it was very relevant indeed as he expected to develop from it the subsequent neuroses of the heroine.

That is what he said and also some other things, but I argued against literature that attempts to gain popularity by appealing to the same giggly and prudishness-on-vacation spirit as does a dirty joke, whose lack of humorous merit is easily exposed by cleaning it up, and our argument descended to almost childish acrimony. To the devil with the neuroses of the heroine. It would be simpler to develop it from an early fall on her head when she was a baby. However, and to clinch things, I said that if I had anything to do with the translation, I would not tolerate any more of such passages which could only offend the ears of the English reader and create the wrong impression about our fair sex and our country where we can be as mid-Victorian as the best. I ended by pouring myself a smug fathom of the brandy.

Garcia glanced at the bottle and me: "There is also some regular whiskey if you want any."

I had had my say and calmed down, so I kept my peace and told him that he did not have to get me drunk in order to read to me.

"I thought it might wash away some of your old-fashioned ideas and loosen up your inhibitions."

"Never mind my inhibitions. You just go ahead and read."

He turned over five pages, no less, and then:

All this created a strong bond of friendship between Julieta and Trini. The maid was the most intimate companion of Julieta. She was her confidante, shared her emotions and became indispensable to her. Between them a strange relationship was developing and who knows where it would have ended had it not been for the interfering incidents which follow.

Fernando Sandoval discovered one good day that his sister's maid was exceedingly likable. He assayed one or two tentative advances which met with but a very weak rebuff and the siege began. He spied on all her movements, approached her whenever the opportunity presented itself and forced his attentions mercilessly behind every conspiring door or portiere until she rushed away to the safety of her mistress's room.

Once, as she came out of that room, she met Fernando in the corridor. Her naturally pink complexion was glowing with a flush of excitement. Fernando made for her hungrily and held her in his arms.

"No ... please ... Señorito ... oh God!"

She could resist no longer and met Fernando brutally, pressing herself against him with all the force that mighty nature can command at times. It was a nerve-shattering kiss. She experienced the sensation of rolling backwards and sinking in an abyss where she could exercise no control, a wonderful, wonderful abyss, and by force of instinct, as anyone who sinks, she pressed more that which she held.

Their love affair progressed rapidly from then on. She was no longer free. She was entirely at his mercy.

At first they did not leave each other a moment's peace. It was a tempestuous affair. To live in the same house, to have constant opportunity to love in a clandestine manner, acted like a whip on their desires, urging them, driving them to one another. Trini seemed to have forgotten Julieta. Those conversations and intimate sessions which had constituted their mutual delight ceased abruptly. Trini limited herself to her strict duties as a maid and had resumed her position in regard to her mistress cruelly. If Julieta broached the subject they used to like so well, Trini answered:

"Don't think so much about those things. It is not good for you."

Julieta could not understand what had happened to her maid and this was the first emotional shock, a strong shock to her tense feelings.

In the house everybody had noticed more or less the change in Fernando's behavior. No one can help noticing a person whom one has scarcely seen for years and who suddenly appears at the dinner table every night and then does not even rush out. Even Don Mariano noticed it and once said to his son while at dinner:

"What is the matter, Fernando? All this sudden seriousness? Have you repented like Saint Francis for all your worldly sins? Are you getting ready to enter a convent?"

"No, it is nothing particular, simply that Madrid life is getting boresome, always the same thing over and over again. Haven't you noticed it?"

"Me? No! I never notice those things."

"I decided to take a little rest. That's all."

"Hmm—it does not seem to agree with you at all. You look paler and thinner than ever."

"I? Why, I never felt better in my life."

"Perhaps it is my imagination and you really are redder and fatter. I have not seen you for such a long time that I almost forgot what you looked like, but I have a vague recollection that you looked healthier."

"That is because I was much younger then."

Fernando grew uneasy. He began to view the matter from a different angle. His meetings with Trini began to take place outside the house at a certain dwelling in the Street of Jardines where a discreet lady accommodated any couple in a cozy room, but this too was difficult. In Madrid too many people could recognize them.

He had thought that he could enjoy the young maid for a while and then tire of her. But she clung to him. Every day she grew more passionately in love. She was a perfect pleasure machine and Fernando became hopelessly entrapped.

His meetings with Trini were more difficult and dangerous. He was now in love with her and the once enticing situation became unbearable. He wanted to have more of her, to have her all to himself, somewhere where he could love her freely all he wanted. He resented her subordinate position as a maid, to see her treated as such. This made him realize things which he did not want to realize and as a consequence began to consider his family as an obstacle.

By this time he used to help his father at the jewelry shop sporadically. He would go in and work on the books or help wait on customers. Of late he had worked more regularly.

Once he was in the store alone with Ledesma. Ledesma was always in the store, always at his post like a good watchdog. He was administrator and had full control of the business. Ledesma was still quite young but he was so serious that he looked much older. He had always been understanding. He spoke in a low voice, in a sententious manner, but seldom advised. He was loyal, perhaps too loyal. This was the drawback. But he loved all the Sandoval family more than they loved each other among themselves. Fernando went to Ledesma.

He told him everything. He explained his whole situation thoroughly and Ledesma listened attentively. Fernando was almost in tears and then he asked Ledesma to let him take a large sum of money in order to go away, to say nothing and then he would replace it somehow.

Ledesma was not indignant; his voice was a little lower, more sententious: "I could not do that. Even if no one ever found out. I could not do it. It is not my money."

"But it is in your custody. You can do as you please. Father has implicit faith in you."

"That makes it impossible. I am here to guard your father's interests."

"But I tell you I am mad. I am living in hell. If I can't take Trini away from this I'll blow my brains out. I have tried to fight it but it is impossible. I can't help myself, please, please!"

Fernando offered a pitiful spectacle. He had fallen on his knees embracing Ledesma's legs and crying like a child. Ledesma felt for him, but he was inflexible. He helped Fernando rise and steadied him:

"Yes, you are mad, my boy, but this kind of madness will pass if you try and let others help you. Why don't you speak to your father . . ."

"You know that is impossible, you know that very well." He was truly frightened.

"You are right and you cannot blame him, should he find out what has been going on under his roof. But perhaps I could talk to him without telling him everything. He might send Trini away. That would help."

"No, that won't help. That will kill me. I'll blow my brains out. Oh, Ledesma! You have always been so good to me and Julieta. You have been almost a second father. That is why I came to you. You are my only hope, please, please!"

But Ledesma argued and persuaded and for once advised. He was by far the stronger character of the two and in the end he had Fernando under control, or so he thought. The latter promised to try his best and even yielded to the suggestion of a short trip to the north, but when he left, Ledesma was no longer very confident.

That night when Ledesma was closing the store, he locked the safe as usual and then stood before it. He knew Fernando had a key to the safe and one to the store, but the safe had an extra lock that was never used and to which only Ledesma and Don Mariano had a key.

Ledesma stood before the closed safe with lowered head. He reached for the other key and then shuddered and rushed out: "He wouldn't have asked me—he wouldn't have asked me."

The next day the thing had happened which all Madrid knew so soon and

Señor Sandoval stood before Ledesma with a crumpled note in his trembling hand: "You knew it, Ledesma, and you did not warn me."

"Sir, you know how I loved the boy," and Ledesma looked away because he knew he was about to lie. "I never suspected that your son . . ."

"Don't say it, Ledesma. I can understand more than is apparent, my good Ledesma," and Don Mariano embraced him tightly as if seeking protection from some invisible foe. The thing had happened which cast the first cloud of disgrace upon the Sandoval family.

Fernando and Trini went to the Argentine. They wanted to put as much distance as possible between themselves and the scene of their delinquency. They remained in Buenos Aires for some time, spending freely what Fernando had stolen from his father.

Trini's vulgarity had influenced Fernando more than his pseudo-refinement had influenced her. One must rise, men say, and experience teaches that to rise is difficult. Does this not prove that one should descend? Fernando did. He and Trini always sought the company of the lower classes and felt more at home with them.

They frequented the cafés in the arrabales. Trini had a habit of looking at people, and especially men, in a provocative and insolent way which for a moment angered Fernando and then acted as an added attraction.

In the café to which this particular case refers, there was a dark gentleman with high cheekbones and the manner of a professional procurer who had been examining her for a long time. He spoke to some friends and said something impertinent about her.

Fernando was excited with the atmosphere of the place which invited braggadocio. He addressed the man loudly and called him a lousy Indian.

The man walked over and very politely promised to perforate his guts and the trouble began.

Fernando, without giving the man time to accomplish his threat, smashed a heavy bottle on his head and the man fell bleeding like a stuck pig.

The place was in an uproar and it was all Fernando and Trini could do to escape with their clothes torn. Fernando was sure he had killed the man and so that night they packed the few things they had and left Buenos Aires for a village in the interior.

It was a painful and sad trip. They quarreled all the time. They had reached that stage.

"It was all your fault for looking at the man the way you did, you cheap . . ."

"I had not even noticed the man."

"You had not, eh? I'd like to see the man you don't notice, you . . ." He held her in his arms and kissed her mouth, biting the thick lips.

"How you hurt, mi negro."

And they went on quarreling more fiercely than before.

They arrived at the village which was in an appallingly primitive state and they took a sordid-looking dismantled house, isolated from the rest. It stood at the end of a plaza in the middle of which was a fountain, and at the end where the house stood, it was walled by thick woods.

The whole village seemed to be submerged in the immense forest. Every street ended in the same impenetrable mass of green, except the one through which they had come and another one, both fading like snakes into the woods. It was like a great nest sunken forever in the jungle.

They remained there too some time and felt horribly lonesome. The villagers were hostile. They knew no one.

Their quarreling had assumed fearful proportions. They lived like two caged beasts, blaming each other for their misfortune, until once, after a particularly ugly scene and as they sat silently in that gloomy house, Trini spoke the first calm words in a long time:

"Fernando, why should we behave like enemies when we are so alone? We are so forsaken. We have nothing but each other. Let us be friendly and make this thing more bearable. I am afraid."

And for the first time Fernando embraced Trini with tenderness, a deep tenderness exempt from any other feeling, and he realized that they were irrevocably bound.

Then an epidemic broke out in the village and, with the difficulty of obtaining help from the outside, it took a terrible toll. People died like roaches everywhere. They fell where they were struck and died there without help. The epidemic gained headway and there was not a single house where candlelight did not burn at night while some person mourned and kept watch over a corpse.

People migrated from the village until after some time there were more dead than alive. Fernando and Trini did not dare to go out into the wild country. They had no more chance to survive there than in the pestilent village; they knew not what to do and felt like trapped rats awaiting their doom. They dared not leave the house, imagining that the hideous disease respected windows and doors—as if it were not in the very walls, in the very air, in the sun itself which penetrated through the dusty windowpanes like a pale, clammy, insidious thing.

The streets were deserted, the houses full of corpses and the vultures had descended upon the dead village. Every time a cart went by carrying some of the dead into the wilderness, a flock of the hungry birds mobbed it and a gruesome battle ensued between the almost crazed cart driver and the horrible birds, and the man lashed away at the vultures and lashed furiously at the horses, the funereal load bouncing and diving into the woods, among a cloud of dust and a cloud of maddening birds.

The vultures had descended upon the dead village. Every night they alighted on the roofs and windowsills and screeched long and lugubriously, begging for the abundant flesh, until Trini almost went mad with horror and clung to Fernando:

"I am going crazy, I am losing my mind with these accursed birds. They seem to be calling me. I know I will be next. Drive them away!"

Then Fernando staggered to the windows like an enraged drunkard and pounded and cursed the vultures as if they were men.

It was under these adverse circumstances that Trini gave premature birth to a boy whom they named Enrique. Without a single skilled person's help, only with the clumsy aid of Fernando whose nerves could not hold out much longer and who went to pieces during the delivery, the child was miraculously born.

Their fears were redoubled. Trini, who was a strong believer, was in panic: "The poor little angel. He will die without baptism."

"If you believe at all, you cannot think your God that bad. This thing has not got us yet. It will not get us," Fernando cried stupidly.

There was only one thing to break the monotony of their existence. Every night at the same time a faint young voice was heard singing, increasing in volume as it neared the house. It was a young native who came to the fountain in the plaza for water: to fetch and drink the poisoned water with the same indifference with which he sang, as if the ghastly happenings had nothing to do with his life.

They waited for him every night. As they sat talking or silent, one of them would say: "Here he comes now. Listen."

He approached singing with a beautiful clear voice and the vultures were silenced. Then he stopped to fill his jug. They heard the water running melodiously and then he went back, always singing, his voice fading away in the distance, as if his life wore an impenetrable armor of indifference. When the voice had faded completely, the vultures resumed their fantastic serenade.

One night they waited for the little singer. They waited long but he did not come and the vultures screeched longer and screeched louder that night.

At last Fernando and Trini could stand no more and one day they rushed out of that place of death. It is not necessary to fill more paper with an account of their disastrous journey. They finally arrived at La Plata and from there Fernando wrote home.

It was an abject letter begging forgiveness, giving a gruesome description of their experiences and sufferings, promising to work until he had paid his father back, if only the latter promised not to prosecute him when he returned to Madrid.

Trini added a sentimental postscript to the letter, telling of her little Enriquito who wanted to know his grandparents, and also begging forgiveness for all the trouble she had given them only because she loved their son so much. The letter ended with the usual clause, demanding money for the return trip.

Don Mariano Sandoval had forgiven them long ago, but the letter renewed his anger and he called Trini unprintable names: "He expects to bring this washerwoman's daughter into the family just like that. What will Madrid say?"

"Madrid always says the same thing no matter what one does."

Julieta interceded in their favor, saying that Trini had always been a good girl and was not to blame for the bad education she had received: "After all, she can't help that."

"That is the worst of it. At least, if she could help it, there would be some hope, but this way . . ."

Don Mariano softened. Ledesma also interceded in favor of the fugitives in his ponderous manner, stating that to forget is to be born again and then Don Mariano sent the money for the return trip and a letter containing his forgiveness.

When Fernando and Trini returned shamefacedly and having aged ten years in eighteen months, the Sandovals went to embrace them and meet little Enrique.

All this had taken considerable time and it was late, or more properly speaking, quite early in the morning. There had been interruptions and autosuggestions by Garcia and he had stopped frequently to make notes and changes and to elaborate certain points, indicating that the reader may not notice the things which the writer has unconsciously left out but never fails to notice the things which the writer has not consciously put in. There had been comments, digressions and even some more arguing that had led through generalizations to very unrelated topics. If it had not been for the brandy, I might not have shown so much interest, but alcohol can make so many things tolerable and even engrossing. But by now, Garcia could not keep his eyes open and finally the papers he held fell at his feet and he was fast asleep leaning against the cushions of the couch.

I poured myself the last drink from the bottle and drank it to the accompaniment of Garcia's snores. Then I realized that I should be doing the same thing and got up with foggy aches running here and there through my anatomy, picked up my coat, went over to the couch and pulled the covers back over Garcia.

When I reached the door I looked back at the scene of intellectual debauchery and my eye caught Garcia's glass still untouched on the table. Feeling chilly and, of course, in order not to waste it, I went back and drank it. Then I left the room. In the hall I stopped at the bathroom and on the way out took one look at the mirror. This hastened my departure and I went down the stairs much faster than I should in that condition. Outside it was open, undeniable morning, the first rays of the sun pointing accusing fingers. But I did not care, I walked away loggily, unashamed and with maudlin visions of a mattress against my body.

Boy! When I got home I was going to sleep like a son of a gun. All things considered, the bed is the payoff.

What I like about Garcia is his ability at loitering. He is a past master and can do it anywhere, day or night. We have often commented on the little loitering done in this country, or at least in the part we know of it, which is mostly New York. The way one lives here does not lend itself to it; there is no café life as we understand it, that is, cafés where one is certain of finding one's friends or acquaintances between hours ample enough to permit a leisurely meeting and miss no one by simply remaining there long enough. There is not, for that matter, any tacit gathering place, some favorite spot or bench in a park or a stretch of an avenue or boulevard, where one cannot fail finding people one knows if only to escape at times a feeling of loneliness, of inevitable solitude among the many.

Garcia has reminded me of a certain sidewalk in Madrid where almost everyone knew everybody else. Between late morning and early evening, one was sure to find whomever one was looking for, but as it might not be convenient to spend all that time walking up and down, and in some cases, one might even have something else to do, there was a fellow who had created a fine job for himself. He worked that sidewalk continuously, accosting the passersby in keeping with some special formula:

"Caballero," or perhaps addressing the party by his name, if he knew him well, but always tipping his hat deferentially: "Any little service I can have the honor of rendering?"

"Why, yes, now that you mention it. If you see so-and-so, will you tell him, please, that I would like to see him? I will be at such-and-such a place at such-and-such a time."

"At your service," and the fellow darted away to find the individual unerringly or to attend to some of the same business while waiting for the time where the person would be accessible. He knew when or where to find anyone and his services included such information as a new girl in some particular house, or when the medical visit would take place for those who wanted to play it safe. He had everyone perfectly catalogued as to his habits and tastes, and I don't know whether he kept any notes but he never approached the same customer more than once the same day unless he was delivering a message, and he could be trusted implicitly. After a few such services, every customer gave him some money depending on the importance of the services rendered. Never, however, as payment but merely as a token of appreciation. This was very important. Once some new man committed the unforgivable breach of etiquette of asking him how much he owed him and the fellow dropped him from his list instantly and never approached or delivered any message to him, until the poor man, helpless, in a state of social ostracism, practically incommunicado, had to apologize handsomely.

Now such a situation, conditions making such an occupation possible, could never be found in this city. During many hours of loitering, Garcia and I have tried and failed. True enough, they have cafés or their equivalent here, and parks with benches and avenues with people walking through them, but the social, club-like atmosphere which miraculously partakes both of the casual and inevitable is missing. One either has to take a taxicab or the subway, with a premeditation that spoils the whole thing, to see but some specific party, or else make a series of telephone calls well in advance, which lends the thing an importance beyond all proportion and dilutes all spontaneity.

Perhaps in this case one tends to particularize and many of these things which one claims typically Spanish are perhaps Latin, or even European, but to return to the loitering of Garcia: he could only indulge in it here with one or two of us as a rule, and usually me, because I lived nearest him.

From this, it is easy to see that Garcia did not like to work at anything regular. He would do so only in desperation. He lived with his land-lady, an imposingly domestic German woman who held him in sublime worship and awesome respect for what she termed his intellectual pursuits. This took care of his room and board, but the humiliation he felt and her plebeian manners and the secrecy in which he considered he must keep this relationship, only revealed to his closest friends, was to him an exorbitant price to pay and grated his temper. His attempts at extracting a living from writing in this country, battling the set ideas, preferences and patterns of the literary world, had left him as frustrated as a woodpecker in the petrified forest. But still he wrote most of the time and occasionally sold to lesser Latin American reviews an article invariably about New York, a short story invariably about Spain, or a poem invariably about himself. This could be construed by those faithful to him into a semblance of independence and a flicking caress to self-respect, but the irritation was there and this precipitated bitter quarrels in which his pride rose to soaring heights of despair and he decided to go to work. This he attained with the help of a fellow roomer.

This was the only other roomer in the house. All the others had fled soon after moving there and the reason was simple. During the day they could scarcely move about without the handle of a broom banking under their feet or the hefty knuckles of the landlady rapping imperiously on their door and demanding sepulchral silence because the master was working or resting and any noise disturbed him and, when night came, they could not sleep because that was when inspira-tion often assaulted Garcia and he would punish the typewriter mercilessly. More maladjustment and more quarreling.

But this one roomer did not mind. He was a fellow who worked as a dishwasher mostly at night and slept during the day and when the order was reversed, he could sleep through anything anyway. He was a carefree and perennially happy individual without much sense of responsibility and a nature that permitted him to disregard all the minor annoyances of life. He had even let Garcia read to him and like most Latin Americans felt dutybound to enjoy poetry and consider it the one justification for any man to reside on the surface of the earth, and he liked it there because it was one of the few places where he was permitted to bring a girl now and then, provided he was not too shameless about it. When he was tired of a restaurant, he quit and went to work in another. If he managed to accumulate a little money, which his nature made very infrequent, he quit altogether until he needed some more. This then was the chap who could always get Garcia a job as a dishwasher whenever Garcia suffered an attack of pride and decided to leave the house with phrases such as "pride is more pressing than hunger."

Of course, Garcia would only work a few days until the attack subsided and then returned swearing that work of that nature destroyed his spirit and would lead him to suicide, and the landlady must have timed his returns chronometrically because she always had ready a gallon of Rhine wine and a good-sized sauerbraten and I understand that it takes over two days to prepare this dish. Then Garcia ate, drank and held forth about the social system.

During his absences from the landlady, he stayed either with Dr. de los Rios or Don Pedro Guzman in brilliant and luxurious surroundings, or with me who only disposed of a room with an extra cot. In either place he could find a typewriter and paper and these were things he could not be without. If his pride had not been too badly mangled, he only made believe that he was going to wash dishes and spent his time in one of our places writing or reading when we were not there, but if there was any remark about his imposing on his friends, which the poor woman threw as a last desperate obstacle to his departure, he sallied forth with his own portable typewriter and a bundle of paper, his only traveling array—and as Don Pedro called it, his intellectual paraphernalia—to render the accusation unjust and lend his exit an element of finality.

It was during one of these absences from his home, when it was my turn to be honored with his company, that we were loitering in Central

Park. The quarrel was due this time, I believe, to the irritability induced by the season of the year. Spring in New York was the despair of Garcia. He could not stand cold and had a pet theory that any temperature below thirty-seven degrees centigrade, the approximate temperature of human blood in circulation, must be necessarily unpleasant. Anything above this only increased the joy of living up to certain limits, such as the boiling point of water as he used it in his bathtub. All winter he had to carry on his loitering indoors with lightning-fast dashes between one place and another, bundled up to his eyes, and when spring arrived officially and still no warm weather, he felt cheated by the malevolent forces of nature and became impatient, lugubrious and unbearable. One day the sun would shine brightly and the day would be warm, filled with glittering humidity, like a harbinger of the spring, and Garcia was optimistic and talked lyrically of hearing in his mind the thunder of ice breaking and being carried along by the irresistible force of the season, roaring in its streams again like sap through thawing lands. The next day the temperature dropped, the skies were overcast, it might rain or even snow, and his hopes were ruthlessly dashed to the icy ground by buffeting cold cruel winds whispering like needles in one's ear that winter was still in command. Then he was seized by a fit of depression, swearing that the warm weather was never coming and one might as well be resigned to spend the rest of one's life in this climate hibernating, or else pack up and flee to any place on the equator. He could not understand why all the biggest and most important business centers should be built in climates capable of discouraging the hardiest and he frequently exclaimed at such times:

"What diabolical stubbornness got into them that they did not move south after the first winter? With all the coastline from Hudson Bay to Patagonia, they had to pick this godforsaken locality."

All the minor annoyances of the cold weather accumulated and grew in his mind to the proportions of a conspiracy directed against him, the running nose, the overactivity of the kidneys when out of doors, conniving with the scarcity of comfort stations.

He could never forget the occasion when driven by the cold and an even more pressing need, he went into a barroom and with a drink, bought himself some heat and an admission to the washroom, but soon after he left the place, he was in the same peremptory situation, perhaps stimulated by the drink. He dove into a subway station and found the lavatory locked with a sign giving two remote, unheard-of choices of one station uptown and another downtown. Then he knew despair. Damn it all! To take a subway ride every time one has to do that—if one can last that long. He bolted out of the station, ready to ask the first policeman to do something, anything, like holding his hat for him. Then into another barroom, only to have to repeat the operation again and again because he was far from home. He had never been so drunk for the benefit of the sewers and did not remember how he got home at last, but he was dizzy and developed an irritation either from the alcohol or from the cold washrooms that kept him up a good part of the night.

His landlady was fond of the beach and swimming, which is characteristic of most buoyant people, and he accompanied her sometimes, but only once did he venture into the water. No true Madrileño can swim, coming from a city in whose only river, the Manzanares, one could dive with no danger of drowning but with the certainty of breaking his skull against solid ground, or, this failing, choke to death from the dust he would raise. Garcia was no exception. That time he stepped into the water gingerly, exploringly, prolonging the agony, taking hold of the rope and submerging with a slow deliberation that was literally painstaking. A few moments after, he was back on the sand shivering, blue, frozen to the marrow and consuming quantities of hot coffee and whiskey. He could not thaw out for the rest of the day and, as these humiliations repeated on him, he would exclaim:

"Damn it again! I am going away. I swear I won't stay another day."

But he stayed. The next day was bright and warm and all was forgiven.

And so we were in Central Park enjoying the sun and loitering in this weather. We tried sitting on the grass but it was still damp. Since he had come to stay at my place and for a week before that, the weather had been foul and only the day before there had been an unpleasant experience.

We were walking home in the rain but it was not cold and I for one did not mind it. Also the rain has its beautiful aspects. It reduces the field of vision, lending intimacy to things, and all scenes appear imprisoned in it, as in a cage of crystal bars. People skipping along under umbrellas assume the precariousness of tightrope dancers balanced on all sides with the doubtful help of these fragile sparkling rods. A light rain is about the most discreet and charming of nature's phenomena; it intrudes on tiptoe.

But then we saw the dead dog. The cheerful cage became a dark prison and the rain chilly and lugubrious, like the one that should accompany a funeral procession. The dog lay by the curb, stiff, swollen, his teeth bared with the final pain and horror, holding the last tragic moment, the last memory of life a terror riveted there to disappear only with him.

This upset Garcia beyond description and when we reached home, he sat by the window looking out at the rain and saying nothing.

We gave up the damp grass and contented ourselves with a bench and our conversation. Then a squirrel appeared in front of us and stood attentive as if listening to our talk. It wore a collar with a bell, and as we had never seen a squirrel in the park with a collar, Garcia surmised that it must be somebody's pet that had escaped. Studying the squirrel I agreed because it looked very scrawny with very little fur on its tail and a hungry, forlorn look, showing that in captivity it had forgotten how to get along in freedom. We regretted having nothing to give it and commented about it. The squirrel continued to look at us, its head to one side and then to the other, almost as if it understood our conversation. Then it started to run away, only to turn and freeze into that ready alertness, and continued to watch us. One could swear that it understood Spanish. In the end, it seemed to make up its mind about us and darted away.

The spasmodic agility of the squirrel had made us restless and we decided to walk to Riverside Drive. Coming down one of the side streets and out into the drive is a classical experience and illustration of the greatness of nature dwarfing the greatness of a metropolis, and even if one has seen but few big cities, the view creates the conviction that not many of them have anything comparable to the grandiose dimensions, the proud high banks of this majestic river whose dignity and magnificence proceed deliberately, undisturbed even by the grimaces and yelpings of industrialism, whose unkempt and wounded limbs it deigns to lick with noble humility.

Garcia's arm swept from north to south and back in silent tribute, and then he spoke and dwelt on Henry Hudson and his feelings in a great moment of exploration and imagined him at the bow of his ship improvising an ode to the beauty of nature, in the style of Garcilaso or Camoëns, to the accompaniment of *La Africana*'s "Oh Paradiso!"

After he had delivered himself of this we began to watch the people passing by: the old moving slowly, analytical in their appreciation, absorbing as much of the sun's rays as possible, and the young fast, uncritical and only aware of growing exuberance, whistling some popular tune or discussing their immediate interests; nature, happiness and generalities taken for granted.

Seeing Garcia in good spirits, I suggested a reconciliation with his landlady, but while swearing that he would never return there to resume such a debasing and humiliating existence, he observed that on a fine day like this, there was no point in going home yet and that she would in all certainty be at the beach and would not return until late. We both shuddered at the thought of anyone throwing cold water on this banquet of heat. Then he admitted that he might go home that night for a change of clothes, but to resume that relationship, never. They were too different. She liked swimming, to feel the water. He liked to look at it and he gestured toward the river.

I knew that he was happy, and relenting and to make him happier because one can never let well enough alone and in a moment of recklessness possibly induced by too much sun and panorama, I asked him about his writings. It was not long before I found myself regretting my abandon.

Without a word, and with the quiet determination of a driver who sees the green light, Garcia extracted a thick bunch of papers from his inexhaustible pocket, selected part of it, and put the rest back. Then he spoke and referred to the first part of his moving picture story inspired by the item in the newspaper we had seen together and which had culminated in the fellow Ramos finding himself in New York by some remarkable sleight of hand. He said he had that written out in full but would spare me as it had been considerably elaborated that time during our walk, and besides he was not satisfied with the section describing the feelings of the fellow when he saw the miracle happen and found himself transported from one continent to another. He said he wanted to lend the passage more power because an experience like that was not to be taken lightly and as a matter of fact, that he must lend it credence and realism as it would be so difficult to believe. Here he was again sticking to his guns and insisting that the thing had really happened. Like many persons with an overactive imagination, to put it diplomatically, Garcia suspected a confabulation of incredulity among all his listeners whose tacit incredulity became patent by virtue of being told something by him. He was creating a problem for himself that admitted of no rational solution.

I told him that I did not see how the situation could be helped because it was too late to get an affidavit from Ramos, and even if he could do that, Ramos could not get one now from the fellow who appeared in the mirror in his room in Valencia that unforgettable night and that if he had believed Ramos, there was no reason why he should not expect to be believed in turn and that if he had not believed—well then, the game was among the boobs, as we say. Anyway, if he had a good yarn, it did not matter much whether people believed it, but I did not mention the converse.

He insisted that even if a story were unbelievable, it should be presented in a convincing manner. We argued back and forth about this and about literary styles, and for a moment I thought this might get me out of listening to his reading and save me from the just deserts of my own folly, but I think he divined my intentions, or deduced them from past statistics, because he suddenly decided to go into these matters some other time and begin to read where we had left off the last time:

Upon first arriving in New York, Ramos roomed in a house on Batavia Street patronized by Spanish laborers. His funds were low, he did not speak English, he felt lost, and although the place was worse than his last pension, he had to clutch at it like a drowning man. There were many Spaniards in that neighborhood and Spanish cafés and restaurants. There was one of the latter with stairs running up one side of the building where he ate regularly. The streets looked worn out, the houses old, and at that time New York was not what it is now. To Ramos, his surroundings were not very different from neighborhoods he had seen in his native place, but he was alone. Not many people like him lived in that neighborhood. The Spaniards he met were not his kind, nor the American laborers around there for that matter. This was a rough neighborhood where his ignorance of the land had cast him.

Every day and night there were wrangles and fights at most of the saloons and in the streets, and one afternoon he saw in front of a tavern on Water Street a man being beaten half to death. A small section of the pavement was being repaired and there was a patch of sand. Ramos saw the man fall there and the blood first sucked up by the sand and then congealing over it. His thoughts reverted to Spain, but there was no real regret or nostalgia. He had come to the wrong place, or the wrong people, and that was no reason for turning back. He wanted to find a section of the town and of its people more in harmony with himself. He realized that it was more important to find one's class of compatriots than one's country compatriots, but his ignorance of the language deterred him.

With English grammar and dictionary in hand, Ramos sat in his room as he did in Valencia, night after night, making superhuman efforts to learn, but time passed and his progress was insignificant. His funds had given out and he was working on the docks of the Spanish line, a type of labor he had never done before, for which he was not suited, labor that took every ounce of energy out of his small supply. It was necessary to speak English in order to obtain work at the offices of the line.

And then impatience made its presence known once more. He wished to get away from there in a hurry and wished to speak English with uncontrollable desire. He had almost forgotten how he got to New York, but only almost, and a wave of fear came to stay the wave of impatience. He reasoned with himself that the previous experience had been but a hallucination. No one could really have the power to skip conscious time. The other time he probably had lost his memory of previous actions. He had read that such things happened to people, but still he feared. What if he really had that power? He might want to reach a certain point in the future and between now and then, something might be waiting for him, something perhaps terrible, to snatch him, to crush him, some unsuspected trap into which he might fall to even end his life in his flight to an assumed, hypothetical future.

But then, one afternoon impatience won. He was in a saloon in the Bowery at the corner of Doyer Street, not frequented by his countrymen. He had grown tired of their company, of their presence, and he thought that perhaps hearing English spoken, he might learn it sooner. He was leaning against the bar, an untouched drink in front of him, still debating with himself the subject uppermost in his mind.

A group of men were drinking near him and the one nearest took Ramos's drink and drank it, winking at the bartender. Ramos awoke from his thoughts and tried to protest, but could not find the words. He stammered, he gulped, and a stream of Spanish escaped him. The man and his companions laughed loudly and answered back in words which Ramos could not understand. He knew that they were English and suspected that they were mocking, possibly insulting, but he could not make them out. Madly groping in his mind for the few phrases he knew, he blurted out one or two inadequate words, surrounded, lost, neutralized by those violent gestures with which people have always expected to be understood anywhere. His display only increased the general mirth and the whole saloon joined in the joke at his expense. In despair he turned appealingly to the bartender, but the latter also laughed and with bowing politeness removed Ramos's empty glass, refilled it, and with a flourish placed it upon the bar.

Ramos was dizzy with exasperation. In impotent rage, he shut his eyes and his clenched fists pounded the bar. Oh! How he wished he could speak!

There was a sudden hush in his ears and a rapid tapping sound that came from about him. He heard his own voice speaking and then opened his eyes. He did not fall because he was leaning on a desk, in a large room where several girls were typing, and he was protesting in very fluent English to the general manager of a very large business concern specializing in the manufacture of sewing machines, and the man appeared quite convinced, quite conquered.

Ramos halted, his back to me, regarding me over his shoulder. Again he pointed at me almost accusingly. He had the manner of one who sees the inner man in his interlocutor and talks to it. He pointed as if accusing one of having so transparent a soul. He held that pose well into his talk:

"Yes, that is right," he answered my mind. "I also had this time a dull memory of things lived between both moments of consciousness. It was like awakening and knowing one has dreamed, but being unable to remember the dream, except for some dim flashes. Some of the visions took definite aspects but always like objects sensed in the dark, or seen in very poor light." He relaxed, his hand dropped, and turning fully, he resumed his restless pacing.

"I saw myself laboring at the docks and there is a clear picture of a classroom, probably some night school I attended. Then I saw myself scrubbing floors at some railroad station under artificial light and again saw a classroom by daylight. I heard insisting, screaming whistles which made me grow taut, intent, alert, or made me relax and sigh with relief. I found myself speaking another language, surrounded by new acquaintances, but I did not know when I had learned one single phrase, where I had met any one of those people. At times they referred to things which had happened before, and sometimes they brought back a swift memory and sometimes they brought back nothing. They must have thought me strange."

And strange he was, this man Ramos, I thought. I offered him a cigarette and lighted it for him. When the match went out, the growing darkness of the room was more apparent. We smoked a while without talking, Ramos leaning against the wall. He looked right through the smoke, at something very distant. Perhaps he had tired of looking into my soul and was looking into his own.

"That experience was repeated. I did not want ..."

"Before I forget," Garcia interrupted himself, "now you see why I think this would be better as a moving picture. It could show the shifts and changes of scenery and action much better: close-ups, fade-ins, fade-outs, you know. Much more elastic than any other medium."

I said that I agreed with him there, but that even at the risk of dampening his enthusiasm, I must remind him that things for the moving pictures had to be written in a special way, scenarios or something like that, with technical indications, in which case he should not be writing his story the way he was doing it because much of his literary points and style would be wasted anyway, as in pictures one only heard dialogue or noises made by actors or other things like on the legitimate stage—that is, unless he intended to have a narrator, which, I thought unreservedly, would be very silly. I concluded that moving pictures might be very flexible indeed but perhaps for that reason they were also very difficult and one should not be carried away by ease of scene-shifting.

Nothing could dampen his ardor or admiration for the cinematograph. He lunged into a discourse praising it. The actors could concentrate in one capital performance to be recorded permanently for all to admire, the human element reduced to a minimum. He declaimed that it was not only the most flexible and efficient way of presenting a story but the most flexible way of absorbing it. He lauded the cheaper prices, continuous performances which permitted the public to arrive when it pleased, the fact that one could smoke during the picture, take any seat available and then change it for a better one if the opportunity presented itself, instead of being assigned to one place like a school-boy. He gestured again in the direction of the river. Nature was its stage, real cities, real buildings, mountains, woods, prairies and rivers.

That was the real legitimate stage and not the other which was not only illegitimate but inadequate as well, and he embarked on a tirade against the theater proper, accusing it of cramping the author and cramping the audience, and when he got through with it, all the playwrights in history from the Greeks, or whoever were the first, to the most recent ones, who had gone to join them in condemnation, would have turned over in their graves to hide their faces and all the movie magnates would have joined hands and broken forth in a fandango for sheer joy.

Now he told me! I wish he had felt that way the night he took me to the Spanish Theater of Tia Mariquita.

Having thus delivered himself, Garcia looked for his place on the page and resumed his reading:

"That experience was repeated. I did not want it, but I could not help it. I would endeavor not to wish, but sometimes I wished before I had time to think. You see? It was always a very strong wish, almost a paroxysm of desire that did it, and that always darkens one's reason. The experience was repeated as I say and although still fearing, I was more familiarized with it. The amount of time skipped was on occasions negligibly short and on occassions dangerously long. Sometimes there would linger an almost aching sensation of fear that rose to the surface from unknown recesses, and then I knew that I had been in imminent danger and come close to my doom. A shadow of impending disaster hovered over me. I did however exercise the utmost degree of self-control that I could muster and even succeeded in developing some discipline. It was arduous, hard work. The conquest of oneself is always the most difficult because one sympathizes so with one's foe. But it was the only near salvation. I saw myself growing old in what to me was but the space of a few days, a few conscious scattered days. My life was not my own. I was feeding huge chunks of it to the gaping jaws of my impatience, endeavoring to appease its constant hunger."

Ramos recalled his gaze from distant regions and entrusted it to the smoke of his cigarette.

"I heard things which sounded familiar or found myself in places where I must have been before and then by checking up on such things, although without definite recollections, I would come to the conclusion that they had been squeezed some place between the moments of lucidity, or been displaced into some other dimension, some latitude of time." He shuddered:

"At times it was horrible." He grew restful once more, his eyes always following the smoke: "But there must have also been happy experiences during those moments, because at times there was a feeling of elation and at times of regret. They must have been few, but very happy. Out of that turmoil of vague memories, a beautiful vision emerged, condensed. I found myself with a woman, a woman I must have loved or wanted very much."

Those were probably the happiest days in Ramos's life. He was quite adapted to his surroundings, to a different country and different people. He could go to the theater or to music halls and laugh at jokes on the stage with the rest of the audience. Man must laugh in company. This is his happiest communion with his fellow men. A man may laugh alone, but this is at most bitter for him and sadder for the rest of the world. A man may feel superior when he laughs with the minority at the majority, but he is happier when he laughs with the many at the few. Then his laughter is not a misleading aspect of despair, but a true expression of well-being.

This, nevertheless, did not last long. Ramos felt intimately alone. It was the question of love. While several women had already passed through his life, that was the trouble: they had passed. He wanted something more stable. He took to walking and sitting in the park by himself. He was alone but for a strange company. He knew that his impatience had found him again, that it had singled him out once more from the world with which he had already almost blended. As he walked he felt it following behind, gradually overtaking him. If he stopped or sat, he knew it stood there, on constant guard, and every time nearer, always approaching, closer and closer.

Then it overtook him. He was sitting on a bench in the park and he felt it next to him. He sensed the heavy grip of its iron arm about his shoulders and its hot breath searing through his ears, setting his soul aflame. He almost screamed. He shut his eyes.

The clear laughter of a woman cooled his ears like a cascade. He opened his eyes and for a few moments there was untold relief. He was sitting on the same bench, the surroundings, the day, were the same, a very clear and reassuring day. He thought that at last he was free from that thing. He felt impatience drained from his whole being and then he noticed the strange laughing woman sitting on the same bench, looking at him, and there was something familiar about her that set the old fear scraping at his very marrow. He stiffened and stared at her for a long time. Her laughter died out and he saw her grow puzzled and then heard her voice, which something within him began to suggest as a little vulgar:

"Gee, Julio, but sometimes you are funny!"

A part of his mind was trying to compose him, to smooth surprise away from his countenance, and he heard himself saying mechanically:

"You know, Jenny darling? I sat on this very bench one day before I met you and I wanted so much to meet a girl like you! That was the reason why I wanted to sit here again today, at the same hour with you."

"Are Spaniards always so romantic? I'll bet you say that to all the girls."

He sat without uttering a word, trying to remember, to find some opening, no matter how small, in the wall which separated him from his memory of the particular contributing circumstances to this moment.

Two young blades went by leisurely, one of them, bowler hat carelessly and miraculously hanging from the back of his head, his thumbs thrust in the armholes of his fancy waistcoat. He was singing:

> "While strolling in the park one day
> In the merry merry month of May . . ."

The stare faded from Julio's eyes which began to crease at the corners, the growing light of a smile illuminating them like sunrise.

"That's better, honey," Jenny said.

Garcia stopped and for a mute moment we looked at one another blankly, he because he was perhaps still turning things over in his mind and I because I had not been paying very close attention and could offer no critical comment. Maybe Garcia felt that he was wasting his time on me because he said he thought that was enough for the time being and that he would perhaps continue later. The afternoon was nearing that horizontal hour of long recumbent shadows that bind one's path to sleep like a striped caterpillar, or lash it into lively action like a bolting zebra and when the sun reflected in windows, beats the budding electric lights into hopeless inadequacy.

After a while Garcia suggested that we go to the Armenian district for supper. His partiality to Oriental or semi-Oriental food matched his fondness for street lamps and was involved with poetic misconceptions and ascetic dreams complicated by a rebellion against his practical surroundings of sauerbraten, knockwurst and kraut which cried out for a purifying bath with a jug of wine, a loaf of bread, unleavened, and anything else on the side that aroused gastronomical curiosity. I remember his consternation when Don Pedro informed him that Omar Khayyám was also a mathematician; Garcia, for whom mathematics was absolutely unknown territory and who with the sublime authority of ignorance damned it as the ultimate distillate of the prosaic, had been shocked, disconcerted and unbelieving, considering the revelation a gross slander, and I think it was from that day that he baptized our friend Don Pedro el Cruel.

We boarded a bus and sat on the open top. All the way down to 72nd Street, the sun coming through the trees beat a tattoo of light and shadow on our faces that produced the exhilarating confusion of a shower of sparks or confetti, of a disorderly activity directed by nature toward one's person, of buffeting flattery; and then out of that luminous gauntlet of burning swords and corridors of gold, into the gloom portals of the city where a few embers from the great bonfire outside had rolled in. A sunny corner here, a store window there, the incandescent crown of a tree at an intersection and looking up, one could see the tops of the buildings already on fire. All the way down, the shadows of the trees kept growing to immense proportions until they were the shadows of the buildings and the streets themselves were ropes of fire holding down a prostrate giant. The great conflagration would burn itself out beyond to leave a few distant sparks floating in the sky and then continue to smolder in the city lights all through the night.

This is as much as I can remember and convey of Garcia's comments on that occasion until we reached Madison Square. There we got off and walked along the north side of the park toward Lexington Avenue.

There is something about most of the East Side, rain or shine, that lies somewhere between what we call reality and what we call a dream. It is the quality of a memory that has lain forsaken like an unattended grave. Nowhere else in New York can one find so everpresent the spirit of the has-been, of the window of a shop on Sunday inhabited only by our own reflection as we go by. It has the eerie texture of a sudden breeze on a calm day. Garcia suggested once that it seemed as if the tradesmen, the children, even the domestic animals there were saying: "I remember, I remember," without speaking, but I think that what they are really trying to say is: "Remember me?" And "remember" is one of the saddest words.

Perhaps it is the crowded conditions that turn many of its sections into something like a junk shop heaped with faded, dusty, useless things of yesterday. Perhaps it is the bridges that trample down those parts like a fallen drunkard. Perhaps it is the proximity of the morgue or a combination of all these things, or perhaps to be cautious, this is the way it affects some people. We decided to forget all this as we entered the restaurant.

We sat through a protracted and variegated meal of morsels impaled or shrouded in leaves with innuendos of the sacrificial lamb, or even suggestive of historically famous French chefs speared in self-immolation because of royal culinary contretemps: immaculate rice, salad dressed with oil that could have come from the Mount of Olives, vinegar worthy of a scriptural sponge, and bejeweled with pomegranate grains like holy drops of blood, the end sweetened and punctuated with honey and almonds. The gastronomical lyricism of Garcia did not exclude quantity; it was rather Wagnerian.

And it was after this edifying meal, with a feeling of savory righteousness, while sipping coffee emulsion and arrack in a dining room that was emptying as fast as our bottle and while considering how Garcia would look with a long beard, that he regaled me with some more of his writing. This was about that Spanish family. He drew faster than a Western hero, and without any preamble he fanned at me:

This is the day of the week when the Sandovals are at home to their friends. The bell rings incessantly and people pour into the house shedding their hats and overcoats all over the antesala. A little graceful maid with white gloves keeps one hand on the doorknob; another one attends to the guests as they come in.

There are presentations, not as many as people because most of them know each other. The hum of conversation fills the air of the drawing room. One can't hear anything—it is just as well—there is nothing to hear.

There is a lull at the door during which the two maids look at one another and take a deep breath. Then the bell rings again, perhaps for the last guest.

The first maid gives the door a lazy pull and then stands at attention.

A handsome gentleman saunters in caressing her cheek as he passes her. He places his coat, hat and stick in the hands of the other, looking at her intently. She is a pretty creature. He takes her by the chin and she blushes.

"Do they keep you working very hard, preciosa? You can go now and rest. I couldn't allow anyone to arrive after me." He kisses her swiftly and with two agile leaps turns toward the drawing room. At the door he meets

Fernando Sandoval talking to a group of gentlemen.

"Hola, Paco."

Outside the two maids look again at one another: "Well! What did you think of that?"

"I think we can go now. Señorito Serrano is always the last one to arrive."

At the door of the drawing room Fernando said: "I think you have met most of these gentlemen, haven't you?"

"More or less. I can always stand a second introduction."

Fernando produced a shrunken little gentleman whose face was all wrinkles when he smiled.

"I don't think you two have met yet, have you?"

The little gentleman did not think so and extended a hand as Fernando made the brief introduction:

"Señor Ricardo Echenique: Señor Francisco Serrano. You know? Señor Echenique is a lawyer like you, Paco. Perhaps you would like to talk of your profession."

Paco kicked Fernando's foot very obviously and said aloud that he hardly thought so. The other man's face shrank to the limit.

Paco surveyed the room and located Julieta surrounded by young men and women. Without bowing to the gentlemen about him, he walked in her direction. It took him fully fifteen minutes to reach his destination. A buxom lady giving out a cloud of perfume addressed him with a voice like molasses:

"Where have you been hiding yourself lately Pa— Señor Serrano?"

"I have not been hiding at all, but perhaps you have not looked in the right places."

"I know what kind of places."

"In that case you must have appreciated already their importance, my dear Madame Pacheco."

A taciturn gentleman approached the buxom lady scowling, and her smile faded immediately. Paco hastened away.

For a few moments all the attention was centered upon him, upon the graceful smiles he bestowed right and left. He was detained here, granted a passing introduction there. He remembered vaguely, yet obligingly, an admiring individual and made an anemic girl happy with a close scrutiny of her person. He eclipsed everyone by his witty and bold answers. He was the suave gentleman allowing short roaring bursts of the social lion.

An elderly lady who sat in the company of several older people held him by the hand as he went by: "Since when is it the fashion not to greet old friends?"

He looked at the lady and grew apologetic. He held her hand in both of his. "Why, Doña Rosario, please forgive me. I don't know where my eyes are."

"I know," she laughed jovially and shoved him along in a friendly and familiar way.

"I want to talk to you after, Doña Rosario."

"After what?"

"After—after tea."

He rushed on but was soon detained again. A little interruption, a short repartee. By the time he was free he had to change his direction because Julieta was no longer where she had been.

He took her hand and put it to his lips, prolonging the action as much as possible, but he did not speak. He only looked at her very long.

The people around her began to talk among themselves. Julieta and Paco found one of those confidential settees and there they spoke in whispers for a long time. Then Doña Rosario called her daughter and Paco stepped into an adjoining room where the tea was being served.

There he found more people and among them Trini eating heartily. She inquired in a nice hoarse voice with her mouth full: "How is our simpático Paco?"

"All right, and you?" he said, inflating his cheeks to imitate her.

"Never better. Here; help yourself."

Paco looked at her cynically: "No thanks."

He entered the smoking room glowing green from the light right above a billiard table. There was Don Mariano, Ledesma and several other old gentlemen. Ledesma always sought the company of older people.

Paco heard Charles Darwin mentioned and immediately turned on his heel and made hastily for the door.

"Wait a moment, Paco, wait a moment, don't run away."

"You are discussing serious topics and you know that I . . ."

"Come over here, we need your advice. By the way, you have not met General La Calle yet."

The general stood on tiptoe trying to disguise his height. His eyes drooped at the sides and gave him a permanently afflicted air. Paco looked the general over and one side of his face shrank sympathetically: "I don't think he has suffered that one more imposition."

"Well, this is Paco Serrano, General, and he knows more about women than the whole bunch of us together."

The general made a doubting sound and his eyes drooped further.

"We need your advice, Paco."

"If you boys are still in need of advice, it is not mine that will help you."

"Be serious! General La Calle insists that women should be granted the same rights which men have. A rather drastic view for a military man, don't you think?"

"But what have women done to deserve such a fate?"

"Never mind that. Ledesma here claims they would not know how to use those rights. What do you think?"

"In matters of women, it is better not to think but act." Paco looked at the group of old men insinuatingly and they all laughed.

"What did I say?" Don Mariano exclaimed: "He knows more about them than the whole bunch of us."

The general did not like to have his theories taken so lightly. The conversation changed.

"And tell me, General, why didn't your daughter Corito come today? I have not seen her around."

"She had an accident this morning and is resting up."

Everyone assumed an expression to suit the circumstances.

"Yes, she fell down the stairs and," with a martial gesture he pointed with his finger to a spot on his own anatomy, "hurt herself right here."

"The devil you say! Right in the best part too!" said Paco distractedly. The drooping eyes of the general became those of an infuriated bloodhound and Paco came to: "You'll excuse me now, won't you, gentlemen?"

Outside the room he met Julieta and held her hand: "Listen, Julieta. It is unbearable not to be able to see you without all this chaperoning. You don't know how I want you." He was talking close to her. "Is there any way we can be together? Alone? You will not repent, I assure you."

"It is impossible, Paco. You know how I would like to . . . but it is impossible."

"We must marry right away, then. Anyway, Mother is coming tomorrow to ask officially for your hand. By the way, do you know that Father died in San Sebastian last week?"

"What?" she gasped.

"Yes," he went on quietly. "That is why Mother will come in his place. After that . . . I hope we don't have to wait long. I want to tell your mother so that they will expect her."

Julieta was looking at the charming gentleman before her as if he were very puzzling.

The marriage of Paco Serrano and Julieta Sandoval was one of the brilliant affairs of the season. They were both popular and well liked. The Sandovals were happy with the wedding. Paco was running for deputy and faced an enviable future. After their return from their honeymoon trip, Don Mariano and Doña Rosario gave the newlyweds a beautiful villa situated in the Street of Lealtad near the Prado, one of the truly beautiful spots in a central residential section of Madrid.

These happenings marked the retirement of Don Mariano from business. He and Doña Rosario moved to the villa with their daughter. Madame Serrano, Paco's mother, also came to spend some time with them. Don Mariano left the jewelry store in the hands of his son Fernando and Ledesma continued to administer and supervise the business.

Paco furnished their new home beautifully and hired the service with care. There was not a single good-looking maid in the house and the butlers and grooms seemed to be ready for the old men's home. The only young one had a very high-pitched voice.

Paco seemed to care sincerely for his wife, and as for Julieta, marriage was the realization of a long wish. She felt as if she had discarded a tremendous burden and naturally regarded Paco as the one responsible for her happiness, as the one who had brought her this new joy of living. Now, in full womanhood, she had entered marriage with deep sincerity and eagerness. Upon returning from her honeymoon, her younger friends had crowded her, demanding savagely:

"Tell us, tell us all about it."

And she answered flatly: "Don't be so curious about such things. It is not good for you."

At La Gran Peña, where he seldom came now, a friend asked Paco: "Serrano, you certainly have grown serious with marriage. How is that?"

"Why not? Marriage is a serious thing."

"I bet there are many broken hearts since your wedding. But I cannot believe that you are entirely true to your wife."

Paco, sunk deep in the chair, answered with a sigh: "My dear fellow, I have nothing left to be untrue with."

"And so forth and so on," Garcia concluded and flipped over a few pages, making those humming noises people often make when skimming over reading matter. "I am not too satisfied with this and want to work on it some more."

I suspected he knew that the passage that followed might not meet with my approval and that his appraisal of my standards might be degenerating into something more depreciating than flattering, but that he hoped to get around me eventually, and I made a mental note of stiffening my stand.

Garcia stacked the sheets lightly against the table and resumed:

Don Mariano Sandoval was very old. Everyone knew that he was going to die soon. He did not know it, but he told everyone that he was going to die and everybody told him that he had never looked so healthy in his life. For the last ten years he had been saying that he was going to die soon, but now they all knew that he was right. He did not know it though.

Julieta's first baby, Luisito, cheered his last moments. The old man lived only for the child. Fernando and Trini were jealous of Luisito. After Enrique, they had had a girl, Rojelia, who was about the same age as Julieta's boy and already showed a short curly mane of red hair, but the grandfather paid little attention to her. He only liked Luisito. He said it was the only thing that held him here, the only reason for living, but nevertheless the child hastened the old man's departure from this world.

They played incessantly, strenuously. The child was lively as an eel and Don Mariano grew fatigued and sat on a chair exhausted, choking from asthma.

One night the child woke up very sick and one week later was on his way to the cemetery escorted by other children and by his grandfather.

When old man Sandoval returned from the burial he said: "This has killed me."

Julieta, crying as she had never cried before, said: "No, Father. You must not leave us too. There is another one coming. You must wait to see it."

But old man Sandoval shook his head: "That child was the only thing I had to live for. It has killed me." And it did.

Thus the older generation of the family began to fade. Madame Serrano—Paco's mother—died soon after from cancer, and Doña Rosario followed her husband one year after his death.

Julieta had given birth to a boy, Ricardo, and then to another, Jacinto. Life was filling its vacancies.

"What shall we do now?"

"Nothing. One last drink and then to bed," yawned Paco.

"Since you are a deputy, you are keeping most respectable and regular hours. To bed at dawn and up at sunset."

"Regularity means success, La Torre. But tomorrow I have to be up frightfully early."

"That's right. You have to feed us in the middle of the day. Poor Serrano!"

"And what shall it be now?" La Torre turned to a young man who was in their company and looked at them with undisguised admiration. "What would you like?"

"Anything you do," the young man answered with all the fervor of a tot playing follow the leader.

They decided on a round of manzanilla. The waiter placed a tray on their table with about a dozen tall thin glasses full of the pale liquid. Manzanilla must be consumed in this manner: in commercial quantities, slowly but without intermissions to refill the glasses. They began to sip silently, ritually, isochronously.

Paco then stepped to another table where a very low type man with all the earmarks of a chulo was sitting with two girls and began to talk to them with familiarity. The young man nudged La Torre and whispered:

"I am invited also for tomorrow. I think he is very exacting about fashion. What do you advise me to wear?"

"I can see you don't know Serrano well enough yet. Wear anything you like. Come in your nightshirt for all he will care."

The young man looked genuinely amazed: "But I want to create a good impression!"

"Then you might add a top hat. Listen: you have created enough of an impression already. Serrano likes you very much and he thinks you are a very smart young man."

"He does?" The fellow's eyes were almost watering: "I think he is the smartest chap in all Madrid."

"The second smartest," La Torre corrected.

"And a real and perfect caballero."

"That . . . of course."

When they left the place, the young man insisted on paying for everything.

The next day, when they were all sitting around the table, the young man was not wearing his nightshirt. On the contrary, he was very carefully dressed according to the latest fashion and wore a tremendous white flower in his lapel. He looked at Julieta and at Paco with an admiration that was all but drooling superstition.

There were two other ladies: Madame Gerard, whose husband was connected with the French Embassy at Madrid and had been unable to appear, or perhaps ordered out of sight by his enterprising wife, and her daughter, a somewhat common-looking brunette who wore everything that should go about her neck hanging on her back from her arms and who moved her shoulders as if their supersensitiveness registered all her impressions. She also walked with an air intended to make her ankles seem too weak to support her weight.

At that moment, however, she was not taxing her weak ankles. She was sitting next to Paco and all her energy was concentrated in her responsive shoulders which went up and down at every syllable that Paco uttered.

Her mother, fat, yet with wrinkled complexion made up as if for the stage, was melting under the gallantries of La Torre who looked intently at Julieta and was obviously telling the old lady all the things he dare not tell his beautiful hostess.

Intermittently the Madame looked at her daughter and made a covert sign and the Mademoiselle immediately changed her pose. She was perfectly trained.

"Oh! Señor La Torre. I think you are terrible."

"Exactly as you expect me to be, Madame. I could not disappoint you."

"But my husband has heard of you and he says that you are very bad, very, very bad." In a stage voice. Undoubtedly Madame Gerard had been an actress sometime in the dim past.

"And after telling you that, he lets you come without him! Did he know I was going to be here?"

"Everybody knows where you are going to be, Señor La Torre."

"You are as charming as your husband is foolhardy."

"Ah! but he trusts Señor Serrano and knows he will protect me from you."

"He will not have to, Madame Gerard. I am going to behave today. Besides, I am on a diet."

"You are horrible, Señor La Torre!" she screamed.

Julieta spoke little. She had complained of a slight headache and listened with a set smile to the stupidities of the young man who was doing his best to create an impression. She looked at Paco and Mademoiselle Gerard and frowned on one or two occasions. Paco had laid his knife and fork down and bent closer to the sensitive shoulders. The rest of the people did not exist for him until after the repast ended.

Madame Gerard had said that she liked Spanish shawls and Julieta offered to show her and her daughter some she had. They all rose:

"Julieta. Join us in the shooting gallery. We will be there. Perhaps the ladies will like a little noise after dinner."

The ladies went with Julieta and the gentlemen remained chatting over their liqueur and cigars.

"Don't you think she is good-looking, La Torre?"

"Yes, quite, but she will be the dead image of her mother when she grows old. A mother like that can ruin any girl's chances. She is a terrible old hen."

"An old hen makes good broth, as they say."

"Possibly. I am not particularly fond of that kind of broth. I once had it and, as a matter of fact, lived on it for one year. It turned into good meals, rent, clothes and spending money. It is a miraculous kind of broth, but now—well, I don't need it and it is hard to swallow."

Paco laughed. The young man did not understand and looked on blankly.

Julieta's suite was furnished in the Empire style. It looked very light after the austere old Spanish dining room. The walls of her boudoir were completely draped with Spanish shawls, a bizarre amalgamation of bright colors which should prove strenuous and tiring after a time. They were all draped symmetrically and caught together in the center of the ceiling, all their exuberant colors clashing and melting into the dazzling cut crystal chandelier.

The Madame and her daughter looked somewhat superciliously about. Julieta walked around the room pointing out the shawls.

"This one is very good. The fringe alone weighs I don't know how much. That is why I think they are better on the walls. One has to be an athlete to wear these things."

"But they are beautiful. I think I must take some shawls back to Paris with me when I return."

"I don't think you will have much use for shawls in France, except as a decoration. The only place where people can wear shawls properly is at a bullfight or a verbena and that as a concession and tribute to an old Spanish tradition. Only the working girls wear them at other places, but then they are black and that would be too mournful for you." The sarcasm could not be missed.

"Don't be silly, my child. We shall wear ours at the Opéra in Paris and they will be the flashiest ones we can find in Spain, the ones that are too gay to wear in the country of the Inquisition."

Julieta burst out laughing. It was the same clear, beautiful laugh which had called Paco's attention the first night he saw her. Madame Gerard and her daughter looked a bit annoyed and finally Julieta calmed down.

"Excuse me, Madame Gerard, but a person going to the Opéra with a shawl . . . It is comical."

"That is because you Spaniards respect traditions very much and this is a royalist country, but France is a republic, a free country where everyone can do as he pleases."

With unexpected, probably unintentional tact, the Mademoiselle exclaimed: "Look, mother! Look at this one. How quaint!"

She was standing before an old shawl. It had little figures of Chinamen embroidered on it and their heads were made of ivory.

"That one is a real Chinese specimen. It is something like this one here. Some people consider them the best, although some might not consider them bright enough. It is strange how an industry originally Chinese has become so identified with Spain, although by the way you speak, it seems that someday it will also become part of the Opéra." She was teasing the Madame almost too pointedly.

Madame Gerard ignored the dart: "And how did you manage to make this collection?"

"Given to me at different times. Paco has given me some of the best."

The Madame looked at her daughter: "Well, shall we join the gentlemen?"

The shooting gallery was a wide, long, threatening hall, hung with weapons of different types and periods and several hunting trophies. At the entrance were a couple of settees and some chairs as well as small tables and . . .

"What is the proper name for those things where they keep guns and pistols and the like, do you know?" Garcia asked me. "You must have seen them in pictures."

"I don't know. You see? That is the trouble when writing about things you know nothing about."

"It is not important anyway. I can always look it up and the readers will not know the difference. Very few have been in any shooting gallery, much less own one. Excuse the interruption."

A servant was laying dishes of sweets on the tables and uncorking some bottles. At the other end, the bull's-eye inevitably arrested all the attention. It had a couple of holes in it. Paco and La Torre each held a pistol in his hand.

Mademoiselle Gerard entered with ankles giving way under her. A smokelike piece of fabric hung from her arms and floated down her back. Her mother and Julieta followed.

"Listen, Paco: Madame Gerard is going to revolutionize France all over again. She wants to wear a Spanish shawl to the Opéra. What do you think of that for asserting one's freedom in a republic?"

Paco was aware of the sharpness in her words and decided to smooth out the situation by taking it lightly.

"One does not have to live in a republic in order to wear what one likes where one likes. Next year, when I go to America, I will return with an

Indian costume and wear it to a bullfight."

"In any case you are a most generous husband, Señor Serrano. What a beautiful collection of shawls you have given your wife."

"That is not the best I give her."

"I think you men are getting more impossible every day."

"Now, Madame Gerard," La Torre interposed, "don't talk badly about men. As you see, we are prepared to defend ourselves heroically," and he pointed his pistol at her.

"Oh . . . Please, Señor La Torre! Not even in jest. I will faint. It might go off."

"Don't worry. I have perfect control."

Julieta spoke to the young man: "Are you going to join in?"

"No. I am not good at these things. I would much rather talk to you."

La Torre was pointing to the head of an antelope on the wall, right behind where Julieta was sitting with the young man: "I say, Serrano. You should not have this sort of thing around, being a married man."

Paco was standing at the other end of the gallery. He had changed the bull's-eye and was loading his pistol. He looked up and smiled. Julieta had taken a piece of candy the young man offered her. It was a dainty, long, thin bar with yellow and red stripes. She took a small bite when suddenly the young man snatched it from her and was about to put it to his mouth when a loud report was heard and the candy bar shot from his fingers. An ugly hole appeared under the antelope's head. They all gasped and stared at Paco.

The smile was still on his face and his pistol was smoking. The young man was pale and had stood up. Julieta very quietly met her husband's eyes.

"I am very sorry," Paco apologized. "The darn thing just went off."

Madame Gerard was finally able to speak: "My Lord! I nearly fainted. This is too dangerous. I think we had better find a safer place."

"Please don't go yet. We will be careful. Stay and see the match between La Torre and myself. This won't happen again, I assure you." He had come over to where they all stood and took the old lady solicitously by the arm: "Here. This will restore you." He poured her a glass of jerez.

"Very well." She drank the jerez with avidity. "We will stay to see you shoot once. That is enough to judge a man's ability. But be sure that you aim in the right direction."

"We always do. Don't fear."

La Torre had taken his position. He extended his arm with the pistol and then turned to the audience: "Cover your ears, please."

They all obeyed and then, without looking, he shot.

"Bravo!" they all shouted. He ran to the bull's-eye and then called Paco.

"What do you think of that? Only one centimeter from the center."

Paco admitted that this was very good indeed and difficult to beat: "Let me see what I can do," he said when he had returned to his position, and without aiming, he shot.

La Torre stepped up to the bull's-eye again and examined it. There was but one hole.

"Say, boy! That was some shot! It went right through mine and did not even make it larger. I bet you could not repeat that," and Paco, who had followed him, said: "Of course I can, as long as I shoot with blank cartridges. I am not really a good shot."

La Torre whispered: "But the other one was not a blank cartridge."

"No, that was a real bullet."

Madame Gerard and her daughter were taking their leave. La Torre and the young man offered to accompany them. Paco and Julieta met at the door. For a moment they were alone; the others had preceded them. She looked at him with scrutiny and he returned her gaze very carefully wrapped in a cynical expression, holding the door open for her.

My applause startled Garcia and also the cashier who was the only other person besides us still in the restaurant: "I say Bravo! like your characters. You certainly got it cursi, boy! Bull's-eye cursi." I poured the rest of the arrack into the cups and held mine up: "To the great cursi art which in your hands becomes a science or vice versa."

Garcia looked doubtful and then decided to take it as a compliment and wash it down with the arrack, but he said nothing. Probably he wanted to save his mind for the reading:

La Torre, the painter, was a tall, broad fellow with an abundant mane, a slightly drooping mustache and an impertinent air that verged on the obscene. He was supposed to be as skilled with the sword as with the brush, perhaps more so, and sought duels for the mere publicity of it. The elasticity of his conscience may be appreciated from the following incident.

One night at the opera, he had laid his cloak on the chair in front of his. The occupant came and claimed the chair, asking La Torre politely to remove his cloak. This occupant had had the misfortune of courting the lady who was La Torre's model at the time.

La Torre answered something very insulting and the other man slapped his face.

La Torre scratched his cheek very ostentatiously and then selected a card with utmost care. He carried his insolence so far as wiping some imaginary dust from it and then handed it to his aggressor.

The other man knew nothing about duels and consequently, that night, he visited a fencing master. As there was no time in one lesson to teach much, the fencing master taught him only one resource pass.

La Torre entered the fencing academy right after his opponent had left and inquired from the master which pass he had taught.

News like that travels fast and the master knew that La Torre was going to fight the other man next morning and said that his honor did not allow him to betray a professional secret.

La Torre disregarded the objection. He took out his wallet and said: "I did not ask the statutes of your profession. I simply asked you to tell me what pass you taught that young imbecile. However, I take it that you are a caballero and that is worth something, but somehow I have forgotten the price."

And the fencing master told him.

The next morning La Torre met his opponent in a secluded spot in El Retiro. They crossed swords and the pass the poor fellow had learned was his passport to oblivion.

When La Torre saw the young man lying on the grass, bleeding and very pale, he recalled his face. He murmured: "Serrano scared you with a well-aimed shot for the same indiscretion, but you went too far with me."

It had been a gentlemen's affair.

Since that time many serious people called La Torre an assassin when they spoke of him and refused to shake hands with him. Some would get up and depart when he entered a place where they were. This seemed to please La Torre beyond words.

It was at the studio of La Torre that Paco Serrano met Clotilde Bonafé one afternoon.

Clotilde had been posing for La Torre all afternoon but he had painted very little. She was reclining on a couch when Paco rang the bell.

There was some confusion and Clotilde started to hide. Her husband was no less a person than Don Melitón Bonafé, the famous Bonafé, a ferocious congressman who boasted a beard like a bib. He had introduced the scola di bravura in the Spanish congress, and when swept by inspiration and eloquence, his voice thundered, his white hair and beard shook threateningly and people compared him to Moses. At such moments he was irresistible. It is said that once, while talking about some taxes, the two lions at the entrance of the building walked wearily away to the zoological gardens and there talked two other lions into taking their post.

As has been recorded, when the bell rang, Clotilde tried to hide, but La

Torre, who was fond of theatrical situations, stopped her with authority:

"Why hide, my dear? If it is your husband, I will introduce him to you and then kill him. If it is somebody else, they are not going to find out anything they don't know already. They will have to take me as I am. I am never ashamed of anything I do."

"But I might be ashamed."

His eyes outlined his own figure on a big mirror: "What? Don't be such a donkey," and indignantly he flung the door open.

When Paco entered La Torre exclaimed sadly: "Of course; it had to be the one person that would not be shocked. Next time wear a big white beard, Serrano."

Paco looked tired and showed a great deal of white at the temples. He sat on the couch close to the naked figure of Clotilde.

La Torre, in a light jacket and balloon corduroy trousers, was pouring some drinks while relating an anecdote which concerned the respectable person of Don Melitón Bonafé.

It seems that La Torre had painted Clotilde as Mary Magdalene, very lightly clad, and the picture appeared among others in an exhibition.

Congressman Bonafé saw it. He liked it immensely and he bought it on the spot. The picture found a place of honor in the marital bedroom at the head of the solid, methodic bed, and Don Melitón praised it constantly. Next to Saint Joseph, Mary Magdalene had been his favorite character in religious history, according to La Torre.

On the money from the purchase of the picture, Clotilde and La Torre had a noisy time, but the painter never forgave the inspired congressman for not discovering the likeness between the picture and his wife. It involved a bad implication for his art and besides had robbed the situation of possibilities. He contented himself with calling him a bearded ox.

La Torre, having finished his anecdote, handed a glass of brandy to Paco and held another one for Clotilde: "But listen, Paco, you must have seen her husband at the congress."

"I never notice anything at the congress. I always go to sleep there from the moment I enter until they wake me up when the session is over. It is the only opportunity a good deputy gets to catch up on sleep."

"But with the noise he makes, you must have noticed him. He must have awakened you sometimes."

"Is that the one?" Paco laughed loudly and La Torre caught up with him. "I should have known it. He has interfered with my sleep more than once and I wish I could even matters with him." His hand drifted to Clotilde's thigh.

"You will." He offered the drink to Clotilde. "Drink this one. It will brace you up." He spoke to Paco: "You know? This woman is played out today. When she arrived this afternoon she pleaded exhaustion. I have never known her to be like that before. Perhaps it is because her husband arrived yesterday."

"Did he bore her, or amuse her?"

"You had better ask her that."

Clotilde told them: "He got back last night from Paris where he had been for a week on business and . . ."

"And he was not as old as you thought," they chorused.

"Not a bit," she cried in a pampered voice. "He . . ."

"Now, now!" I shook an admonishing finger.

"All right, all right," and Garcia hummed quickly through a couple of pages: "It wasn't so much, see?" He continued:

"With that big beard, too. The rogue!"

"I think we will all have to grow beards, La Torre, to save face before this competition." He drank the brandy at one swallow and handed the glass back to La Torre for a refill. "But doesn't he know anything about this arrangement between you two?"

"You know the old rhyme." La Torre quoted: "All Madrid knew it, all Madrid but him.' "

"I suppose he would be jealous, eh?"

"In private I don't know, but in public for sure. He is one of those typical husbands who walk with their wives, their chin nailed to their shoulder, watching them."

"And with that beard hanging down his shoulder, he must look like a hussar."

"Hmm . . ." handing Paco his drink.

"Some people take marriage too seriously."

"Are you speaking for yourself, Serrano?"

"No, of her. What the devil! She does not give me a moment's peace. It is all right during the honeymoon, but not years after."

"You know? For some people marriage is but the official acknowledgment of mutual obscenity."

"Poor boy! I don't blame her. You are so very, very . . ."

"So very what?" lifting an eyebrow.

"You know," stretching herself.

"I would like to crave peace with a woman like yours." He looked at Paco who was caressing one of Clotilde's hairy thighs. Her eyes were closed. "If I can relieve you," he pointed at Clotilde, "we might swap for a while."

"Impossible. I wish we could oblige you, but she can't see that. No detrimental implication intended for your charms, but merely a matter of principle."

"Well, I thought it would only be fair. You are going to get Clotilde anyway. Tomorrow you will be together and I shall be left to look for another married woman model."

"Please!" I stopped Garcia. "Don't go and transpose the words now. That would be the last blow."

With astounding docility, he crossed out a line with his pencil and then said that he might tone down the whole thing in the final draft. When he resumed his reading, I think he missed a few lines:

"It is hell to live with her. She is a neurotic, a case for a doctor . . ."

"Or for a painter."

"Perhaps, but she certainly is a case of bad nerves."

"From what I know, I think it runs in the family. Look at her brother for instance."

"But he is not quite as bad. He is the type that won't jump out of a window and I wouldn't stick my finger in his mouth. He is an idiot, but Julieta . . ."

"And say, how is the jewelry business coming along?"

"Not so well. If it had not been for old Ledesma, who is the only one who uses his head, it would have gone long ago. I advised Fernando in some deals, but he did not want to heed my advice."

"I don't blame him."

"At any rate, we have not been on speaking terms for some time, and that is something good. It happened since I compelled Julieta to take and realize her share in the business."

"Naturally."

"Certainly. I did not want the poor innocent girl to lose all her money and . . ."

Clotilde seemed to have passed out completely under Paco's ministrations. La Torre drank another glass of brandy, stood up and said: "I am going into the next room."

"You don't have to leave."

"It so happens that I have to dress for dinner. Otherwise I always like to observe a good seduction. Live and learn, you know."

When La Torre emerged from his room, dressed, shaven and perfumed, Clotilde was putting on her clothes and talking with no affectation in her voice to Paco who answered distractedly.

"Children, we are ready. I am taking both of you to Botin to help me eat a roasted suckling and celebrate your engagement."

"You know I can't go," she adjusted her hat. "I am quite late as it is."

"I had forgotten that the bearded ox is back and you still have to comply with your marital duties. We two will go then and oblige Botin."

While she finished dabbing at her face, La Torre pulled Paco gently to him: "You know, I could have very easily killed you, but why spoil a good situation?"

"Why indeed?"

They chuckled and La Torre filled two more glasses: "To a happy affair." La Torre sighed and enveloped Clotilde in a sidelong glance. Paco was drinking his brandy with relish that banished any other consideration. "Not bad, eh, Serrano?"

Paco interrupted his operation long enough to answer: "No, excellent brandy."

La Torre's thoughtful expression evaporated: "So that's all you like now?" and Paco answered with the glass still to his mouth: "Aha."

Garcia looked up: "I can see that you don't care too much for it. Do you?"

"How can you see? You were not looking at me."

"But I could hear your fingers on the table. Go on, admit it."

"No—it isn't that—it is that the whole scene could have been handled more expediently by saying that Serrano was a scoundrel." I waved aside an objection: "All right, and if you want to give an example, you could have said that he went one afternoon to see a friend who was a painter and there seduced his model who had a trusting, if ridiculous, husband, and his friend, who was a very unscrupulous fellow, did not mind, and to make matters worse, they reveled in their sinful ways and celebrated afterwards."

"Oh, well! If we come to that, we could reduce everything to saying that the world was created, then it lasted for a long time and then ended. That would take care of all happenings and stories, what the devil!"

"Now. Don't exaggerate. . . ."

"You are the one who exaggerates. . . ."

"Look," I said patiently. "What I mean is all this dialogue. I feel that when there is too much dialogue, it is disguising something that without it would boil down to very little or might not be so easy to swallow. Like coating a pill. I feel that the whole thing—this and much of what you have read to me before—has too much dialogue. Takes too much paper."

He was in a temporizing mood. He said that he agreed in principle but that he had done it intentionally as part of the presentation, in keeping with the times when the action took place. Stereotyped style, situations, phrases. You know: cursi, and he reminded me that this was not the final draft and that he expected to improve it.

We would have commented and discussed at greater lengths, but there were unmistakable signs of closing the place for the night and the cashier seemed impatient to call it a day. In these semi-biblical surroundings, Garcia had assumed the leadership of a missionary and, although I knew that his funds were low, he insisted on paying the check and leaving a handsomely posthumous donation to a long departed waiter.

We left the tabernacle and walked slowly, passing a free theater on the way, where we had been once before. In this proverbially commercialized city, it was a contrast. It cost nothing to see a performance there, like listening to Garcia's stories. The same artistic, unprofitable level, but by a natural association of ideas, it made me think of the theater of Tia Mariquita and I was glad that it was too late to go in. We strolled back to Madison Square where we sat on the bench closest to a street lamp that Garcia's practiced eye could select. We spoke of things not worthy of recollection and then Garcia mentioned a person no less than the American writer O. Henry. Every time he is about to read or discuss his own stuff, Garcia always prefaces things with comments on great writers, thus creating an unfavorable contrast.

I tried to keep the conversation on this auspicious level, to hold it there, deferring the inevitable beyond the limits of our negligible knowledge of American letters, but in the end he won handily as usual. The man goes about armed and carries more paper with him than a newsboy. I have tried to retaliate, carrying something about with me, advertisements, tracts, news clippings, any kind of equalizer that will give me a chance to fight back, but when my resistance has been stubborn, Garcia becomes adroit with: "Shut up and listen," and the net result is that he reads and I listen.

Garcia said that he thought I had had enough of the other story for a day—very generous of him—and that he would read what he had left of his moving picture story which, I learned with dismay, was not yet finished:

Ramos dropped the cigarette butt and ground it with his foot on the bare floor with distracted determination and for a long time.

"You know?" he said: "Those were happy days."

To speak of happiness in our surroundings was so incongruous that he must have noticed my expression.

"Yes, they were happy, but for one thing. I could not remember my courtship. Mind you, the girl was not worth a damn, as I found out later, much later unfortunately, but that is beside the point. A courtship is one of the happiest moments of love, or so we have been taught to think, and I had missed its charm. A man fears to miss happiness almost more than to encounter trouble. Otherwise men would never seek adventure or take a risk. I regretted having missed the only part of the affair that was any good. For the first time I began to think of all the happy moments I must have missed during those dark hours. Like diving from the day into a great cavern full of wonderful sights and rushing through in complete darkness, seeing nothing, to come out at the other end into the light. If I had only brought along the torch of consciousness. Did I love the girl? Considering the fantastic manner in which she entered my life and what my life had been, this is one of those things I cannot answer. It is something which you may debate in your mind as you please. Some people may opine that one only thinks one is in love. I am old now after all these wasted years and it seems to me that love is not to be discussed, but to be felt. It is for the emotions, for action, not for meditation or reasoning. I don't know whether I loved her, but I feel I loved her, at least at one time." Ramos half raised both hands in a deprecating gesture which held infinite tiredness.

But at that time Ramos was younger, less tired, and he questioned such things. He could not understand why he was in love with the girl. Indeed, he doubted very much that either one was in love with the other. Yet they remained together. The reasons for this, at least his own, must have been strongly planted during those unconscious moments when he supposedly met her and undoubtedly loved her. He could feel the aftermath of a profound passion in his whole person. As for her reasons to remain with him, very early in life Ramos had concluded that women did not usually employ what one might call reasons for their actions and he looked for none.

They did not precisely quarrel, but there was a perennial smoldering disagreement between them. To her he was introspective, "dull" and "gloomy" she called it. According to that girl, smiling and laughing were something at which people should always be exercising regardless of motives. Hers was an insane obsession with laughter. But after all, he must appear puzzling to her. There was something very definite which prevented him from having a normal relationship with others: these periods of time which he skipped. She called it absentmindedness, but perhaps she already suspected something else she did not dare or could not formulate. . . .

Garcia continued to read but my mind wandered and I was not paying close attention. I remember not too clearly that his story went on to deal with the differences of race and background between Ramos and his girlfriend and their growing incompatibility. That he was serious and she frivolous. I caught one or two things that did not seem well-founded or convincing, but was not inclined to further discussion. Then there was something about a serious disagreement at some party where there was a certain Charlie something-or-other, a Spanish fellow who had become very Americanized, which irked Ramos and also gave Garcia food for some character study. Also there was some hint about an affair between this fellow and the girl. This Charlie had appeared out of one of those blank moments in Ramos's life with several other things, even as it had appeared to me who had not been following the story.

Garcia continued to read and I continued to look around me and think of nothing too important. There was something about Ramos wanting to marry the girl Jenny and her raising objections, probably calculated to trap him better, and then Garcia read something about Madison Square which arrested my attention:

They argued while walking along Madison Square, the argument becoming more and more heated. Julio's resentment increased; he did not want to wait. Jealousy at her liberty, at her other men friends, gnawed at his very entrails. She was unflinching; her mind was made up. And then impatience began to invade his being. He was walking arm in arm with her and heard a clock's bell sounding the hours away, time passing, and he realized that he could wait no more, that to convince a stubborn woman would take eternity. He released her arm and clenched his fists as if to drive his fingers through the palms of his hands. He shut his eyes.

The clock's bell had turned to solemn organ music. The sidewalk under his feet felt soft. He opened his eyes and continued walking with Jenny on his arm, along the luxuriously decorated center aisle of a church and out, in time with a wedding march.

And this time the impression was less. He only missed a step, a thing which did not surprise her under the circumstances, and he continued to walk very erect and out of the church.

"You see?" Ramos said, "I had already become more used to it. One becomes used to most anything in this world. I had grown weaker, my defect, my impatience, stronger. It is always that way." He was walking again and I could see his shadow pass outlined against the livid window and then almost disappear again. It was much darker. He noticed it: "I have no light here. You must forgive me." He walked on and then:

"I took my life as I found it, where I found it."

The man standing in front of us was the personification of fallen and unvanquished dignity, of reluctant mendicancy. The full beard, yet the head respectfully hatless, the stoop due to the weight of years and misfortune, that could yet spring back erect in long-forgotten flashes of a regal past. He spoke to us in proud and nostalgic Castilian:

"Forgive the intrusion, little masters," a flattering appraisal of our age despite Garcia's prematurely white hair and my other timely and less becoming signs: "but I heard you speak our language and was certain that you would help a poor old compatriot with a few coins to fill this bota." He patted an object he carried under his arm and which in the imperfect light I had taken for his hat held deferentially in this fashion.

"Is that a wineskin?" Garcia exclaimed: "I have not seen one for I don't know how long."

"That it is, sir, and it has accompanied me in my peregrinations all the way from Spain. It is thirsty now and as empty as a wretched mother's breast. Will you gentlemen help to fill it up, so that I may have a drink to your health?"

His frankness in asking, as we say, for vices was disarming and I began to reach for my pocket, but Garcia stopped me. This honor would be his. I gave him a dissuading nudge which went unheeded and then to my surprise and consternation, he brought out a ten dollar bill. I nudged like a pneumatic drill, but Garcia was pachydermic:

"Look: I have no change. If you can go and change this someplace in the neighborhood, I shall be glad to contribute."

The beggar took the bill and stood more erect: "Thank you, little master. I know a place nearby where I can get this bota filled up for very little and I will bring you the change right back. I knew you would not let a compatriot down," and with this he walked away and disappeared around some bushes.

I knew this was Garcia's last money in this world. Either he was going to follow my advice and bring about a reconciliation with his landlady that same night, or else he wanted to go back to washing dishes sooner than necessary, because I was certain that this would be the last he would ever see of that bill. Undoubtedly we had drunk too much arrack.

Garcia read my thoughts like one of his own manuscripts: "Look: perhaps it is the drinks, but what is the purpose of drinking aside from the taste? This is an experiment for my own, and maybe your, satisfaction. Here we meet a compatriot, in this big city, at this hour, in this square of memories. To fail him is out of the question."

"Of course it is out of the question, but you did not have to give him all you have. I could have given him some change."

"I have not given him all I have. He will take what he needs and will bring the rest back."

"He may decide he needs it all."

"Oh no! When you give a Spaniard a foot, he does not take a yard, but returns eleven inches, and that is the experiment I am talking about. If he returns with the change, I know that Spain still lives. If he does not return . . . But tonight the opportunity has presented itself, and I must find out. It is worth much more than all I have. If he broke faith with a countryman, I wouldn't give a damn what happened to me . . ." Garcia was moved and his eyes were bright in the semidarkness: "But I am sure he will come back. A faith like mine cannot be unfounded. I'll bet my bottom dollar that he returns . . ." His voice broke.

"You have, literally," I thought, but did not say it, and then we fell silent and waited. Time dragged on, perhaps because we were waiting or because we did not speak, but Garcia smiled confidently to himself. He slid a little on the bench, his legs, one over the other, stretched before him and his hands in his empty pockets. I looked in the direction where the beggar had gone, started to say something and left it unsaid. We waited some more. One could not see the clock in the Metropolitan tower because of the trees. Garcia closed his eyes and bent his head down, a lock of white hair fell forward, and the contented smile remained. He was awaiting the verdict with serenity, with confidence.

And as I was about to plant the final stamp on my condemnation of mankind, with avowed contempt and abhorrence of all its members and an oath to trust no more such hypocritical duplicity, the man appeared walking from the opposite direction, his steps accelerated by solicitude as much as his age permitted.

"Sorry to have kept you waiting, little masters," he announced, "but I had to try a couple of places." He patted the wineskin bursting under his arm like a fat jolly suckling and spoke to it: "Thank the gentlemen for the transfusion," and addressing us: "She can't talk, she is too full." Then he took out some bills and handed them to Garcia: "There you are, little master, nine dollars and a little change."

Garcia took the money in a matter-of-fact way. He had scored and I looked away. I was ashamed before him and the beggar, and to avoid thinking of it, I considered that wine must be pretty bad for that price, but that only made me feel worse.

"Good night, little masters, and may God repay you for contributing to the milk for an old man," and he departed in yet another direction, merging into the shadows with furtive greatness, the wineskin held against his breast like a kidnapped child.

"Well!" exclaimed Garcia, coming to life with elation: "shall we move on?" He bounded along triumphantly and I tagged along somewhat contritely. At last I forced myself to say:

"Of course, I knew all the time that he would return. Never doubted it a moment. Once a Spaniard . . ."

Garcia allowed me to come abreast of him and held my shoulder in a generous clasp: "I am glad to hear that, because I am ashamed to confess that I doubted."

Again he had scored and then we both laughed and walked on very happily.

We crossed west and took the subway uptown. During the ride Garcia entrusted to me the last pages of what he had written on his story of the family, but had not read because of the interruption of our comments and the closing of the restaurant. He told me to look them over the next day or even that night if I wanted to stay up a little later. I got off with him at his station, which was the one before mine, and I suggested that we sit on the park side and smoke one last cigarette, but he said he was in a hurry for a bath. When we reached his corner, there was indecision and we only waved our departure without speaking. If I had mentioned seeing him later, this would have created compulsion, and if I had said good night, it would have acknowledged his weakness. So I walked the rest of the way home slowly. Then I noticed the roll of pages in my hand which I had been holding absently. I should have realized when he gave them to me that he was going home to stay and had decided on a reconciliation, but with the noise in the subway, one can't think very clearly. Anyway, I was glad I had said nothing.

I crossed the street and walked alongside the park still conscious of Garcia's manuscript in my hand. When I came to a bench, I sat down and began to thumb the pages. I did not want to go home yet. It had been a long winter and now one could not get enough of the outdoors. Also I felt well-disposed toward Garcia. He probably wouldn't be around for a couple of days, then would call to ask peremptorily where had I been and invite me to come over to his house for dinner and to meet some of his landlady's friends and perhaps her very young niece from Pennsylvania who was supposed to come for Easter and looked like my conception of a Valkyrie. All plain and merry people with whom I would have—what the devil!—a rousing good time, shoveling under the nose, as we say, and gulping Rhine or May wine with happy unconcern for the fine points of libation, out of sweeping pilsner glasses.

It was with these cuddling thoughts that I decided to go home to read the pages in my hand, at first carelessly and then gathering detached attention.

This part of the story described a trip that Serrano took with that

Clotilde Bonafé, during which time he left Julieta without explanation and without money, and then it elaborated considerably on the obstinacy of her love for this undeserving and libertine character, harping strongly on the pathos of a woman abandoned with her ill-nourished children by her husband, a woman who has seen this thing coming and blames herself for loving him more the worse he treats her and for this passion which consumes her and drives her mad. The manuscript went in for much abnormal psychology and stormy emotionalism, leading to some more risqué passages on which my sight bounced along to something else, or had to digest without an opportunity to voice a protest. Garcia must have had this in mind when he left the pages with me. Then the story said something about Paco gambling, contracting debts, mortgaging and eventually losing all his property, and wound up with a moralizing discourse in which he was pictured as a man who, having risen to an important and respectable position in society, falls prey to his vices and slowly but surely sinks to the lowest depths of moral and financial collapse, dragging down his household with him.

I found myself in disagreement with much of that section: its inconsistency, its presuming to lay bare and dissect what goes on inside the soul, or the head, or the heart of a woman, a thing which to me has always appeared pedantic in the extreme whether it applies to women, men, or animals, and a task to which, in my opinion, Garcia did not show himself equal, but rather dogmatic and scarcely qualified by his record. His cursory treatment of the subject, the masochistic delusions, the bait of salacity under the guise of pseudoscientific analysis and many other things. This section was corny, all right, and I suspect that this time it was not intentional. However, there was nothing I could do about it and I continued. Then I came to an amusing passage where Paco, having reached the nadir of depravity and spiritual callousness, tries to gamble with La Torre for his wife's favors without bothering to consult her and La Torre answers:

"No, Serrano. My women I don't win and I don't even earn. They must come to me of their own accord, preferably without my deserving them, and also preferably without the official knowledge of their husbands. Don't forget that I am a caballero."

Garcia had succeeded in making Serrano even a worse brigand than La Torre and, in doing so, had made up for some of the latter's failures and disclosed a saving grace of innocent self-deception, both La Torre's and Garcia's. I read on:

It was at that time that Paco called on the Count of X. with the obvious purpose of obtaining money from him.

He betook himself one good day to the Count's residence at Recoletos, where the old man lived with his daughter Laura, both of them lost in the immense mansion which to all appearances housed a regular army of servants rather than the masters. It was one of the most lavish places in Madrid. The main staircase alone was a masterpiece and worth a fortune. The banister had been designed by a great sculptor of the time and represented a waterfall in which cherubs rolled and swam with foaming joy.

Paco ascended the staircase appraising its value and was led by consecutive servants to a small library in the rear of the building where he found the Count buried in a huge Spanish chair, the lower part of his person wrapped in a llama blanket and his feet resting on a merino skin dyed red. The Count was reading with all the comfort of a priest. Upon the table there was a silver tea service steaming aromatically.

The Count was a very old man with a magnificent head of white hair which was neatly combed. His white beard melted and faded into a white muffler submerged in the folds of the blanket. He had a penetrating gaze and all the traces of being ill-tempered.

With a hand he waved the servant away, always looking at his book, and then he regarded Paco with the tail of his eye: "I knew you wouldn't be gone long."

"Splendid! That eliminates the element of surprise, which is generally somewhat upsetting."

"No. Some surprises are very soothing, as for instance, if you had decided not to see me again."

"I had, but the decision has abandoned me completely. It is fortunate, for I see I come in time to inquire after your health. You seem to be ill. All these blankets, mufflers and steaming tea. These are bad signs at your age. Hmm— you are a very old man, and you had better be careful."

The Count was always irritated at being reminded of his age: "Old, you say? Don't worry. I will live longer than you would like."

Paco whistled and sat down: "And how is my dear Laura?"

"She will probably be down soon. That fool servant always advertises everyone who comes here all over the house."

"Most embarrassing when the guest happens to be a charming one with skirts."

The old man disregarded the allusion: "And she still has that stupid tenderness about you."

"It is none of your fault if she still has, eh?"

"No. I admit it. At another time, it was different. Now you are married and you threw your chance overboard."

"What do you mean?"

"You know very well what I mean. That girl has loved you with a faithfulness of which I never suspected a human being capable. She has suffered on your account and she remains single because of you. If there is a man who never deserved that love, it is you, but you could never appreciate a fine thing."

"But this is the first news I've had on the subject. Why! How flattering!"

"You knew it all the time, but you can act unconcerned and most candid when it suits you. As they say, acting dumb as if you were not . . ."

"I assure you . . ."

". . . and you have been a fool. You could have married her and had everything you have been after for such a long time. You chose the other road and now you can take the consequences."

Paco stood up in true surprise: "But do you mean to say that you would have let your daughter marry your own son?"

"Why not, if she did not know it and it could have made her happy? That is only a superstition like many others—but now it is too late. Now she knows it and she suffers from that superstition and now she is very unhappy because she has lost all hope."

"You have told her, then?"

"How clever of you! Yes, I have. And now that I have learned the kind of life you are giving your wife, I am glad that things have ended this way. Now she will grow to be an embittered old maid, but that is better than being your wife."

"I am not sure of that."

"Your opinion is immaterial to me, as is everything that concerns you. I have been lenient enough with you. Not because I did not know you for what you are, but because of my daughter. She has been a good daughter and I love her much, and I owe you also the most painful moment in my long life, when I had to confess to her who you were. You have been a fool and I am finished with you."

"I have done what I like and I don't think that is being a fool."

"You might have liked this better and that is what you don't know, and now you will live in the uncertainty of thinking that perhaps you might have been happier."

"Uncertainties have never bothered me."

"Because you have never been down, way down. But you are going to be very soon and then you will know the proportions which a doubt can assume. Your mother was also a fool. If she had listened to me, everything would have worked out for the best, but she also had the superstition about brothers. She was sentimental and grew maternal with you."

"If she had not been so, things might not have worked out so easily for you."

"Perhaps, I don't know. But Serrano, your . . . father, was different. He was a clever fool and I think he is the only man who has ever understood me and one of the few who understood life. However, they are both dead and these vagaries concerning the past lead nowhere."

"That is right. I am glad to see that your logical faculties have not abandoned you yet. Let us get down to the present. I came to see you because . . ."

"You don't have to tell me. I know why you came and let me tell you that there is no hope. I am finished with you. Don't even count on my death. I think I am being fair to you by letting you know in time that your name has been erased from my will."

Paco threw his cigarette down and stamped his foot on it.

"Mind the rug, my boy."

"But this is an abuse! I am as much your son as she is your daughter. Simply because of a benediction, a meaningless sign in the air . . ."

"Not so meaningless as you think . . ."

"Yes, as meaningless as the scraps of paper which make an innocent child legitimate or illegitimate. I am your blood as much as she is. All the rest is nothing but a superstition."

"Now you want to discard a superstition and a little while ago you were considering another superstition as something insurmountable. How you change!"

"That is different. This is merely social. The other is biological."

"Big words. But you know very well that people respect the social much more than the biological, at least officially. But we are not going to discuss that now. You have been disinherited and that is all that concerns you."

"Wait a moment. Don't think that you can discard me as easily as that. I have papers which may support my claims, or at least spoil your good memory after your death and create a painful situation for your daughter."

"You may have papers, but I have influence."

"I have influence also, and besides, remember that you will be dead and stiff, and a scandal is a scandal."

The Count had stood up in rage and threw the blanket aside: "You will not show those papers. You will not stoop so low. You will not acknowledge publicly that you are a bastard and that your mother was . . ."

"Yes." Paco's teeth had appeared: "I will acknowledge what I please." He was calm again. "After all, that is also another superstition. It seems that today we are doing away with many superstitions."

The Count was drawing his breath in short gasps. He extended his arm and pointed to the door: "Get out! Get out of this house."

"I am waiting to see Laura."

"You need not wait for her. She will not come down after what she knows."

"Yes. She has strength of character and she will come down."

"Don't think that she will intercede in your favor. Nothing will change my decision. And she will not try to change it. She is also finished with you."

"She will not fail me."

"You will not see her."

And then the door opened and Laura stood there. She was of medium height, very dark, with black curly hair and large green eyes like those of a cat. Those who believe psychological qualities break through the skin like an eruption would have looked in vain for strength of character in her.

"Hola, Paco," and then she looked at her father and inquired with composure, "What is the matter?"

"Nothing, my darling. Nothing. This man has come to upset me as usual."

Paco had approached Laura with an afflicted air. He held her hand and declaimed theatrically: "Sister—yes, sister! At last I can call you that and it is the saddest moment in my life."

The Count had dropped back into his chair and was looking at him with contempt, shaking his head: "Hypocrite, hypocrite!"

"Don't listen to him, sister. He is furious with me and I don't know why. I am innocent. I could not help it if I was his child."

"Paco!"

"Yes, sister. That truth has embittered my life." He was acting his part splendidly. "I could never be proud of my mother like other boys. No, I only knew shame from the very beginning."

Laura was looking down. The Count had covered his ears in desperation. Paco went on:

"But that is not the worst, Laura. I knew of your love for me, I knew it all the time, and all I can say is that it was not as deep, not as intense as the one I felt for you. But I had to seal my lips. I knew the truth and I could not reciprocate it. In despair I married . . ." He broke down effectively.

Laura had stepped to the window and her back could be seen shaking. The Count stood up again: "Liar—dirty liar. I never thought a man could be so low."

Paco smiled at him politely, bowed, and then became serious again because Laura had turned about.

"Father. . . .!" She extended her arms. Paco walked over to her and held her hand.

"Yes, sister, please defend me. See how he treats me. See how he insults me and I cannot retaliate, because I am his son."

Laura looked at her father in silence, long, reproachfully.

"But damn it all! Don't be such a fool. He is a liar, a hypocrite. He was laughing behind your back. Just this minute he was laughing— Oh! He is such a . . ."

"Don't believe him, sister. He wants to turn everyone against me. He has cast me into the world, a helpless illegitimate son, and as if that were not enough, now he wants to disinherit me, to leave me in utter misery— Oh! how unjust, how unjust life is with some people!" He produced a handkerchief and put it to his eyes.

"Father. How could you do such a thing? How can you be so cruel?"

"Yes, Laura, how can he be so . . ."

"Enough!" The Count was shaking all over, almost foaming at the mouth. "Get out, you damn liar! Get out! You have come to make her unhappier still. Get out or I will call the servants to kick you out!"

Paco had opened the door with a dramatic gesture. He stood there, his arms open, a crucified victim:

"Yes, I will go away. You are turning your son out of your house. That is your last abuse. I shall empty my cup of bitterness to the dregs, but I shall never lower myself to discuss money." He addressed Laura: "Good-bye, sister. You are my only hope. You are the only one I have in this world."

The Count laid a hand on a heavy crystal inkwell and Paco, hurriedly, as if to hide his tears, rushed out.

Laura was about to run after him.

"Stop, Laura! Don't go after that man! Someday you will know him for what he really is."

She slid to the floor against the door and cried for a long time.

As Paco left the palace, he felt a strong desire to kick the sumptuous staircase, but he considered its massive hardness and gave up the idea.

There followed another long-winded and pathetic analysis of Julieta's feelings and Paco's misbehavior. I select a few paragraphs at random:

Julieta sat alone with her children in the big house and saw the works of art, the furniture, leave piece by piece. The numerous gifts of jewelry which her parents had given her had been sold. Even her collection of shawls was sold, some of them given away, to adorn gay happy women, all but a very bright one which she liked more than the others and had hidden away.

This gives a fairly accurate idea. Here is some more:

One day a friend came to see her. Julieta had retired from society as if ashamed to face anyone she knew. This was practically the only friend she still had.

The lady saw Julieta old and worn but was too discreet to comment, a rare exception, and then Julieta told her everything, slowly, calmly, with scarcely any expression in her voice or in her action.

"He was not like that before. He was so serious when you married!"

"Yes, but the goat will go to the mountain. You see, Virginia?" And Julieta showed her friend an ugly bruise. "That's him."

"But I thought he was a gentleman, Julieta."

"I wonder if he ever was. You know? He was thrown out of La Gran Peña for stealing there. Do you hear? For stealing! At least my brother stole from father and the shame remained at home, but this was public. They were kind enough not to send him to jail. They only threw him out like a filthy thing, and the few jewels I had left had to go toward paying back. He owes money to everybody."

The interview of the heroine and her friend went on like this with more self-punishing confessions on the part of one and increasing pity on the part of the other, to end with this bit of dialogue:

"Poor Julieta!"

"Don't pity me. Let me feel that I am also to blame, lest the injustice be too great to bear."

Paco announced to Julieta that he had closed a deal and would have the villa torn down and an apartment house erected in its place. This would pay more.

Julieta said nothing. For some time they lived in different places while the house was demolished and the building erected. They scarcely saw each other during that long time.

When the building was finished they moved to one of the apartments while the others were yet to rent. Although it was a good apartment house, it seemed to her, after the way she had lived, a dingy sordid place. In her loneliness she thought that perhaps the new rooms coincided with the old ones, with the rooms that were. Although the rooms were smaller, she tried to imagine that they occupied the same spot of the former ones. She walked about trying to conceive that, although walking on new floors, she was moving in the same space which had once been so dear to her. She tried to conceive it but the idea escaped her; it puzzled her, it obsessed her.

Then she knew real misery. The apartments did not rent and heavy mortgages became due and took away what they had. She resorted to her brother, impelled by Paco, but his help was very slight. The jewelry shop had lost greatly; it also had big debts to meet and threatened bankruptcy. Only Ledesma's administrative skill kept it afloat.

Fernando's family was also larger now. In a short interval Trini had given birth to two more children: first one boy, Jorge, and then a girl, Lolita. All these things meant expenses, particularly considering Fernando's and Trini's vanity. They had more than one governess and several tutors for the four children, and the only one who seemed to profit by the costly education was Rojelia.

The house above the jewelry shop had also been remodeled, almost rebuilt. Fernando had all the floors connected by ornate staircases. The whole house was redecorated, even the outside, in a showy wedding cake style. Rather than have rented or bought a residence in a better spot, they seemed to like the vulgarity of that location, to be right in the heart of the city with all its disagreeable noises.

When Julieta asked Fernando for money, he was insulting and persistent about her leaving Paco. He said: "I don't mind helping you, but I don't want to feed that crook when I also have a family to look after." Julieta left blushing with shame and indignation. She still resented having her husband insulted.

Ledesma tried to help her but Fernando reproached him in a manner that was almost disrespectful, and Ledesma continued to help her as best he could, out of his own pocket, and also to comfort her.

He, a decided misanthropist, who had never sought her company when she shone in society and who seemed to avoid her, was generous in his visits now that she was forsaken.

Once he was with her in the small sitting room. Although they did not speak, all those happenings were in their minds and they knew what they were thinking of. They were almost following a conversation in their minds. Then he said as if answering: "But then you should go away with your children, if only for their sake."

"I can't leave him, Ledesma, you do not understand." She held his hand and looked at him very directly: "Have you ever loved, Ledesma?"

He held her eyes very intently and his lips moved in silence as if trying to say something that he could not pronounce.

Ledesma had never shown any particular age. He had looked mature ever since she had known him, but now he seemed to her very old and tired. He looked away and relaxed: "Yes, I have loved. I still love and I have never hoped."

"But if you have loved like me, without attaining, how could you always be so calm? I never noticed anything."

"No, you never did."

"Because you did not really love, Ledesma. You never loved as madly as I have." Ledesma was looking at her and his eyes were very open and very dull and there was anguish in his face. "Oh no, Ledesma! If you had loved, you would have killed yourself already. You would have wanted to kill your rival, but one cannot kill the whole world. Then you would have wanted to kill the one you loved, but in the end you would have killed yourself knowing you could not live. People who really love and are not loved kill themselves. Love is a storm of life within and, if checked, it turns against one and destroys. Those who love in vain kill themselves sooner or later."

"Not all of them." His voice was hollow. "You say that because you are young yet. When one is old, when one has conquered the storm of a young, secret love, that storm turns into gloomy days, hopeless, endless, gray, dull days, and one waits and one knows one waits in vain. One does not kill oneself then through conviction or despair. One kills oneself then because one has realized that it was death one was waiting for."

At that time Julieta used to take long walks in the Retiro with her children. She walked fast, with resolution, frowning, like someone in a hurry to get somewhere, and then, all of a sudden, stopped and sat on a bench, her head down, while the children played about.

It was thus that her friend Virginia met her once. She noticed Julieta looking frightfully aged, careless of her person and dress, the one thing she once was so exacting about.

They embraced one another a long time and then Julieta spoke, but this time she was sober in her manner and scarcely spoke of her life. This composure was even sadder to her friend.

When they parted, Virginia hesitated and then said: "Julieta, I hope you know that if you need anything you can come to me, like a sister. Promise me."

Julieta looked long and blankly at her friend and said, "Thank you." Then she looked down again and shivered in her thin, shabby clothes. It was a chilly, somber autumn day.

The friend was about to say impulsively: "Julieta, I know that you don't like to wear a coat, but . . ."

But Julieta had already called the children and was walking fast away.

"That Virginia was my mother," Garcia had said once to me very solemnly, as if this lent matters an authenticity that justified anyone in crashing the literary gates and then condoned his misconduct, once inside.

I dallied a bit longer thinking about these things, then stood up, stretched, and walked home with determination.

When I got there I noticed the light in my room and wondered if Garcia had changed his mind and returned after all. I went in and sure enough he was there, but it was a very different Garcia. He stood in the middle of the room as if he had heard my key in the door and come to meet me, and he looked very strange:

"Where were you all this time?"

"Sitting on the park side reading this." I laid the manuscript on the desk. He stood there wanting to say something, I was sure, and not knowing how to say it, and I asked him what was the matter.

"She is dead." He choked on it and his whole expression seemed to disintegrate. His mouth, the flesh all over his face, trembled.

I knew he meant his landlady and for a moment I entertained the stupid thought that he might have killed her, but soon the idea vanished of its own accord and I asked him what was it all about, to tell me more.

"When I got home I found a note from the Cuban roomer telling me to call some number. He had to go to work and could not wait for me." Garcia produced the note. "They told me that she had drowned, that she was at the morgue and I must come down to identify her, or something like that."

"But then why didn't you go right down? Perhaps it is somebody else. What will they think if you don't go right down?"

"Oh, it is her all right." He appeared to be regaining some control: "They had all her stuff, and anyway the note was left this afternoon." He looked away from me: "Think. She was dead all that time, drowned —that horrible tragic death, and we were— I can't go down there all by myself. You must come with me. I could not go alone."

"But of course. Let's go." Then I had an inspiration and told him that the person to accompany him should be Dr. de los Rios.

"It had not occurred to me, but Dr. de los Rios—to burden him with these personal matters . . ."

It was obvious that, even now, he was ashamed of his relationship with the woman and still more ashamed of his shame.

"Dr. de los Rios understands much more than you think and is as much your friend. I am going to call him."

As I made the call he insisted: "But you are coming too, are you not?"

"Naturally. You don't think I am going to go to sleep at a moment like this and let you go out by yourself—" The voice of Dr. de los Rios interrupted.

I explained as well as I knew how and he said to come right down. It would be simpler that way as he lived on the other side of the park and farther down than we did.

We went out and hopped a late-cruising cab and rode across the park and down to de los Rios. All Garcia said during the ride was: "And to think we were in that neighborhood this evening and tonight."

Dr. de los Rios was waiting at his private entrance and his car was ready at the curb. He got hold of Garcia by the shoulders and studied him. Then he told me that he had made a telephone call and everything would be all right.

We all piled in the front seat and were off.

I will not easily forget that scene at the morgue. Going down the narrow stairs to the basement of the building we met a chauffeur coming out. At the foot of the stairs we met two men whom I surmised were the police or something like it. They greeted Dr. de los Rios and moved a little away with him and spoke in a low voice. De los Rios motioned with his head in our direction and for the second time they gave us a careless glance. Then a voice behind us said to get out of the way and we turned, and it was an attendant wheeling a man stretched out on a curved tin rack. He looked small, shriveled. I noticed the blood, the bald spot on his head as he passed. He looked so puny and vulnerable, so incapable of coping with life and so easy to eliminate by death. The pallor of Garcia was ghastly to see in that light.

"What are we waiting for?" he whispered and his words caught in his throat, but when Dr. de los Rios and the two men approached us and we started walking along the room, he held back shaking and saying that he could not go on, could not do it.

Dr. de los Rios held one of his arms tightly and propelled him gently forward. One of the men moved ahead of us and we followed.

We did not find her in one of the boxes as I had expected, but in a room at the far end, on a table. Sometimes the dead look small, shrunken, and sometimes they look big and swollen. She looked big and imposing, her whole body saying: "Here I am. It is your problem."

Garcia stood like a swaying stone pillar. Here was the woman of whom he had been ashamed and there probably was a futile and sad attempt to control his emotions. I am sure that if he had been alone with the two men, it would have been easier for him, but we were there, his friends, Spanish, creating a self-imposed conflict of loyalties and inevitable embarrassment.

And then he leaped forward and threw his arms about her, the side of his face against her breast, his eyes shut.

One of the men moved toward him, but Dr. de los Rios was nearer and lifted an unresisting Garcia. He looked at Dr. de los Rios as if he could not make him out, as if nothing in this world made any sense to him, as if he could not understand his own emotions. His sorrow, crushed between bewilderment and shame, was horrible to behold, and suddenly his tenseness melted away. He sagged against de los Rios's chest, buried his face in his shoulder and wept like a child. His muffled voice cried that he loved her, that he wanted to admit it to us at last, that he loved her and owed her that last confession.

Now that we were going out again, Garcia did not want to leave her there but stay with her or make better arrangements for her surroundings and he babbled that this was his duty, but again Dr. de los Rios prevailed and eventually we were outside. Once more we all piled in the front seat and Dr. de los Rios said that Garcia would stay with him.

During the ride Garcia mumbled persistently whether we thought it was suicide, that she was a good swimmer: "This last quarrel we had— I could not live with that on my conscience."

Dr. de los Rios told him not to worry, that it was not suicide: "I got the whole report and it was an accident."

"But she was a good swimmer."

"An accident can happen to anybody. A cramp, an unsuspected weak heart, any number of things, and it is not likely for a good swimmer to drown on purpose. Don't worry. Don't think that way, Garcia. I assure you that it was an accident."

When we arrived at de los Rios's place I wanted to leave, but he nodded toward Garcia and asked me to come in for some coffee. We went in and de los Rios told Garcia that he was going to give him a sedative. He prepared it in a glass and told him to drink it. He coaxed Garcia to a couch and threw a rug over him. Garcia turned to the wall and we saw him shake with sobs. The sobs subsided gradually and then his breathing came regularly. Dr. de los Rios's big dog came in, went to the couch and sniffed, and then he stood as if guarding Garcia. De los Rios opened one of the windows and I opened the other. The spring night air came in and it was still quite warm. I looked at the sky and although it was already paling, the stars were bright. I stood there while de los Rios prepared the coffee and thought that this would be another warm day, the kind that Garcia liked.

We did not say much as we drank the coffee. Once I said: "You knew about the affair and how he felt about it?"

"Yes, I knew that and I know Garcia."

I was thinking that he was understanding. He may not have been sympathetic but he was understanding and tolerant. This was one of his marked characteristics differentiating him from Don Pedro. With the Moor one could discuss personal emotions and find him sympathetic and ready to generalize them into racial or national traits and even encourage and champion them, but one felt that acting these emotions, showing them to him, would have been a waste of time;

they would have gone unheeded in his mad plunge after the explanatory and esoteric formula that would bring them into line within the vaster domain of philosophical generalization. He gave the impression of being personally not above or below emotion but outside of it. With Dr. de los Rios, one was aware of the Spanish characteristic which precludes intimate personal discussions, to which he seemed unresponsive, indifferent, distracted, and he even discouraged and shrugged away any rhetorical confessions or sentimental theorizing, but one felt that one could break down before him and give way to one's feelings as one would in the embrace of a father. With the Moor, one could discuss onself. With Dr. de los Rios, one could be oneself; but thinking it over, I am not certain which one of them was understanding and which one sympathetic. I know that neither one was both.

Dr. de los Rios rubbed his eyes, then stared with them wide open, a habitual gesture with him. I moved to the door. He said that he was going to take a shower, and since he was up already and it was too late to go to sleep with all his early appointments, he would take this opportunity to catch up on some of his accumulated work.

At the door we shook hands, a thing which Spanish friends seldom do, and I said: "He will be all right, won't he?"

Dr. de los Rios looked past me at the quiet avenue, the crepuscular opal of the park where, in this silence, the birds could be heard already: "Well," said he. Then he released my hand and I departed.

I decided to walk across the park. The drives and pathways were violet under the fresh green trees. I looked, listened to the birds, and for once did not think about anything. When I reached my place, the light was still burning, the manuscript on the desk, yesterday still imprisoned in the room.

This day when I met Don Pedro, the Moor, he told me that he was on his way to see Bejarano and asked me to come along, and since I had nothing to do, I went with him. Bejarano was the male half of the dancing team Lunarito and Bejarano. The Señor Olózaga, the one who backed up the Spanish Theater and was said to own El Telescopio, a man with a remarkable interest in business, had brought them from Spain to New York on a brief engagement, but their dancing had soon captured popular fancy and after appearing several times with the Moor, I mean, Pete Guz and his band, they had gone into musical comedies, visited Hollywood, taken part in moving pictures and, now back in New York, were riding the crest of their success without knowing very well, according to the Moor, what it was all about, taking everything for granted in what the Moor described with one of his favorite phrases as seraphic optimism, refusing to have their style of life changed by this civilization, sincerely on the part of Lunarito perhaps, but more as a convenient pose where Bejarano was concerned, because as Don Pedro said:

"Culture does not have the merest information regarding their minds, and in the words of that Spanish philosopher, one could say that, at most, their ignorance has lagoons, but they are clever in matters of life. They may not know how to sign their names properly, but try to put anything over on them. Just try."

They lived in a large apartment with several other transient people who came uninvited, stayed, and then left, and then there was always some Spaniard down on his luck whom they befriended and who helped with some chores and little favors.

The last time I had visited them I went there with the Moor and Garcia. I remember that when we arrived the door was open and we went right in. We heard voices in the kitchen and went along the corridor there. It was around noontime and the preparations were going on for dinner. Lunarito and Bejarano had never been able to keep servants for long and it seems that they did not like or trust any. It was a large kitchen as kitchens go here, but everybody complained constantly about the smallness of all rooms. In fact, Spaniards always find in this country a lack of space and a lack of time. One can obtain any number of gadgets which was the privilege of the very rich to have in Spain, such as automobiles, cameras, vacuum cleaners, etc., but no space or time, which is what one has plenty of in Spain.

Leaning against the kitchen door, glass in hand and an eye on the proceedings, was Bejarano. Inside was Lunarito doing something at the kitchen table and in a corner, sitting on a chair with her arms folded, was the old lady Doña Felisa. The woman practically lived in the kitchen and only left the place to go to bed. No one had ever presented her to anyone and she scarcely spoke at all but sat there looking at everything with resigned understanding and a smile reminiscent of the Mona Lisa.

Bejarano greeted us and stepped aside, pushing us hospitably into the kitchen. The Moor said: "Not late for dinner, I hope." This was another aspect of the Bejarano ménage: anyone could arrive at dinnertime and bring whomever he pleased without previous invitation. The Moor continued:

"Paella again, I bet. From the looks of things and from past experience: paella."

"Yes, paella again," came with lugubrious patience from Doña Felisa.

"So it is paella again," Lunarito said, "and you seem to like it well enough. Don't you want to eat it, Moor? It will save me trouble. I won't have to make more."

"Oh, to be sure. In fact, I will prepare it myself inasmuch as I and my friends are going to eat it. That will save you more trouble. Let me see what you have here. If I am going to eat it again, I am going to have it cooked right."

This precipitated a violent argument between Lunarito and the Moor, Lunarito swearing that she would not lift a finger and he could do everything by himself, including the unpleasant attending chores of washing and peeling this and that. Meanwhile Bejarano was pouring drinks for everybody, including a surprisingly tall one for Doña Felisa. Don Pedro recoiled from his:

"Not that. I am not going to drink that at this time of day and before dinner. You are supposed to be so castizo and you drink that thing! A true Spaniard never drinks anything Spanish before meals. He drinks Italian vermouth. You have some Cinzano there, I know. Bring it out but use the same kind of glass, big."

"There is some lemon there too," put in Lunarito, "although I don't see why I should bother with you."

"No. No lemon. Only plain and in a big glass." He got what he wanted and went straight to the refrigerator. He placed his shillelagh on the nearby table and then brought out two chickens and laid them on the table. He began to squeeze and poke them with expert fingers: "Hmmm—they could be more tender, but they'll do. The technique of the old maestro will tame them. You know." He reminisced about those people in Spain who grow chickens for eggs on roofs. When one of the chickens won't lay or is slow, they hold it over a bed and squeeze for all they are worth. He pantomimed while talking:

"Come on there, you lazy chicken, let go of that egg— These Spaniards are inimitable and most of the time they get their egg." He addressed Lunarito: "I am going to cut up and clean these chickens. You get the olives and rice and fix more peppers and chop a lot more garlic, and don't go foreign and independent on me. You and your pressure cooker for the chickens—it is formidable. They could sell all of them in Spain, but not for cooking but to press the eggs out of the lazy chickens— The National System, always use everything for what it is not intended. Put the pressure cooker away. I cook this in the black iron casseroles, although a paella should be cooked in a paella. Where are the casseroles?" He found them under the stove. "There seem to be enough chorizos," he mused to himself.

"Better put in more chorizos," chimed in Bejarano. "I like them and I am hungry."

"More chorizos it is," sighed the Moor. With remarkable speed, no doubt born from long experience, he was cutting chorizos in slices and dissecting chickens like a surgeon. Lunarito, her argument forgotten, had obediently done as ordered and brought all the ingredients. Don Pedro picked up the bottle of olive oil:

"This is Italian, but no matter; just as good." He interrupted himself with a start: "Where are the clams and the shrimps?"

"The clams are right there in front of you and here are the shrimps." Lunarito brought a bowl of shrimps from the refrigerator.

"These are the clams? In these jars? All shelled? Have you lost the last vestige of mind you had left?"

"I like them that way. One gets all clams and not shells mixed up with the rice and taking up room, and while we are about it, that's why I like the pressure cooker; one can cook a chicken in it so that the bones come out easily and then one does not have bones taking up room and . . ."

"All right, all right. You win." He lifted his shoulders and then let them drop with a deep sigh: "I still say a paella should be cooked in a paella, but . . . this is what things have come to. Paella Newyorkina—

I tell you, these Spaniards—" He took a good swallow of his vermouth: "I need the stimulant, but as I was saying: they were living in Spain, in primitive bliss, with those things which could not possibly be improved because they were born perfect, and when they leave Spain, they begin to think. They try to simplify and that's when the complications begin, because they lose track of the original plan. It's hopeless. They join all the foreigners in that absolute incapacity to understand the obvious, they become reasonable, traitors and forsaken by God."

"Such sanctimonious words coming from the Moor." It was Dr. de los Rios standing at the kitchen door: "Don't let me interrupt while you are in such a mood."

"The Dr. Jesucristo," Don Pedro cried, "to my arms." He limped over with arms outstretched and then stopped. "I can't. My hands are all messed up, but christen your gullet and watch me do what I can with what I have. You, Lunarito, put some of the juice from those accursed clams in some container and soak some saffron in it." He limped back to the stove, poured the oil in the casseroles, and then in went the garlic, the pieces of chicken, and the seasoning. He kept a running commentary: "We'll give it a little more time, to tame the chickens," then he eyed the large refrigerator with disgust:

"That ridiculous white elephant. Like the pressure cooker, it is only a domestic example of the second law of thermodynamics. In one, time passes fast; in the other, slow. No wonder people live in such confusion. The old-fashioned cool room was much better. Foods developed more flavor, you know?" He chuckled to himself. "It reminds me of an extraordinary business venture on which the Chink was going to embark." He always referred to the Señor Olózaga as the Chink. "We baptized it the Case of the Vanishing Refrigerator—that Chink! Simply no one like him. You know how things are here about advertising all these gadgets. Lunarito and Bejarano here have been long enough in this country to learn only the bad things." His head nodded toward the clams: "But you know about this advertising pressure—your pressure cooker, Lunarito, that's good, double advertising pressure. Get the eggs out of your chickens faster—but you don't know what it's all about anyway. The Chink learns fast, even if his materialism is purely illusory. This was a fitting counterpart for his other inspiration of selling the sand in the Sahara Desert as a cleanser and at the same time forming an international combine to fill in the space with water and make a sea out of it. A great idealist, but this time it was the refrigerator. You must remember how some enterprising manufacturer discovered that when a solicitous housewife approaches her refrigerator with both hands occupied, she cannot open the door. So, he thought up a pedal that would do exactly this. However, this had the drawback that some people might lose their balance and fall, breaking dishes, hurting themselves, and then, you know? They have all learned about suing in court—the International System, of course. Well, the Chink thought up a better one. Have a refrigerator without a door and maintain a lower temperature. See the connection? One can see what's inside without opening the door, use more electricity, obtain a commission from the electric companies, and at the same time save in the manufacture of doors. Beautiful, I tell you; a non-existent source of profit and a good selling point at the same time. Oh! The combinatory powers of the Chink. But having conceived this, he went further; there was no stopping him now. He said to himself: Why a refrigerator at all? Why not market a nonexistent refrigerator? Step by step, the refrigerator has vanished—an irresistible selling point, and the profits, immense. One can lower the price considerably, claiming that the space saved in shipping this nonexistent refrigerator, as well as the savings in manufacture, are being passed on to the consumer and competition is smashed. Besides, it has the undeniable advantage of taking no room at all in the kitchens of the consumers. No doors to open, no fatal falls, no lawsuits. But besides, in the space left by this refrigerator, one can install one of those, by that time, wonderfully fashionable old-fashioned oaken iceboxes purchased at some auction upstate with the savings from the vanishing refrigerator. Masterfully rounded, eh? That Chink—but I suppose that by now he has forgotten all about it, like he did about the Sahara Desert. His is a love for the business itself. Once conceived, once planned and solved, he loses interest. He wants the general solution. The numerical solution is for the lesser mortals who must be shown. His business ventures have been refined until they vanish like his refrigerator."

By this time, Don Pedro decided that the chickens were cooked enough. He called for the rest of the things, cooked the peppers a while, poured in the rice, the shrimps, pitted olives, and finally gave in and shook the clams out of the jars and onto the whole thing. Then he doused in the saffronized clam juice, added more water ostentatiously without measuring it and with an air that said, "That's only for beginners." Then with a grand swipe of his hand he turned the burner on full blast.

As he washed his hands under the tap, his whole back consoled: "Just a little more patience, my children. I have done my best to feed you and after all, my best—" He picked up his shillelagh from the table, once more the conductor, and we moved to the dining room. As we crossed the door he shot over his shoulder: "When the water boils, cover the pots and turn the fire very low. You can take care of the rest, I trust, Lunarito." He kept going without seeing the murderous look of Lunarito.

As he entered the dining room with the rest of us in tow, we heard the end of a sentence spoken in English with a shrill voice: ". . . why, she ought to be spanked!" There was something about the voice of rejoicing, suppressed baby laughter that practically tickled one's tonsils.

The man who had spoken the castigating line was middle-aged, very happy and antipático—I can't find another word. He was remarkably pink and rotund, like a piggy bank, with kinky reddish hair growing far back on his head and very bulbous eyes. Another one was a striking-looking woman. She was very dark, with black shiny hair and low narrow eyes set aslant over prominent cheekbones. She was dressed all in black, stockings and all, wore large gold rings in her ears and around her neck, like a necklace, a magnificent rosary with beads and cross made of rubies. She also wore a tortoiseshell comb in her hair, of proportions somewhat large for these parts.

The antipático man greeted us all with vociferous merriment, his words almost massaging our backs. The woman acknowledged our presence with a smile that was so mechanical and forced as to be an insult, and the other fellow who waved at us absently, looking up from the Spanish paper, was a young and languid-looking chap, very much at home, wearing no jacket or necktie. This one, as I learned, was Gaston Bejarano, alias El Cogote, older brother of the dancer. Although much fairer, he bore a general resemblance to his younger brother, but for that matter, so did the woman, although in her case, it may have been the dark complexion which marked her and Bejarano as the Gypsy type.

El Cogote was what is referred to in Spain as a winter bullfighter and wore the badge of his profession: the coleta, a pigtail that when seen in profile made him look like the old lady Doña Felisa, who had very sparse hair knotted into a small bun at the back of her head. Like his brother, he also wore the small gold ring in his left ear.

The indefatigable promoter Señor Olózaga had brought him to this country with some fantastic idea of introducing bullfights here. The idea had been, of course, a total failure. They had run into difficulties with organizations whose purpose is to make life as dull as possible for all animals and, in the Moor's own words, deprive them of their right to a glorious and tragic life and death.

In view of the opposition encountered, the Señor Olózaga at first had thought of eliminating the suertes of banderillas, picas with horses and sword killing, but even with these concessions the anti-cruelty groups proved adamant and, in any case, a bullfight without these three suertes and consisting only of capework would be either too short or too tiring for the diestro, or too dull, and it would prove nothing at all because it would be no bullfight. As a last resource, the Señor Olózaga had thought of rigging some sort of a contraption resembling a bull with an oversized pincushion where the estoque, the banderillas and the picas could be thrust and give a performance at Madison Square Garden, no less, but again Dr. de los Rios had pointed out the ludicrous aspects of the whole idea and the Moor, the great purist in matters tauromachial, had denounced with righteous indignation this obscene mockery, this unmentionable travesty, this unthinkable sacrilege.

The result was that the Señor Olózaga found himself with a bullfighter on his hands for whom he had no earthly use, but the younger Bejarano made more than enough as a dancer to take good care of his brother, so that he would be no financial burden to the Señor Olózaga whom they had come to look upon as their kindly Maecenas and advisor. This then was the other fellow at the table. As for the woman, all I knew was that the bullfighter addressed her, without regard for the author's rights of Bizet, by the name of Carmen.

There was another fellow sitting very circumspectly on the edge of his chair and looking quite like a bad student who has been punished. He was small, inconsequential, a fellow by the name of Fulano something-or-other, his complexion putty-like with violet shadows, and he wore glasses with the thickest lenses I have ever seen. It was the one thing about him that arrested one's attention at first sight. When we entered he had jumped to his feet with a certain servility and officiousness, murmuring:

"Doctor— Don Pedro—" and to Garcia and me: "Caballeros—" and then stood smiling, blinking behind his thick lenses, attentive and pitifully trying to make himself pleasant, until the Moor waved him back to his seat with one of his gestures that spoke for him and for a whole race. The hand, the arm, the head said:

"Be at ease, man. Don't try so hard. You are under no obligation. I am sure the Bejaranos like to help you if you are in difficulties, and we all like to befriend any countryman who is in need of reassurance. Remember that you are a Spaniard, remember your pride—and also ours."

Bejarano with innate, easy good manners was saying that of course, everyone there would stay for dinner.

"Not me. Oh, not me!" the antipático man shrieked in English. I don't know why he insisted on speaking English there when we were all Spanish and the Bejaranos scarcely understood one or two words of the language. "Don't mention Spanish food to me. I tried it once—" and he began a gloating, nauseating description of a past attack of indigestion, with much accent on fainting, being a mess and puking— of all the synonyms, he would pick that one—all in English. "But go ahead. See if I care. Ruin your stomachs and your complexions and disgrace yourselves in public. See if I care," he challenged with almost libidinous, flirting condemnation, his voice reaching for the ceiling. He finally quieted down, fanning himself with his handkerchief.

The Moor burst into a prolonged, loud laugh, slapped his knee and pointed at the man with his shillelagh:

"The green man. Look at him there, acting his part. There is no one like him. Don't you know him, fellows? Why, he is the one who could stand nothing Spanish since he took out his first papers, and now he is back for more. Why, more American than the Americans. He was living in blissful confusion, like so many others. They come here and immediately acquire the art of picking out and liking precisely those things which Americans would most like to get rid of; they unfailingly repel them with their ingratiating imitations. Completely misinformed. They never miss—could drop in the middle of an international group and instantly arouse unanimous dislike that would cause the group to disband and leave them alone like the illustrations of some well-known advertisements—and this one is the champion, my friends— He is wise and he knows. He has learned everything since he left Spain and now he is properly ashamed of his past ignorance and doing his best to live it down—the perfect example of the repentant foreigner. No more garlic or wine, no more chamber pot under his bed at night. Oh, no! He freezes gymnastically on his way to the bathroom and back because he also sleeps with windows wide open, believes in fresh air, dieting and exercise, and also in the equality of the sexes, when one well-directed look could convince anyone who still needed convincing of the fallacy of the assertion. But don't let it confuse you, my green friend. Take a good look before you make a pass—the equality of the sexes—haa— And he believes it like the gospel. Completely misinformed. Doesn't know what it's all about and has overlooked one thing that we have been saying in Spain for a long time: that there are no more Indians in America—that is good; Indians indeed—what he wants to be. He wants to be more American than the Americans, so he will have to be an Indian. But Indians are red and this is the green man—no more ignorant old-fashioned Spaniard, but the green Americaniard—" The Moor collapsed in a chair convulsed by loud, impudent, brutal laughter, a picture of Satanic mirth: "The green Americaniard—"

Then I knew who the man was because I had heard the story several times. It was like this. This fellow was an enthusiastic follower of every new fad. Once he was speaking in the presence of Don Pedro and the conversation touched on the legend that in Spain people don't know how good the sun is for them and they avoid it like an evil emissary of the devil, parade around overdressed in black clothes in the shade and therefore grow pale and anemic. This riled Don Pedro, who decided to play a joke on the fellow. He told him that the latest thing was a chlorophyll compound that had just been discovered. He gave one of his pseudological expositions on how this substance in plants synthesized the sunlight and said that by covering one's body with this compound, one could obtain in a few moments as much benefit from the sun as from continuous exposure during one year. He said that the stuff was not on the market yet, but that he would obtain some through Dr. de los Rios. All very seriously.

A day or so later, he brought him a large jar of some kind of green greasepaint and the fellow, who was an easy mark for all such novelties, believed him, and they tell me that he put on a pair of bathing trunks, smeared himself with the greasepaint from head to foot, and went up on the roof of his house, where he almost created a riot among the neighbors living in buildings overlooking his when they saw this green apparition. Someone called the police and a radio station, fearing some kind of interplanetary invasion. A great mob gathered before the house. The riot squad rose to the occasion and, under the cheering crowds and with every conceivable precaution, surrounded the building and then assaulted it, while the poor fellow paraded about, oblivious of the commotion he was creating. In the end he was arrested on a charge of disorderly conduct and Dr. de los Rios and Don Pedro had to vouch for him and bail him out.

The poor fellow—even an antipático under attack becomes less repugnant—was trying to smile and was visibly embarrassed. His words immediately cost him what little he had gained: "I still think that Spain is a country of darkness and I feel what every Spaniard with common sense must feel when leaving: that he has come into the light."

"That's it; into the light and then turn green—"

"Never mind that. Anyone can fall for an evil joke, and as for my citizenship, I repeat that I am making a living in this country—"

Lunarito's voice came from the kitchen: "Carmen, come and help me carry these things."

The woman called Carmen, who had been setting the table indolently, went to the kitchen.

"What living are you talking about? Man, you are killing yourself with all this fresh air, cold baths, exercise and dieting, and growing more spherical every day. A man's mode of living is determined by his race and not the medium where he finds himself—with certain exceptions, you know? One must not be too radical—but simply because a cat has kittens in the oven, one cannot call them muffins. Why, man, everybody knows that garlic is the best thing for anyone, including a Spaniard. It lowers arterial pressure, promotes longevity—"

"I wouldn't believe you again if—" The man looked with hopeful doubt in the direction of Dr. de los Rios, who contented himself with whistling while the Moor held the floor:

"I tell you, you are killing yourself. You leave Spain and see the light— No more garlic or olive oil. Nothing but all kinds of insipid food à la mode. Everything with a ball on top— Wonderful! You can play golf with it and get your exercise at the same time." He swung his shillelagh: "Watch it go: golf à la mode. That's it; the Spaniard conquers America, the land of the red man, and immediately turns green and begins to play golf à la mode— The enormity of it. You have seen no light. The moment you left Spain is when you were plunged in total darkness and you don't know what it's all about."

The man stood up with a forced dignity that was all the more ridiculous because of his shape: "I think I will go home now."

"Listen to him. The ambiguity—he thinks. And then he claims he is no longer Spanish. He knows that he is not going home at all, that he is simply running away because he can't stand his countrymen, especially since he got that Junior at the end of his name—that's good; Junior at his age."

"I am going away!" the man almost screamed, and he rushed toward the door where he met Lunarito and the woman Carmen bringing in the casseroles with the paella. Lunarito stood aside, holding the heavy casserole with both hands, a towel wrapped around it: "Are you not going to stay to eat?"

"No. I ate already. I believe in eating at a civilized hour and in the middle of the day only a light lunch. I, for one, watch my figure." It was pitiful.

"But if only for the company, stay a while."

The woman called Carmen said that she was not going to stand there while they argued: "This thing is heavy and hot." She walked to the table and planted the casserole on top of a pad.

"No. I am going. I wouldn't stay anyway and eat with this man—and I still think that Spaniards are backwards and crazy, and when they insist on remaining the same after they have the fortune of leaving

Spain, I think they are crazier still. So there!" The man was indignant in earnest. He stood at the door surveying us all superciliously and then spat down his shoulder the words: "Good-bye, Spaniards," and walked down the corridor.

The Moor greeted that parting shot with triumphant and louder laughter. He had attained his point and now was wiping his eyes and still laughing some more.

When we heard the front door bang, Dr. de los Rios regarded the Moor reproachfully and said without much conviction: "Satisfied now? You made the poor man go away in a huff. What a Moor!"

"Yes, you know? Very satisfied. That is not a man; it is an emetic, and although one knows the inclinations of which Moors have been often accused, that is not one of mine. One gets tired of the fellow and of stepping on his verbal droppings. It has reached the point that whenever he arrives someplace, people go away. It is high time that one begins to stay and make him go— But let's attend to something more pleasant, like this paella." He reached unceremoniously and began to pile his plate: "Look at that rice! I tell you—" He frowned at a clam speared in his fork and chewed it with concentration.

"All right, eh?" said Lunarito. "No shells to bother with, and if only the chicken had no bones—"

"And perhaps you would also want the peppers and the chorizos without the skins? What kind of a paella is this? If we continue with the refinements, it is going to be like the refrigerator—the vanishing paella." He began to pour the wine all around while the others were helping themselves to food. He had a way of becoming the host wherever he was. Everybody began to talk, mainly on the subject of this country. It is the usual thing in front of new arrivals from one's land. It is the necessity of explaining a different people and its different habits and sense of values and also of explaining one's own minor concessions and surrenders, almost like giving them a new tariff on life. The bullfighter, however, was not listening. He was telling and seemed well satisfied with his rash appraisal of the country which he was almost explaining to all the others with that authority which comes from lack of familiarity with a subject. Without hesitation, he listed what was wrong with the country, what was right, and what was fantastic, insane and incomprehensible to any person with common sense. Because of his misadventure with the Señor Olózaga, he had soon found out about the ASPCA—he pronounced it Aspca—and was talking about it. He mentioned that he had seen a moving picture of a bullfight in Mexico and that the part when the torero kills the bull as well as the placing of picas and banderillas had been suppressed, but not the part where a bull gored and killed the torero: "Well, I think a man is at least as deserving as an animal," he concluded with moving candor.

"It is not the Aspca you are thinking of, but the Society for the Extermination of Men, of which Dr. Jesucristo here is president," the Moor was bantering. "The trouble with you is that you have no conception of foreign sportsmanship. Have you ever heard about fox hunting? Of course not. You are a torero of sorts and have no feeling for the chase."

El Cogote pursued his theories with obstinacy: "They are crazy, but absolutely crazy. From home to the office and then back home. No life at all, but only work from morning to night. No loitering, no killing time, no nothing. Only the other day in the subway—you know—one of those big crowds was waiting and then the train arrived, and when the doors opened, the people inside rushed out and the people outside rushed in, all at the same time. Like two bulls in a head-on collision and no one gave ground. They stood there and fought it to a dead heat, toe to toe, knee to knee, shoulder to shoulder; and in the end, the doors were closed again and those who were in stayed in, and those who were out stayed out. Now I ask you—" He interrupted himself to eat some more but held up a hand all the while to forestall any objections: "And the restaurants— Last week with Carmen here. She will bear me out— You know they don't put a bottle of water on the table as we always do." He pointed at the bottles of water which, incidentally, no one had touched. "And they don't drink any wine with their food, and so I forgot myself and asked the waiter in Spanish to bring some water and of course he looked blank, which was not surprising, so I repeated only the word, mind you—I know now that the word in English is 'water,' but I didn't know it then—and I repeated as clearly as possible 'agua' and went like this, you know." He pointed with his thumb toward his open mouth. "Nothing. So, and I am very patient, I repeated the word slowly, almost spelling it out.

You'd think anyone would have understood, but not that waiter. He stood there, stiff as Don Tancredo, until Carmen here picked up a glass—mind you, they put glasses on the table and no wine or water—and showed it to him and then he understood. I ask you again— This lack of water everywhere. I have never been so thirsty—and also lack of public places where to get rid of it." I looked at Garcia, remembering an experience that I am sure he wanted to forget. "Once more, I ask you—" but he barred any answer with raised hand while chewing rapidly. He went on to praise highly the status of women in this country, that they could go about the streets by themselves without the men pinching them or dropping obscenities in their ears. This seemed to impress him very much, but immediately he regretted having found a tendency in the majority to flat chests, being too tall and having exceedingly long feet. This worried him and he was not certain what to attribute it to:

"I don't know whether it is due to the independence, or maybe those sensible shoes they wear, which I think make for an ungainly walk. I still think that independence or no independence, the only sensible thing for a woman is to look pretty. I remember some of those women back in our land, walking so gracefully and lightly; as they say, like a bit of paper blown by the wind. But I think it is wonderful for women to be so self-reliant. Just like men, you know?"

Don Pedro stopped eating just long enough to say: "If you continue along that line, you will soon be talking like the green man. Look, you have only been a few months in this country. You still don't speak or understand the language and cannot even read the newspapers, but already you know what is wrong and what is right with the whole country. A lifetime is not enough to understand a country, or anything for that matter." He spoke to de los Rios: "I tell you, these Spaniards are ineffable. One glance at a situation and they know all about it."

Dr. de los Rios was temporizing as usual: "That is not an exclusive Spanish trait. You can hear most people, when they are in the mood, not only finding what's right or wrong with a country, but with life itself."

"This Dr. Jesucristo, always with the cape to the feint." He moved his arm imperceptibly, yet his gesture was so eloquent and well-aimed that for a moment one could see the bull coming out of a pica and being suctioned by the cape in the most decelerating veronica. Instantly El Cogote was on his feet. With his serviette, he made two very stylized low passes and ended with a half veronica that as far as form could not be improved: "And I could show you a farol—but I have no room here." He sat down again: "Excuse me. I was carried away. It is a long time since I have felt the tools in my hands."

I was looking at Garcia and remembered a description in his novel of a bullfight, full of stock situations and cast-iron sentimentalities and impossible feats of courage and skill; something in the manner of "Casey at the Bat," or the Kid's last fight. He felt that in English this should prove very edifying and instructive to readers and help them understand the Spanish soul. We had argued the advisability of introducing it in his story and in the end, I convinced him by saying that it would be as silly as getting sentimentally technical in Spanish with descriptions about baseball, or to translate the Merriwell series.

Then my attention was disturbed by the meek, servile fellow, Fulano. He had spoken little and with great respect, prefixing every sentence with Doctor when addressing de los Rios, or Maestro if addressing the Moor, and Diestro and Bailador if addressing El Cogote or his brother. Garcia and I were still caballeros, and apparently he did not dare address Lunarito and the women Carmen unless spoken to first.

He had finished eating and was looking attentively at my dish and then, in order, at the dishes of all the others. He was one of those persons who eat with rapid voracity, as if trying for the title of the fastest thing on teeth, and then, having won the race, sit contemplating longingly, with deep regret and unconscious indelicacy, the plate and the mouth of those about them. They do not make good dinner companions and this particular one was one of the best. Even Lunarito, who was very much engaged in conversation about women here and in Spain, and asking innumerable questions of Dr. de los Rios, noticed it:

"Have some more paella. Why don't you help yourself? Go ahead; you are in your house."

"Oh! Excuse me," he answered, startled out of his reverie. "I really don't want any more. It is only—" His arm dropped to his side and he half turned his head as if to avoid facing the audience while baring a secret: "— This habit acquired from a life of privation and misery, of hurrying to get it while one can—absolutely uncalled for here with your generosity and — You have the souls of hidalgos—" The man was almost in tears and thirstily took a long drink of wine. It was good acting and I bet he was enjoying it, feeling it was in the manner of a partial payment for what he alone priced as a debt of honor.

The consequent embarrassment fanned the fire of conversation, but I was not listening. Something extraordinary was happening. Dr. de los Rios's eyes were sweeping from me to Fulano and back again, not focused upon us but going through, far beyond us, expressionless, cold. His gaze was like a blank abyss upon which we oscillated dizzily. I averted my eyes and looked at Fulano and for a moment felt as if I were falling into a deep well, rushing past strange visions that gradually took on very clear shapes. Perhaps it was his insignificant yielding personality which offered no resistance, perhaps it was the thick lenses of his glasses that were like little transparent wells leading into his head. I even wondered if Dr. de los Rios had anything to do with it, but I could swear that I had entered the man's mind and was seeing and hearing him think, and at the moment he was casting himself in a sad role.

He was a heroic martyr sacrificed in the interests of his country. He was not definite on which his country was. He considered this irrelevant to the generality of the formula.

In order to carry out a secret mission that would save his people, he had endured untold tortures in silence, both physical and spiritual. He had undergone floggings and public dishonor. He savored the intimate secret scene with the ruler when he had been entrusted with the mission.

Guarding his secret against superhuman odds, he had witnessed his friends, his family and his wife cast him aside in revulsion as the treacherous man he must pretend to be for the sake of his great mission. Only the ruler of his country knew the truth, but must keep silent, because the country came first and this would in addition to his country save the world.

This inhuman torment went on, the little man seeing himself kicked from cell to dungeon, every right of a decent being denied him, until in the end, when the mission was accomplished, the whole world found out the truth and he was publicly reinstated and acclaimed.

Then a great ceremony was held in a public square and the moment of public and glorious recognition arrived. He marched very quietly between great dignitaries, at last wearing once again his beloved uniform, but he was a faltering, shaking, broken and prematurely old man and he knew everyone was saying or thinking: Look at him, see what duty has done to this man, this greatest of all men who was dishonored for the sake of honor—a pleasantly involved idea which pumped fast the lump in his throat.

Then came the great moment. He, everyone, stood at attention and the great ruler spoke:

"You, greatest of all patriots, man of unequaled courage, pride of your country, valiant—" and then: "All men will long remember—" Only the telling phrases of the speech appeared clearly: "We can never give you back your—" and ending: "—but your country, the world, will—" and the great ruler embraced him and pinned a special decoration made for the occasion, because no decoration big enough existed.

The lump in his throat was already like a goiter, his eyes were misty, and then, with great solemnity, the flag was raised for him alone, or they did whatever it was that had never been done for a man before, and the thunder of applause was deafening, but he did not hear; he looked down that long vista of suffering, leading darkly to a broken cross. His task was finished, his duty performed, but the price exacted had been too great and he knew that he was through, that the man had been the task and was finished with it. To all these honors heaped upon his broken frame, he simply answered:

"Long live my country."

By this time his self-pity and exultation had reached the overflowing point and he wiped a furtive tear. I could not believe it myself. I was actually seeing a human being's mind at work and, in this particular instance, it was rather foolish.

I shook myself from this, which I still considered a hallucination induced by too much wine or too much paella, or perhaps a state of self-hypnosis due to the way light struck the thick lenses, but the thing that left me uneasy was that Dr. de los Rios was no longer looking through him and through me at some unfathomable distance, but only at his plate, and he was eating with great repose.

The conversation was running from tall women to tall people in general, which all admitted were more frequent in this country than in Spain, and the Moor was expounding a theory about a race of lilliputians which he insisted would be the only salvation of the human race. He contested that producing big people by the method of eating and living was a suicidal error, racially speaking, in which the Nordics could unfortunately indulge because of their greater material facilities. By Nordics he meant Anglo-Saxons, Teutons, Scandinavians, and so forth, regardless of the latitude where they lived. He claimed that Spain was saved from this fatal error because of its lesser degree of industrial development, but that the true salvation of the human race must lie in the opposite direction, by becoming smaller and smaller in size. He predicted dire results for those who, insisting on developing bigger and bigger people, must necessarily come to the stage where they cannot have enough food or room in their own place and will have to expand at the expense of others. But even this is no salvation. A time would arrive when the earth itself would not suffice, and even long before that their own size would prove their undoing. He pointed out that as every structure grows, it must reach a critical point, depending on the qualities of the material, beyond which the result must be unwieldiness and collapse. An elephant will be badly hurt by falling a few times its own height, whereas a mouse may fall many times its own height without any considerable damage, and as for a flea— It has often been said that one of the main difficulties with this world is that there are too many people. And yet science, which is supposed to use a modicum of common sense, continues to do everything possible not only to increase the span of life but the size of people, and immediately must concern itself with the production of food and the solution of traffic and living congestion problems which it has created. Completely absurd. They don't know what it's all about. It is logical to increase the span of life, because with its growing complexities, the lifetime of a human being is already too short to find out, if not what it's all about, at least what some of it appears to be about, and even this would reach a dangerous limit for reasons similar in some respects to those applying to size. What should be done, and without any waste of time, is to develop a miniature human race. This would eliminate, or at least postpone for a considerable time, the problems that face it. Food would go much farther, a room would be like a building and a building like a city, a park like the jungles of Brazil, and one could go on making such comparisons for a very long time. Any of the machines which we consider necessary could remain the same. It should not be difficult for any of these miniature men to run any of them with but a few adjustments.

"But what about so many other dangers?" I think this was Garcia speaking: "People would be proportionately weaker, and any animal, even domestic ones, would become a terrible monster, a source of continuous danger."

"Nothing of the kind. Physical strength is losing more importance every day. Certainly tigers and lions and bulls are big and strong enough to be as dangerous to us now, but one sees nobody worrying about them, except bullfighters like this one."

"Wait a moment." This was Dr. de los Rios: "Now that you mention bulls, and I am confident El Cogote will back me up, how could we have bullfights without also decreasing the size of bulls? And we don't know how this shrinkage might affect their other characteristics. We all know that the smallest changes in breeding may affect their fighting qualities. You started all this claiming that Spain would be saved from the horrible fate of countries developing big human beings because of its lesser industrial facilities, and now we are led to a Spain without bullfights. The death of Spain! We cannot attempt to save the human race at the expense of our own country. We would be the hardest hit people by this policy, and as the well-known foreign black legend would put it, Spain rises again to hinder progress and block your brilliant solution of the problems of mankind, but dispense with bullfights? Never! Or not so long as there is a drop of Moorish blood in us, eh, my friend?"

El Cogote was backing Dr. de los Rios enthusiastically. He walked through the French doors into the adjoining room and from a sideboard took a cape: "Oh! It is a long time, a long time." He stood like a statue, looking fixedly at a point in space, and suddenly the cape burst open.

Bejarano had joined his brother in the other room. He executed some dancing steps and his heels beat a tattoo on the floor with incredible speed. It was fortunate that they lived on a ground floor, a preference shared by most Spaniards. Then he charged the cape and finished with another dancing step.

"Olé!" cried the Moor: "A bull dancing flamenco—the desideratum. One has to come to New York to see bullfighting as it should be done."

"I think I will stick to dancing and not play the bull any longer."

"Listen to that, Dr. Jesucristo. The fear of being identified with anything that has horns is one of our best-rooted national virtues."

But El Cogote had not had enough. From the same sideboard, he took a muleta and estoque and made a natural pass. Then one with cambio, shifting very smoothly the estoque and the muleta from hand to hand. Don Pedro, however, did not approve of the style; he picked up his stick, stood up and went over to the other room:

"Not good enough. Here, let me have that muleta, you can keep the estoque. I'll do it with the shillelagh. See? The natural pass is the most natural thing in the world when offered from the port side and stepping with aplomb on the ground reserved for good toreros."

Despite his lameness, there was aplomb and such a theatrical grandness in his movements that we all knew he had made his point. Perhaps because he was a conductor and also because of his strong personality, his gesture carried more suggestion and conviction.

"And if it were not for this accursed leg that does not let me turn properly, I could show you something with the cape that would melt you." He handed back the muleta. They continued to argue while he returned to his place at the table and leaned back in his chair:

"You see? The way you were standing, any bull would say to himself: Now there is a fine leg right in front of me. Why should I go for the muleta? Why indeed? Me for the leg, and you wind up in the infirmary if you are lucky. No, my friend. I have seen most of them since Lagartijo to modern ballerinas, divas and prima donnas like Oleares, Pintueles, Mesenguita, but I never saw one of them break one of the three fundamental laws of bullfighting and get away with it for long. Those laws are basic and ineludible: parar, templar y mandar. That is bullfighting and nothing else—something like with mathematics and the three fundamental laws, associative, distributive and commutative, which has always struck me as very scientifically castizo, except that in higher mathematics, which attempts to reach a little beyond bullfighting, they may not all hold at times. But you follow your rules, my boy, and then—maybe—"

"Bravo, professor," Bejerano applauded from the next room, but El Cogote was thoroughly aroused. He wanted to show something good so he made one more pass and then the muleta fell and the estoque rose. He sighted along the blade and lunged. The estoque went clean through the back of an easy chair.

"Toreador, don't miss the cuspidor," the Moor chanted in English, but the scream from Lunarito rose high and stood wavering at first like a saeta, and like it descended, breaking into exclamations, invocations and appeals to the Celestial Court and was followed by pandemonium and longer recriminations.

"See what you have done. Now look at that chair, and that's the third time. He has it in for the furniture in that room and has almost knocked all the stuffing out of it. It has gotten so that I call that furniture the ganadería."

Bejarano strode from the room and at the door he turned: "You don't have to show off so much. You come and plant yourself in this house and then have to go around breaking things up." The polite veneer was peeling off fast under the heat of savage temper: "I wish you had tried that on a real one and maybe you would have lasted as long as the Catalonian— These things cost money, damn it!" His was an unprintable word: "I should think in your position you could use a little more consideration." He went back to his place at the table and poured himself some wine.

"You don't have to get so flamenco about it," said El Cogote, somewhat subdued, and he placed the things carefully back on the sideboard.

"Oh no? I know where I would like to place that estoque."

There was an embarrassing silence and we felt out of this family quarrel. Dr. de los Rios, temporizing as usual, admonished El Cogote: "If you had killed recibiendo, as this purist Moor would claim one should, this would not have happened, because the chair would not come to you." The Moor followed this with: "Dr. Jesucristo always with the verbal cape to the feint," and Garcia, changing the subject, said to the woman called Carmen:

"That is a beautiful rosary you are wearing."

"I have had it quite some time. They gave it to me at the Convent—"

Bejarano set his knife and fork down with resolution: "And I suppose they also gave you at the Convent all the other valuable things: the copones, the eucharisty, everything—and to think that father went to jail for something he never did while others go about enjoying and displaying their loot." His bitterness and repressed fury were such that everyone was surprised and there ensued another silence. Garcia's attempt had been ill-fated.

"Stop picking on her, will you?" shouted El Cogote: "Always digging up the dead. Every time anyone mentions anything, off we go. So everybody has his shames in his family. What do you want us to do now, start a procession on our knees around the table?"

"Of course we all have our shames," Lunarito was saying: "Look at my own father—and even the columnist who said something about bums' row on the Bowery playing host to someone who claims to have sired Lunarito of the well-known team Lunarito and Bejarano—but what good is worrying?"

Bejarano had his head in his hands and was scowling silently at his salad. He lifted his head as if to say something, but then thought better of it and resumed his pensive pose. We all knew what Lunarito was referring to.

She had brought her father from Spain soon after she and Bejarano began to be successful. Dr. de los Rios knew him from Spain, and Don Pedro also knew him and considered him one of the real castizos and liked him very well. Garcia and I had never got to meet him. Everyone referred to him as Don Laureano.

The whole story was rather sordid and there should be no reason why Lunarito herself should have brought it up, except that there are some Spaniards who have the pride of suffering and delight in matching sorrow for sorrow, shame for shame, opprobrium for opprobrium, always hoping to make good and emerge someday undisputed champions, but they are always being thwarted by someone who comes up in the end with a devastating and tragic disaster that tops their best.

The life of her father in Spain had been a pretty shady affair and he would have been correctly described as a Caballero de Industria—the English translation Industrious Gentleman being scarcely accurate, to say the least. Upon his arrival, Lunarito had exhorted him:

"I hope that long vacation you spent in jail before coming finally taught you a lesson. Please do not try any of your tricks here. Remember: there are no more Indians in America, this is a different country and things here are very different."

"Different, my eye! Everywhere they cook beans but," he hastened to add, "don't worry, I am retired now and don't expect to cook up anything. I brought you up, educated you, took good care of you, and now I will let you take good care of me."

"Well, if you want to engage in something honest, please consult the Señor Olózaga. He has lived here long and knows things well. Besides, you and he were partners before."

"Hmm—so we were— We'll see. I am a different man now. I have reformed."

"I hope you have, because don't forget that we can have you deported if we mention your jail sentence. We have influence with the police too. We have danced at many benefits—"

"So you have? Well, well—don't you worry about your old man."

At first Don Laureano behaved to the point of doing nothing, including nothing for his keep. Of his old habits, he had kept the most trivial ones, such as never separating from the wineskin he had brought from Spain as his only luggage and filching now and then some belongings from Lunarito and Bejarano, or perhaps a visiting acquaintance, and a trinket or two from the apartment, all of which went directly to the pawnshop. He went frequently to the park and sat in the sun with his beloved wineskin, only to return home when it was empty, just in time for supper and a refill. Sometimes he took his lunch along and bought peanuts to feed the birds and squirrels. The squirrels amused him for he had never seen them in Spain. One in particular fascinated him and they became fond friends. He even bought a collar with a bell for it and this delighted the children when they discovered it. That squirrel was a smart one and waited every day for him in order to climb on his knee or his shoulder, and then he fed it and held long, one-sided conversations with it in Spanish and got it to understand and obey many of his gentle commands, but he never took it home. He knew that Lunarito had never harbored anything more than a cat and now that she was harboring him, he had learned in his old age the value of independence. A passing observer seeing him thus, with his venerable white beard and sharing his food with the animals, would have taken him for a kindly, patriarchal, almost bucolic old man and a direct descendant from Saint Francis of Assisi.

Once while thus resting, his hand fell idly on a new green leaf torn by the wind and carried to his bench. Absently, he lifted it and found that, by coincidence, it was resting on a dried old leaf, no doubt from last year and also carried there by the wind. He contemplated this long and thoughtfully, smiling to himself. Then he let the new leaf go and took another swig from the wineskin. The squirrel settled on his shoulder and, fondling it, Don Laureano began to share his confidences in whispers with this, the only friend he had made on his own since he left Spain.

Reminiscences of his old life drifted into his mind and, with every swallow of the wine, condensed and assaulted him with visions of past and sinister splendor, of the times when he had been known in Madrid as the Prince of Beggars and the Grand Old Man of Knavery. Always shrewd and calculating, his methods had consistently avoided violence and trusted skill and, in his long and arduous career, he had but once been carried in a moment of senile, impatient greed, to the utmost limit of transgression and paid only partially a penalty he considered light for the stupidity he could not forgive himself. Quickly he passed over these gruesome details, to recall his most clever ruses and masterful strokes, swindles and deceptions. He could not remain idle long. Begging and the life of a rogue were in his blood, and old as he was, there was still battle in him.

At an advanced age, it is very difficult to change one's personality, and regeneration is by definition out of the question. His old and less trivial habits began to assert themselves. It was inevitable. Insensibly, without apparent difficulty, he became involved with the police.

To hear the Moor tell it was like listening to a fairy tale.

One of the first things was the chlorophyll salve with which the Moor had caused so much embarrassment to the antipático man. Don Laureano heard about it and immediately took his daughter's advice and consulted the Señor Olózaga. Together they formed a haphazard partnership to market the stuff. Out of cheap ingredients they manufactured large quantities of it and began to sell it on street corners through the so-called pitchmen. One could hear the spiel on any of New York's corners:

"It prevents sunburn. Takes the sun out of the skin where it does the most harm and carries it inside the blood where it does the most good— Wake up to the new Sun Cult and be like a plant— Plants don't eat eggs or steaks or salads, but get all their energy directly from the sun. Think of the money you and the missus will save in food— grow strong as an oak— No special training required; slap it on, spread it on, the more the better. It will impart a brilliant green color that will make you the sensation of the beach—" And so on, on any sidewalk.

It was unbelievable. The thing caught on and sold like hotcakes. The business grew. It sold by mail and the department stores held demonstrations on their main floors and sold tons of it. The five-and-ten stores were swamped with emerald jars. It was a colossal hoax that exploded with a boom all along the seashores. If beaches like Coney Island had looked on warm holidays like huge tracts of macaroni, now they looked like spinach noodles, or as if they had been overrun by some kind of moving plant life. It will always be remembered as the green era, and had Columbus looked upon this, one wonders what his thoughts might have been. No more red men in the Americas, but green, bright green. The Moor interpreted all this as an example of his theories about spiritual territorial conquests and pacific penetrations.

When things reached this point, the police stepped in and the Señor Olózaga went for an extended vacation, and Don Laureano, due to some technicality, got off with nothing worse than to find himself right back where he had begun.

But the pair had tasted blood and would not be discouraged. The next thing they picked up from the Moor's fertile imagination was the idea of selling toy balloons filled with some very light gas in order to lighten the luggage of airplane travelers, so they could carry more, or even lighten themselves or anything they had to lug along. Again the police stepped in. Then the Moor sold them on the racket of peddling dehydrated water. It turned out to be bicarbonate of soda in this case. Just a pinch in a gallon of fresh water and there you are, a whole gallon of water. Wonderful when camping, or on picnics or hunting trips. Don Laureano embraced the idea with omnivorous greed and the Señor Olózaga with that indomitable optimism of every born businessman and inveterate promoter. I hear that they managed to sell some. The great Barnum would have smiled wisely. Once again they found themselves standing in front of a judge. However, it appears that there was someone by the name of O'Moore connected with the police department who claimed an archaic family relationship with the

Moor. This must have helped the unholy pair on more than one occasion. The Moor had a genuine liking for them and considered them the last of a great and fast-disappearing breed.

Lunarito and Bejarano were both indignant and frightened, thinking of the immigration quota, deportation and who knows what horrors in a country they knew so little and which to them was mysterious in its methods and perhaps with a clemency beyond their reach in the strict application of its justice. There was a loud final scene with screams, tears, oaths and mutual accusations. The old man, his wineskin tenderly clutched to his breast, left, saying that he was being thrown out of his own daughter's home like a tramp abandoned to the mercy of a strange country, and when his well-aimed histrionics failed to temper their decision to rid themselves of him and they stood in the corridor grim and adamant, in one of their most hostile dancing poses, he cursed them, swore that he would never again look on their renegade faces and stormed out banging the door.

After that began the constant pelting with minor humiliations. He had been seen panhandling in the streets, there were those veiled and unveiled paragraphs from a couple of columnists. He had made his head- and sleeping quarters on the Bowery where he had soon gathered a good following and connections and where his foreign methods, albeit mastered and worn threadbare after a lifetime of practice, had in the new surroundings a certain novelty and freshness that were greatly admired and had earned him a comfortable popularity.

But this had not broken the relationship entirely. Every so often the old reprobate slipped back on his promise and caused them untold embarrassment at stage doors, their house, holding forth when in his cups about his daughter's talent, and on one occasion he spied on a restaurant they frequented after their show with friends and admirers and came in to beg and had the affrontery to beg at their table.

This caused another and more violent row. When the manager summoned the police, Don Laureano stood tragic, crucified, his beard agitated by a wind of fury; a veritable King Lear, his wineskin held protectively against his heart like a badge or a threatened baby, and he thundered:

"That's it. First thrown out of your house, now throw me to the bloodhounds. From the height of your opulence, not an extended hand, not a crumb, but a slap, a stone—that's it; trample regally over the prostrate remains of your own father on your way to happiness."

In the end the filial affection of Lunarito won and she and Bejarano pleaded in their broken English with the police to let the man go free. In embarrassed haste, they whisked him away in their car and dropped him someplace along the way, but that scene made the front pages and gave the tabloids just the necessary injection to carry them through a slack season.

The conversation had dwindled around the table but there was still an aftermath of little rumbles, sharp remarks crossed between Bejarano and his brother, like receding thunder after a storm. The Moor looked ostensibly at the ceiling and quoted from *Don Juan Tenorio*: "Son pláticas de familia de las que nunca hice caso."

This seemed to touch the spark again and the argument revived stronger than ever with references to intimate family matters that reached the most indelicate limits. It went on endlessly with lamentations of the past and dark predictions for the future until it appeared that it should never end, but then it began to abate and subside and gradually everyone's attention centered on the Moor, who was engaged in some little game of his.

He had caught a fly with surprising skill and now held it prisoner under an inverted glass. Then from a cork he cut two slices, ceremoniously filled a dish with wine, and pushed his sleeves a little up his arms. After that he carefully floated both slices of cork on the wine. On one he placed two matches and on the other some sugar dampened with wine. With great care he lifted the glass and recaptured the fly which seemed to be hypnotized: "Watch now carefully. This is the most difficult part of the trick." With infinite gentleness he placed the fly on the wine-soaked sugar: "Quiet, everybody." He struck a match and picked up the glass again. Then with smooth adroitness he lit the matches on the cork and brought the glass down over the whole thing without a tremor: "Behold! The raft and the lighthouse. A tragedy in the red sea." The wine rose slowly in the glass and the fly flew inside momentarily and then alighted on the sugar once more and lay still while the matches went out and the glass filled with smoke.

Lunarito screamed and looked away; El Cogote moved farther into the room and craned his neck; Bejarano was leaning forward, his argument forgotten, watching fascinated; the woman called Carmen remained calm. She looked on puffing at her cigarette and only one of her eyebrows went up. The meek man with the thick lenses murmured: "This maestro, this maestro!" But Garcia protested loudly:

"No wonder I call you Don Pedro el Cruel. Why torment the poor fly? Let her go."

Don Pedro bided his time unmoved and then lifted the glass slowly to let the liquid seek its level without too much disturbance, and the miniature rafts remained right side up. The fly lay on the sugar, still and apparently dead. He leered at all of us: "The Aspca, remember? What about flypaper?"

"Poor little fly," whimpered Lunarito. "She choked to death. You killed her."

El Cogote said that perhaps the fly was only drunk from the wine, but everyone showed consternation as if some minor tragedy had occurred that affected all personally, and the silence was tense.

Then Dr. de los Rios waved his hand over the plate. The fly flew away and straight for the ceiling. Everyone heaved a sigh of relief.

"This Dr. Jesucristo always to the rescue, but the fly is dead. That is only her soul that has gone to the ceiling, which is the heaven of all flies."

With that we began to adjourn to the more comfortable if also more punished furniture of the next room, and due to some of those associations of ideas that always seem mysterious, Lunarito exclaimed: "The soup! I forgot the soup and I had a large bowl full of gazpacho in the refrigerator."

"Gazpacho. Oh Lord! These people continue to live in Spanish territory and to be gradually conquered by the pacific penetration of the refrigerator."

"It does make fixing the gazpacho more easy with all those ice cubes."

"Easy, that's it, easy. Ease is what brings about the downfall of a country." The Moor collapsed on the chair that had recently played the part of a bull and pointed his shillelagh at Lunarito: "It is little things like that which are dangerous. First a refrigerator—easy. Then flat shoes—easy. Then after that, the vanishing paella and you forget your language, you forget yourself—" The shillelagh fell dejectedly across his knees "—and you are nothing, but then the refrigerator also vanishes and everything comes to nothing."

Lunarito and the woman called Carmen began to clear the table and carry things back to the kitchen, Lunarito doing most of the work. The fellow with the thick lenses excused himself saying that he was going to see someone who had promised him a job. I watched him go, walking gently on the bias, his head slightly to one side, his back a picture of clandestine humility.

I was still thinking about my experience with him, questioning it as much as its alternative dictated, while his footsteps faded in the corridor, and after an interval, I heard the front door close. Although I did not know it then, that supernatural experience was to be repeated. I looked at Dr. de los Rios. He was pacing calmly back and forth, conversing with the Moor, the personification of peripatetic postprandial innocence.

The bullfighter, after a soulful look at his trastos on the sideboard, had gone back to his newspaper. That left Bejarano and myself sitting on the large sofa with Garcia who was, of course, closest to the window.

With feline smoothness Garcia reached, and I threatened: "If you read to me, I'll read to you."

"Please, gentlemen," came from Dr. de los Rios, "sheathe your respective literary weapons. I am sure that everything can be settled amicably."

"Be a good fellow," Garcia was saying. "This is the end of the first part of my novel and it is almost ready for final correction. I want you to hear it."

"But you are imposing on Bejarano also. He has just fed you and this is no way to show your gratitude."

"Nothing of the kind." Bejarano was politeness itself again: "I like listening to literature." And immediately he frowned and his face assumed a look of attentive concentration which he must have thought fitting to the circumstances and to his interest in cultural things.

Too full of paella and wine, the world could have come tumbling down without arousing me from that comfortable and lethargic position and while Garcia began, the words of Don Pedro ran through my mind: "Ease, ease—the destruction—your undoing—the vanishing paella—"

One day Trini broke into Julieta's apartment wildly. Her hat was unintentionally on one side, her face congested and her dyed hair in disorder. She was in a frenzy:

"Is that beautiful husband of yours around?" She crossed the room like a tornado and looked into the next.

"No, he has not been home since yesterday."

"Of course. Just as I thought. I knew I would miss him. The low dog!"

Julieta looked at her sister-in-law blankly. Nothing seemed to surprise her anymore.

"Do you know what? That chulo, that thief, is carrying on with that French girl, the charming Mademoiselle Gerard who called herself your friend. She and her mother are nothing but rampant, lousy peseteras. Monsieur Gerard, the poor fool, has gone back to France because he could not stand the life they led him. He should have knifed them as a Spaniard would do. And your darling Paco has brought that puta and the Celestina of her mother to live right here in the apartment two flights up."

There came a rhythmic, rumbling noise. Garcia and I looked at Bejarano, who was fast asleep. Garcia regarded him silently, his mouth tight and drooping at the ends, his eyebrows raised, his forehead wrinkled. Then he expelled his breath with heavy resignation and resumed:

Julieta did not answer. She listened to Trini, who vented her fury in indecent language. The children looked on bewildered, and only then Julieta said:

"Don't use that language, Trini, before the children."

Trini left as she had come, like a whirlwind. She ran up the stairs and, with a piece of chalk she must have brought for the purpose, wrote on the door of the French women "Zorras" and departed.

That evening Paco came in and did not touch dinner. He changed clothes whistling all the time and went out without a word.

Julieta heard him ascending the stairs. She waited and listened. Then heard him descend accompanied by a woman's voice and steps.

Julieta listened until the voices and steps faded and then laughed long.

Her laugh was the same silvery laugh but somewhat strident, and the children, seeing her laugh, laughed too. Then she sent them to bed.

That night, when Paco returned late, he found Julieta awaiting him. She wore a bright shawl and a high comb. Her face had a very strange expression.

Paco looked at her quizzically: "What is the matter? Going to a verbena?"

"Look, Paco, look!" She cried with a high, shrill voice: "I am as beautiful as they, more beautiful then all of them. Why don't you love me?" Her eyes stared and darted straight to him and all around him.

Paco was quite drunk and his sense of values deranged, but through his fog, he felt that something was wrong. He moved toward her: "Come on, Julieta, what is this? Don't talk so loudly."

But Julieta continued with rising voice: "It was my fault, Paco. I don't blame you. I was careless about myself. No man likes a shabby woman. Dear Paco." She caressed his cheek and he averted her touch as if it were an intended blow. "But now I will take care of myself for you, only for you, to win you back. It was all my fault." She tried to embrace him and he drew away with annoyance.

"Why, Paco? Why don't you want me? Is a little love so much to give?" Then she staggered to the bed where she fell crying.

Paco laid a hand on her: "Pull yourself together, Julieta. I am tired and want to sleep."

She slid off the floor and, on her knees, held his coat: "Don't treat me like this, Paco. You are killing me. I never thought that I would beg, but you have the upper hand. Nature is on your side. It has made me low. Help me— Oh God! Help me!"

"Come on, Julieta. I am tired." He began to remove his clothes.

"But how can you do this?" She held on to him.

"Let go, Julieta! I am losing my patience." He wrenched himself free.

Julieta was deathly pale, her hair undone, the comb had fallen down. She pointed at the ceiling: "But with her yes, with that accursed . . ."

Paco's hand crossed her mouth: "Don't ever say that about a lady," he said contemptuously.

Kneeling as she was, Julieta drew back livid as a corpse: "Coward, coward!" she repeated with obsession, her voice rising. "Coward, coward!" she howled.

Paco expelled his breath very slowly, then finished undressing and turned the light out, leaving her kneeling in the darkness, her voice subsiding, still repeating: "Coward, coward!"

What thoughts go through the head of a suicide before the critical moment?

What thoughts swarm in that desperate brain while the preparations are being taken for the climax? Are they fully awake? Do they go through it mechanically, like somnambulists?

What terrible moments to live through, when one knows that one is going to die by one's own hand! In those last moments, how do they see the day? How do they regard life? Will they look in a mirror and recognize the face of the assassin who is going to murder them? Will they think of their past? Will they remember their childhood?

What force compels them to put an end to themselves, to conquer that instinct for self-preservation which has carried them through the most dangerous paths of their lives? How horribly unbearable life must be to the one who is driven to suicide! And yet, how can they go through with it? Or are they always insane?

Suicide—oh saddest of all tragedies! When a being resolves to stop his own existence, when a being puts a check to the torrent of life that flows within. When a being turns against himself in that black moment of despair and in this loneliness becomes his own enemy, to commit the most unnatural act of existence.

Suicide! How many have sought peace and rest, persecuted by life, in the dark clouds of your night? How many have defended their crazed minds by wrapping themselves in the cold armor of your shroud?

The next morning Paco was awakened by the ringing of the doorbell. It did not surprise him to note that Julieta was not in bed because she always rose earlier. He went to the door still dizzy from alcohol.

Two men from the floor below said that the bathroom there was locked and they could not get in. Paco looked for the key but could not find it.

Together they descended the stairs and stopped before the bathroom door. Paco tried the knob.

"It seems to be locked from the inside." He turned to the men and he was very pale. "I think we will have to break it down." His voice was insecure.

One of the men applied his shoulder and pushed, but the door held.

"You don't mind if I break the frame a bit, do you?"

"No, go ahead. Hurry!"

The two men looked at him curiously but did not move.

"Stand clear then. I am going to break it down."

He hurled himself against the door which gave way. He stopped on his toes holding on to one side of the frame and gasped.

The two men looked over his shoulders. They did not look long and then backed away.

Julieta lay on the middle of the floor, wrapped in the bright shawl as if asleep. Upon one of her hands there was a white glove stained black. The window was closed. In one corner was a stove. The place looked white, bare and cold.

The two men bore her body reluctantly up the stairs to the apartment, and after a short moment of hesitation, they laid it on the floor. Paco walked unsteadily behind, as if still drunk from the night before. Then the men rushed out to call a doctor and Paco remained on the threshold of the apartment, not daring to enter the room. He remained there alone, like a waxen figure, waiting.

The doctor arrived and then Paco entered with him. The doctor examined Julieta rapidly and pronounced her dead from asphyxiation and then departed hurriedly to fulfill the necessary formalities. At the door he met Fernando, who was in a fearful condition.

"How did Fernando get there?" I interrupted. "Did anyone summon him, or did he have the gift of premonition?" To be perfectly frank, I did not care, but I was afraid that Garcia might notice how sleepy I was and I wanted to show him that I was paying attention.

"Why, yes. Perhaps you are right." Garcia made a quick note: "I will fix that later," and he went on undaunted:

Fernando stopped before his sister's body, staring at her as if making an effort to grasp the meaning of this scene, and then raised his eyes to Paco who sat in a chair on the other side of her body, his head between his hands.

Fernando said in a dull voice: "Assassin." Paco looked up blankly. "Yes, assassin. What have you done to my sister? You have killed her. You have murdered her. You are responsible for this. Accursed criminal!"

Paco stood up, his legs scarcely able to hold him. His arms went out appealingly.

Fernando was disfigured, his features distorted, his mouth drooping on one side. He hissed through clenched teeth: "You low bastard! You son of a bitch!"

Paco's face flushed. He was standing firmly now: "No man will call me that, you neurotic whelp!"

It was disgraceful. They stood with the corpse between them, hurling insults at one another. Fernando squared himself and spat in the direction of Paco:

"For you and for your lousy mother!"

Paco was ready to spring and then a commanding voice was heard at the door:

"Stop!"

Garcia did. He looked at me and said that perhaps I might find what followed somewhat of a stock situation. As if one could not see it coming. He read it:

They turned around with livid faces. There stood Ledesma in his long black overcoat. He advanced toward them and stopped before the dead woman:

"Is there no respect for death? Out! All of you, out! Do not desecrate things to that degree."

He bent down and with difficulty gathered Julieta in his arms. Paco took a step as if to help him: "Stand away! Don't touch her!"

And staggering under the heavy burden, he carried her into the next room and laid her on her bed. He laid her down with care, as a mother lays her child to sleep. He kissed her brow and said: "Forgive whomsoever is to blame. Forgive us all, because in this world no one is responsible for anything."

And respectfully, tenderly, he covered her with the bright shawl.

I knew it. It was exactly as I had expected, but I was still too sleepy to protest. Garcia conceded that perhaps he did spread it on a bit too thick, but that this was the original idea of his story, to make it cursi, corny, remember? I said nothing. There was nothing to say. He had stolen my reluctant thunder and went on unhindered even by his own conscience.

That last scene must have been more than I could bear in my condition and I must have dozed off momentarily because Garcia's voice faded and I only recall very obscurely something about Paco Serrano disappearing after his wife's death and no one except his many creditors caring much, that the doorwoman of the house where they lived took in his two boys when she found them abandoned, and that none of their relatives did anything to help them because they wanted nothing to do with any Serranos. Then Garcia's voice came back into focus:

They grew and developed in the sordid atmosphere of the portería, mixing with other golfos, running through the city and reappearing at the portería when they pleased, for the portera was either too busy or did not care enough to do anything about it.

It was Ledesma who in the end decided to place them in an orphan asylum. After the death of Julieta, he had wanted to leave the jewelry shop and go away, but Fernando pleaded with him to stay if only for the memory of Don Mariano and in order that the business he built should not perish. Ledesma was moved and in the end decided to stay, but he did not mention to Fernando having placed the boys in the orphanage.

Nature had been little generous with Ricardo, the older of the boys. He was undersized, ugly, almost repelling, and spoke little. Perhaps this was due to his unfavorable upbringing, or perhaps he was that way, considering that Jacinto, the younger, brought up in the same environment, was good-looking, with large eyes, well-developed and with a delicate complexion.

They were as different in temperament as they were in appearance. While Ricardo was humble and shy with his superiors at the orphanage and wanted to learn what they taught him, Jacinto was of a dreamy disposition and did not care about what went on around him, but in the end he always seemed to know more than his brother and to guess things with amazing perspicacity and no effort at all. He was by no means humble, and once when he was upbraided for his behavior, he said calmly:

"I don't have to put up with bad treatment, because if I don't like it, I can go away."

"Oh no, you can't. Don't think it is so easy to get away."

"Don't you think so? Wait and see."

His superior was angered by this impertinence, but after that he did not scold him so often.

Ricardo took up printing at the orphanage. Jacinto did not study anything. His main occupation was to observe, but seemingly without paying much attention. One could only judge all he knew by his remarks. Although the younger, he was the leader of the two and his brother did anything that he told him.

One day Jacinto said to his brother: "I don't like this place. I don't like any place where they tell you what to do as if one did not know what one likes to do, where there is no time to loaf, and where they even tell you the time when you can play. I miss the times we used to have at the portería. I am going away. If you want to come, we can leave together."

Ricardo hesitated: "After all, we learn something here and they take care of us. I have learned printing."

"You have learned it already, haven't you? Why do you want to stay any longer then? At least you know a trade now, which is more than I know. I am going away tonight. If you want to go, all right."

And Ricardo, although afraid, followed his brother.

They found things a little harder than they thought, as is usually the case. They learned that eating was something extraordinary, and they slept on the rope. This is a special device to accommodate the least exacting of sleepers. It consists of a hall with a rope stretched from one end to the other. The men lay their coats on this rope and then their heads on the coats and thus go to sleep. In the morning the keeper loosens the rope and the sleepers are rudely but efficiently awakened by the consequent fall.

Jacinto did not mind this kind of life and even thrived on it. He had discovered all kinds of methods to obtain money without working. He learned to imitate cripples and beg for alms. He found a café where they kept a mechanical piano. Jacinto sat at the door and listened to the jingling music with avidity. The piano constantly played old selections from operas, musical reviews and zarzuelas. It played things from *La Gran Via*, among them, the "Jota de los Ratas" which was Jacinto's favorite. He liked the impudence of that piece; he had known it for a long time and it reminded him of his brother whom he had not seen now for some time. He remembered singing it with Ricardo. He would step out and recite:

"Soy el rata primero."

Then Ricardo echoed: ". . . y yo el segundo," but as they never had another boy with enough memory to take the part of the third pickpocket, Jacinto always had to take it and add: ". . . y yo el tercero," and that always made them laugh and they always stopped there.

That music reminded him of his brother and it reminded him of himself. He felt a grossly obvious affinity between that and his own and his brother's life, and then he did not hear the music anymore and thought of his childhood and felt something surging within him, very much like pride, pride in things for which inferior people felt shame, and he felt that he was very much like those three ratas who jingled and made merry inside the mechanical piano, because they did not dare cry as he dared smile now, to assert his contempt for the sadness that was eating his heart away.

In that café there was also a machine where one inserted five centimes and by pressing a lever one might or might not get one peseta. He studied this machine and discovered that the peseta always came out after forty five-centime coins had been inserted.

He waited and observed the people come in and out of the café and insert coins in the machine. He counted carefully and when the count reached high enough, he stepped up, inserted up to forty and pocketed the peseta.

Then one day, a man who had missed repeatedly and then seen Jacinto win the coveted silver coin approached him:

"Listen, boy, how did you do it?" The man spoke in a melodious voice, used very high heels and licked his lips when he spoke.

Jacinto looked at him impudently: "Brains, my dear sir, brains."

"You seem quite fresh, my lad."

"I am quite young yet, am I not?"

"You certainly are, but I'll bet you know a great deal already. I wish you would tell me some of the tricks you know."

"It is a pleasure, sir, to enlighten those who seek knowledge."

The man laughed and took Jacinto by the arm: "Let's have some vermouth together and then you can tell me everything. I wouldn't ask a boy of your age to drink but I feel differently about you."

"I know you don't, but your generosity overwhelms me just the same," and Jacinto bowed and headed for the bar.

"We had better sit at that table. They can serve us there and we can talk more easily."

Not so long after this incident, Jacinto could be seen very well-dressed— in fact, overdressed—and to all lights having solved the problem of living.

As to Ricardo, he had not been able to endure the life Jacinto led after they left the orphanage. He went back to the portería, but the woman was no longer there and he returned the same way he had come. He went from one place to another. He worked in some printing plants but the air he inhaled there only served to weaken his lungs further. He sold newspapers and did odd jobs, his health failing him.

One afternoon when he was at Recoletos, hungry, bewildered, not knowing where to turn, he met his brother strolling arm in arm with an elderly man.

"Lo and behold!" exclaimed Jacinto, opening his arms. "If it isn't my dear brother who has become visible once more."

Ricardo opened his arms also and advanced, but then stopped short. He looked at his brother slowly from head to foot. He noticed that his eyes and face were made up, that he wore a shirt very open at the neck and a pink scarf, that his coat fitted him tightly about the waist, and he wore pumps with large bows. Ricardo turned his face and regarded his brother sideways:

"Maricón," he whispered.

Jacinto still held his arms open dramatically. Some people were looking on. He also regarded Ricardo carefully and noticed his haggard expression and shabby clothes:

"What holds you there, my dear brother? Does this unexpected meeting stupefy you? Did you not expect to find me still in the flesh after the days and nights we passed together?"

Ricardo was turning away. Jacinto walked over to him and held him by the hand. His companion was standing a few feet away and looked on annoyed.

"Never mind. I can understand. You feel slightly embarrassed because you think you don't look quite your part. I think you are in need of a good meal. Come on, let us celebrate this happy encounter."

Ricardo shook his hand free violently. He looked squarely at his brother and said with rage: "I don't need your dirty food, do you hear?"

"But, my dear brother, one has to live." He pronounced this so as to lend it a double meaning. "I can understand you are proud and all that, but one has to live."

Ricardo had been seized by a paroxysm of coughing. He held his chest and said brokenly: "I don't want anything from you—and don't call me brother —do you understand? Don't call me brother," and he went away, his weak frame racked with coughing.

The elderly man placed a consoling arm about Jacinto's waist: "Don't mind him. He has no gratitude—and besides, he is very ugly."

When the Count of X. died, Paco Serrano reappeared on the scene for the litigation of the will. He produced papers which he claimed entitled him to part of the inheritance and on their strength he managed to appease some of his creditors. However, the matter was soon hushed up, and to the surprise of many, he gave way easily. It was officially stated that he was an imposter and entitled to nothing. The fortune of the Count passed to his only daughter, Laura, and Paco Serrano disappeared once more. People said that he held papers which compromised the Count's daughter, that she helped him because she feared he would make public certain embarrassing facts.

This gossip must have been founded upon certain visits which he paid Laura undercover—one may accept this part of the gossip—whenever he came to Madrid.

Serrano did not live in Madrid by this time. He lived in Paris and some said that he was linked with the underworld there. La Torre, his old crony, was the first one to bring news to Madrid concerning the life which Serrano led in Paris.

According to him, he was returning to his hotel late one night and, as he passed a doorway in a dark street, a man came out and ordered him to stop and hand over all his valuables.

La Torre turned to face the bandit. He saw a man slightly shorter than himself but much thinner, wearing a cap and dark glasses, with the collar of his coat turned up. This was winter.

La Torre said: "My dear fellow, I am sorry to disappoint you. I have been gambling tonight and have lost my last cent; otherwise you don't think I'd be returning home on foot? If you can find anything on me, why, I'll share it with you for the service."

The speech is of course too long for any hold-up man to tolerate. However, La Torre has the floor. His story goes on:

The man had approached La Torre and dropped the hand which held the gun. He scrutinized him closely and said:

"Can it be you, La Torre?"

"I did not know that I was so popular among your class. That is my name. May I inquire who has had the honor of holding me up?"

The man removed his glasses and turned his face to the light.

"Se . . . Serrano!"

"Exactly, your old friend Serrano."

"But . . ." La Torre extended his hand to shake Serrano's.

"You don't mind, after this?"

"On the contrary. You know I always considered it a privilege, and by God! I congratulate you. I thought that I only knew lounging puppets in this world."

"It is fortunate that the first person I have met who knew me has your moral standards. Even if they are not sincere, they are comforting."

They embraced each other fondly and Serrano took La Torre to a café. La Torre had not bluffed when he said that he had lost his last cent.

According to La Torre, it was one of those cafés one sees in moving pictures; of course, less theatrical, but quite as effective nevertheless. There Serrano related his adventures to La Torre and then inquired after some people from Madrid.

"And how are the Bonafés?"

"They seem to be quite happy now. They go everywhere together. He has accumulated quite a fortune. The bearded ox! And she behaves like a model wife."

"How the world changes!"

"You remember how she acted when you left her for your little Frenchy? Well, when she learned that you had disappeared and heard some rumors about your death . . ."

"What do you mean, my death?"

"Yes, some people believe you are dead. Anyway, when she heard all that she was in a sea of tears and looked more than ever like the Mary Magdalene

I painted of her. I believe she reformed since."

"And what about my family?" He tried to make this question offhand, but it was only stiff.

"Your boys? No one knows where they are."

"But I understood they had been placed in an orphanage."

"They escaped from there long ago and no one knows where they are."

"Oh, I see."

"As for your brother-in-law and his family— He is as ostentatious as ever and making an ass of himself in society. They say that the oldest one of the girls is quite a beauty, red hair and all that. I have not seen her except once at the opera and from a distance."

Paco was not listening to La Torre and the latter studied him:

"Tell me more, Serrano. How did you come to step into this road of virtue? Tell me more about yourself."

"There is nothing to say." Serrano had arisen and paid. La Torre was following him. "You see me here. You knew me in my days. This is what I have come to. That's all."

"Then, Serrano, let's get together, say tomorrow night, and do something."

"Listen, La Torre: I don't think I will see you again. You know? We have drifted apart, we don't belong together anymore. Tonight, well, I wanted to find out some things. You are as good a fellow as ever, La Torre, but I don't think I will see you again. If I bump into you . . ."

"Look well before you shoot." They both laughed.

"Good-bye, La Torre."

"Good-bye."

And they never met again.

Here Garcia stopped to say that he only had disconnected notes on the section that followed which he had not worked together yet. He wanted to describe Serrano's extralegal activities, his life and associations in the Paris and Madrid underworlds between which he traveled frequently, and his sinister missions—international intrigue and mystery stuff—and he wanted to describe in detail one of the smuggling trips from Paris to Madrid, but first he intended to document himself well in order to give his narrative more authenticity.

I told him that his story was supposed to be truly authentic: the facts, the people, as told to him by his mother, if he remembered, but that if at last he was ready to break down and confess, to concede that the game was up, it was perfectly all right and in that case he could see more moving pictures and get all his standard situations right.

"Maybe I will," he taunted. "But now listen to the last scene. This is the first draft, but it is stereotyped enough." He laughed shamelessly: "It will kill you." The word he used in Spanish was not "kill" but "pulverize."

I waved his right-of-way. Felt too heavy to bow aside.

One night he arrived at the palace, having previously notified his sister. When he knocked at the door, Laura opened it for him. She was in an evening gown. He entered the small library where they always held their meetings, the same one where he had seen his father for the last time.

Paco sat down, removed his glasses and rubbed his eyes with a tired gesture. He looked old, old and worn out. He must have been near fifty then, but he looked older.

"God! I am tired. I have been on my feet all day and must take the express back tonight. What a life!"

"Why don't you stop it? Why do you keep this up?"

"I can't stop. I am too far in it now. It is too late to get out."

There was the sound of music and Paco listened . . .

Garcia looked at me puzzled and said:

"I cannot make up my mind whether to have them play here 'The Blue Danube' or leave it the waltz from *The Merry Widow* as I have it here. 'The Blue Danube' might be carrying things a bit too far, might show lack of originality, but on the other hand, the reader might imagine some foolish implications in *The Merry Widow*. What do you think? For the life of me, I can't decide."

If I had been drowsy, this woke me up and I exploded: "At this point you worry about that! It should be the least—use either one, or use another waltz. It doesn't have to be one of those two, or simply say that they were playing music and let it go at that."

"I'll see. I can always change it," and he went back to his reading. What a man!

"What is this? Did you prepare a serenade to receive me?"

"Don't you know? This is my opening reception of the season. You know everybody holds it about this time of the year."

"That's right. I see you are all dressed up, but God! I don't notice anything. I don't know what is going on in the world I used to know. I don't know what is happening to me."

"Never mind—now I have a surprise for you."

"What is it?"

"Guess who is here."

"A lot of imbeciles, I am sure. I could mention them to you. I still remember most of them."

"No. Your son is here."

"Legitimate or illegitimate?"

"Oh, quite legitimate."

"Which one?" Paco had stood up: "Is it Ricardito?"

"No. Ricardo died at a hospital in Barcelona last year."

"Oh, he did. . . ." Serrano said this flatly.

"Yes, from consumption."

There was a silence.

"Then it is Jacintito. How did you find him?"

"I met him tonight. The Marquis of N. introduced him. When I heard his name, of course I knew who he was, together with other things I had already heard. I did not tell him you would be here in case you did not want to see him. Shall I bring him in?"

Paco hesitated, he pressed his lips together and joined his fingertips. Then he swung around and sat on the arm of the chair looking down at his dirty attire. "I don't know, I don't know . . ."

"Don't worry. He won't be more ashamed of you than you will be of him."

"What do you mean?"

"Paco, what a family!" She had laid her hands on his shoulders: "Paco, do you really think it is too late? Have you lost all hope?"

"Too late for what? Hope for what?"

"Everything, Paco. You still have me. You will always have me. Say the word and you will be master of all this. You will own everything I have."

Paco looked at her but his gaze was centered upon his own soul: "You know, Laura? There is greatness in what you say, but I think I would rather have your charity. It has been worth living until tonight to see what a great character you have. I don't think I will see you again. Perhaps I only came to hear you say what you did and also to find my son."

"Do you want to see him?"

"Yes; bring him in."

"But remember my offer, Paco. Think it over. I shall always be waiting with open arms. But if it is going to annoy you, I will never mention it again."

A wave of music flooded the room as she went out, then it was silenced again by the closing door. Paco stood still. For a moment he felt an overwhelming desire to run after her, to cry, "Yes, I accept!" but he checked himself and the fear of his decision descended upon him like a cold draft. He slid down into the chair, adjusted his clothes and brushed off his coat with the palm of his hand. Then he lighted a cigarette and waited.

He listened absently to the music that filtered into the chamber. He straightened himself and listened more attentively.

They were playing the waltz "Caballero de Gracia" from *La Gran Via*. The music brought back his whole life. He remembered the first night he had heard it. He too was a caballero then, a graceful caballero, pampered by Madrid. He had thought that when old, he would be as graceful and neat as that old crisp dandy who sang it on the stage, like the gentlemen he imagined listening to it now, dancing to it, without hiding, shining in society as he had shone once. And what was he now?

He heard a transparent, silvery laugh behind him. It was so vivid that he almost turned around. It was a mocking laugh, the same laugh he had often heard since his wife's death— Yes, what was he now? Perhaps still a caballero, a gentleman in the Spanish sense of the word. His hands were fine, his fingers long, although his nails were broken and dirty. He was a caballero, but not graceful. He was a disgraced caballero.

Now, in the intermission between dances, they were playing the "Jota de los Ratas." It pierced through his ears like a jesting deadly gimlet of persistent sarcasm. Was he a caballero? Perhaps, but he was this now: a rata, a petty thief, a crook. It was not the shame of it, it was the failure it represented that wounded him; to be a rata, hiding from the light. In a few moments the music had framed his life, had brought a realization of things upon him, of the wretchedness that was his. It was a cruel parody of his truth. It had happened as if carefully prepared, as if it were a sentimental snare, a trap where he had been caught like the rat he was.

The music had changed. They were playing a well-known tango. He had heard it in Paris a few nights ago, where the whole city swayed to its rhythm with the tango fad above and below street level. His present rose before him. He threw the cigarette in the fireplace and buried his face in his hands until another flood of music filled the room. He lifted his head. In the door stood Laura and Jacinto.

Paco rose slowly. Father and son looked at one another for some moments, the son with superficial curiosity, the father probingly:

"Jacinto."

"Father."

They embraced tightly.

"Jacinto— Jacintito— It has been a long time. I suppose you did not even remember your father?"

Jacinto leaned his head on his father's shoulder and played with the dirty lapel. Paco looked down and frowned slightly. There was an incipient smile on the lips of Laura worthy of the Gioconda. She said: "I must go back to my guests now. I will leave you two alone. You must have a great deal to talk about—and Jacinto, don't keep your Marquis waiting too long." Her laugh was drowned by the music.

Paco had disengaged himself from his son and his eyes narrowed and seemed to stretch as if to grasp the whole scene, its meaning and the meaning of this entangled world. His look was abstract. Then he said to his son: "Jacinto, I gather that you have managed to keep ahead of the times—but one has to live."

"Possibly. And I notice that you have remained behind the times—but one must not die."

"Very probably," and Paco's face grew horribly cynical. "Perhaps we can get together and synchronize ourselves to life in the happy medium of convenience."

And so they did. The last that was heard from them is that together they were leading the same outlaw existence and that the father was speculating on the eccentricities of the son.

Then they say that they joined the famous band of Bonnot, and that in the last raid on this band, they died fighting like fiends to the last.

La Torre, who was fond of making round sentences, used to say that Paco Serrano as a caballero had proved to be a regular bandit, but that as a bandit he had behaved like a true caballero.

Some other people said that it was only Paco who died in that raid and that his son Jacinto escaped, and during the war of 1914 he was raided with other apaches in Paris, that he joined the army and died on the field of battle.

Whether he died bravely or not, no one says, and since one has accepted so many novelistic touches, shall one give him the benefit of a glorious ending?

Garcia pocketed his papers satisfied, and I stretched and shifted my position on the sofa.

The women had not returned since they went to the kitchen. El Cogote had turned on the radio some time before, which was the signal for the Moor to leave, carrying Dr. de los Rios with him without bothering to say good-bye. It had also awakened Bejarano, who sat up while Garcia finished, again frowning but not listening. It was not his professional frown, it was the ferocious scowl of bad temper, of one gathering his wits after a heavy sleep. I thought he must have had a nightmare which shattered all his good intentions of being a polite host, but later I learned that he always woke up in a terrible mood. He mumbled something about having to get ready for his show and we left.

On our way out Garcia confided: "I think I will leave it the *Merry Widow* waltz. It must have been at the height of its popularity about the time of these happenings."

But all this happened the last time I had been at the Bejaranos'. On this particular occasion and what I began to say is that the Moor and I went to see Bejarano at another and smaller apartment he kept for himself, where he could entertain his lady friends under more auspicious circumstances.

When we rang the bell, there was some commotion inside and the unmistakable sounds of hasty preparations. The Moor began to laugh without making a sound.

The door opened and there stood Bejarano holding a broom and dust rag, an expectant smile on his dusky face: "Oh! It is you— I thought—" He motioned us to come in.

"Yes, it is only us and not the Department of Sanitation with skirts. You can relax now and put those things away."

Bejarano laid the broom and dust rag within easy reach and went to the kitchenette, and while he was gathering bottles and glasses, Don Pedro decided to banish my wonderment at the mysterious greetings and elucidated:

The arrangement was this: Bejarano could not manage to have a cleaning woman come to fix the place. For one thing, he never knew much in advance when he would be there and even if he did, he would not go there only for the express purpose of letting her in. There were two objections to giving a cleaning woman a key. One was that she might arrive at an inopportune moment, because Bejarano never had any set hours for his gallant life; the other and perhaps the strongest reason was his gypsy nature which made him suspicious of servants and their respect for the property of others, although he did not keep anything of much value there—but that is the way he felt and consequently he had developed a subtle system. He could not come out and ask one of his lady friends to clean up things for him, but he could hint. When one of them arrived, if the place needed cleaning, he would receive her with broom and dust rag, or with a mop in hand, and the scene developed something like this:

"What on earth are you up to, darling?"

"Only trying to tidy things up a little before you came. This place gets so messy—but you caught me before I finished." This looking ashamed.

"Now you give me those and let me do it. Why, it looks as if you had not even begun."

"Oh no, I couldn't think of letting you—"

"Come on. You look foolish with that apron on. You men are all alike, so helpless— A woman can do this in a jiffy. Here, let me show you."

And the thing was done. As simple as that. Sometimes, he would be found with thread and needle, or at an ironing board he had procured: "Nothing, only this button— The laundry, you know—" or: "Ran out of shirts and I thought—" It never failed.

The Moor said that once one of his girlfriends was late and he fell asleep, still clutching the broom just in case, and he forgot the electric iron on the board. When the girl arrived and rang without getting an answer, she used the emergency key that was left under the doormat —the key he always took inside with him if he had feminine company —and she went in. She found the place full of smoke and Bejarano sleeping placidly holding the broom. She got a good fright thinking that the place was on fire and the fellow choked to death. She ran to throw the windows open, discovered the source of the smoke and disconnected the iron. Then her pity knew no limits: the poor boy asleep, exhausted from working so hard to make his apartment presentable for her and the place still looking so dirty and untidy! Bejarano, who had awakened with a start, also got a good fright that time but even this failed to cure him. It was a good system.

He came back from the kitchenette and placed two bottles and glasses on a coffee table. He had been listening to the explanations of Don Pedro with pride:

"Clever, don't you think? It saves money too, and you know us gypsies . . ."

"But, Bejarano," I interrupted, "I should think that this method would occupy most of the time allocated for a gallant occasion and tire the girl out."

"Nonsense," said the Moor. "Have you forgotten the spirit of Don Juan? You know—the conquest for its own sake—never the realization, the foregone conclusion. Not the concrete, but the algebraic viewpoint, and the Moors developed the science and we are all half Moors. It is the national system. The assignation is a ritual, a formality, a tribute of good manners to masculinity, as when we say to someone who admires any of our possessions that it is at his disposal; yet he would never dream of availing himself of it. The Spaniard is fundamentally ascetic, almost frigid, and never in a hurry for sex, food or money. He likes the full table, the abundant wine, yet he is frugal. If he attains power, he disdains to use it; he upholds the theory of the harem but his heart is only with one woman while his body sleeps in the serrallo, because being mystically concerned with the spirit only, he knows that no place in his anatomy is the site of his fidelity, that only the soul can be faithless. Indeed he appears boastful of his masculinity and militant for the privileges of pornocracy, but only because he is modest and practices what others should at least know: that one must not boast of one's virtues but belittle them, be almost ashamed of them— It is Calderonian, but the national system."

Bejarano was basking in all this and taking it as a personal eulogy. He had even assumed the air of one long misunderstood and at last redeemed. His was the manner of one who has long known the truth but prefers to let his actions and, if fortunate, others more articulate, speak for him. His smile had that smug repression one seldom sees except in the faces of cripples, which is supposed to reflect their inner satisfaction and conviction in their own indomitable courage, the only thing left to help them navigate the storms of destiny.

I could not hide my derision and the Moor, sensing that he had enlisted the undying gratitude and unconditional support of Bejarano, put on the pressure: "It is quite simple. The combination of the Moor and the Christian, and I concede that my own example might lead you to doubt, but don't forget that I am more Moor than Spanish. I don't think that you, or many others for that matter, understand a man like Bejarano. He is castizo. He is Spanish."

I'd swear that Bejarano was ready to break down and sob shame-lessly. He gulped his wine and choked on it but not as much as I hoped in my impotent indignation at this farce. Had the Moor been standing instead of sprawling, Bejarano would have embraced him: At last a kindred soul, redeemed at last, at last cleared, the outcast once more welcome, paradise regained!

We stayed there the length of two or three drinks and Don Pedro invited me to an early broadcast he had and then to dine with him and Dr. de los Rios. Bejarano usually had a nap at this time unless he had something he considered much better to do, and as a rule he never ate until after his show.

It was after the broadcast and while dining with de los Rios and the Moor that they decided to call on the Coello family and asked me to come along. All this happened—oh, quite some time ago, and since then I saw that extraordinary family several times and learned a few things about them. Dr. de los Rios had attended to them professionally and also as a friend, because although they were very poor and his fees very steep, he always forgot to send bills to his poor patients, especially those of the Spanish colony. It saved his conscience and bookkeeping. The Moor, who had met them through de los Rios, considered this one of the most castizo families, after their own fashion, that he had met outside of Spain, something that according to him only a Spaniard could appreciate, and he liked to drop in on them occasionally to chew the humble rag.

But this family deserves to be considered especially, and emulating Garcia, who for some remarkable reason has not written about them, I might tell their story and preface my narrative with the erudite and ominous lemma:

"Memento homo, quia pulvis es, et in pulverem reverteris."

A family like that of Coello would be inconceivable except in two places: Spain, where they came from, and New York, where anything goes. This is not intended as a play on words but as a preparation for the incidents preceding the demolition of a building in Harlem, where this family lived, incidents which some members of the Spanish colony in that neighborhood considered incredible, while others considered highly significant and which, not having taken the trouble to doubt, I pass along to those enjoying the same lazy distaste for systematic disbelief.

The story might open on the day when Mr. Robinson called on the Coello family with the unselfish and civilizing purpose of illuminating the darkness in which this foreign family undoubtedly existed, of preaching to them some good modern sense, of rescuing them from their foolishness and of rendering them an invaluable service by, incidentally, selling to Don Hilarión Coello a life insurance policy.

Mr. Robinson did not know that day when he took derby, umbrella and briefcase and departed on his way to the Coellos, that his visit would be fateful and the starting point of events which he never suspected and never learned. He walked in one of those New York spring showers that last all week. As he crossed Lenox Avenue, the wind blowing caused him to lower his umbrella, blocking his view of traffic and he nearly walked in the path of a fast-moving taxicab and came close to putting an abrupt ending to many subsequent events. He heard the noise of brakes forcibly applied and of English forcibly used, all of which he disregarded with professional philosophy.

He turned into 123rd Street where Don Hilarión Coello lived.

The Coellos were a very proud and very mournful family. They lived in one of those apartments with an endless narrow corridor onto which small rooms open like cells and one cannot walk through without instinctively accelerating one's steps for fear that something may be lurking in one of the treacherous rooms, ready to spring, to snatch, as one passes.

If Don Hilarión called out authoritatively from one end of the house to his wife at the other end, she would have to journey that long corridor looking into every room repeating: "Where are you? where are you?" and she always grew a little afraid.

It was sad to look that way for a person, it was like one of those melancholy fairy tales or a dream, and yet it was an everyday affair.

That apartment, with all windows overlooking a court that was in itself a nightmare, could have turned the happiest person into the most helpless hypochondriac, let alone a family with the propensities of this one.

Black garment encased, somberly proud families like the Coellos, whose poverty has gone to their heads and are intoxicated with failure, were common in Spain and this was the paradox of the Coello family as of so many others. Unable as they would have been to remain themselves under changed conditions in a country of which they were a typical, if old product, they could be unmolested in New York and even contribute to its typically heterogeneous population. Here they could mourn the glad tidings about their country brought by the newspapers, they could wail and deplore to their hearts' content, remain in their pure unadulterated state, like calamares in their own black sauce, with all their militant, though aesthetically justified defensive chastity, worshiping traditions which dictate to cover the greatest possible area of human bodies. Don Hilarión Coello sported an abdomen like a balloon, and his wife one like an apron which would have permitted her to remain chaste even in a nudist camp.

As one of their friends said—an individual who having arrived here six months before them felt entitled to become their spiritual cicerone in the labyrinth of American life:

"That is the convenience of New York, Don Hilarión. On one side you have progressive Nordics who do gymnastics and read science, and on the other you have retrograde Latins who procreate behind shut windows and read the catechism."

"You have said it." Don Hilarión spoke with a very profound and important manner: "On one side you have one thing and on the other you have the other thing. On one side the wrong and on the other the right."

Don Hilarión felt very important, and his family thought that he was and therefore they also felt very important. Don Hilarión was a notario, not a notary, mind you; that does not quite convey the meaning, but a notario. A notario in Spain, at least in Don Hilarión's day, was a title given to a man having achieved the summit of his career in the field of law. It was the coronation of every law student. When parents addressed good children showing particular brilliance, they always said: "Study law, my boy. It has many applications, among them the diplomatic service, and you may even someday be a notario and always be respected and looked upon as an important citizen, not to speak of the good profits you will derive." And the good children always imagined themselves with beard, silk hat and a frock coat, walking along the street acknowledging the deferential greetings and respectful salutations of the admiring crowds.

Don Hilarión had been one of those boys.

He had studied law.

He did not enter the diplomatic service because he only had studied two dead languages.

He did not wear a silk hat and a frock coat, because his friend and spiritual guide had advised him that in this country one did not have to be ceremonious, but do as one pleased; a somewhat exaggerated statement, but safe where Don Hilarión was concerned.

He did not have any greetings to acknowledge, except occasionally those of the janitor and of one or two acquaintances, because the rest of the population did not know him from Adam.

But Don Hilarión was a notario. He felt important. His family felt important. But they were Spaniards of the old school and therefore were gloomy.

Their obvious reason was that Don Hilarión could not practice law in New York because he was not a citizen and besides, his knowledge of English was very limited. However, he had set up one of his rooms as an office, with all his law books, solid cabinets, large imposing desk and heavy chairs. The room was small, Don Hilarión fat, and consequently it was difficult to move about the place. Once he succeeded in sitting at the chair behind his desk, it was not easy to induce him to abandon his post and leave the room, and Don Hilarión sat there all day, reading newspapers from Spain, and it made him feel like a very busy man. This room was at the end of the long corridor and it was from there that Don Hilarión, finding it difficult to extricate himself, called out to his wife who was most of the time with Vicenta, the servant, in the kitchen, unfortunately located at the other end, and she had to look in every one of the rooms, when she very well knew that he could be but in one, held there at the mercy of his furniture.

Doña Dolores arrived breathless: "What is it, Hilarión?"

"Nothing, woman, what can it be? The usual thing. Can you lend a hand? I want to get out of here and I am in a hurry. Where did you think I was?"

By this time she had already got hold of his hand, heaved and given him a good start. "That's enough now, woman. I can manage the rest by myself."

"Such small rooms in this country! In Spain this furniture was lost in that office you had, remember?" Her voice was very throaty, very weepy.

"No use complaining, woman. Nothing gained by that," Don Hilarión finished, heading for the bathroom, newspaper in hand.

Doña Dolores walked back swiftly along the corridor wailing at her memories, at her wretched present: "Those were rooms! At least one had that in one's poverty." She assumed a very resigned air, very brow-beaten. "But when one is so poor one does not even have the right to complain . . ." She reentered the kitchen and ably turned her lingering remarks into a fitting continuation and confirmation of her inter-rupted talk with Vicenta:

"I should say one has no right to complain. With sufferings, one finally does not mind anymore. But still there are things that reach your marrow. Don't think I don't notice, Vicenta. I did not want to say anything the other day about the incident of the shoes of Hilarión—but the procession goes on inside."

She referred to her husband having had a patch placed on one of his shoes. Then he had met some friends and they had walked. One of them was a Spanish writer who wrote chronicles about New York for South American papers and was always making bad suggestions. This time he suggested that they all examine their feet, right where they were, on Seventh Avenue, to determine who had the largest.

Don Hilarión suspected that the writer had spied his repaired shoes and was calling attention very indelicately to the fact. He had arrived home feeling very depressed and had discussed the incident with his wife in front of Vicenta. The matter had gradually diminished in his mind, but in Doña Dolores's it had behaved like a rolling snowball, reaching the phenomenal proportions of a unanimous world com-fabulation to vex them, to mock their honorable poverty.

Vicenta tried to soothe her with the usual speech: "Don't think about it, Doña Dolores. A writer! Like all the rest of them. They are always talking for the sake of talking. Who takes writers seriously?"

But Doña Dolores persisted. She relished such experiences that made her feel like a martyr. She resented Vicenta's lightly discarding the matter, simply because she had no appearances to maintain, robbing this succulent humiliating morsel of all its imagined seasoning. She skillfully misinterpreted:

"All right, Vicenta, you let it go at that. It does not hurt you. When one is poor, one does not even have the privilege of complaining. Being poor is the worst sin I suppose, which must be constantly expiated, paid for, when one can pay for nothing else." She compressed her lips and a wistful smile sent her eyes in search of remote places of mournful reveries.

Vicenta, whose salary had not been attended to for the last six months, misunderstood sincerely: "Doña Dolores, you know very well that I am not one to think of certain things and I am very happy to work for you as it is. But what you do is like someone stabbing you and then you take the knife and twist it around."

"Now I twist it around! When one is in my position, one must be even accused, held to blame for one's own sufferings." She shifted to the other section of her servant's speech which offered opportunities too tempting to pass over: "And as for the other matter, Vicenta, you will be paid. Don't worry." Her voice rose to eloquent heights: "you will be paid even if I have to tear the flesh off my bones like that famous merchant of Italy, and you can have the blood too."

"Please! Doña Dolores! I am not worrying—" Vicenta gave up in hopelessness and turned to proceed with her chores and made an attempt at changing the conversation: "What shall we order from the grocer's today?"

"Anything," said Doña Dolores, disgusted with her servant's reluctance to continue her pet type of talk. "You know better than I. That is, if they want to send it. We also owe them money and—"

An interruption was advancing tumultuously along the corridor and invaded the kitchen. It was her two children, a boy and a girl, Jeremias and Angustias, both thin, sallow-complexioned and darkly sad-eyed. Both spoke with the same tearful throatiness of their mother and showed already strong-inherited and well-encouraged tendencies to gloom, contrasting with their noisy if not cheerful behavior. This last strange and unexpectedly inconvenient attitude for Doña Dolores was resignedly explained in her mind by what she considered the vulgarizing influence of the environment. Superficially, both children had become thoroughly Americanized in an amazingly short time. They were even called Jerry and Angie in school, a thing which extracted most devilishly from their names all the glorious, tragic implications.

"We want lunch!" Jerry shouted brutally, but with elegiac overtones.

"And in a hurry!" Angie completed with even worse manners and heart-rending harmonics.

Their mother withered them with a well-planted look: "I don't know what has come over these children since we came to this country. They were never like this in Spain. They have changed so!" In Spain they were half their present age, and never left home.

The children had sat at the kitchen table with drooping mouths and heads humbly to one side, to eat the lunch that Vicenta was preparing for them.

"Mama, can we have some money for carfare?"

"Yes, teacher is taking us to the Museum of Natural History and each one is supposed to provide his own carfare."

"Now you want money for carfare. When it is not one thing, it is the other. In that school they are constantly demanding money. We are poor and can't afford it."

"Oh, Mama! All the other children are going. Must we always be thus humiliated before others?" Their chins quivered, their voices shook effectively.

"Yes, I know. You have begun to suffer privations early, but you must be resigned. Being poor is no shame when one is honest. You go back to school and tell that teacher that your father cannot afford these luxuries like the rich parents of other children, but that you don't mind, that your father is a respectable notario and that in our poverty we base our pride." Her voice was decidedly damp.

"But Mama, you know they won't understand all that." They appeared to have given up melancholic displays as useless.

"Well, they should. It is high time someone woke them up to the fact that this life is not a novel. In this country they have no consideration. All they think of is money and good times, always telling one to be gay and keep smiling." She made an effective pause. "Smiling! Yes, while the procession goes on inside. These women teachers here never marry, never have children, they don't know what suffering is, what privation, what life is."

"All right, Mama, but can we have the money?"

"Go on now," Vicenta stepped in: "You have enough museum pieces with those bespectacled old hens who teach you—"

"Miss Finch is not an old hen and she does not wear spectacles," Angie charged.

"Never mind that. You go back there and tell them that you did not get the money. Come on! Finish that omelet. You have appetites like millionaires. We can't be throwing food away in this house. Your father—" Vicenta checked herself. This pessimism was contagious. "Go ahead now, hurry! Run along and take an umbrella. It is raining."

And so it was and at this time, under another umbrella, Mr. Robinson was fatefully walking toward their house.

No sooner had the children left than Doña Dolores resumed her interrupted litany: "I suppose I should also laugh at the question of the cream puffs. I should be very cheerful about it."

"There you go talking about that again," Vicenta said while looking into the icebox and kitchen closets to see what was needed. She knew the incident by memory. For some reason it was one of the selected tear-jerking, bitter-smile-squeezer pieces in Doña Dolores's repertoire.

It seems that a friend, knowing Don Hilarión's precarious financial condition, had given him some matter to investigate concerning Spanish law. It turned out to be a very simple matter and Don Hilarión felt that it detracted from his importance as a notario to do a piece of work that could have been attended to by any law apprentice, any law office amanuensis. However, when he was paid, he made his grand gesture. He went to a pastry shop run by another Spaniard in the neighborhood and bought some cream puffs.

"To sweeten the bitterness left by this humiliating job," he said as he laid them on the table before his wife.

That night they had dinner accompanied by the usual lamentations all around. When time for dessert arrived, the children greeted the appearance of the cream puffs with vociferous sadness.

"You must be grateful for this little luxury, my dears. It has cost your father very trying moments, but do not be common. Poverty is no excuse for bad manners."

Angie was the first one to make the nefarious discovery. She held up the puff she had opened, under the overhanging lamp, for all to see: "This pastry is bad. Look, it is green inside."

Doña Dolores looked, they all looked. Vicenta had appeared at the dining-room door and also looked. This was a real crisis and Doña Dolores rose to it:

"Rotten!" she exclaimed in piercing tones. "Even that! Poor people must be given rotten things, because they have no money to buy at the right places—" She was beside herself. "That is too much. We may be poor, but too proud to permit such insolence!" The children's mouths were already drooping and trembling at the corners. "Take them back immediately, Hilarión!" Angie began to bawl shamelessly, a true Desdemona, and her brother bit his lip and cast his eyes down, a little man in distress. Doña Dolores fell prone upon the table, wiping aside the guilty puff: "Mockery, Hilarión—rotten mockery!" she wailed prostrate by the shock.

Vicenta surveyed the scene in perplexity. Don Hilarión gathered the offending puffs back into their box of shame and left like one walking to his doom, muttering between his teeth: "How long, my Lord, how long?" He returned the pastry, got his money back, and bought himself some cigars instead.

That incident had been one of the high, cherished moments of the Coello family.

"Just when poor Hilarión, happy at having earned some money, wanted to celebrate by giving his children something sweet, which they so seldom have." Doña Dolores concluded: "I am supposed to dance a fandango for sheer happiness."

At that moment the doorbell rang. Mr. Robinson had arrived.

Vicenta walked the length of the corridor wiping her hands on her apron and opened the door. Mr. Robinson introduced himself and in that roundabout manner which every salesman considers deceptive and enticing, he hinted at the purpose of his call. Such linguistic subtleties were beyond Vicenta's neglected knowledge of English and she called her mistress:

"Doña Dolores, please come and see what this man wants."

Doña Dolores was slightly more successful than her servant and understanding that the man had something good for her husband, she led Mr. Robinson, who had not removed his derby, into her husband's office: "Hilarión, this gentleman has come to see you."

Don Hilarión removed his gold-rimmed spectacles and regarded the gentleman. He assumed his most important manner, meanwhile trying to rise unsuccessfully: "Please have a seat, sir. In what can I serve you? Forgive me for not rising, but as you see, this furniture—"

"Don't bother. It's perfectly all right," said Mr. Robinson, squeezing past some furniture and into a chair. "My name is Robinson of the ——" he gave the name of some insurance company, and with that he opened his briefcase and spread his subject's literature before the prospective client, right over the newspaper that the latter was reading. Then in a speech not too short to be unimpressive and not too long to be wearisome, he stated his case, being careful to make himself clear to this foreigner.

Don Hilarión and his wife, who stood in the doorway, listened, the former pompously, the latter politely. Then when Don Hilarión thought naively enough that Mr. Robinson had finished, he cleared his throat and began: "You see, Mr. Robinson, I do not believe in life insurance policies, I—"

The other took ready advantage of Don Hilarión's halting English to lunge confidently onto well-trod ground: "What do you mean you don't believe? I don't care how rich you are. No one can afford to be without this protection. What about your wife, your children? Suppose you die one of these days. If you have the policy I have been speaking of, your wife won't have the added expense of your funeral, and she will get some money besides—"

"Holy Virgin!" Doña Dolores cried on the verge of a faint. "Listen to what this man is saying. He is talking about your death, and he dares suggest that I profit by it." Her face had gone from pallor to deep red. "Listen, mister. We may be poor, but we are no ghouls and when anyone dies in this family, God forbid, we shall obtain the money somehow to give them a decent, Christian burial. Listen to him!"

"Please, woman! Let me bear this cross alone," Don Hilarión said, while Mr. Robinson looked from one to the other endeavoring to make out these foreigners. "Pardon, Mr. Robinson, but as I said before, I do not believe in life insurance. No one can insure his life. One never knows when one will die and therefore there is no use—"

"Listen, brother. You don't know what you are talking about. If you would let me explain—"

Don Hilarión had succeeded in rising: "I don't know what I am talking about? Did you say I don't know what I am talking about?" He smiled a superior smile and deliberately placed his gold-rimmed spectacles upon his nose. "Perhaps you don't know whom you are talking to, sir. I happen to be a notario. Do you hear? A notario."

"So what? What's so wonderful about that? I am a notary also, and I can prove it."

There was a silence. Doña Dolores approached, Don Hilarión removed his glasses and leaning on his desk scrutinized his visitor, hat and all.

"You are also a notario?"

"Sure! What's wrong with it? Anybody can be one. All you do is pay a few dollars and you are a notary."

Don Hilarión staggered and, holding on to the arms of his chair, he slid down into his seat slowly, dejectedly, like one crushed to dust that settles gradually. Another silence followed, a longer one, like the kind that comes after an explosion.

"For a few dollars—anybody—a notario—" he managed to whisper hoarsely.

Doña Dolores precipitated herself forward and reached across the desk, a hand gripping her husband's shoulder: "Hilarión, Hilarión! Oh my God!"

"What did I do now?" questioned Mr. Robinson, puzzled. These foreigners were too much for him.

"What have you done?" Doña Dolores had turned on him like a lioness: "You have killed him!"

"But madam, I only—"

"Go away, please. Can't you see that he is ill? Go away!"

"All right, lady." Mr. Robinson picked up all his papers. "I'll be back when he is feeling better." He walked out hurriedly despite the furniture. He had nearly sold his best policy to a man who could die at the slightest provocation.

Doña Dolores was hovering over her fallen husband: "What is it,

Hilarión? Speak to me."

Don Hilarión heaved a sigh that was like lifting a ton of bricks: "Nothing, woman, nothing—I prefer not to speak now," and then he began to talk. That man usually of so few chosen words began to talk rapidly, carelessly, in a manner his wife had never heard before. He poured out his soul. He spoke of his life, a subject he had always skipped with dignified reticence. He spoke of his hopes and illusions, of his disappointments and subsequent pessimism.

"Forgive me," he ended. "I have been talking a good deal and one should not burden a woman with one's troubles, but sometimes a man talks as he swims: to save himself from drowning. Talking is for the soul what motion is for the body. The body moves, does; the soul speaks, explains. I had to talk, but now I have to rest. I feel very tired. You go about your things and let me rest awhile." And Don Hilarión leaned his head on a hand that also shielded eyes no longer adorned with gold-rimmed spectacles.

"My poor Hilarión! What a blow!" said Doña Dolores, or rather, her lips formed the phrase silently, and silently she left the room, and once in the corridor she walked with more resolution to the kitchen.

Don Hilarión remained in the same position for a few moments. Then his eyes opened and he noticed once again the Spanish paper he had been reading. In sudden rage, he crumpled it up into a shapeless ball and hurled it against the walls lined with his law books. Then he sat back, his breath coming in gasps, and his eyes roved over those books. For only a few dollars anybody could be a notario!

He felt an uncontrollable desire to tear those volumes from the shelves where they reposed, to trample them, to smash them. He made an effort to rise and something snapped inside of him sending a sharp pain from his chest along his arms. Everything reeled, everything went dark: "Dolores—Dolores—!" he cried with despair.

Doña Dolores was rushing along the long corridor, looking into every room: "Where are you? Where are you?" She finally reached his room: "Hilarión, what is it, Hilarión?"

Don Hilarión did not answer. He was leaning back in his chair, his head drooping on one shoulder, his arms hanging lifelessly down the sides.

"Hilarión, are you sick? Hilarión, speak! Hilarión—! Vicenta!

Come!" she howled.

Don Hilarión was dead.

To try to convey in words the extremes to which Doña Dolores went in displaying her just, unquestionable sorrow, would be impossible and if possible, useless, since no one could conceive of it more than of the stellar light-years in a book of astronomy. One can conceive possibly the feelings of a panhandler who is seeking five cents for a cup of coffee and suddenly finds himself owning the treasures of Ali Baba, then one could raise that to the nth power, but it would do no good. One cannot conceive that, and yet this is but like an orange compared to the earth if one considers the sorrow of Doña Dolores, the full measure of her bereavement.

Even she felt that it was quite impossible to do complete justice to her position, and like a clever actor fearing that a role may lie beyond his dramatizing potentialities, she wisely and conveniently for the surrounding world chose to underact her part. In all her sympathy-acknowledging answers she was sober and introduced simple phrases such as: "No, nothing, my dear. He left us nothing but his good name and the honor of bearing it," and "Yes, my dear, quite unexpected, but those who live honestly in spite of their poverty are always ready when the moment arrives," or "That is right, my dear. Death is the common leveler and no amount of money can pave the road to the kingdom of heaven and it is easier for a camel to pass through the eye of a needle—" But her expression was a thing to behold and she always ended with the same words: "Ay! They did not baptize me Dolores for nothing!"

But throughout all this Doña Dolores smiled wisely, sadly and to herself, as one who is keeping a secret. She was preparing her great coup, her fitting and masterly stroke. When words failed, it was time for action, and since tears, sobbing, nervous attacks and bellowing could do no justice to the situation, she, Doña Dolores, the champion mourner, would not be caught napping. She would do something, she would do something that would show how she could feel such a thing, something that would break all previous records set by the loudest mourners in this world, something memorable that would put to shame the most rabidly unfortunate characters in history.

Two days after the death of Don Hilarión, Doña Dolores summoned a Spanish undertaker by the name of Zacatecas. They remained a long time closeted in Don Hilarión's office, where the body lay in state. When they came out, enigmatic phrases were heard:

"You must reconsider the price, Señor Zacatecas. We are poor. He left us nothing but his good name and—"

"I know, madam, but this is a special job and besides, I may get into trouble and the least that could happen would be losing my license. Also remember that you would have had to buy a coffin."

"Very well, Señor Zacatecas. Please hurry and do your best."

"Oh, don't you worry about that. I will do my best. Now I am going for lunch and to my office to get some things and will be right back."

The Señor Zacatecas having left, Doña Dolores walked up and down the corridor several times, an unfathomable and resolute smile upon her lips.

When the Señor Zacatecas returned as promised with a large black case, she ushered him again into her husband's office and left him there behind the closed door. After that she had to perform what she called the painful duty of taking some nourishment to remain alive for the children's sake and then she sat surrounded by friends and acquaintances like a queen on a throne to bask in their admiring sympathy and discuss and comment at length with undisputed authority upon the exemplary past actions and never well-praised virtues of the illustrious and important defunct, while some black-attired guest summed up matters with a deep remark such as: "The real trouble with life is death."

Time passed and a few close and dejected friends sat at her sadly regal, if materially poor table to "do something for life, since one can do nothing for death" by eating a hasty supper prepared and served by Vicenta with red swollen eyes and unsteady hands.

The children sat through all this together, their thin faces paler than ever, Angie crying intermittently under the protective arm of her brother.

"Vicenta, please see that the children eat something."

"Yes—Doña Dolores," she said shakily and she went to the children and, holding them tightly with trembling arms, she disappeared with them into the kitchen, sobbing.

The mournful gathering remained repeating the same words,

singing the same praises until well into the night. The children also remained up, Doña Dolores affecting an adequate disregard for anything not connected with her bereavement.

And then the Señor Zacatecas emerged from Don Hilarión's office where he had been all that time and called Doña Dolores, who responded immediately, reentering the room with him.

They remained there mysteriously with door closed quite a while and then she reappeared, followed by the Señor Zacatecas and closing the door carefully behind. Then she summoned everybody.

All the guests walked in single file along the corridor, Vicenta and the children bringing up the rear. They arrived as the Señor Zacatecas was taking his leave noiselessly like a shadow, and standing in front of the closed room, they met Doña Dolores, arms folded, beaming upon them her despair, her tragedy:

"I have summoned you all to witness the proof of my devotion." She quoted the old saying cryptically: "Things you will see of the Cid, that will cause the stones to speak." And she flung the door open.

The grief-stricken gathering crowded in the doorway and gasped.

Don Hilarión was sitting at his desk, in typical pose, pen in hand resting on a sheet of foolscap, his gold-rimmed spectacles balanced on his nose. There was even a frown clouding his noble brow as if it were laden with the problems and responsibilities of justice. The Señor Zacatecas had done a good job.

The wall behind his chair displayed a Spanish flag, adding to the sad arrangement a touch of glorious brilliance. It was a perfect picture of dignity, sacrifice and important futility. Doña Dolores had risen to unsuspected heights of genius to meet the challenge of the occasion:

"From now on," she said throatily but with appropriate self-control and an edge of fatigue in her voice, "this will be his shrine, his sanctuary. He will sit among his legal books and papers, in the atmosphere that was his life." She grew stern with the assurance of the cruelly wounded person before an appreciative, almost envious audience: "They shall not take him away from me. He was our only and most precious possession in our poverty. He was all we had. His exemplary life, his important achievements, no longer appreciated in these materialistic days, shall guide us in our dark hours of sorrow. He was a notario as you all know and he will remain one. Indeed death is the common leveler and all dead notarios are equal. In the new fields he is conquering, his well-justified ignorance of a vulgarly modern language will no longer stand in his path to glory. Here you behold Don Hilarión Coello, Notario."

"Doña Dolores—" came from every mouth like a murmur in response to her funeral oration. It sounded like "ora pro nobis," and involved an admiring recognition that was worth living for. The children hung on to Vicenta's apron, their faces a deathly white, their eyes like saucers. Doña Dolores raised a hand in the classic mob-stilling gesture:

"I propose to pay him homage once a year on the anniversary of his departure. He shall remain here, where he can be respected and honored as he deserves, but I appeal to your honorable sense of secrecy to keep this from misunderstanding outsiders as it would be very sad to have him who was a respected and important man of law involved in legal complications." There was a strange leer on her face as she lighted two candles which had been placed on the desk and knelt in front of it.

"Doña Dolores—" The murmur rose again, and again it sounded like "ora pro nobis," which smoothly turned to general prayer trailing among the kneeling figures along the corridor. Then Doña Dolores rose, and all, knowing that the audience was over, filed out silently, still crossing themselves with reverent fear.

When they had all departed, Doña Dolores put out the candles and locked the door of the shrine. Vicenta was standing in front of her, the children still grasping her apron. They looked like a petrified group and Vicenta said hollowly:

"I wouldn't do that, Doña Dolores. It does not seem right."

"Let anyone try and take him away," Doña Dolores responded with threatening finality as she pocketed the key.

The next two days Doña Dolores spent several hours enclosed with her dead husband. On the third day she only stayed a few minutes and when she came out she telephoned the Señor Zacatecas to come immediately.

As soon as he arrived she took him into the room: "Look here, Señor Zacatecas. There seems to be something wrong with your work. There is a strong smell and then also stains in the face and hands. I have not looked further because I did not want to disarrange anything until you got here. Come and look for yourself. Don't you notice the smell?"

They struggled past the furniture. The Señor Zacatecas bent close to the figure, he looked, he sniffed, he finally straightened up: "That cannot be helped, Madame, the job is good. I worked for hours on him. If you had called me sooner it would have been easier, but when you called me, he was already in pretty bad shape and it was hard work to get him in the position you see him now. I had to use special chemicals and after a while they react that way. But this is nothing. You keep the windows open for a while and it will wear off. I really don't want to know any more about this affair. I may get in trouble. I only did it because we are both Spanish and must stand together, but I want no more of it." The Señor Zacatecas departed.

Doña Dolores opened the window and looked into the pallid abyss of the court. Her gaze then remained suspended in space for a long time and then she also left the room.

That first year went by slowly at first and then it gathered speed uneventfully. In the beginning Doña Dolores's visits to her husband were frequent and the children lived in constant fear, stayed away from the house as much as possible and at night insisted that Vicenta sleep with them. Then after a few months the visits of Doña Dolores grew more scarce. She seemed to prefer to pour her eternal lamentations enriched by this magnificent new addition into the faithful, though inattentive ears of her servant. Then a few days before the anniversary, it was decided to pay a call on Don Hilarión to see that everything was as it should be.

They discovered that all the furniture had accumulated an alarming amount of dust, as had Don Hilarión. They considered the matter at length and finally arrived at the conclusion that everything had to be dusted, including the old notario.

"I thought it might be disrespectful," said Vicenta, "but what can one do?"

"It is more respectful to clean him, to perform that duty instead of allowing him to accumulate dirt. After all, Vicenta, cleanliness is next to holiness."

They left the room and Vicenta returned to it with duster and broom. She swept the floor as well as the furniture permitted and then dusted every piece with expert hand. When she came to Don Hilarión, she remained a while, duster in hand poised in midair, and then with a shrug of the shoulders, she began vigorously.

At the first stroke the duster caught the gold-rimmed spectacles and sent them crashing against the desk, one of the lenses breaking. "Now I've done it!" poor Vicenta said in distress. She picked up the spectacles and with some effort she managed to balance them upon Don Hilarión's nose, which seemed to have shrunk. Indeed, the whole figure appeared slightly shrunk and distorted out of position, and then she also noticed Don Hilarión's face. It had also changed, for it seems that time passes even for the dead. His lips had receded somewhat and began to expose his teeth, with the suggestion of a macabre smile. The frown in his forehead was a bit accentuated. The whole face and hands looked much darker. Vicenta studied the whole thing for a while shaking her head and then left the room closing the door.

When the anniversary arrived Doña Dolores invited a few friends. They arrived endeavoring to cover their curiosity with an air of great reverence and when Doña Dolores opened the door of the sanctuary, they all crowded in with almost abject hurry.

Doña Dolores was about to deliver the speech she had prepared for the occasion when she caught sight as well as all the others of the expression on her late husband's face. The lips now fully exposed the teeth in a decided broad smile and the frown had become marked to the point of ferocity. The contrast was, to say the least, disconcerting.

Doña Dolores approached the sitting figure and eyed it. She overheard snickers and giggles and even a remark or two from a couple of American guests about the skeleton in the family closet. They all seemed nervous, fidgety. A young lady became hysterical.

And then Doña Dolores's eye fell upon the broken spectacles: "What is the meaning of this? Vicenta, come here. Explain!"

The dejected servant advanced twisting her apron in embarrassment: "Well, madam, the duster caught on the spectacles and they fell and—" She broke down and rushed from the room crying, her apron already a sausage in her hands, to seek refuge in the kitchen.

Doña Dolores looked at her husband's face again and mused: "I wonder what chemicals that Zacatecas used?"

The guests seemed unable to restrain their risibilities. Their rampant fear had created a nervousness which found only this outlet. They gulped, inflated their cheeks, coughed applying their handkerchiefs to their faces, and grew purple.

Doña Dolores turned upon them, the livid image of righteous indignation: "Shooo, imbeciles!" she emitted with all her might.

And this was too much for the guests. With howls and roars, they stampeded out of the house, convulsed by loud, open, ribald laughter.

The ceremony had ended.

The second year went by even faster than the first. The family activities had progressively invaded the room. There were things there which had to be used. At first Doña Dolores or Vicenta entered on tiptoe and left silently, but later they hurried and forgot to close the door on their way out and the door was open most of the time. The children appeared to have lost their fear. They played in the corridor and once when their ball rolled into Don Hilarión's office, Jerry walked in boldy, retrieved it, and as he was leaving, he stopped to study his father.

"Come over here," he called to his sister and when she came: " 'S funny, but doesn't he remind you of someone, with that mustache and all?"

Angie looked carefully, her head to one side: "That's right! That portrait in the principal's office in the school."

"Doesn't it though?" They both laughed and then, forgetting all about it, resumed their play right in there.

Doña Dolores, who saw them as she came in from shopping, scolded them that time, but the scene was repeated often later and she minded it less each time and eventually noticed it no more. She was going through that critical age in which women sometimes become slightly stupefied.

Vicenta dusted Don Hilarión regularly like another piece of furniture. Once while thus occupied, she noticed that the pen had fallen from his hand. She tried to replace it but the fingers had contracted or separated and wouldn't hold it. She tried to press them together and one of them came off in her hand. Vicenta contemplated this minor disaster stoically. She remained undecided with the finger in her hand looking for an adequate place to deposit the relic. At last she dropped it in the wastebasket. When Doña Dolores eventually spotted the missing finger, she simply sighed and said: "That Zacatecas—that Vicenta—!"

More time passed and one day when Doña Dolores had to use the desk, she discovered that her husband was in the way: "Come over, Vicenta, help me with this."

Together they shoved Don Hilarión and chair and when Doña Dolores finished whatever she had to do at the desk, they forgot to replace the throne and master, and he remained in that position, on the side of the desk, like one applying for something to an invisible provider.

The family moved and lived about that corpse as if it were but an object, one more useless object which Vicenta had to attend to protestingly. One could often see Doña Dolores sitting there writing a letter or one of the children doing homework, with the vigilant, immobile figure next to them, frown, spectacles, mustache, smile, teeth and all.

The third anniversary passed unnoticed and when Doña Dolores remembered, she realized that it would have been an anticlimax to open a door which had been open already for such a long time. Besides, her friends were already completely familiarized with the presence of Don Hilarión. He had been very often included in their visits and two friends left the house once talking like this:

"But how is it that the authorities have not found out about this irregularity? Or if they have found out, why have they done nothing?"

"Well, you know. These foreign families can live in New York in their own colony, completely isolated from the rest of the town, like in an independent state. As long as they do not bother the rest, the city does not bother to find out. The thing remains among the group, but if anyone outside their circle has learned of it, it has been probably discarded as an old Spanish custom."

This explanation was as good as any, and as for the children, they were entering that age in which they felt ashamed of being connected with anything different from the rest and they did not mention it. Perhaps they did not give it enough importance anymore.

Don Hilarión was still holding together in spots, but on the whole, he looked quite bad and threatened to disintegrate completely at any moment. Every time he was moved, one could feel something snap, crush and roll down to accumulate in the folds of his clothes, in small particles, like crumbled fragments of old cork that sometimes found their way to the floor and had to be swept up.

One day Vicenta said to her mistress: "You know, Doña Dolores? This thing is falling apart, and it is only in the way here. I think we could put it in a trunk and send it down to the basement. Then we will have more room and we certainly need it with all this heavy furniture."

Doña Dolores pursed her lips and looked her husband up and down: "Yes—I suppose so. The purpose would be the same. I only promised not to let them take him away, and I am a woman of my word, but I suppose he will be better off that way."

And Don Hilarión, in the collapsible condition he had reached, was easily crammed into a trunk and sent down to the basement.

Time moved on to the melancholy accompaniment of Doña Dolores's lamentations, seasons followed seasons, and years pursued years with gradual acceleration, and the story might close one day when Mr. Goldstein, the landlord, called on the Coellos, thus saving them from perishing under the ruins of the building which had to be demolished, and incidentally to render them the service of another apartment in another building which he also owned. Mr. Goldstein did not know that day, when disregarding coat and hat he left his office on the other side of Mount Morris Park, that his visit would bring to an end the incidents of which he fortunately had never learned. He walked on one of those splendid New York summer days that last about an hour and was thinking big, generous, humane thoughts. His heart was warm toward his fellow man. That building had developed a weak spot and was unsafe. He might as well tell the tenants to move, since the building had to come down anyway. He wanted to keep a clear conscience.

As he reached the park's sidewalk, he was nearly run down by a speeding car and one wonders what he thought of worrying about other people's troubles.

At that moment Doña Dolores was speaking with bitterness to Vicenta: "I suppose I should be happy enough to sing, after all the misery I have known, after all the misfortune that has piled upon my head. I did not want to say anything the other day about the incident of Angustias's party dress, but the procession . . ."

The usual, unavoidable interruption was advancing loudly along the corridor.

Jerry entered the kitchen and suggested in comically deep tones: "What about food, Mama? I have to rush back for the meet." His voice was changing and his gloom only seemed increased by his puberty.

"It is high time you thought of something else besides playing. If your poor father were alive . . ."

The bell rang. Mr. Goldstein had arrived.

The moment he explained the object of his visit, Doña Dolores put her hands to her head. "Ay Dios mio! Vicenta! Listen to what this man says. The house is going to fall down. This is the very dregs in the cup of bitterness which has been my life. Even the house where I live is going to fall on me, all because poor people cannot afford to live in solid buildings. Oh my God, my God, my God! When a person is as unfortunate as I am, she has no reason for living. I may as well die right now. Let's get out of here this minute!"

The magnanimous offer of Mr. Goldstein to move to another of his houses was accepted as soon as he had reassured Doña Dolores that all his other buildings were sound, solid as a rock, and the preparations for moving were begun at once.

The next day as Doña Dolores stood on the sidewalk and saw the two moving vans drive away packed with their belongings and heavy furniture, she turned exhausted on Vicenta: "Did we forget anything?" she asked feebly.

"I don't think so, Doña Dolores," the servant answered through a yawn that nearly turned her inside out.

"Well; it would make no difference anyway. We are too poor to own anything of any value. . . . How tired I am!" She addressed her two children who stood there looking very bored and dutifully sad. "All right then, let's go."

The group walked slowly in the direction of the new house.

And the last incident one may accept since one has accepted so many others is that one day after the old unsafe building had been duly demolished and nothing remained but abandoned foundations replete with debris, a tramp was rummaging through and came upon a bundle of dark clothes covered with dirt and dust. He picked it up, shook it and more dust dropped from it, mixing with the other. Having found the clothes acceptable, he walked away still brushing and shaking from them the last traces of dust, without bothering to think whether it was the stuff houses are made of, or the stuff men are made of.

By now I have allowed these things to fall out of chronological step, but it is just as well. Possibly the order in which incidents happen may not always be as acceptable as the pattern they form when seen in their totality. But be that as it may, I go back now to things I got ahead of in this haphazard account of recollections.

After the death of his landlady, there followed several unpleasant days demanding Garcia's attention to details he did not like. A will turned up which left to him the house where they lived and also most of her money, but Garcia suffered an attack of Castilian pride and wouldn't hear of it. I suspect that it was due to fear created by seeing Latins often depicted as graceful pimps and also in the way of an atonement for his past weakness. He had been weak, allowing his impractical dreamy nature and circumstances which he considered himself incapable of conquering to place him in the suspected position of a man living off a woman, a woman of whom he had felt ashamed, but not ashamed enough to do anything about his position, and he had even allowed that shame to carry over to her very end. Perhaps he had been only human but he was in the mood to judge himself sternly. In his own eyes he had been weak in her life and weak at her death, and now he was twice as ashamed of himself. He knew that she had a sister in Pennsylvania and communicated with her. She came with her husband and at first they were unfriendly and belligerent and threatened to bring matters to court without bothering to find out his attitude in the matter, but when finally it penetrated their minds and they realized that he was giving up everything in their favor, they became all beaming and effusive courteousness, calling him a fine Spanish gentleman and scholar, and the husband arranged everything with a lawyer and paid for all expenses, funereal and otherwise, mentioning that Garcia was in no condition to be bothered with sad financial details and showing the generosity of one who insists jovially that this round is on him.

Then Garcia, who had brought to my place what he considered his valuable personal property, most of which were his manuscripts and notes and his typewriter, said that he was going away, but he did not say where and I did not ask. I knew him well. The man was ashamed after the ordeal, like one unmasked, to have his position openly and officially discussed as the object of legal consideration when he signed his claims away. He was ashamed the way one who has suffered an accident is ashamed of his torn, dirty undergarments exposed to the public gaze. He went away with his eyes averted, but only from his former haunts and stayed in town. I did not see him for a long time but heard from him now and then through various sources.

This was the beginning of what he considered his long expiation, the downgrade epic into the mud bath. His sentimentality led him to all established situations of romantic degradation, and from his material suffering he must have derived some spiritual satisfaction.

The amount of anonymity and tolerance dispensed in these parts is amazing. He could never have gotten away with it in Spain. Hours spent on public benches with the bottle of self-justification, waiting for the final crucifixion when the policeman on the beat told him to move along to wind up naturally on the Bowery, the acknowledged Mecca. He had the romanticism of the Bowery and I had heard him speak of ending his days there in wretched, sentimental glory. The life of a hobo fascinated him as it would anyone who has not tried it. It was inevitable. One can imagine days of dark, exultant, alcoholic confusion culminating in the peregrination over the Manhattan or Brooklyn Bridge, from the benches of one city hall square to another, and then on to other side streets, but never, no matter how bad the stupor, down Atlantic Avenue and Columbia Street to any Spanish café where he would be seen by his countrymen. It may pass to be a bum to strangers, to play the role for foreign consumption as he would say, but not in front of those with whom one has closer bonds, even if they are impersonal. You cannot let your own people see you when you are wallowing in your own mess.

I fought the desire to look for him through some common acquaintance. I had heard that the only Spaniard who had seen him was our erstwhile friend Don Laureano, who held court in the parts Garcia frequented and who probably lent a helping hand to him and must have piloted him expertly in the new existence that Garcia had chosen, and I also suspected the Moor of having found some means of helping Garcia without offending his racial type of delicacy and formalism. But if I had sought him out in this direct and open manner, it would have been the unforgivable sin. I know that this type of loyalty in reverse is difficult to put across; the closer one is, the more outrageous such liberty becomes.

The case of Garcia was, according to the Moor, a complex one and should be allowed to play itself and straighten itself out. He had an intricate theory that when a Spaniard takes to drinking and bumming in this land, it is due to an Anglo-Saxon psychosis. He has absorbed too much of his environment, is saturated with it and requires the native, domestic antidote—must take the cure that has been perfected for this condition. Although Garcia could not speak English well at all, the barrier of the language in his case, as in that of many others, had acted only as an osmotic membrane: the words had not gone through, but the fundamental ideas and feelings had, and he was suffering from an Anglo-Saxon psychosis. The Moor concluded, with his habit of generalization, that every new language one learns, or every new environment one joins, stimulates new centers of the mind and new emotions, creates new associations of ideas, new viewpoints, and therefore produces an additional psychosis.

Nevertheless, I hoped for a chance meeting which could be brought about accidentally on purpose. This would create a scene that was sure to delight Garcia, if I knew him as I thought I did, and once in an unguarded moment while passing the time with the Moor, I suggested that we go down to the Bowery where at the moment it appeared the most natural thing in the world that we should run into Garcia. The Moor, who liked to encourage all such absurdities and acts of illogical futility, agreed readily. We were luxuriously transported in his dark Hispano-Suiza as far as Cooper Square, where we left it. Then, fortified with some ale drunk from china mugs at a very old barroom on a side street that deserved the Moor's endorsement and with true Spartan resolution, we walked the whole length of the Bowery as far as the Manhattan Bridge and, of course, never met Garcia. We met several bodies on the sidewalk and in doorways but only examined closely two of them because of the long white hair. The second of the two was in a particularly dark spot and I walked around him bending and peering without being absolutely sure because his face was hidden in his arms. Finally the Moor grew impatient and told me to turn him over, that he would not mind, but to be careful not to hold the match too close to him—the usual sally. I felt sure that the Moor knew readily how to find Garcia if he had wanted to, but he was letting me be the victim of my own folly. We walked on and ended drinking doubleheaders of unashamed bar whiskey at Chatham Square in a bar where the Moor and the bartender appeared to be bosom friends. The Moor gave him tickets for his broadcast.

Those drinks made us hungry and the Moor took me to a Chinese place on Pell Street where we found the Señor Olózaga at a table talking to the owner of the place in his native language. This was one more piece in the jigsaw puzzle picture I had of him. He greeted us affably and we sat at the same table. They immediately began to speak Spanish. The owner of the place, who seemed to know the Moor quite well, spoke it fluently but with the same padded silkiness as the Señor Olózaga. The Moor did not seem at all surprised to find the Chink, as he called him, there and the vague feeling I had had since the beginning of that evening began to take concrete shape in terms of a cat playing with a mouse, just for the fun of it.

While the Moor and I disposed of a dinner for four, the conversation around the table might as well have been in Chinese for all I understood of it. They spoke in mock mysterious sentences, a frequent habit with the Moor but which seemed contagious on that occasion, and I suspected that I was being the subject of some kind of mild practical joke that concerned my quest for Garcia, particularly when the Moor said something about Spanish gestures and the national system. I felt distinctly outclassed and to regain my poise, drank considerably of some exotic wine that the Señor Olózaga was planning to market and which he praised lavishly both by word of mouth and elbow action. Everything was very polite and tranquil and the dream-like quality that had palled the whole evening like a fog became denser and soothing so that when we left the place, I was not surprised to find the fateful Hispano-Suiza with the Cuban boy all smiles waiting to drive us home. I did not care whether I had been foolish in looking for Garcia, but on being dropped in style at my very door, decided not to look for him again.

Enough time passed after that for spring to arrive.

Then, one day I was in that section where the quiet, though gradually surrendering dignity of Brooklyn Heights is ignominiously crowded by commercialism down a steep hill to meet the lugubrious Furman ravine at the foot of Fulton Street, when I saw Garcia, the fallen bard, as he would have put it, and he was truly a bad sight. He was lying near the curb in front of a bar which might have seen younger if not better days, and he was in a state of complete inebriation: his clothes dusty and torn, his face blackened by soot and unshaven, a patch of caked blood matting his white hair. It was the regulation uniform and he would have passed the inspection of the king of bums with flying colors. He was the wounded soldier of misfortune and paladin of the scum. Next to him, and but one shade less of miserable glory, was another fellow, still upright from the waist up, who kept on shaking Garcia with that characteristic truculent yet affectionate persistence, calling to him to "get up, you . . ." followed by some foul epithet. There was a dog nosing about Garcia. Probably belonged to the other man.

Garcia only rolled from one side to another and groaned his contemptuous disregard for the whole damn respectable world, while the man continued to push and pull ineffectually. There was something about the man and the animal, the suggestion of the loyal watchdog, something in this sinister scene, in the common bond of degradation uniting two outcasts, that sent a wave of pity through me that washed all revulsion away. Even at this point, Garcia, who had always aroused the protective instinct in anyone who knew him, had found someone to sit by him and try to pull him up to his slightly higher level of indignity.

I rushed to Garcia and managed to bring him up to a sitting position, but his head rolled and if he recognized me, he may not have been able to distinguish the situation from a dream. The other man smiled his cockeyed recognition of our mutual interest and patted Garcia on the back with a manner that said: "Good boy—good boy—"

Talking to Garcia and trying to make him understand was a useless task and I did not know how to take him in his condition to better surroundings, so, as usual under the circumstances, I thought of Dr. de los Rios and decided to call him up and ask him to come down and help me.

I left Garcia to the thankless ministrations of his companion and entered the barroom and there put a call to de los Rios. This was his hour of consultation, but nevertheless he said that he would be right down and to stand by Garcia, so I sat at the bar from where I could watch him, feeling quite confident that he would not run away and that the indifference of the city would let him lie there where he was, and ordered a drink and then another while waiting, and although Dr. de los Rios arrived with miraculous speed, I was feeling pretty good myself by the time he arrived. He stopped the car right in front of Garcia, and when I came out to meet him, he was already by his side. I lent him a hand and between the two of us we got him to his feet. Then despite his groans and protests, we propelled him forward and into the car. Garcia drooped in the back seat like a sack of flour. Before taking his seat, de los Rios looked around and what I saw in his face, I could not describe.

This whole thing had made me forget what I had come to this neighborhood for, and I went along for the ride and to see whether I could be of some help. I wanted to be near Garcia as much as possible after not seeing him for such a long time. We crossed over the bridge and then rode up to de los Rios's house. There he called an attendant and I decided that I was not needed and took my leave.

A few days after this incident Garcia arrived at my place looking like a new man: new clothes, clean shaven, well-combed silky white mane and, although he had never been the picture of health, he looked much better than I had ever seen him. He made no reference to the past happenings, and even though I had not seen him for about a year, since our last recent meeting did not count, he tried to act as if we had been together the day before and nothing had happened. He was the least bit shy and I could not help quoting from Fray Luis de León: "As we were saying yesterday—"

He gave me a smile and then said that he wanted to gather his papers and things and that he had already imposed enough on me. I showed him where they were piled up and he began to rummage among them, and then I said that the occasion called for a drink and went to fix a couple, but he was too absorbed in his work and I don't think he heard me. I handed him his drink and he took a sip absently, set it down on the desk and promptly forgot all about it. This was the old Garcia. He was drinking again like a Spaniard.

He was holding some papers in his hand and there was the enthusiasm of the inveterate writer in his face. He said that he had to get busy and work on his stories. The past experiences he considered, I am sure, a contribution to furnishing what he would operatically call his nest of memories, and he was raring to go. I could already see myself involved with translations and manuscripts and subject to litanical readings. He certainly was the same old Garcia. One can't keep a good man down.

During the days that followed, Garcia busied himself with his writings and in particular with the second part of his novel about the family, and at that time he had not finished the first part yet to my knowledge, for he did not read the end of it to me until sometime later following a meal at the Bejaranos' which the Moor prepared and I have recorded already. But this was the way he worked. He assaulted a story from every angle at the same time; it was a general offensive all along the front. Where a sector yielded, his forces concentrated on the attack. If a particular section of his work suited the mood of his inspiration, he labored on that, finished with it and then lay it aside to be fitted subsequently in its proper place—well, not always.

This may serve as a justification for the disorder I have allowed to invade my narrative. In order to preserve the sequence of Garcia's stories, I have sacrificed my own. It is a good excuse anyway.

One of the first things Garcia completed was the draft for his moving picture story and immediately began to cast his eye around for someone who could make a scenario from it and to pester me with entreaties to make at least a rough translation. He wanted to ascertain up to what point I remembered the story and I told him that during his absence I had reread many of his writings because having no one to loaf with, I had more time to myself, and then he reproached me for not having translated some of his work with all that time on my hands, but I countered that one could not embark on a task like that without even knowing whether one was ever going to finish it.

"You should know better than that," he said acidly. "Now sit tight because you are going to listen to the end of the moving picture story and after that you are going to get busy with the translation."

If he had changed at all, it had been for the worse, but even so, having Garcia back was good. I had really missed him, and realizing that everything has its price, I listened:

He found himself living in Chelsea and, to all appearances, quite prosperous. He had fleeting recollections of arguments and more arguments with Jenny and of having a Charlie held up before him as a paragon of practical success. Then blanks and more blanks and more brief visions of working and again scheming and eventually owning the company for which he worked and of Jenny always coaxing, goading him with relentless ambition.

Those were hectic days of his rise to prosperity. He was associated with Charlie, an association born from a contract which he never remembered having signed, but now Ramos never bothered to question his past actions. He had found himself during his life with so many things, in so many positions which he could not explain, that scarcely anything surprised him anymore. Besides, with time, Charlie had grown softer, he was no longer the potential and never-proven forcible character he had been assumed to be, and he was now in the subordinate role. Ramos had proven the stronger of the two by a wide margin, almost a revengeful margin.

He and Jenny had then a short and belated honeymoon trip. She had insisted on arranging it even as she had insisted on delaying it. All he remembered from it was a vertiginous amount of water falling before his astonished eyes with a deafening roar.

Upon his return he had to face a delegation of South American business-men who, in a tumultuous meeting, accused him of monopolizing the Latin American market, flooding it with American products. They spoke of unethical business methods. One of them was particularly offensive. He threatened cutthroat competition, a formidable boycott:

"My group is large. We shall fight you with your own weapons. We will fight you for years if necessary. You will have to give in."

"You think?" queried Ramos, already in the grip of impatience.

"I know. You will give in. You cannot afford to wait that long."

Ramos knew the man was right, that this would be a long, wearisome war, intolerably long. The tone of the man's voice, its challenge, irritated him beyond proportion. He could not wait. He forgot himself. With fists pushing against the conference table, he rose, he closed his eyes.

The noisy voices subsided, the irate Spanish words turned to polite English words. Julio opened his eyes. He stood at the head of the same table, or one very much like it, and he was bringing to a close a very successful conference with a group of American bankers in which a very profitable loan for all concerned had been negotiated with a Latin American republic.

He remembered then portentous days in Wall Street, unnecessary days of trouble, of multitudes of people losing all they owned, of absurd panic, and from all this turbulent crisis he had been one of the few who had emerged successful. He saw like one sees from a fast-moving train his financial position extending to cover other fields, his business connections growing to a dominant position.

When the bankers filed out majestically, Ramos sat down again and regarded the span of the long empty table before him. He sat that way alone in the conference room for a long time and finally came to with a start. This time he had skipped a long time, he had cast a handful of years aside, a good handful. He could not go on like this or death would be upon him in no time at all. What if he should close his eyes, never to open them again? He rose slowly and leaned on the table. The glass top sent back his reflection, clear enough to show deep changes. It seemed like only yesterday that he had seen it like this in the mirror of the old pensión.

"Listen, Garcia," I interrupted. "With scenes like the ones you describe, it ought to be a cinch and you will not have to bother about a scenario. They probably have made them thousands of times and all they would have to do is to clip them off old pictures. You have it down pat."

Instead of being annoyed, Garcia was delighted: "That's fine, fine. I might go over the whole thing in the light of what you say—easier to find a producer. Cheaper, you know?"

I knew I couldn't win and let him read on:

He had to put a stop to this. He had to take life calmly now, take care of himself, his time, be quiet, be patient. That was it: be patient, and he continued to repeat this as he left.

He had the chauffeur drive his limousine slowly even for those days. They rode up Broadway. He surveyed the passing scenes with contented close attention and repose and was aware of the immensity of the changes in town. For several years he had seen in a few passing glances the whole city change before his very eyes. He had walked in a serene avenue to be brutally awakened by the roar of the elevated train overhead where there had been nothing between one's eyes and the sky. He had opened his eyes to find himself rushing through what he knew was the road to infernal regions in the tunnels of the subway. He had looked skywards to stare at cruising airplanes and had seen enormous buildings appear where slums had stood a few moments before, and what is more, he had seen world events parade in the same absurd and disconnected manner, without cause, without effect.

He would never skip time again. He had to be patient.

At 23rd Street the car continued along Fifth Avenue. He was not surprised at the new direction taken. He was ready for anything. All the way to the Sixties he continued to contemplate things with peaceful curiosity, as if he were seeing them for the first time or perhaps for the last, and he kept repeating that he had to be patient, to nurse time.

He was still repeating this when he arrived at his residence, a splendid, sumptuous building facing the park. He let himself in quietly and although he never remembered having seen the place before, his muscles, his senses seemed to recognize things, to guide him. He ascended the stairs, his epidermis calling out for a warm bath. His body knew there was a luxurious and restful bathroom in this strange palace. That was all that mattered for the moment.

As he passed Jenny's room he heard conversation inside. He recognized Charlie's voice and her eternal laughter. The door was sufficiently ajar, but the hall was dark and the floor carpeted. He could neither be seen nor heard, but in turn he saw and heard enough to confirm a suspicion whose roots seemed to lay in one of his dark moments.

For a few moments he stood still, chilled through. Like precipitous torrents coming from distant, forgotten sources, his old traditions, instincts and prejudices converged to feed and agitate the wide stream of his turbulent rage. They rose from the rocking ground, twining themselves about him, to reach his head and burst in it. How much of this had gone on during those unknowing moments? How much shame had he skipped with time? For this men killed, his mind repeated, eroding his soul.

But one had to be cool. He would obtain all the proofs. He turned and silently went downstairs, his head held high as if literally endeavoring to keep it clear from a mounting sewer. He entered his drawing room and walked instinctively toward the windows, to seek light and air. He lifted one window gently to avoid making noise. The bars on the outside irritated him. He recalled having them placed there under the pretext of an added protection, but truly because they reminded him of the windows in Valencia, and now they irritated him, he did not know why.

He had to compose himself, he had to think cleverly, to spy on them. His hands closed on the window bars, yearning for their throats, his hatred burned his chest, his breath hissed spasmodically through dilated nostrils. He heard her laughter again through the window, pouring out his dishonor. His teeth appeared. He hated them! He had to stop them now! It was impossible to wait, to reason. No! He could not wait. His hands tightened on the bars, he shut his eyes. God! For this men killed—

Coolness descended upon him and he heard isochronous steps upon a hard floor. He opened his eyes. He was holding on to the bars of his prison cell door. A guard was walking along the corridor in front of the cells.

Ramos had been leaning against the back of his chair while talking. The room was quite dark except for some light from a street lamp coming through the window and illuminating mostly the ceiling with a reddish light, but in the corner where Ramos stood, it was dark. He felt his way around the chair and sat down once more:

"And that was the time I regretted least having that power. For once I had encountered the often-dreaded pitfall awaiting my mad unconscious rush and had fallen in it, but I did not regret it. That time my recollections of the period erased were more and clearer. With time I have acquired gradually a greater capacity to recall those moments, to bring out things from my subconscious. I remembered quite clearly the scandal covering front pages in the newspapers. I remember also much of the trial. I had money and influence and hired the best defense counsel that could be had. He was a brilliant man, that lawyer. In the end he got me off with a comparatively short sentence, but it did not make any difference." Again I heard his laborious breathing.

"But I must not hold you here any longer. You must go back to your Sociedad." He noticed my expectancy: "No, there is nothing more. After I regained freedom I saw the downgrade of my life extending ahead uninterrupted, but even had life held something for me, I had nothing for life. Yet, I had no impatience, I knew that I was finished and kept going with the dying momentum like the hair, like the nails that grow on a corpse. I was only mildly curious. I wanted to see my life a few days before the end and I took a long chance, the longest and safest in my life. I could not lose— And here I am. Now I know the wait will not be long. It does not matter, you see? That is why your Sociedad must not bother with me. I need no help or charity now. I have all that counts now: memories. I am living over now all the moments of my life through which I passed unconsciously. They are all coming back now, emerging from the shadows with tremendous power, clear, dazzling, some horrible and some magnificent. I am sitting and resting, waiting, living and being conscious of every moment of this last and short wait."

I knew that anything I could say was superfluous. This was final. I tiptoed out of the room shutting the door noiselessly behind and, unable to turn away from it, held on to the old banister and thus descended those dark stairs backwards, hypnotized, eyes fixed where that door should be that could not be seen.

I was on Cherry Street once more and walked away slowly, the feeling of depression increasing with every step, and suddenly I could stand it no more. I wanted to go home and almost broke into a run. Hailing a passing cab, I plunged in shouting my address. I sat tensely on the edge of the seat and in my desire to be home, shut my eyes and pounded my knees with my clenched fists.

A sudden screech of brakes and a swerve caused me to open them. The cab was standing in front of my house, and the driver was speaking to me over his shoulder and saying that it was a pretty narrow escape we had had back there.

When Garcia finished, he walked to the desk, gathered what he had read with the rest of his story and placed it in a large envelope. "It's all yours," he said, sending it spinning across the room to me.

Also during those days Garcia gave me several cursory descriptions of the second part of his novel, particularly the beginning. Concretely, he was not decided on how to open the second part, but he favored a family gathering that would permit him to show the younger generation of the Sandovals, with comments he expected to be of deep social significance regarding the new generation after the war of 1914 and also considerations regarding the older set of the family and the changes which time had wrought on each. The profound social comments had not yet materialized in black and white but that did not efface Garcia's literary optimism. He also hoped to expound a theory to the effect that the nineteenth century had not really ended with the year 1900 but with the First World War. All these ambitious philosophical plans must have gotten sidetracked in his subsequent attempts, because I never found them in what he read or made me read or, if they were implied somewhere, I did not notice them.

Garcia finally settled on opening with a family gathering which, besides being a well-tried method, would permit his character studies of the members of the family and would present as the central figure the heroine of the second part of his story, who was Rojelia, the oldest daughter of Fernando and Trini Sandoval. He was all set on making it a musical soiree where the heroine played the harp, one of the accomplishments of this girl whom he wanted to describe as beautiful, proud and talented as well as discreet with lofty ideals that contrasted with the rest of her family. Also this he expected would give him an opportunity to discuss music.

Garcia had become interested in music through his association with the Moor, but his knowledge of it was sadly inadequate and he contented himself with saying very modestly that he simply liked good music. He was confident that he could get all the necessary information and facts from the Moor.

I told him that he knew the Moor disapproved of his literary activities and that perhaps he had better consult someone else.

"I know, but I will have to swallow my pride and spruce up my patience. The Moor can be approached. I can tell him, for instance, that I want to write about music but that I don't know what it's all about, get it? That will win him over."

I winked my assent: "That's the boy! You tell him that. The Moor is after all a good scout even if he—knows it."

This encouraged Garcia, if he had needed it, to begin to read from his notes. There was a platitudinous character and physical portrayal of the heroine and a sketch of the mental vacuity of the two younger members, Jorge and his sister Lolita. It was a standard description that could have fitted any other contemporary youths. I told Garcia this but he stated that generalization of characters, making them universal, was one of the acknowledged virtues of great literature, so I let that pass and he read a description of Trini where she appeared considerably refined by maturity, a thing which was reflected by the more tasteful decorations of the house and probably tied in with the musical soiree on which the Moor was to collaborate with his learned advice. What had been once in the woman plain vulgarity was now an earthy exuberance with suggestions of nature's nobleman, breaking at times like a geyser through the shell of acquired culture and ripe composure which held it in precarious check. Her voice had also remained a deep, rich, heartwarming contralto. These are, of course, Garcia's own words.

He took less kindly to Fernando Sandoval. His description in this, the second part of the story, came down to that of a weakling and neurotic, but Garcia elaborated at length on the psychological and pathological aspects. He had a weakness for this sort of thing. I said that he should not commit himself in writing about things he knew so little about, but he insisted that he knew more than I gave him credit for and that anyway he would enlist the advice of Dr. de los Rios. This, I argued, was foolish, as his knowledge of de los Rios should make plain to him. The good doctor would be glad to help him in any serious problem which concerned his person, but he would never indulge such a waste of time and attempt to teach him in one easy lesson what he had accumulated in a lifetime of studies. He might tell him to read up on the subject, and even allow him to attend some of his lectures, and all this would take too long for impatient Garcia, but more probably, he would tell him to forget the whole thing or he might have a relapse and wind up once more on the Bowery.

This made Garcia laugh and he said that there was no danger of that. He had wanted an experience and he had had it and that was enough for him. Instead he was going to work earnestly, and to prove this he went on to read a section which dealt with the oldest son of the Sandovals:

Enrique Sandoval was a tall, thin boy, the darkness of his complexion nearing a sinister shade. There were decided contrasts among the members of the younger Sandoval generation.

Enrique had an aquiline nose, sharp features, sunken eyes, very thick eyebrows and very black hair.

His intelligence was very limited. Compelled by his father, he had with great difficulty studied a business career, although as a child he had wanted to be a general of artillery and later a physician. His father, however, thought better of a business career and Enrique took it up. He took the examinations twice and the second time he managed to come through. He then graduated to his father's shop to help him, gain experience, and complicate matters.

He did not seem to profit much by his education. The pursuit of pleasure was the sole object of his existence, whether at a gambling table, a café or in bed.

His somewhat warped nature was first encouraged when still a child by the maids of the house, who in more ways than one were responsible for his later development. From a very early age he showed a marked degree of discrimination about being punished. When his father did it, he showed very plainly that he did not like it, but if it happened to be his mother or one of the maids, he did not appear to mind it much but rather taunt them into it.

As a matter of fact, at the age of four or five, he was in the habit of going into the kitchen and addressing a husky washerwoman, after ascertaining that no one else was around:

"Spank baby," he beseeched her and presented his buttocks with all the meekness of a monk before an irate abbot. He had developed a predilection for being spanked, particularly by the husky washerwoman.

She would spank him once and then send him away: "Go on, you little—" she would say wonderingly. "And don't come back in five minutes and make me waste time. One of these days I am going to spank you real hard and then you won't like it so well."

"I wish you would. You never spank me hard enough."

The description was built up out of several other such foolish incidents, then a cursory description of a life of excesses which in the end turned the boy into a full-fledged victim of epilepsy. I suggested to Garcia that he check up on his facts. He acknowledged my remark with a nod of his head without stopping:

It was soon after he began to work at the jewelry shop that he made the acquaintance of a certain girl who exhausted both his scanty vitality and abundant money and soon made a worse case of him. He was absent from the store for days at a time, burying himself in the room she kept on the Street of Jacometrezo, there to smother his epileptic attacks in her arms.

When he showed up at home, he was haggard, his eyes were more sunken than ever and he looked like a corpse. Then his mother would flare out in a fusillade against the girl:

"Look at him! See how he comes! That cheap *puta* is killing him. He could get better ones for one peseta, but who knows what she is doing to him. A boy in his condition! She is killing him."

"Don't talk that way before the girls, Trini. And please let me handle this, will you?" Fernando shouted.

"But look at him!" And then shaking Enrique by the lapels as if he were a rag: "What do you think you are? You are not even half a man. You can't stand that life. You haven't the physique for it. She will finish you like any other woman would and then throw you aside. Tell me, what is she doing to you?"

Then Enrique lost his temper: "Leave me alone. I tell you to leave me alone. I am not a child anymore and I suppose that I can take care of myself. You are driving me crazy with your constant bickering. I am going to leave this accursed house someday and never return." He went into a frenzy and collapsed on a sofa, sobbing and cursing.

"Trini! I tell you to let me handle this. Who is master in this house? Or are we all going crazy too?"

Fernando's handling of the situation only served to make things worse. He limited himself to an avalanche of insults and oaths, offering as pitiful a spectacle as his son, if not more so.

"Is that the way you are dragging our name through the streets with that prostitute?"

"I don't allow any man to call my woman a prostitute, do you hear?"

"And damn it! I don't allow any son of mine to get cocky with me. If you want to settle this matter as man to man, you can forget that I am your father, but remember that I am as much of a male as the next one."

Trini could restrain herself no longer and joined in. This was too much to miss: "Now you are going off the main track, Fernando, and losing your authority."

"You keep out of this. Does he think he is going to scare me?"

"No, I won't keep out. I am his mother and I also have a right."

"I am telling you to keep out."

"Who do you think you are? You are as bad as he, boasting of manliness! I would like to see you before a real man. If the boy is that way, it is because he takes after you."

"What do you mean? Let me tell you that my pants are well placed, very well placed, and the only way he takes after me is in having taken a street woman seriously."

Then the fight became general. Lolita and Jorge joined in, Trini shouted and Enrique went into convulsions.

"What do you think you are?"

"Who is master in this house?"

"He is going to die!"

"My pants are well placed!"

"You are not even half a man."

"We are all going crazy."

"Help, help!"

It ended as usual in ridiculous noise, the neighbors listening and people gathering in the street below. Enrique was carried to bed in a fit and the doctor was summoned. The only one who kept out of it was Rojelia. As soon as one of these quarrels began, she locked herself in her room.

I stopped Garcia to ask him whether he had nothing to say at the opening of this second part regarding good old Ledesma, the administrator of the Sandovals' interests, but Garcia dismissed him summarily by saying that he had not changed; he was still the same good old Ledesma. I insisted that the fellow deserved a little more attention and recognition and that he, Garcia, was in fact teaming up with the rest of his Sandovals in disregarding this fellow's many virtues and displaying ingratitude for his long and faithful services.

"Never mind," Garcia said impatiently. "I tell you the man did not change, he let me down. What can I do? And since you are so interested, let me inform you that I have a note somewhere about showing him asleep in an easy chair during that musical soiree I mentioned and then he wakes up when it is all over and I comment that he looked the same but older, and someone asks him whether he has enjoyed his after-dinner nap and he says yes, that he enjoys dreaming, brings back the past, lets him forget the present—memories, you know what I mean." Garcia fumbled among his papers and came up with one: "See? I even expected to philosophize on the subject and had taken this down:"

As one grows older, one prefers what has been, scarcely tolerates what is and decidedly abhors what is going to be. The greatest virtue of a thing, then, is that it has passed, the greatest defect, that it is yet to come. In one's opinion things are bad and are growing constantly worse. Every coming event means certain disaster. Among the things that are going to be, the vision of one's own death looms as the most execrable, tainting the horizon with the most somber and depressing hues. One sees every future event through these funereal shadows, everything appears wrapped in ominous clouds of pessimism, whether it be social changes, new ideas or even the smallest change of routine. One dislikes everything modern, everything new, including young people, because all these things represent the flow of time, because everything that enters this world is taking the place of something that is leaving it. One becomes a conservative and wants things to stay as they are because perhaps thus one will stay as one is. All because the future harbors one's death, man's most implacable enemy of which one only becomes emotionally aware with maturity. One lives on memories because one does not dare look at such a dismal future . . .

My hand went up in an instinctive gesture of self-preservation: "All right, all right, I have had enough."

"There is more to it, but I think this will hold you. Are you satisfied? Now let me go on with this."

In the part that followed, Garcia's story introduced the first serious love of his heroine, but I will let him do it himself:

One afternoon, she was out on her balcony when she saw a young man crossing La Puerta del Sol.

He had all the ease and dash of an individual who shares not one single binding convention with the rest of the world, an air which, as everyone knows, commands sincere admiration.

He stopped in the middle of the street and looked up at her openly, the light shining upon his unique features, his black hat to one side, one end of his long bow tie blown by the wind over his shoulder. No character in romantic literature could do better.

Rojelia tried to look away but his fascination held her. He remained there looking up until a car that had been forced to stop almost on top of him began to honk its horn.

Rojelia smiled. Then he calmly stepped onto the sidewalk and removed his hat with an ostentatious bow.

Rojelia realized it was time to go in, but all that evening and even that night, she thought of the young man with his black loose clothes and that life-defying air, so different from the stiff, pattern-cut gentlemen dipped in brilliantine that she often met.

Garcia had cast this leading man in a role and atmosphere shamelessly suggested by *La Bohème*. He lived of course in an attic, with illusory Spartan paucity of material possessions: wooden cot, working table—where the word "working" is given a very special and flattering meaning—shelves for books of course, fireplace and the irresistible added touch of a cage with a canary. A nightingale would have been more suggestive of the role of a poet, but perhaps Garcia realized that he could carry things only so far and settled for the canary.

The portera of the house, a devoted admirer of Urcola—that was the name—was responsible for the white linen, occasional flowers and the well-fed bird. She had a pale daughter who wore spectacles, read romantic novels and always looked at Urcola with the eyes of a beheaded lamb, as they say. The more one saw of Garcia's production, the more one suspected that many of his ideas had been developed abroad and he had forgotten much of the Spain he knew. But again I will let him take over:

One day Urcola came down from his attic in excellent spirits. All morning one could have heard him whistling as if in competition with the canary. That was the day after he had seen the wonderful woman on a balcony at La Puerta del Sol. That night he had composed a poem dedicated to her entitled "La del cabello rojo," meaning the one with the red hair, and he was quite satisfied with it.

At the door he met the daughter of the portera: "Good morning, bard. I see you are happy as the birds in the spring, singing to life and nature."

Urcola assumed an afflicted aspect. The girl produced a piece of paper and her eyes were cast down, exactly upon his worn-out shoes. He bent his knees so that his trousers would cover more of them.

"This is my first poem and I want you to be the first one to read it and tell me what you think of it."

Urcola, standing as he was, looked like a man about to spring upon his victim. He took the paper instead and read its contents:

"Hmm— If I were you I would not write poetry but help my mother around the portería. And by the way, my dear Sappho, don't call me 'bard' anymore, will you do me that favor? I resent it. It is embarrassing, as if I called you Saint Peter simply because you are always at the door."

The girl dragged herself dejectedly into the portería.

But the poetry of Urcola had filtered into the daughter of the portera; it took root in her and sprouted so convincingly several months after that Urcola and two ferocious brothers of the portera, not having ever expected the girl to take him so seriously, decided it was high time to do something. Yet, this is getting ahead of time.

Garcia went back to describe the relations of his heroine and the poet, their clandestine meetings, carefully arranged with the complicity of her personal maid. The only thing he had worked out in this section was a dialogue in Madrid vernacular between Urcola and the maid when he gave her his first letter to his beloved. Garcia was quite enthusiastic about the typical words and phrases he had collected in that dialogue but I argued that it could not be put successfully into English, and its virtues, if virtues they were, should be lost in a translation. Strangely enough, Garcia could not see the point and insisted that English also has a vernacular and therefore the thing he proposed should not be so difficult. We argued back and forth. He was stuck on his piece of dialogue, proud of it, and probably for that reason he could not see the absurdity of his stand. Then he also wanted to introduce a scene where the heroine, Rojelia, whom he had described as a fine musician, put some poems that her lover had sent her to music and sang them from the music room with windows wide open so that he stood in the street and listened to them. Considering that her windows faced the Puerta del Sol, with so many people and so much noise, this serenade in reverse was insane. Garcia said that he had intended this for foreign consumption but I quoted our saying that there are no more Indians in America and this time he saw the point.

A few days after that we were sitting in the park with nothing to do and I was in a good mood because it was something we had not done for quite some time. It was the good old days all over again. Garcia passed me a stack of papers which I had learned to recognize even without looking at them. He said this was a section he had almost ready for the final copy. I read it:

Tonight is a great night. The whole of the Sandoval country residence outside Madrid is ablaze with gaiety.

Cheer long! Cheer loud! It is Rojelia's birthday and she is the most beautiful maiden in Madrid.

A big costume ball is taking place. The garden in front of the house is brilliantly illuminated with lanterns, like a verbena. They hang from the trees and from garlands of flowers. There is a long table at one side with many candles and heaped with exquisite foods and rows of bottles with delightful wines, the whole table strewn with fresh dewy petals.

Even the moon and the stars look on with envy and have come closer, wanting also to participate in the amusements and congratulate the happy girl. What a magnificent fair! What a wonderful summer night!

Cheer loud! Cheer long! It is Rojelia's birthday and she is the most beautiful maiden of the region.

The máscaras are arriving in luxurious carriages drawn by fine horses, and they fill the garden. There are young and gay Pierrots and Columbines and mischievous Harlequins and old serious Polichinelas and sullen Dominoes. Most of the famous characters in history are also assembled there, and even heaven and hell are represented by angels of indefinite sex and fearful red devils. The whole world has come to rejoice and wish Rojelia a happy birthday.

Fernando and Trini are dressed as two members of the Borgia family. Jorge appears as a clown and Lolita displays her substantial limbs in the tights of a page's costume.

There is a little theater at the other side of the garden where a pantomime will be presented, and it is also gaily illuminated. Everybody talks and laughs and all eyes glitter and scintillate behind black masks. The pale bluish light from the moon and the warm light from the lanterns make a fascinating contrast and create fantastic effects. What a night!

Cheer loud! Cheer long! It is Rojelia's birthday and she is the most beautiful maiden in Spain.

Rojelia comes out of the house to greet her friends and all are taken aback by her splendid beauty. She wears a white pompadour costume and carries a tremendous white fan, but she wears not the wig and her red hair flames like a bonfire in the night.

How many men would gladly jump into the crater of burning passions that woman must conceal! But perhaps this is only the glamour of the night when one dreams infernal fantasies which fade with dawn.

A clown tinkling with bells approaches Rojelia, makes a deep bow and, saying a funny rhyme, stumbles purposely and everybody laughs. Then a melancholy Pierrot kneels before her and sings her praise, fingering a lute, and an old Polichinela kisses her hand and pays her a compliment showing that his heart has not cooled with the years or else has revived in the proximity of her glowing womanhood. A jumping devil then tells her that a look from her eyes has redeemed him, and a colorless angel exclaims in heavenly transport that if fire in hell is like her hair, he will gladly seek eternal condemnation.

The whole world is at her feet in admiration. There are Nero and Julius Caesar, the Great Captain, Columbus and Napoleon, to say nothing of half a dozen other kings and emperors, all wanting to be nearest her.

But no one commands more than her polite attention. All these great figures with their historical background, glory, titles and power cannot move her. They are only máscaras, colorful, empty rags that live while the wind blows on them, that shine only for a night.

Who will attain this magnificent woman? Who will pass over her unyielding feelings, breaking them loose like a squall? Only one being can arouse her and cause her deep emotions to fall at his feet like the petals of a flower, one by one. Only one man of flesh and bone, only her lover. Only for one are all her thoughts, only for one is all her beauty, only for one she lives tonight, only for one. For that free poet who belongs to no time, for that eternal poet who knows no law, who with a burning hand has reached and crushed her heart, who has caressed her soul with melodious words, luminous and perfumed words like flowers at dusk.

Cheer loud! Cheer long! It is Rojelia's birthday and she is the most beautiful maiden in Spain.

She is twice as beautiful tonight, because it is her birthday and she is happy to live. She is happy to live because she is in love and that makes her three times as beautiful. Her poet is coming in disguise, under cover of the night, and she alone knows it. He is coming to tell her how he blesses the day that she was born.

Everyone is growing happier and noisier. The abundant libations have kindled a flame in every heart. They all sing and dance madly. The men have grown bolder and their faces glow like the faces of satyrs. The maidens are no longer afraid and are generous with their favors, and the garden blazes in the pagan night.

Cheer long! Cheer loud! It is Rojelia's birthday and she is the most beautiful maiden in Spain.

Lolita appeared on the stage. She had exchanged her page's costume for a bright shawl which she draped about her semi-naked figure and had taken a pair of castanets. The small orchestra played seguidillas for her and Lolita began to dance.

She undulated slowly, rhythmically, and moved from one side of the stage to the other like a wave. Her castanets rattled evenly and smoothly, fading like a distant echo and then increasing like the approaching drums of a conquering army.

The shawl opened up about her like the cloak of a torero, exposing her exorbitant limbs, or closed about her displaying curves that caused one's heart to sink. Her black hair brushed her face in which the red full lips glowed with maddening lust. The men looked at her and their nostrils dilated and their eyes grew dull.

Jorge was standing in a dark corner of the garden and a girl dressed as an infanta clung to his arm, but he did not notice her. He was looking at Lolita with a strange expression in his eyes and his breath was coming fast.

The infanta said: "You should not look at your sister that way."

"I like the way she dances."

Oh dusky and voluptuous Lolita! How far will you go? Poisoning feelings and trampling instincts, awakening things which if latent had better be left undisclosed. But you arouse the most dangerous emotions. You lure them to the surface and they emerge gaping, appealing, like hungry sharks in the sea. Do you not fear, Lolita? Do you not think it is wiser to stop?

But Lolita went on in the mad swirl of her dance. She knew what she was arousing and enjoyed it with infernal delight, with thirsty curiosity. Oh tempting, perverse Lolita! She danced like a witch in a Saturday's dream. Jorge looked as if held in a spell; he looked and he sank in her abyss; he looked and was burnt in her hell.

But perhaps these are but deceiving fantasies of the moment. What a night!

Cheer long! Cheer loud! It is Rojelia's birthday and she is the most beautiful maiden in Spain.

They are playing the pantomime in the little theater, but no one pays much attention to it and least of all Rojelia. She is thinking of her poet, who at this moment is probably jumping the back fence and with his face hidden by a mask will mix with the others unnoticed and tease her by letting her guess which one he is. Rojelia is so distracted scrutinizing every máscara that they have to fetch her when her number is called.

Rojelia was on the stage. She was singing a beautiful song and playing the harp and now they all realized how beautiful her voice was. On that stage she looked like something that does not belong in this world. The men looked at her and their brows grew smooth and they became peaceful. The women looked at her speculatively and pressed their men's arms. And she sang wonderfully because she was singing for him.

Suddenly a potent voice answered her song, a deep, rich voice. They all beheld the svelte and somber figure of Mephistopheles with a black mask, coming from nowhere as if he had emerged from the ground.

Who was this unexpected visitor from the infernal regions? Who was this intruder who had cast a spell of surprise upon the audience with something that was not in the program?

Like a dark cloud, the stranger had invaded the small stage where Rojelia sat, almost covering it with his great black cloak. He continued to sing beautiful verses with a powerful voice and Rojelia, entranced, accompanied him on the harp.

Kneeling before her with his weird horns, he was the devil himself tempting an angel.

Rojelia was pale and trembling. She had recognized in that sinister figure her lover, her poet, the undaunted conqueror of all conventions who broke all laws and came to her ruled by love only, who came like a hurricane of fresh and youthful romance, to enthrall her and to mock the stupefied audience, to frighten that historical and fantastic array of masqueraders without reality.

Everyone was afraid but his voice was so entrancing and his verses so delicate that all were held in ecstasy, and Rojelia played mechanically but she played more melodiously than ever.

Indeed it was Mephistopheles, who lured mortals with honeyed words and then poisoned their souls.

The curtain came down among a soft murmur of admiration. It had been a magnificent and unexpected performance and when the curtain went up again, he was not there, he had vanished as he had come, and Rojelia had also gone.

Then they were no longer afraid. It had all been a hallucination, it was the intoxication of the wine and the wonderful summer night, and they all laughed and applauded with delight. It had been a grand jest. Even Mephistopheles had been reincarnated that night of nights for the benefit of Rojelia and no one was surprised at her disappearance from the stage. They all laughed and applauded madly.

Cheer loud! Cheer long! It is Rojelia's birthday and she is the most beautiful maiden in Spain.

Enrique was dressed as Charles V in a gleaming red costume. It fitted him beautifully, but he had danced so much that it had become disarranged and one of his garters had burst. He decided to go to his room to fix it, but as there were so many people around the front entrance and he was vain, he chose to use the back door.

He had scarcely placed a foot on the first step when he beheld a couple sitting on the lawn beneath some bushes.

It was his sister Rojelia in the arms of a man. No! In the arms of the devil. Undoubtedly this was the evil spirit who had come to tempt and demoralize her.

She who was so circumspect and pure lay now in utter disorder like a bacchante, sprawling on the grass under the volcanic assault of Lucifer. Her dress was opened and exposed a milky shoulder glowing like a white flower in the shadows, and Mephistopheles kissed the shoulder with impure, burning, demoniac lips. One of her perfect legs was exposed.

Enrique could stand no more. He approached them with clenched fists, trembling with fury.

Rojelia jumped up and arranged her costume. The devil looked up. He wore no mask and Enrique recognized in him Urcola, the insolent tramp of Madrid. The poet's face beamed with an impertinent smile, truly devilish:

"Well, well, if it isn't my future . . ."

Enrique did not let him finish. Possessed of insane rage, he leaped forward, foaming at the mouth.

Rojelia uttered a faint cry and ran into the house.

Enrique had the strength of a maniac, but Urcola was hardened by life and many fights. The struggle lasted a while and the devil gave Charles V a sound thrashing. He finally tripped him and hurled him to the ground. Then he jumped over the fence and faded into the night like a blast from hell.

When Enrique stumbled back to the guests, his face was scarcely recognizable. One of his eyes was blackened and his nose and mouth bruised. His beautiful costume had been torn to shreds. He was a pitiful sight.

His mother ran to him screaming: "My son, my son! What has happened to you? Talk to me! Are you alive?"

The guests had surrounded him and looked on astonished.

Enrique was still shaking with anger. He pushed Trini aside and, with all the dignity he could muster and with his only available eye flashing, he addressed the gathering, panting from exhaustion:

"It was — that tramp — that intruder, that Mephisto — pheles. He was seducing Rojelia, staining the honor of this — household, but I gave him what he deserved. I — pulverized him! And then the coward flew away because he knew I would finish — him. Yes, that is what I will do to anyone who dares stain — the honor of this family. Do you all hear me? Yes, I will kill — him, anyone. Do you hear? I will — annihilate — him!"

And then he was seized by an attack. He grew tense, moaned and collapsed. His mother cried like a madwoman and then his father came with two servants who carried the convulsive Charles V into the house, followed by Trini who behaved like a Mater Dolorosa.

Everyone was silent. The gentlemen looked at one another and shrugged their shoulders and smiled.

Polichinela said to Harlequin in a nasal voice: "The impertinence! Giving us that sermon about the honor of the family, as if we had anything to do with it."

"It is too bad that such a beautiful fiesta should be so completely spoiled with this disagreeable ending."

And Nero, still holding his lyre under his arm, laid a hand on the shoulder of Napoleon, who scratched his chest thoughtfully: "I think he deserves the beating the other one gave him. The crazy imbecile! Addressing us as if we were children."

"And who is not a child? We were all enjoying ourselves tonight like children and now we are all like children who have lost a toy. Too bad, too bad."

In a corner of the somber garden, leaning against a tree, the pale figure of Pierrot looked sadly at the lone forsaken harp on the stage.

The stars were fading. Crestfallen and with bowed heads, the strange figures left one by one.

Be quiet! Cheer no more! Rojelia's birthday is over and she is the unhappiest maiden in the world.

And slowly, with gloom, the fantastic gathering paraded sadly into the dawn.

The next day as they sat at late breakfast, Enrique came down, his head swathed in bandages. He had spent the rest of the night dressing his bruises and was in a fearful humor. He entered the dining room however with the air of a hero. Jorge and Lolita were not up yet.

"My poor boy," declaimed Trini. "How are you feeling? Could you sleep?"

He bellowed with rage and sat down to attack the food.

"Look at him. Look at your poor brother, all because of defending the honor of the Sandovals."

Rojelia sat with dignified calm. She was paler and there were shadows under her eyes, but otherwise she was calm and even cheerful.

"What shall we do, decorate him? Those are only bruises that will heal easily. It is a good lesson for not minding his own business. If he were so ill, he wouldn't be eating so much."

Fernando was drumming on the table. Now he pounded his fist on it: "So that is the way you take it after having dragged the family name in the gutter with your wanton ways. And still you tell him to mind his own business?" He had stood up, upturning his chair and upsetting a glass of water. He was in a fit of fury: "Isn't honor the business of every Sandoval?"

Enrique mumbled some unintelligible words with his disfigured mouth and helped himself to another buñuelo.

Rojelia also stood up. She could say a great deal but it was no use. She looked at the three of them as if they were objects of contempt and left the room.

Jorge appeared at the door and the servant asked him how he wanted whatever he wanted.

"In commercial quantities," he answered cheerfully and slapped the servant on the back.

Trini scowled: "I don't see why this sudden happiness after what has occurred, after the humiliation we have all suffered before all our friends." The servant had gone back to the kitchen. "And besides, Jorge, you know I don't approve of certain liberties with inferiors."

Jorge subsided until he reached the point where his expression fitted the circumstances: "And tell me, Enrique, what did you do to the other fellow?"

"I think he will spend at least three months in the hospital." His swollen mouth could scarcely pronounce the words: "If it had not been for his accomplices, he would now be in the cemetery."

"I didn't know he had anybody with him."

"Certainly. There were three husky fellows hiding behind the fence and when they saw that I was finishing him, they jumped on me. I gave them what was coming to them, though, and they all ran away, dragging the tramp with them."

They all looked at the weak body of Enrique but registered no expression. It was ridiculous. Fernando was walking up and down with his hands behind his back.

And then they all heard a loud laugh. It was Lolita looking at her brother, lifting her hands and then bringing them down on her knees:

"Oh, you look so funny, Enrique! You ought to see your mouth when you talk."

Enrique looked at her with murderous eyes and said nothing.

She was little, excellently well-shaped, perhaps too much so for her age. Her complexion was as swarthy as that of a Gypsy, her hair furiously black, her eyes quite large and heavily lashed. She was a happy little being. Most of the time she was gay.

Jorge looked at her intently, an almost boobish expression on his face, oblivious of his surroundings, and he lost all interest in food.

Fernando was still angry about the scene with Rojelia. The exuberant laughter of his daughter irritated him. He felt that she was attractive with that selfish and cruel attractiveness of youth and that made him more indignant:

"Young lady! Your uncalled-for mirth is entirely out of place. If your brother is like that, it is because he tried to defend the honor of the family which apparently the women do not guard. You should feel sorry for him and not take his misfortune so lightly, and besides, to laugh so frantically at a man's troubles, even if he is your brother, is, to say the least, somewhat—" He was going to say "whorish" but he said "indecent" and then walked out.

Enrique had finished. He stood up looking hideously at his young sister. He said: "I am going back to Madrid." He turned to the servant who was waiting on Jorge: "Order my car, will you?"

Trini approached him: "You should stay here today and rest. I hope that you are not going to look for that criminal. He does not deserve it."

"I look for him? He is probably in the hospital. I finished him well. I am only going to Madrid because I am bored."

"Can't you let a day go by without amusement? You are in no condition to run around. I bet it is that—woman again."

"Oh hell! Are you going to begin with that again?" He walked out, followed by Trini. They quarreled loudly all the way to the hall. Then the door was slammed and he was heard outside calling for the car.

Lolita and Jorge remained alone. She had not eaten yet and reached for her brother's dish coquettishly: "Let me taste it. How is it?"

"I haven't touched it. Why don't you take it?" He helped himself to some coffee. "I am not hungry this morning."

She ate two mouthfuls and then pushed the dish away: "Neither am I. Pour me some coffee."

While she drank it he placed an arm about her waist: "I am sorry you got that scolding from father, but you shouldn't have laughed so at Enrique."

"He looked so funny, didn't he?"

"Yes—but . . ." His hold tightened.

"You are going to make me spill this," she whispered, and then she laughed again loudly.

Jorge forced a laugh, loosening his hold. She finished her coffee in silence, almost seriously, looking over the cup at the trees beyond the terrace.

"Shall we go out in the garden?"

They went out and spoke of the night before in the fashionable manner of their set which consists of using the opposite word to that which expresses a thing correctly and also using vulgarisms.

Then a town car coming along the driveway stopped before them. Their father and mother were in it. Fernando sat without looking at them. Trini spoke: "We are going to Madrid and I won't be back until this evening. If you want to come you had better get in now."

"If I want to come I'll use the motorcycle."

"But what about you, Lolita?"

"I can ride back of him."

"No you won't. If you want to come, get ready now or you will have to wait until tomorrow."

Fernando impatiently struck the floor of the car with his stick.

"I was only joking, mother. I don't want to go today."

The car moved slowly and Trini called back: "Tell your sister that if that man appears, I have told the servants to throw him out."

Lolita and Jorge followed the car a few steps: "But I overheard Enrique say that he was in the hospital."

"Never mind that. Tell her what I said."

"All right, mother. I'll help with a kick also."

They remained there watching the car drive away. Inside the car Fernando turned to his wife: "We shouldn't have let them stay in that house alone."

"The servants are there and Rojelia too."

"The servants are all idiotic and Rojelia will be locked up in her room all day long. I know her."

"But they are not so young anymore."

"Precisely."

Here followed a scene between brother and sister over which I pass hastily. Their strange relationship had been hinted at clearly enough without having to throw the details in the reader's teeth. It ended somewhat lamely with what Garcia must have thought the palliative of an artistic tableau:

"I am going to pick some of those cherries." She ran toward a group of cherry trees with Jorge in pursuit. She stopped under the cooling shade: "They are higher than I thought—the ones I like."

"I will lift you." Jorge bent down and, embracing her knees, lifted her up until her dark plump hands touched the coveted fruit. Then she looked down and began to laugh again, her black mane covering her face like a dark wave. They formed a beautiful group.

Upstairs, in her room, Rojelia lay asleep and held a poem in her hand entitled "La del cabello rojo," and she was dreaming of who knows what.

In the garden, under the cherry trees, Jorge held Lolita in his arms and she picked cherries and ate them and put some in his mouth and she was laughing, laughing—

Enrique went straight to his girl's room, a sordid room unworthy of a detailed description. She was still in bed when he arrived. She was half sitting, half reclining, covered with a torn nightgown. On a table near her there was a tin of biscuits, a dish with mojama and a bottle of aguardiente. When Enrique entered she looked him over in surprise: "Where have you been? You must have found someone more accomplished than I am. How much did you pay for that?"

"If that is what you think, you are wrong. It was a man this time and I sent him to the infirmary. I did not kill him because his friends interfered."

"Sit down and tell me all about it."

Enrique dropped into an upholstered chair, raising a cloud of dust: "There is nothing to say about it. A poor fellow who wanted a passport to the other world and nearly got it."

"You might have let me know that you were handing out passports last night. I waited for you and lost a good engagement."

"What do you mean, engagement? I am buying all your time, do you hear?"

"Buying all my time! With what? For what you have given me, you couldn't find anybody else to do half the crazy things I am doing. Did you bring me that money today?"

"And did you take a bath?"

"Wait a moment, wait a moment. Do you think I am going to sit here in this filth and not wash myself because of your queer ideas when I don't even know if you are coming? I am fed up with this. Do you hear? Fed up! With all this dirt, having to wear dirty, torn clothes to please you. You can go and give your perros chicos to some cheap puta. I am too good for you and I know someone who will pay what I am worth and let me live in a clean, decent place and bathe all I want and be glad to get me."

Enrique had stood up in a mixture of fury and excitement. He came close to her and tried to embrace her: "When you talk of other men and treat me like that, I don't know what happens to me."

"I know." She repulsed him.

"Yes you know, you know!" He was like a cat with valerian. "And I need you and you know that too. You are the only one who understands me."

She shrank close to the wall: "You act like a maniac when you are like this and I don't like it. If you don't have the money, get out!"

He had one knee on the bed and reached for her with a clammy, quivering hand. He was disfigured: "Tell me that you were with another man last night, with a better man. God! Tell me that you were with the man who beat me up and you don't want me today. I love that!" He rushed to the dresser and returned with something in his hands. It was a whip, a hideous-looking weapon of dark, resilient woven leather. He thrust it in her hands and fell to his knees: "Go ahead, go ahead, I am waiting."

She took the whip and hurled it to a corner of the room. Her lower lip curled as she looked down on the trembling figure before her: "I am not acting today. I mean it this time, understand? No money, no whipping."

He lifted his head: "I have given you all I can. I can't get any more out of them. I have given you plenty."

She said slowly: "Get out and don't come back without the money."

He rose with difficulty. In one of his hands he held one of her shoes that had been lying under the bed: "I hope you don't mind if I take this. It is one of your old shoes and you won't need it as much as I will."

"Oh Christ! You turn my stomach. Get out!"

He slunk away like a beaten dog ashamed of his beating, or perhaps relishing it: "All right—you command."

And there you have it. I have transcribed this scene almost literally so that the reader may judge for himself and not accuse me of unfairness. It bears its own and most damning condemnation, evidencing an amateurishness which should only help to increase the sentence. It is obvious that Garcia wanted very much to be the literary enfant terrible with delusions of being classified as one who submerges boldly into the depths of the human soul, behavior and depravity, startling revelations of the abnormal, lurid passages resolving into profound conclusions which are never disclosed and all such things which no one takes seriously and have long been out of date. I could not help saying all this to Garcia but will not report on our ensuing argument because it was only a repetition of previous ones and I have already made my views quite unequivocal. Instead I will go on with his story, which after this becomes less reprehensible, if not from a literary standpoint, at least in content:

Summer soon ended and autumn descended slowly upon Madrid.

Rojelia had not heard from Urcola since the night of the costume ball and this had proven a real disappointment to her. At first she only blamed her family and for some time almost treated them all as strangers. After that she considered other possibilities.

As she always did when unhappiness seized her, she had retired within herself, with a cool dignity, and tried to put the whole episode out of her thoughts.

Things had not gone well with the family. The jewelry shop did not produce as much as it should. Ledesma worked until all hours and looked older, if possible, and worn out. Enrique drew large sums from the store and on several occasions took jewels also.

Fernando limited himself to shouting at him and engaging in loud disputes which led nowhere. He also let himself be carried away by stupid ostentation and the business suffered all the more for this. Several lawsuits were pending against the business and the future of the family was, as they say, on the ropes.

But outside the Sandoval family, those were balmy, calm, still days. Madrid was beginning to bustle with the approach of the winter season, and the Retiro was more poetic than ever. Old people sitting on benches, storing the last heat from the sun for the coming winter. Nurses with children playing around them while they chatted with a sunburnt soldier wearing some decorations. Lonely young men with long hair and dreamy expressions. The faint rattle of the wheel on the red cans of the barquilleros. . . .

Rojelia and Trini were riding in a victoria along the Paseo de Coches. There were scarcely any carriages and very few people in that most beautiful avenue. The great mass of trees bordering it covered all the autumnal polychromy, from deep red, passing through rich gold, to light yellow—and then the disorder of the dry leaves swirling along the way and flying about the carriage like bewildered butterflies.

Rojelia had noticed a couple walking along the opposite side of the avenue. A man with a woman who pushed a perambulator. Rojelia looked more attentively and then stood erect, her eyes wide open.

The woman had a chalky complexion and looked sickly. She wore spectacles and aimed them lovingly at the child inside the worn-out carriage. The man was Urcola. He walked on resignedly, but was a little stouter. His black romantic clothes fitted the autumnal background. He also saw her and lifted his hat politely, as the most natural thing in the world.

Trini had not noticed the couple, but she was surprised by Rojelia's attitude: "What is the matter?"

"Nothing—nothing."

"You look very pale. Shall we turn back?"

"No. I am all right now. Maybe we could walk a little."

The carriage stopped and they alighted. They walked along the row of small trees which still remained a deep green, the carriage following slowly. The part where they were was deserted and there was a great silence broken only by the rustle of the leaves beneath their feet and the horses' hooves upon the pavement.

They walked without speaking, their eyes following the somber paths leading away into shadows, always receding, always beckoning. They walked thus for some time and then a breeze began to blow and grew stronger and the dry leaves rained copiously in the orchestral wind.

They entered the carriage and returned homeward.

They passed under the Puerta de Alcala noticing the broken stone where bullets had smashed to leave an emblem of quality. They crossed the Cibeles, in the center of which stood the fountain with the goddess of that name, sitting on a cart drawn by two lions, always drawing, always in the same place. Behind, they had left a palace whose windows were always shut and housed a sad legend known to all Madrid and respected enough to be little commented upon. In front and at the right were the gardens of the Ministry of War. Rojelia had a fleeting glimpse of La Castellana, Recoletos and El Prado extending right and left with rows of trees and heavy ornate lampposts in the middle. The victoria began to ascend the slight hill flanked by cafés made famous by illustrious habitués.

Then through the clouds the sun burst and set brightly, turning the street into a river of fire. It shone right in their faces, dazzling, tinting them a glowing red. They sought the shadow of the coachman in front and their heads came together. Rojelia pressed her mother's hand and looked distractedly at the sidewalks filled with people.

At their right they saw the entrance to the Gran Via, the brand-new and long-awaited street which had inspired Chueca and Valverde to write some of their best music and words for a revue featuring it. The broad modern street rose slightly, majestically, cutting its way through an old part of the city, leaving at one side the narrow street of Caballero de Gracia where a delicate romance still dwelt in wandering shadows that trailed a short way from the present and through the past of a sentimental tale, back to the present of prosaic Madrid.

Trini said: "I was at the theater the first night they played *La Gran Via.* It was not built then."

"They have not got very far with it yet."

Trini had not heard Rojelia. Her thoughts were rushing to the past: "That night I was with Fernando and your poor Aunt Julieta. I was happy then— your father and I had just been married. You know? There behind that building is the street the famous waltz is about."

Rojelia knew that part of Madrid well but she looked in the direction pointed by her mother, even though the street could not be seen from where they were.

They had reached the top of the hill and their carriage stopped, held by the traffic. Then their attention was arrested by an amusing scene that was taking place near the sidewalk. A bicycle policeman was chasing a boy. The boy dived into the crowds that jammed the sidewalk and the policeman had to abandon his machine in the gutter and follow on foot. The people, siding as usual with the enemy of the law, made way for the boy and hindered the policeman's path as much as possible. In the end, the boy emerged from the crowd where the bicycle lay, seized it and pedaled swiftly down the street among general laughter.

Trini had turned to see the boy ride down Alcala Street toward La Cibeles. Her eyes rested once more on the entrance to La Gran Via but they seemed to be looking into the past.

Here Garcia talked about the way in which he had worked the theme of the Gran Via throughout his story and spoke of it as if this literary trick were his own discovery, admitting only that he had perfected it more from ideas gathered when hearing the Moor talk about thematic development in music. I suppose he wanted to make sure that no one would miss his virtuosity and he asked whether I had noticed it: "Something like the principal song in a musical comedy, you know?"

I told him he need not worry, that it was quite clear and therefore he should not overdo it. We spoke a while about this question of development of ideas and then he proceeded:

The traffic began to move again. They were descending mildly onto La Puerta del Sol. Every sunny afternoon this place lives up to its name. They were blinded by the glare of the sun, deafened by the noise of traffic and people. Rojelia felt tired of all these things. She knew them all by heart. They bored her and she had a strong desire to go away. She wondered how her mother could relish the past of such things, having lived among them so many years.

When they arrived home, Trini went directly upstairs and Rojelia entered the shop. A gentleman who was coming out held the door open for her.

At the bottom of the store was Ledesma behind a glass counter. Rojelia advanced and over the counter took both of Ledesma's hands in hers:

"How is my good Ledesma?"

"Not so well, my child. Troubles of age. That gentleman who just went out is a customer and while he was here, there was a terrible row going on upstairs between your father and your sister. These things are embarrassing. The man was listening to it. That creates a disastrous impression."

"I understand, Ledesma, but don't worry. This can't go on forever."

"That is why I worry. I know it can't last and I see the end coming fast. I am doing all I can to hold it back, to fight against the inevitable, but I can't all alone. I am too old now. Are they all blind?"

"Ledesma, you are doing your best. So am I. I have tried to bring equanimity into this insane household, but it is impossible. They are all mad with vanity and nerves. But we must not worry. When one does not worry, half the adversity has been conquered."

"But even if it were only for selfishness? What will become of me when this sinks?"

"Ledesma, where I go, you can always go."

"Ah, but that does not worry me. I know I will have nowhere to turn, but I will be too old to care. Then the end is at hand and one can always precipitate and make sure of it—"

"No—not that, Ledesma."

"—but what kills me is to think of what will become of you and your younger sister. Especially you, Rojelia. You know how I have come to love you. I have known you ever since you were just so high and you have always been so good to me. Although you are a different type from your Aunt Julieta, may she rest in peace, sometimes you have exactly her expression, and then I don't know what I feel. When you came in and held my hands, you looked so much like her—! And she was so unhappy—!"

"Don't worry about me. When the time arrives, I trust I will be out of the wreck with someone who will teach me to walk again on the road to happiness."

"You will, Rojelia. You will find someone very good. He will have to be very good to deserve you. In the meanwhile be strong and calm."

"I will if you don't work anymore, Ledesma. I don't want to see you working anymore. I want you to have more time for me. I am happy with you." Two tears rolled from her eyes and shone upon the glass counter.

"Rojelia, this has been my life. When it ends, I shall end also. Then I will rest."

"Wait, Garcia! Let me finish it for you." I recited: "And the two tears sparkled among the gathering shadows like the best gems in the store."

Believe it or not, that is exactly the way he had it written down. Garcia was amazed, stumped. For once I had scored a bull's-eye, made my point convincingly clear by implication, and won a smashing victory. One does what one can.

After this I did not mind what followed of Garcia's novel, which was a jumble of notes with references and more references, sheets with small slips of paper pinned to them as intended insertions, with red penciled marks and much of "this goes here and this there." I watched him as he tried to assemble all this rough work and make some sense out of it. Most of it he told me and some he read.

The next chapter introduced the character who was destined to become Rojelia's husband. He was an officer in the Spanish colonial army in Morocco, and it was against this background that Garcia attempted to present him in a full chapter. Garcia lacked all the necessary preparation and equipment to handle the task. All he knew about war was to lay down a barrage of clichés that would have discouraged the most desperate offensive of foolhardy readers and listeners. The thing contained every known situation of swashbuckling heroics, men who talk and act tough, tyrannical discipline dished out with aching heart and unwavering hand, disillusion in the great cause and in the chosen career degenerating into hard professional militarism salvaged in the nick of time by the sporting gesture, and everything generously sprinkled with foul words.

This has been done by masters of the trade and Garcia had taken in every stock situation with amazing powers of retention, but he had not put things together right and had used extraordinary discernment in not adding one single touch of originality.

These were the most specific defects; the others were of a more general and intangible nature. This fellow, whose name by the way was Albarran, in case one has to refer to him again, was intended as a contrast to the carefree, unpredictable poet who had caused our heroine so much sorrow and disappointment. He was supposed to offer her a sense of stability, of security, to represent her change of course from the foolishly sublime to the wise and soundly prosaic, but as he appeared cast in the role of a soldier and in a manner more or less consciously copied by Garcia from moving pictures and romantic popular yarns, the fellow was inevitably surrounded by an atmosphere of adventure which destroyed the proposed contrast with the other one. It was a meaningless change from devil-may-care to devil-should-worry. I suspect that Garcia considered the military career as something very dependable, which in some ways it is, with regular promotions, increases of salary and eventual pensions, but his logotypes had led him astray and his thesis suffered from inconsistency. In order to maintain a measure of contrast in the face of these essential obstacles and against all odds, Garcia described his hero as matter-of-fact, even somewhat unimaginative and inordinately healthy both in spirit and in body, thus disclosing unintentionally that Garcia, for reasons of his own, considered poets unhealthy in every respect. All this was in direct contradiction with the thoughts and actions of Captain Albarran who, immediately after, is shown as continuously harrassed by dreams of his farm back in Spain, because it seems that everywhere the background of a farm is a guarantee of normality, and who toward the end of the chapter tells his colonel that his soul is sick, that he is tired of the African campaign and wants to return to Spain.

Garcia had intended to make this character healthy and normal and a regular guy, but he had only succeeded in making him vulgar and rampant and unconvincing. In short, a fraud.

But the worst of it, what worried Garcia, was that his character had not turned out simpático. We argued the matter profusely, endeavoring to extricate Garcia from the literary traps to which he had fallen prey, and especially this last one, whose spring was so vague as to defy detection. No matter how much Garcia deleted and inserted, the man would not turn out simpático. Garcia was ready to rewrite the whole thing, and I suggested that perhaps everything emanated from the fundamental inconsistency of his thesis and its presentation and that it would be better not to make his hero a soldier in the African wars, but perhaps a merchant on the peninsula, some kind of a salesman, or even a farmer who goes occasionally to Madrid. I was only trying to help.

"But how many times do I have to tell you that this is a true story?" Garcia was quite exasperated by now: "I met the fellow myself in Madrid when I was a boy. He was already married to Rojelia whom I also met, in case you are interested. He was a captain then, tropa class, you know, had never been to a military academy, but I tell you he was a captain."

"Well?"

"He was very antipático."

After this there was no point in arguing the matter in hand further and we became involved in generalizations and a discussion about the merits of reality versus literature and Garcia quoted from a thinker something to the effect that art is more discriminating than nature and more concerned with arrangement and harmony, and we talked of several things like that which did not help Garcia's problem, and then he went back to his novel.

Toward the end of this chapter Garcia considered the matter of fairness in peoples at war. He told me that many years ago he had been very badly impressed by the comments in the Spanish press about the campaign in Africa. If the Spaniards made a stubborn stand against great odds and died to the last man defending a position, they were praised as heroes, but when the Moors did the same thing, they were criticized as fanatics. He felt that this was not fair and that one should always give the devil his due. He presented this theory in a conversation between Captain Albarran and his colonel. I said that this happened not only in Spain but everywhere, and he said that this was precisely the point he was trying to make indirectly and once more repeated that generalization was one of the great virtues of literature.

"If this thing is going to be published in English, I must give the reader something of general interest. Can't keep it so Spanish that he cannot find the point."

The chapter ended with Captain Albarran finally getting his wish and sailing back to Spain, which is a short sail from where he was. I quote a small section:

And so it came to pass that Captain Albarran sailed from the coast of Africa where he had spent so much of his life, on his way to Spain.

It was a splendid day and when he saw the red and yellow flag against the blue sky, he felt something he had not felt since he first had left Spain, and when he turned and beheld the receding coast, he thought almost aloud:

"Look at me well, as I look at you in the hazy horizon, across the afternoon and the distance, because it is sad to part, perhaps forever, and not have looked at one another enough."

Some loud thoughts for a prosaic character!

Next we find the hero in Madrid for the Jura de la Bandera, which is when the new recruits are inducted I think, and it was thus that he eventually met Rojelia. Garcia had this part written more in full and read sections of it without too much difficulty or hunting for the continuation of some particular paragraph. This is some of it:

It took place in La Castellana. It was in the spring and all the trees along the boulevard were in full bloom. It was a wonderful morning. Everything was bright, everything magnificent. There was still the novelty of seeing the Moorish soldiers parade through Madrid under the Spanish flag.

They advanced in colorful phalanxes. The Moorish infantry with their bronze chests bare, the red jaiques hanging from their shoulders and floating behind pompously, shining bright under the sun, as if the men were torches and the jaiques flamed flattened by the wind.

And then came the Moorish cavalry in all their stupendous African regalia, advancing in a tumultuous and rhythmic disorder. Wonderful horsemen, great white jaiques, dazzling white jaiques and black and white horses, clean, shiny horses and jet-black men, black and shiny faces and bright white teeth, and sound and movement and strange piercing cries and strange pirouettes. Everything against the background of fresh trees that tainted things with their greenish glow. An astounding display of savage glamour, of primitive glory.

There were the famous old Spanish regiments, all stiff and frozen with prestige. Each one was a gallant page sparkling in history, a walking page telling the story in straight lines of men. A magnificent parade with phalanxes of men and phalanxes of trees that stood as if presenting arms.

All the streets leading down to La Castellana from the Hipodromo to La Cibeles were closed. The boulevards were bursting with people whose drab mass spread far into the streets. They were on roofs, on balconies; they stood on the benches, on carriages and carts of all kinds, on top of the kioscos and clinging to the iron fences, and even the children hung from the trees like fruit.

All Madrid was there to see the new soldiers swear fidelity to their country and their flag.

The Sandovals were standing in a carriage at the Plaza de la Cibeles, looking above the heads of the crowd. Everybody was cheering and waving their hats and handkerchiefs in the air.

Ahead of a large detachment of soldiers, almost isolated from the rest, a man advanced on a horse. He wore a white uniform and bright silver helmet. He had a mustache and his lower jaw protruded slightly.

When the man entered the Plaza de la Cibeles, a stocky individual wearing a cap darted out of the crowd. He seized the horse by the bridle and fired two shots. The man on the horse swayed to one side and the heel of his shiny black boot struck the aggressor on the head, knocking him to the ground; then he threw his horse over him and rode on calmly.

The scene had happened so quickly that no one had time to realize it. Other officers also on horseback closed in but their loyalty was no longer needed; the man lay on the ground still clenching the gun, broken by the horse's hooves.

A great disorder followed, everybody rushed and some of the public wanted to lynch the man who was being dragged away by the police. Reporters ran from one place to another with the proverbial pad and pencil, but finally order was reestablished and the parade went on.

Rojelia and Trini looked on, excitement showing in their faces. Trini watched the soldiers march in tune with the pasodoble and shook her shoulders keeping time with it. Fernando had been commenting on the incident of the frustrated assassination with Ledesma and dispatched Jorge to investigate the details. Enrique looked sullenly and almost with resentment at the passing rows of soldiers. Lolita looked on distractedly and seemed to be far away.

"See there now!" Rojelia exclaimed. "The soldiers are taking the oath."

Ledesma stood up and they all looked down La Castellana. In the middle, quite a way off, stood the small figure of an officer holding an enormous flag. It was Captain Albarran. He was calm and impassive and no one could have guessed what his thoughts were.

During those days I got a good deal of Garcia's writings, considerably more than usual and that was not a little. I happened to be on vacation and consequently at his mercy almost twenty-four hours a day. One of the things on which Garcia and I agree is on not going to the country, and much less the seashore, for a vacation, but to spend it in New York. It is not only that we like New York in the summertime, enjoying with contented steadfastness the crises of heat waves that squeeze the stuffings out of tenements and onto their fire escapes, children playing under street sprinklers and water gushing from a fire hydrant opened by the hand of some civic-minded good samaritan, the frequent and ephemeral cool drinks in the company of kindred sweating souls under a sidewalk awning, a sparkling vision of golden heat, of humid shadows and informality that march unhurriedly but straight to the heart; but if besides all this, one does not have to work, if one can roam about in freedom, gleefully pitying the rest of the busy population enslaved by their jobs, with the opportunity of seeing how the city looks during a weekday, what things those who are not imprisoned in offices or factories do, that they always tell us about when we return home from a day's work, there seems to be no reason for going away.

Garcia has suggested many of these things and, in conspiracy with lack of funds, has encouraged me to stay in town and I have believed him candidly and also possibly because I want to believe him, but sometimes I suspect that he wants me around so that he can read to me and this he did during those days and even induced me to attempt some translations of his writings which I don't think he found very satisfactory.

What followed of his novel was still in a more tentative phase and his plans were not quite definite. He introduced another character, a young friend of Jorge Sandoval, with whom Lolita, the younger sister, fell in love. Garcia's treatment took more kindly to this new character than it had to the captain. He was described as an individual of extraordinary tranquility, very detached and indifferent for his age, who had not been very responsive to Lolita's open advances, but had carried his circumspection to what she considered an insulting degree. I am sure that Garcia had wanted to bring these two individuals—the captain and this other boy—as the knights in shining armor, champions of equanimity and composure coming to rescue the damsels from the insane, or neurotic and abnormal atmosphere in which they had grown, and while Garcia, through no fault of his, had managed to make this new character rather simpático, which was also unexpected in view of his determined coolness, again the plot had militated against him and frustrated his ends.

Lolita, aroused by such circumspect disinterest on the part of the man she desired, had quarreled with him, grossly insulted him, and he had left her. Then she heard that his father, with whom he lived alone, had died and the boy had gone to America. Subsequently she learned that there he had become involved in some revolution, mistaken for someone else and executed without further ado.

Here Garcia became quite lyrical about Lolita's feelings. In his absence, she realized the greatness of her passion for him. Here is part of it:

That friendship had lifted her style of love to a plane different from that of the flesh. She realized that besides a carnal passion, he had aroused a tenderness in her that was stronger now in memories.

He had been a great gentleman. With his supreme indifference he had passed over her, leaving her blood a sea of fire, and from that melting pot he had brought out newer, well-tempered feelings which pierced her soul like blades. He had taught her a new side of love and passion, a side that was stronger, more binding—a dangerous side.

And on bright days, she always imagined him, his placid face, his clean-cut features, his kindly eyes, looking from the bottom of his normal, unique soul upon the sea, and an old ship carrying him away. She could see him looking at the horizon, indifferent to everything, this strange man whose unglamorous manner was flat with the greatness of a prairie, this man, oblivious of life and death, who had passed through existence like a cool breeze, like a calm breeze, even as he had passed through her heart, bringing out a new and last flower and then, unconsciously, withering it when only a bud.

Since that day, Lolita decided that she would never allow love to go deeper than the flesh.

Here I remarked that this was a big decision not only for such a little girl to make but even for a writer to make for her, and I also inquired whether Garcia had intentionally made both heroes come in and out of the girls' lives in a ship and looking at the horizon, but Garcia paid no attention and continued to struggle with his papers.

It was a good thing that all this part of the novel was in a tentative stage because the plot again became objectionable. It was not the Peeping Tom kind of pornography, the sicalipsis which had marred it on other occasions, because the subject was dealt with in a more serious, almost tragic vein, but it could scarcely be recommended nevertheless.

Lolita had turned in despair once more to her brother Jorge, and if their very strange relationship had been suggested quite frankly before, it now became an openly acknowledged incestuous situation. The novel at this point became sordid, sinister. It seems that Garcia was intent upon showing in no uncertain terms the downhill path of this family, its complete degradation leading to ultimate material and moral collapse, and he was assiduously heaping every disgrace upon them. I remonstrated with him, but again he repeated that his story was true to life and that what he described had become common knowledge to all Madrid. Seeing that he was dealing with the subject in such earnestness I could not attack his work in this case as being unnecessarily ugly and had to let it pass, but I did tell him that many things sounded in English much more crude than in Spanish, as I believe I had already said before, and that a translation under the circumstances might prove exceedingly difficult and requiring a finesse well beyond my capabilities, so that perhaps he had better count me out.

Garcia only said that his work was still in a very embryonic stage and that he might be able to shorten that section or subdue it somewhat, but that he could not see how he could eliminate it and at the same time save his literary integrity. He added that we would see and with that went on to another section.

This one covered a good deal of ground. The main idea was to show the gradual deterioration of the family and the jewelry business. Here Garcia intended to document himself properly. He wanted to describe in detail how a jewelry business crumbles notwithstanding the skillful efforts of an administrator of the caliber of good old Ledesma, but Garcia had no knowledge of business whatsoever and confessed that he was in a quandry as to whom he should consult. I suggested the Señor Olózaga.

This part of the book was also to deal with the courtship of Rojelia by Captain Albarran and their eventual marriage. This was strenuously opposed by her family because her suitor had no titles or fortune. A series of quarrels took place and the question wound up with their elopement, just before the crash, when she was saved, with but little time to spare, from the general financial ruin by his captain's pay. All through this section Garcia expected to describe minutely the progressive abulia of Fernando Sandoval induced by some kind of disease, which had not been decided upon, in combination with excessive drinking. The specific ailment was something which Garcia's mother had apparently neglected to tell him. She had told him of the symptoms, however: growing irritability, distraction, weakening of will-power and a complete breakdown of the spirit which ended in idiocy and incapacity to recognize people. Armed with these symptoms gathered on such heresay, Garcia intended to accost Dr. de los Rios and obtain a complete diagnosis. I agreed to the plan because I supposed that de los Rios in the end would pick out some disease for Garcia, give him the proper symptoms so that they would fit the general plot, and thus deliver him from his difficulties.

Right through this whole part, of course, and while everyone and everything was going to the dogs, Rojelia and Ledesma stood like two towers of strength, two regal examples of serenity and wisdom, seeing things falling all about them and unable to do anything; but with the entrance of Captain Albarran into the scene, they had another ally in their superiority and nobility of character even if in the end it did not seem to do anybody much good. Rojelia and her husband went to live on his farm in order to get away from all these terrible things. On the farm the reader would meet the captain's mother: an old, wise peasant, a kindly though silent woman—one of those wonderful Spanish peasant types, in Garcia's own words—and the younger brother, a fine upstanding lad, portraying the modern trends in country gentry, who listens to serious music and reads books, who in less ponderous moments, and quoting again from Garcia, could show his youthfulness by indulging in wholesome, clean fun. For this part Garcia had ambitious plans: everybody engaging in philosophical discussions, discussions of music which Garcia undoubtedly expected the Moor to edit, and discussions of books, which he, considering himself an authority on the subject, would handle all by himself. A sort of working-out section.

I felt that aside from the very popular idea that cities are sources of evil and the country the site of virtue, Garcia was leaning heavily on concepts gathered well outside of Spain. All this about wise old peasants and progressive youth on a milk farm where people go to take the cure is nothing but a shameless commercial that anyone can recognize and unmask. I made this clear to Garcia and said that he was on his way to becoming an imitation hack writer and that obviously he had in mind foreign consumption, as he had already confessed once before. We argued the matter animatedly until we got sidetracked from the main issue and reached the irrelevant point where I asserted without proofs and simply because it came into my head at the moment that one cannot get any good milk on farms because the best is sold to the cities where they pay well for it. Garcia was no better informed than I and therefore in no position to challenge my baseless denunciation. He stated for the record, however, that at no time had he said that it was a milk farm and went back to his book.

Here Garcia would have an opportunity to liven up his narrative by jumping back and forth from the country farm to the city dwelling, confront the reader with abrupt contrasts between a place in the sun that bathes our body and soul and the sordid lair of a clan living in discordant greed, lust and ignominy, between mind- and muscle-nourishing walks, discussing topics of intellectual interest among exuberant meadows in which everyone on the farm joined except the old lady who, on their return, greeted them with sagacious twinkling eyes to ask whether they had solved all the problems of the world, and humiliating quarrels over the last material remains of a fortune squandered in evil stupidity, where a brother and a sister lived in sin and their mother was too disillusioned and their father too weak-minded to interfere or even take notice. A blasting contrast between pastoral spiritual meanderings of succulent peripetetics and gloomy retribution of debasing rapacity.

I shook my head in dismay, but Garcia went on elaborating his grandiose plans. It was here that he expected to use what he claimed was a stroke of inspiration. On the farm, Rojelia had her first baby—subsequently Garcia never mentioned a second one—and he had conceived the daring project in those days of shocking stories of describing minutely the last stages of pregnancy and the complete delivery of the child, with country doctor blissfully devoid of new-fangled ideas, the captain as attending nurse because the good doctor with unerring bucolic criterion had concluded that a husband should always be present at his children's births and thus acquire respect for motherhood with accruing interests to his wife, and last but not least, the understanding old lady, a veteran of many such battles—she only had the captain and his brother to show for it—talking sententiously about life.

Garcia expected to dedicate a full chapter, no less, to the delivery and for this he was going to consult books on obstetrics and whatnot. He did not say, but I could see more projected assaults upon Dr. de los Rios's busy schedule. He was convinced that this should prove a sure-fire trick with the readers, a courageous literary challenge to prudish critics. His persistent attacks on the harmless squeamishness of others did not stop there. He had saved for this point his most subtle contrast, what he might call the brochette that bound his plot together, when the reader, who had been dealt with as a pendulum throughout, finally came to well-deserved rest. Garcia here read a scene where Lolita, on her way to some village where she was to meet her brother Jorge, stops off at the farm for a short visit with her sister. There the horror of her life is brought to her with mind-shattering force, she breaks down and sobs in her sister's arms, there she knows repentance and the desire for expiation, there she kisses the captain's hand and blesses him for having saved her sister and made her so happy, and also there she meets the captain's brother and they both fall in love. But the subtle touch, which Garcia thought that of a masterful hand, was that during the whole visit Lolita kept on a dark cloak carefully wrapped about her person. Garcia said that he expected to make his novel magnificently shocking.

The implication, too obvious to miss and too disgraceful to contemplate, considering the background, only seemed to elate Garcia. The love between Lolita and her young intellectual, nature's nobleman, was to culminate in marriage during an epilogue or apotheosis on the sun-drenched farm which Garcia had all but written for the end of his masterpiece.

I was speechless and only continued to shake my head.

"Now what?" Garcia demanded.

The whole thing was ridiculous beyond conception; not only an objectionable plot, whether true to life or not, but the final affrontery of a young Spaniard of those days indulging in clean fun and marrying a girl with a past like that of Lolita's—even if one lets her keep her cloak on. All that obsession with sunshine and normality, health and wholesome living intended to relieve the hangover of pornography, or perhaps to justify it; that true story alibi for militant salacity, disclosing an even more insidious fundamental prudishness; all that progressive youth and ideas nonsense, paraded like a drum majorette in shorts before the ogling eyes of those who would never visit a brothel openly. Everything was absolutely un-Spanish in its well-schooled hypocrisy and, what is worse, it was absolutely unlike Garcia. It reminded me of these diligent dirtmongers, pitchmen of smut with a

holier-than-thou attitude in reverse who, in their craposant exultation, invoke misrepresented laws of biology and even the freedom of
the press to advance the cause and promote the sales of the biggest
industry yet: organized sex with all its ramifications and agencies, from
intimate underthings to the bridal gown, from the peep show to the
maternity ward.

I thought all those things, but I only said: "I think that you are giving
Spain an awful black eye."

This was a great day for El Telescopio. When we arrived the place was
resplendent with decorations and luminaries of the Spanish colony.
The sun coming through the windows added to the gaiety which was
not mitigated even by the joyful gloom of the Spanish music filling the
rooms. There were farolitos, those paper lanterns that look like colorful concertinas, hanging from the ceiling, to be lighted later, and the
whole place was decorated in very Spanish style.

On entering I immediately saw Don Pedro. The old maestro was
holding forth at a table surrounded by an improvised clique and
unquestionably he had begun to test his drinking capacity early.
Greeting acquaintances as I passed, I hurried to join his group and
found a place near him.

The Moor was talking in that voluble, disjointed and kidding way
of his, as he did whenever he was happy or surrounded by several
people, which is the same thing. He stopped in the middle of a sentence
and fixed me with his most theatrical and Mephistophelian look
without saying anything, holding the suspense for no reason at all.
Then without taking his eyes from me, he waved and ordered loudly:
"Wine for the gentleman, and don't throw the bottle; this one is not
very adept." He cut the end of the sentence in midair with the edge of
his hand and the long and dramatic silence continued; he regarded
me, his head and eyes brushing approval up and down my perplexity,
until the waiter arrived with the wine. Only then, he released his grip
on the audience: "Very good, man, very good," and turned again to
the table.

As if this had been a signal to break ranks, everyone around began
to talk and I began to survey the company.

It was incredible. From one end of the room to the other, and most of the tables were occupied, practically everybody was drinking out of a bottle. The scene was one of almost ritualistic bacchanalia. To think that this was happening on Manhattan Island was surrealistically comical. I reached for my bottle.

Don Pedro distinguished me again: "How do you like it? Not bad, not bad; like babies drinking out of the biberón," and with impudent disdain he lifted his glass of sherry in silent toast to the gathering. This was the limit. After he had got almost everybody drinking out of the bottle, he chose to drink out of a glass.

"I tell you," he continued, "these Spaniards are extraordinary. The moment they leave Spain they don't know what it's all about any more than the Americans. In fact, anyone outside of Spain doesn't know what it's all about—" His thumb grazed his lower lid and the palm of his hand slid down an invisible undulating toboggan: "Like this sherry. You see?" The same thumb pointed at a girl sitting at our table who was all smiles and admiration. She was the American vocalist in his band—his Trilby as someone had said once—and obviously a tourist there. She exuded the happy, breathless expectancy of one gloating in the contemplation of a chamber of horrors. "Look at her." He glowered at her with fingers stretched under his chin: "Boo!" he ejaculated and she winced but recovered at once:

"You can't frighten me or anybody else, Gus, old boy. We all know you. Under that exterior—"

"Quiet!" he expostulated with paternal authority. "She does not have much up here," pointing at his head, "but she is good." He gave her a kindly look and lifted his glass to her: "The sherry, remember? Completely misinformed about it. She read some place that good sherry has a nutty flavor— Paradisiac innocence!" He lowered his voice, imparting the esoteric knowledge: "Good sherry tastes of breast, you know, teat. That's what any good catador will tell you in Spain. Put a rubber nipple on the bottle and you are in your second childhood. That's why we call wine the milk of old people— Nutty flavor indeed!" He eyed her sideways while addressing the rest: "Nuts to you, sister!" and roared his laughter. "Not bad, eh? Nuts to you."

"That's not fair," the girl was whimpering. "You talk in Spanish so that I cannot understand what you are saying and then you finish in

English, 'nuts to you,' and I don't think that's fair." But one could see that she was enjoying it all.

"That's not fair, that's not fair," he mimicked. "That's what she is always saying. I tell you: doesn't know what it's all about," he mused thoughtfully. "Fair, fair— The moment one leaves Spain, one finds this obsession with fairness. I never heard the word as long as I lived there—"

I let him ramble on and again began to take stock of the people gathered there. At our table and aside from the Moor, there was no one of particular distinction that I knew of. True, there was Garcia but perhaps I knew him too well to consider him distinguished, and his retiring manner, albeit his prematurely white hair, did not contribute to make him outstanding. He was sitting at the other end of the table in his usual melancholy mood and more than usual dejection, clutching a bottle like an anchor; but again, the presence of the Moor always seemed to make him shrink. He waved at me in dismay. I sighted the faces one by one, along the sides of the bottle. Someone sitting by the windows said loudly enough for me to hear that Dr. de los Rios had just driven up and was getting out of his car. I continued to sight the faces, closing one eye and looking with the other.

And then I met his eyes. He was sitting opposite me at the other end of the long table, near Garcia. It was that Fulano something-or-other, the little meek man I had met once before. There were the thick lenses that met my eyes with an impact which then melted into yielding suction. I could not look away and my hand came down slowly and set the bottle on the table. The thick lenses acted like microscopes focused in his interior and I was once more in the extraordinary position of reading a man's mind, suddenly, without warning, in this incongruous place:

This time his thoughts were not willful daydreaming like the last time. He was concerned and obviously very much concerned with his dreams which had taken place when asleep. He was going through them and remembered them well enough. There was that one about the woman who had kidnapped a child under circumstances that made it the horror crime of the century. He was not clear on whether the woman had been finally located, caught, or had given herself up. His mind concentrated on the last possibility because his thoughts, which had thus far been a hazy jumble, sprang into brilliant colors.

The woman had announced that she would give herself up, that she would return of her own accord with the body of the child to make whatever amends were expected. He was standing on Riverside Drive, looking up the Hudson River, and the whole length of the drive was packed with an expectant mob, clamoring for justice, long cordons of police endeavoring to hold it back, swaying back and forth all along and all the way from the line of buildings to the shore that was devoid of train tracks and had a very narrow beach.

Then they saw the little rowboat floating down the river with the woman in it. The day was very bright and everything on the other side and up the river very clear and there were millions of extended arms, pointing fingers like the bayonets of a marching army.

The boat turned and slowly, with deliberation, made for the shore. As the boat approached, the angry roar of the mob rose, fearfully, brutal, avenging, like a howling storm. When the boat reached the embankment, the woman bent over, picked the body of the child up from the bottom of the boat and stood up facing the mob. He could see her clearly although she was quite distant from where he stood. She was wearing a dirty white sweater, a brick-colored skirt and a black beret. She waded calmly toward the beach bearing the child's body in her arms, walked straight into them and then the mob broke loose and engulfed her.

Then he decided to go home but it was difficult to find it in this enormous city. The town was enlarged and idealized to fantastic proportions. The buildings were like mountains and their lower part carved out of the very rock in immense arches and columns, the roofs so enormous that what amounted to cities were built upon them. And here he must find his own little room, his home, and yet it was pleasant to be thus lost and to look so hopelessly for a home.

Going up the buildings was like climbing a sierra. He knew that his room was not up there, that it was down below, way down, but as he did not know where it was, he could always explain that he was looking for it, should anyone question his motives. It was a good reason and he wanted to go up.

Then he came down and wandered through deserted streets at night. All of them ran downhill and he kept turning toward the east until he came to a building under construction. The street floor was still open, strewn with rubbish, broken bricks and cement-caked wheelbarrows, a forest of steel beams and wooden uprights.

He walked deeper and deeper into the building and with an unexpected feeling of joy knew that he was lost and therefore would reach at last the cellar of the old house. This was the moment when he always began to descend the wide, long ramp which led to the subterranean town. He had been looking forward to this with happy anticipation. It was a miniature city and he must walk carefully so that in places his head would not scrape the rocks on top.

He walked across a square not bigger than a medium-sized room, and through one of the streets that led away from the square he could see a little elevated train pass. It was like a toy train. He saw light shining on the small sidewalks from the doorways of these dollhouses. He was too big to go into any of them, but he did not want to go in anyway. He wanted to find the cellar of the old house.

It was very late at night and he knew that the night would go on and on beyond the point where the sun would have risen and set many times until it would never rise again. Although the puppet town was deserted because it was so late, the air was charged with hostility, the enemy entrenched in the houses. He walked faster and took the street that led from the opposite corner of the square. Here too, the light from the little doorways struck the pavement like a series of hurdles in his way which he must negotiate. Every time he passed a doorway, he felt the same creeping sensation up his back. All this part of the dream was very vivid because he had dreamed it many times. Then he came as expected to the doorway on the frame of which was the face. It was the face of a toothless old man with a sharp nose, twinkling eyes and long white hair. It was a face made of reddish rubber, like some small ones he had had when only a boy, and it was contorted with cackling laughter, laughing at him. He raised a stick he had picked up along the way and struck at the face and the laughter gradually died out like a motor faltering to a stop. He walked still faster and arrived at the cellar.

He went straight to the trapdoor on the floor, lifted it and began to descend to a second cellar and then a third and a fourth, until he emerged into the sumptuous hallway with the long row of elevators on one side and the luxurious lounges on the other. There was much activity and people milling around and, mixing with the crowd, he entered one of the elevators unnoticed. He was carried up and found himself alone again.

He was walking up a steep road on the other side of the Hudson River, which was surprising because he knew that he had been moving east. The road went up, walled by high rocks on each side, and he was dragging a body which might be his own. He walked up the road laboriously pulling at the body which grew heavier with each step and then at the top of the road was his home. The door was ajar and there was light inside. At the threshold he let go of the body and entered. The room was in great disorder, as if a struggle had taken place in it. A lamp was overturned but the light still burned. He looked madly about and remembered his own words very well. He said to himself:

"Is this my life?"

I became conscious of the voices all around me and found myself, without any effort on my part, outside the man's mind, but I was disconcerted and wanted to regain some composure by looking at the outside of other people as one is supposed to do. The Moor was looking at the door, no doubt waiting for Dr. de los Rios to come in, and I realized that my visit into this man's thoughts must have taken an incredibly short time. This did not help my desired composure and I looked at the other faces there more intently, seeking normality and distraction.

At the other tables I recognized the best importations from Spain. There was the dancing team, Lunarito and Bejarano. There was a famous newspaperman and foreign correspondent who had to his credit a long list of deportations from various countries. If one wanted to meet him, the Moor had said, one had to catch him between trains. He was sitting with the best Spanish importer of antiques who owned a very exclusive shop on Madison Avenue and had lent for the occasion the old Spanish tapestries and shawls which hung from the balcony that ran along one wall of the dining room and gave things an air of magnificent refinement contrasting harshly with all this bottle drinking. The other man at their table was the owner of a Spanish newspaper then published in New York.

They were entertaining two women: one old and quite ferocious, watching like a hawk over the other one who was very young, blonde and angelical. The old harridan was talking through much wine-swallowing and lip-smacking about what I understood was her favorite pastime: to sing the graces of her angelical daughter to anyone who would listen. The daughter sat quietly, looking more and more like a picture by a primitive, sipping ojen. Her name went well with her looks. She was the incomparable Angeles Medinaceli, La Niña de los Madroños, currently considered the best flamenco singer in Spain and on a professionally exploring trip here.

At a table between hers and ours were two men and a woman. One of the men was El Cogote, the bullfighting brother of Bejarano. The woman was the Carmen I had met at their house, still dressed in black despite the weather. The other man was a phenomenally strong and candid-looking chap, Pilarte, a wrestler turned prizefighter who had developed his muscles loading and unloading ships on the docks of north Spain and who was advertised as the man who could not be knocked out even with a sledgehammer. This was the very latest importation of the Señor Olózaga. In fact, the Señor Olózaga had brought to this country most of the celebrities gathered there that memorable day, and he had toyed with the idea of exhibiting his strongman and put his advertising to a literal test as a publicity stunt, inviting anyone to strike him with a hammer, but Dr. de los Rios had convinced him that this would not make very good publicity.

It was while pondering these things that I heard the voice coming from a table on our other side. It was pampered, sibilant, yet shrill with faked indignation:

"She ought to be thrashed! She ought to be positively and properly chastised!" The voice was speaking English and perhaps that is why it arrested my attention.

Not having heard what led up to pronouncing this sentence of corporal punishment, I turned to have a look and, of course, it was the green man.

Looking at him the place became for a fleeting moment an ice cream parlor, but looking at the two elderly ladies sitting with him, the place immediately resumed its proper aspect of some café in south Spain visited by English tourists. They were having a regular time of it, drinking dutifully from their bottles.

The green man was doing his level best to appear as if he did not belong there, which he did not. It was not that he was speaking English with the two ladies, because possibly they did not speak Spanish, but his manner, or rather, mannerisms and implied condescension and shamefaced acknowledgment of his familiarity with the atmosphere as something remembered from an assumed oppressed past and wretched childhood, intended to convey very plainly that he was slumming among reminiscences that were sweetly revolting.

He waved and winked at Bejarano and, in an aside to one of the ladies, he was carried to remark loudly: "Some Latins are disgustingly

masculine." This with no apparent connection with anything previously said: "But they can discard conventions and have a bang-up
rousing good time. You bet, girlie—the time of your life!"

"Gracious!" one of the ladies exclaimed. "One can certainly get
drunk in a hurry drinking this way."

"You ought to be spanked, you naughty girl. Don't be silly! You
don't have to swallow it that fast. Fool them. Make believe you are
drinking but take little sips, stopping it with your tongue like this,
see?" and he demonstrated expertly. "I believe you are pretty tipsy
already. You should get a good spanking, you bad girl."

I studied the man. He had that peculiar cast to his upper lip and
over-sensitive nostrils typical of individuals of his ilk. I had heard the
Moor discuss it with Dr. de los Rios. He said that perhaps not all those
with such inclinations had that kind of stigma, but that he had never
seen one with it who did not have such inclinations. Dr. de los Rios, as
usual, had been noncommittal and I was considering it now.

The other lady was eyeing the table occupied by the strongman and
the bullfighter with that daring which alcohol induces in her type. She
whispered to her companions and the green man laughed with exhibi-
tionistic squeals. I looked in the general direction of somewhere else
and a prayer of thanks rose in me at the contrast.

She was all saffron and cream; an extraordinary-looking woman
with titian hair and the most enormous mask-like, green, fishy eyes,
surrounded by thickly blackened lashes. I recognized her from
pictures and posters. So, this was Leonor Amboto, La Colombina,
foremost exponent of classical Spanish dance, referred to by critics as
priestess and vestal, her existence dedicated to her art, a mysterious
woman without family and without love, whose life, the little that was
known of it, was miraculously untouched by gossip. With her was the
Señor Olózaga, a man whose past life was as mysterious as hers, but
because of the conflicting gossip heaped upon it.

This inscrutable man fascinated me because, like Don Pedro, he
was a prototype, but whereas the Moor gave the impression of inaccessible recesses, lost in a labyrinth alive with jutting traps, the Señor
Olózaga gave the impression of inaccessible recesses locked into a
solid stone structure. He was big, fat, with an Oriental countenance
that justified the nickname of Chink given him by the Moor, the hair

around the bald spot as white as the full droopy mustache.

To listen to all the stories and adventures for which he was praised or condemned, one would have thought that the man had lived for centuries. Everything regarding his life was confused and heresay. Some said that he had been a magnate and political boss in the days of the Spanish colonies, which he left during the Spanish-American War in order to reconquer them later on with more complex business enterprises of more or less legitimate nature. Others, that he had owned coffee and sugar plantations in the West Indies and traded in white slavery, all of which seemed to such persons very reprehensible; that he was a polygamist and had become a widower several times under circumstances that had engaged the attention of the police in various countries. Others, that he was Chinese or Malayan and had only taken Spanish citizenship for reasons of expediency. Even that at one time he had been a champion wrestler and sold out to lose his championship, thus creating a scandal that kept him away from this country several years; that he was a gambler of inconceivable skill and daring and had extended his activities to cover all world markets and create economical crises in various countries. Again, that his real name was not Olózaga but Chinelato, with other aliases, and that under such assorted names he had carried on simultaneously diverse evil activities and bold coups, that in truth, he was a sinister international figure, moving governments like chessmen and that whenever great events shook the world, one could be certain that behind the scenes was the masterful hand of the Chink.

Yet, all that remained from all this dark past splendor was this jovial, old, big gentleman with a strongman whose ambition was to compete with an anvil, a stranded winter bullfighter on his hands, surrounded by several performers he had brought to this country and who had then made good on their own, their only link with him now a fast-fading memory of dubious gratitude; a man who played at palming amateurishly poor theatrical productions on a homesick colony and whose very ownership of El Telescopio was only rumored and still in doubt. All one could see was a fat old man sitting there placidly like a Buddha, smoking a cigar, indeed with the aspect of a prosperous planter with a weakness for women and rum, but also with undying eagerness for any petty promotion, ready to jump at the drop of a coin, a man who could not help trying to use people, whose favorite greeting was: "Just in time to listen to a little proposition—" or: "The very person I was looking for. I want you to do me a little favor—"

It may well be that this was only a blind to hide greater activities, but it is also possible that the Señor Olózaga may have been one of the most ill-judged of men. The Moor had described him in his chromathematical style as a polynomial in x of degree n, all whose terms but one have zero coefficients.

I remember the time I had seen him last before this day. I had gone with Dr. de los Rios to the Museum of Natural History and we met the Señor Olózaga engrossed in the study of the butterfly collection there. He commented that he would have liked to have been an entomologist but the rushing activities of life— It was astonishing and touching. Then we walked along Central Park West, and he and Dr. de los Rios must have known each other long and well because they held an animated conversation about old days in which they mentioned the Philippines, but I did not follow the conversation because I was considering the manner of our meeting and I will always remember him like that—a man with an aura of adventure, looking at dead butterflies.

And now he was sitting at a table, smoking a cigar, drinking rum and talking expansively to La Colombina, and she listened detached, with unfathomable smile, her gestures deliberate, clean-cut, like tiles in a mosaic of circumspection, like a witch casting her spell all around her, but very careful to avoid contamination. This was good: Buddha and the Witch.

Then I looked at the man at the opposite end of the room from La Colombina. He was standing, leaning against something, I don't remember what, close to the wall. He was tall, slender, with a beautiful build. Very fair and pale, with cold gray eyes and an unaffectedly patronizing manner, he was all romantic arrogance. This was Miguel Pinto, also considered the greatest classical dancer in Spain, whose rivalry with La Colombina was well known. Unlike her, his life was public property and a continuous chain of furious and spectacular love affairs, but like her, he kept his distance and the chasm of their professional jealousy had grown with their fame. It is a sure thing that their meeting in New York was accidental and a source of mutual consternation and their presence at El Telescopio an imposition played by some irresponsible prankster. I thought of the Moor and the Chink.

Dr. Jose de los Rios appeared, acknowledging greetings right and left, and it was obvious that the gathering was now complete. As he passed our table, Don Pedro said: "Hola, Jesucristo," and de los Rios answered: "Hola, you infidel Moor," and he moved to the other end of the room where he engaged an elderly couple in conversation.

"Look at him," Don Pedro was saying. "Every day he looks more like Jesus Christ, with that clean air about him, those blue eyes and light hair and well-kept beard. I used to think that he was Saint Joseph, you know? because of the José, but now I know that the name only threw me off and that he is Jesus son of Mary—if he only wore his hair longer—and as castizo as they come—but who else but a Spaniard? Why, the very Almighty is a Roman Catholic from the albaicín and as castizo and cañí as the next one." He continued to look in the direction of Dr. de los Rios with fond approval: "Look at him—too bad he does not like me better—and of course, the first one he talks to is the head of the Sociedad Española de Socorro—I tell you: Jesus Christ."

"The head of the Sociedad—why, Garcia," I said, "that is your former boss. Remember the story about the impatient fellow?" Garcia was gesturing covertly but desperately for me to shut up, but Don Pedro had heard and was off:

"What, another story? This fellow Garcia is implacable. I tell you, my countrymen—and considering that this one seems more Latin American than Spanish with all this obsession for writing. You know, man?" He pointed at Garcia across the table: "You'll never go back to Spain or even heaven unless you stop this nonsense. What you have to do is to throw away all your intellectual paraphernalia, build yourself up and lead a clean life. That's all, my friend." He looked at Garcia with mock ferocity: "Otherwise I will bring you personally by the ear into the presence of Satan."

"All right, all right," Garcia was saying helplessly. "I guess you are right. I have often felt like doing that very thing. I mean, get rid of the intellectual paraphernalia, whatever it is you mean by that. All right, you win, but all I ask is that you spare—" he finished in an unintelligible babbling that was all but inaudible, but Don Pedro was not paying attention. With his usual volubility he had resumed his previous subject:

"The funny thing is, you know, that the only people here who know everybody else are Dr. Jesucristo and myself—well, maybe the Chink also, but the point is—of course you know, everything has a point and the point or points in this case are the foci. You see? What I say is that we hold the gathering together. You understand, this gathering is an ellipse and Dr. Jesucristo and myself are the foci, sitting at opposite ends, and hold it together. The sum of the tensions we produce on each individual here is always constant. This could only happen with our countrymen—they don't know what it's all about, but neverthe-less ours is the only people who constantly realize a neat mathematical formula of life. That is what makes the pretty picture, the stage setting that foreigners consider as romantic as a play—but it is the national formula—" His voice faded into high pitch and he slapped his neighbor familiarly on the back: "Don't worry, man, don't worry. It's quite all right."

The Moor often expressed himself in mathematical terms, contrary, as he pointed out, to many modern scientists who like to speak of mathematics in humanistic language, and here I want to make a digres-sion regarding things which impressed me enough to make me attempt to record them, however imperfectly, and which I fear may only throw more darkness on the complex personality of the Moor. I will always remember the first time I had an opportunity of observing this person-ality in its own lair. Then I concluded that if it had been difficult to know this man at first, I would only know him less as time went on.

The Moor lived atop a high building in the East Sixties. The apartment was all done up in Moorish Spanish style and there was the strangest Moorish garden with a fountain in the middle and covered by a huge glass dome which illuminated it sadly like an overcast sky. This trans-plantation, abducted from its natural down-to-earth and sunny habitat to be perched in this cloudy day atmosphere, was a melancholy contradiction, a strange symbiosis, like the master of the house.

And it was in these dreamy surroundings that the Moor fascinated us on that occasion with his wonderful music and also brought upon us a sort of jesting consternation with his great pseudology and strange theories about a rigid or solid universe, and where for once he also spoke directly about himself. As in that Moorish garden of his, the occasion was sadly illuminating.

Everything that time was confused and imprecise. His conversation alternated or combined with his music and burst dazzling like a Roman candle in every direction at the same time. One moment the rooms were filled with the strange elegance of Chopin, the cosmopolitan sophistication of Schumann, and the next permeated with his views on the fourth perpendicular and the nonexistence of motion.

The Moor oscillated between the two pieces of furniture which dominated his study: one, a concert grand piano; the other, a tremendously long blackboard before which he occasionally hobbled with the aid of his stick, rapidly tracing symbols and formulas more for the appreciation of Dr. de los Rios than for the rest of us mortals to whom he only gave the polite attention of a passing self-deprecatory remark. Now and then de los Rios stepped up to the blackboard and would add or change something and then they both laughed. What humor they could have derived from that, I don't know, but there are many levels of humor and theirs must have been different from ours.

I remember that Garcia was also there and that later I was conscious of the presence of the Señor Olózaga, but cannot recall when he came in. I remember that the Moor was playing a section from a scherzo by Chopin which ended with four grand broken chords. He played them alternating: two strong, clearly defined; the other two soft and blurry, like an echo. He had turned to face us: "Not the way it is written but one should take one's liberties when playing for one's own enjoyment, and I don't think Chopin would have minded. The business of romanticism is breaking rules. It is loyal to the spirit if not the letter of the music." Then he was up again, his inseparable shillelagh in hand, and he began playing with another strange machine. Wound about two spools that could be turned at will, there was some black material with translucent lines of different shapes and colors illuminated from below which appeared as brightly colored points moving when seen through the narrow slit of a frame adjusted on top. It was perplexing and ridiculous. The little points moved with gathering acceleration, or stood still, or split into two or more and changed colors only to come together again, to oscillate back and forth with increasing rapidity until they were but a blurred vibration.

"See? There is a parabola." He pointed at a curve and down came the frame: "There goes the dot, like an object falling freely. And there is a sine curve." The frame dropped again: "And of course, it becomes a vibration and the colors change—like so many things. Understand what I mean?" He limped back to the piano: "But everything was spread out there for you to see, if only you could lift the frame: simply cinematographic."

It was a theory about time being a fourth dimension and motion only an illusion created by extensions more or less inclined to our space. I had heard or read something about such things but did not know that it was to be taken literally as he claimed it should be. This made it, for some reason, a bit dreadful. I began to play with the little machine and ask some questions, and the Moor took from a desk some folded sheets and handed them to me saying that if interested, I could look through them when I had time. I sensed the net cast by someone sold on a pet theory which he hopes will settle all the difficulties of life, the proselytism which is ever ready to sign up anyone who unwittingly offers the faintest lead, but I was curious.

I unfolded the sheets and glanced quickly through them. They were typewritten hastily and interspaced with hand-penned equations and formulas and geometrical diagrams which took considerably more room than the text. They ranged from the very simple, which even I could understand, to the formidable and on whose merits I had no preparation to pass judgment. The text was obviously written hurriedly without much attention to order and apparently only as notes to be worked out later. The Moor said to disregard the mathematical formulas which I found difficult, that some of them were rather complicated and looked even more so, that this was a monograph he was preparing for some scientific society, and that in its final form he expected to present it in very simple terms that any high school boy could understand provided he had enough imagination: "All those complicated formulas are nothing but a roundabout way of stating something one has not seen quite clearly yet— Impressive, you know, but not as convincing to intuition as a simple graph. The complexities dissolve once the principle and the generalization are understood. If something cannot be presented in very elementary form, it is often of doubtful merit—the old demagogic stand. This question that these things can only be expressed in higher mathematics is only a bit of propaganda nonsense. First one would have to determine where mathematics begins to be high." He pointed at the papers in my hand: "Don't let it frighten you."

I was to learn later that he had composed and published several such papers and even delivered lectures which, considering his style of talking, must have been something, and it was also later that, on my remarking about his diverse talents, he spoke of himself as a well of worthless information and unmarketable achievements with the exception of his bandleading.

He was sitting again and improvised a short melody followed by several chords remotely connected by suspensions as if to round up his demonstration: "One likes to leave these remnants of music about when in the vein. They get lost among the cushions and the drapes and under furniture and perhaps even in that little machine, and then, in moments devoid of inspiration, one can rummage about, finding a chord here, a piece of melody there, no end. Have found it very useful in making arrangements for my band—a little musical reserve fund, eh, Chink?"

It was then, I think, that I realized that the Chink was there. Old, corpulent, with his marked Oriental look, he moved his head up and down slowly in grave assent as the Moor went on:

"You ought to understand—remarkable, this Chink." He was speaking to the rest of us now: "Long, long ago, like all Oriental things, this fellow used to throw change around his rooms when he was in funds, so as to find it when he was broke. You remember, Dr. Jesucristo." He meant de los Rios, of course.

Next thing he was pointing at the machine with his stick: "A clever little gadget this, a better time machine than any clock for impractical purposes. The slit differentiates, gives the derivative, and lifting the frame is equivalent to integrating, but it is also a rather misleading analogy and very inconsistent. It reduces our capacity for dimensionality instead of increasing it, and the lines were moving behind the scenes when the whole idea is the denial of all motion as such. Very sly and sophistic these little lines and they don't fool anybody, but we'll let them get away with it for purposes of illustration."

His Cuban boy moved about quietly. At any rate I don't remember hearing him and all I recall is his bright smiling teeth. He glided unobtrusively, filling our glasses, placing percebes, thick slices of chorizos, sobreasada on squares of Spanish bread, which they call Sicilian here; all in small dishes.

"Oh, tapitas! Come, Dr. Jesucristo, Chink, everybody. Help yourselves to tapitas. Very castizo, like the cheap taverns of our land. Let's see what we have here—aha, aha—what! No shrimps?" And the shrimps appeared as if by enchantment and, of course, the olives. No true tapita without olives.

Then he was addressing himself to de los Rios while the rest of us tried to follow and he was expounding his favorite theory of knowledge. One can learn only what he already knows. Man knows everything he will ever learn, but must have it pointed out by study, given the tools to measure it, the magnifying mirror in which to see himself. That is why all learning must begin by fundamental assumptions which we accept because we know them to be true within ourselves and in the end everything is referred back to us as the ultimate judge. Thus proceeds all logic, all method. Impossible to learn what one cannot conceive. Our capacity for learning is limited only by our wisdom.

But to everything he gave an air of esoteric necromancy and exalted mysticism, presenting the miraculous as the result of logical understanding. With an understanding of the structure of matter, to walk upon the water should not appear impossible, but only uncommon and perhaps unexpected, like rising from the dead. Passing right through a wall, only highly improbable, only a matter of statistics. His was the habit of inflating a point of logic into a balloon of occultism and sending it aloft beyond the reach of anyone who could explode it.

Sucking on a percebe like a cigar butt, he concluded the first part of Schumann's *Carnaval* in the grand manner, only to remove the percebe and resume his talk:

"Extraordinary, Schumann. The moderns have not caught up with him yet, but his heritage did flourish in Debussy. Not only the preoccupation with the novelty in elegance which constitutes so much of the charm of romanticism, but the romanticism essentially musical in the pursuit of new harmonies and coloring—compare their arabesques—the spirit of acoustic experimentalism"—and he played something about a girl with flaxen hair— "And yet, there is where he might have gone wrong. Those whole tone progressions, you know, deceptive and illicit as the little lines behind the frame. The effect constitutes a novel but fallacious illustration. Every note standing in the same relationship to all the others destroys the feeling of tonality and consequently of modulation—one of the most beautiful devices of musical structure—as in the case of the chromatic scale of equal temperament. It reduces everything to a question of pitch—" there was his laughter again. "Like the little lines behind the frame, reducing instead of increasing."

He played from a very slow waltz, also Debussy, and spoke in gloomy tones of waltzes in general and in particular of a very sad one of Sibelius: "That is not a waltz, it is a dance macabre. People could not dance to that; only the dead could dance to it."

Garcia began to talk to me and although I can't remember what he said and don't think I paid much attention, it created enough of a distraction. The Chink seemed to have gone to sleep but I noticed that he opened his eyes intermittently to help himself to the tapitas or a drink of manzanilla. Perhaps he was listening and concentrating, because the Moor, who was now playing a waltz, said to him: "This is for you. It brings back memories, eh, Chink?" and the Señor Olózaga opened his eyes and smiled a faraway smile and seemed to go into a contented reverie. That was his favorite tune, the Moor said very mysteriously, and the Señor Olózaga's smile broadened and he settled himself more comfortably in his chair. He was enigmatic.

I noticed that the tapitas had been growing in size under the masterful guidance of the Cuban boy, who anticipated all our wishes, until after a while we were eating rice with clams out of regular dishes and the Moor a bowl of garlic soup. Magnificent confusion and disorder. I read from the notes in my hand:

Unlike Newton who claimed to make no hypotheses, one must make one fundamental and radical hypothesis for everything in the world of our experience to fall neatly into place and account for all phenomena. This is the advantage of this view over all others which have been advanced with the same purpose, but are full of patchwork and compromises of reason so that mechanics and cosmology rest—if this can be called rest—on two independent bases and are incapable of solving or explaining the simplest physical facts, including ourselves.

The secret and the key is the fourth perpendicular. Euclid with a fourth coordinate . . .

My attention was arrested by a pause in the conversation that was filled with some Spanish music of remarkable brilliance. Many have characterized the Spanish school of playing as excelling in its filigree delicacy and tenuous shading, crisp and frosty in the icicles of its expression. Not him. His was a style impetuous and abandoned. He played more like a natural musician than a trained virtuoso, where lack of digital dexterity is compensated by overconfidence of understanding and purpose in the conviction of being able to turn any blunder into an improvisation.

. . . but there is no motion; not only absolute motion, as the relativists timidly claim, but no motion at all—only inclinations between the fourth perpendicular and the other three. Only extensions. The reasons for the impossibility of detecting absolute motion become obvious, as this is the same as determining which of several intersecting lines is separating from the others—a meaningless question.

Descartes, with his analytic geometry, gave the key to this simple fact. The obvious clue was there, but almost all failed or refused to see it, and if that had not been enough, the elegant notion of the hodograph conceived by my illustrious countryman and spiritual ancestor should have made matters even plainer, if that were necessary.

I stopped reading to put a few questions to the Moor and in answer he disclaimed any originality in these theories. He reviewed the bold encompassing of Minkowski, the optimistically conditioning analogies of Hinton and crystal clear digest of Ouspensky, as some of the few who were on the right track and then others since Lagrange's well-founded suspicions. He bowed politely to Gauss and bypassed non-Euclidians to end in a swift curtsy before Riemann and run his hands over the piano in irrelevant improvisation that climbed the upper register and kept going to reach for the bottle of wine standing guard there and he continued to theorize. I turned back to the notes. At least I could try to reread their meaning, but to follow his arboriform conversation was too much.

Yet the very great majority rejected it, could not admit that time and motion are but the impression we receive from four-dimensional extensions, and they continued to build their physics and mechanics upon three-dimensional projections and slides and shadows . . .

He was playing again from Chopin, something sad, sorrowful to the point of lugubriousness: "He was a sick man, no doubt of that," he said half to himself, "but in other things he showed tremendous force and rebellion—vitality. Berlioz made a mistake in judging him with a banal cruelty induced by the desire, fashionable at the time, of making one more phrase. Chopin was not dead all his life. He has not died yet." He stopped and spun on the stool to face de los Rios: "It was a hasty judgment drawn from a few instances. Short-sighted, exactly like the others."

Contemporary scientists have tried to compromise, had to admit certain facts that could not be denied any longer, but instead of lifting the frame, they began to look at it through telescopes and microscopes and measure it with sidereal or more or less ingenious chronometers, only to become involved in greater contradictions and end in dismal surrender. Anything rather than let go of the intuitive concept of time. It is that insane fear of the absolute which blinds them. As their contributing concession, they admitted time as a fourth coordinate in the strictly mathematical sense, whatever that means; as if it had not been used already as such for centuries—but never in the literal sense.

Further on I read:

. . . and this apparently formidable and elementary geometric objection to taking higher dimensions literally, because of supposed inconsistency with a change of coordinates, can be easily dealt with . . .

If it was elementary and easy, the formulas and line of reasoning that followed escaped me. I resented the patent implication and rather than put the blame foolishly on my ignorance, I placed it squarely and justly on the involved, obscure and careless style of the author. It was a consolation to know that, had this elementary and easy question been presented correctly and clearly, I would have grasped it without difficulty, but I refrained from asking the Moor or Dr. de los Rios to elucidate. Like Don Quixote with his helmet visor, I did not want to expose my mended vanity to a second test. I imagine that he considered relativists as outmoded and not entirely in good faith. He was poking fun at them in the next note I read:

Newton's experiment with the spinning vessel full of liquid as a proof of absolute motion, never quite satisfactorily explained away by semi-modern physics, becomes positively inconvenient by adding another equally filled vessel revolving at the same time but in opposite direction and the effect on relativists should be devastating— Dizzily they pick up all their popularizing tackle: Fitzgerald "contraptions," elastic and non-elastic rods, fast and slow clocks, light signals, free-falling elevators and sidereal swift-traveling twins who turn out younger than each other, and decide to go home to flatland aboard their equivalence hypothesis and call it a day; when by considering the experiment in the light of this theory, as a helix extension, there would have been no cause for embarrassment.

He was playing again that ending of the *Carnaval*'s first part, running through the rapid dog-chases-cat section that rounded up in that magnificent conclusion. He seemed to like that and spoke about it, but I was paying no attention.

. . . there is no motion, but physicists are too timid to admit this. It is this timidity that makes them give up so easily at the first setback. They experimented with light and without bothering to ascertain its nature and, with the least-founded assumptions about that of its propagation, became utterly demoralized because the results of their experiment were negative. One of the most disconcerting conclusions of the experiment was that light behaved as if the earth were standing still, which after all, it does since nothing is moving, but a conclusion intolerable to anyone donning a snobbish Copernican modesty as a necessary accessory to debunking progress—and they gave up too easily.

The fact that an experiment fails our reason should not disconcert one to such an extent, but only make one doubt the validity of the conclusions it implies and the things which it assumes. One might even consider light as an extension in a fifth dimension, which would account for its crossing all objects at the same rate regardless of their speed or direction. Who knows? Might be worth investigating this line of reasoning. Let us say that it crosses our four-dimensional field and the inclination at which it crosses it is what we measure as its velocity. From experiments, it would appear that this inclination is constant. In short, they have not measured the velocity of light at all, but merely a cross section of it. Got everything upside down. Don't know what it's all about.

All this made me dizzy and I know that Garcia, who had been reading over my shoulder, often holding a page I wanted to turn, was flabbergasted. I was ready to give up, like a timid physicist. It was too complicated and removed from everyday experience, although the Moor did not seem to think so:

... quite simple. Add one more coordinate and the difficulties disappear—the complete panacea that cures all ailments of physics and philosophy. But I don't think they want to take that medicine. They will swallow any other pill, assume anything but higher dimensionalities taken literally. They refuse to make this one fundamental assumption, but instead they assumed all kinds of ethers, when the fear of dimensions—a real case of logarithmic agrophobia that leads them to the most outlandish acrobatics on the parallels of the equality sign, in order to duck any exponent higher than the third—was the anesthetizing ether that rendered them totally incapable of seeing the obvious. They accepted non-Euclidian geometries—more mathemacrobatics on other pseudo-parallels—and produced many innocent and disarming little admissions springing coyly out of a hat like tame rabbits charged with some infectious virus. Everything under the spell of their favorite magic wand which by moving swiftly past our noses like an admonishing nightstick, changed into a stupefying blackjack—the well-known contracting rod, their most reliable weapon—when, on the contrary, one glance even at my little machine shows that it should grow long as a fishing pole with all its implications.
But speaking seriously ...

This made me laugh and Garcia joined me, but I am not sure that we were laughing at the same thing. Nobody else paid any attention.

But speaking seriously, since what we call the length of an object is its three-dimensional section, it is clear that the length of this section varies according to the inclination of the cut, although inversely as they conclude. The real object, the four-dimensional object, remains the same. Nothing is moving, nothing at all. They are utterly confused.

By considering the limiting case—infinite velocity—one can see that an object would be all along the line of motion at the same time (its time extension stretched full length in our space); that is, elongated to the utmost, instead of shortened to nothing as they claim. They have got everything upside down.

All these elongations—or contractions if we accept them for the sake of not arguing—hold no mystery. We are all familiar with distortions in space of three dimensions. The most rigid body can be made to shrink, expand or become deformed simply by receding from it, approaching it or changing one's position, and no one questions which is the real or apparent size and shape and the phenomenon causes no one, except perhaps a high mathematical physicist, the slightest perplexity. This is because we understand perspective, because we can interpret the third dimension.

In the same way, the fourth dimension involves distortions which appear as motion, elongations or whatever you please. It is puzzling because we have not conditioned ourselves to interpret the fourth dimension and understand its perspective, but there is no reason for calling upon special branches of mathematics or trick devices to explain something that an extension of Euclid can explain more concisely, naturally and convincingly.

I assumed that Dr. de los Rios knew all about these things already, but I was not sure of what he thought of them and I don't think the Señor Olózaga was interested, but I felt and I am sure Garcia also felt that this concept of a motionless universe extending in undreamt-of directions was depressing. Possibly the idea was not difficult to grant, if not to conceive, as applying to all external happenings, perhaps even our dreams, all of which appeared to be independent of us, but when applied to our thoughts, to our decisions, our labors, our smallest motions, it seemed very difficult to accept. It conjured infinite, terrifying vistas of changeless destiny—our past and future spread out and coexisting, all foreordained, all inevitable and we pinned, held like flies in this endless spiderweb, or perhaps constituting some of its enormously long filaments. Regardless of any degrees of freedom through all these dimensions, it was a horrible prison, a prison from which there could be not only no hope, but no conception of escape, because it took in everything and one could not even have the consolation of dreaming of an outside or a future.

On the other hand, it appeared as tremendously dramatic that this extension, which might be but one single instant, should create that impression of enduring time, of all history, of all eternity. Only one moment, one flash, all at once, and yet our intuition of it so gradual, so slow, so protracted, creating the illusion that we contribute to creation.

It was at this moment that Garcia rescued me from these useless thoughts by asking the Moor how he became interested in these subjects. In a series of reminiscences shared with Dr. de los Rios and the Señor Olózaga, who had come momentarily awake, he told us.

There were memories of his stormy youth and a brilliant scene one night when, having returned from Ireland, he had conducted at El Real in Madrid one of the most magnificent performances of Gounod's *Faust* ever presented at that venerable and critical opera house, when he inspired the musicians and singers to heights worthy of that romantic and significant opera. Then a concert with the Madrid orchestra where he made history with a capital rendition of Beethoven's Third Symphony, by giving it full rein, letting it play itself, with warmth and turbulence, with serenity and piety, in those days when conductors could still do novel things with time-honored classics. He extemporized on the symphony.

The first movement: a complete thesis—strident and sentimental —sheer glory in all its aspects—a résumé of the whole program. The second movement with all the rotten grandeur of death, of green marble sepulchral dwellings and tearful lamentations. The third movement, a resurrection in memories of battles with horn calls suggestive of the hunt. Many conductors have been tempted to transpose these two movements because of misunderstood reverence for chronology. Beethoven's musical instinct guided him unerringly to the proper arrangement. Not only to sacrifice an unessential chronology to musical structure and unity, but philosophically as well; to kill his hero at the outset and understand that death is the foregone conclusion in the life of a hero which implies it by definition. This was a stroke of genius which sees clearly the timeless pattern of destiny. The last movement: victorious soldiers marching and also rhythms and accents indicative of limping, wounded, tired, straggling soldiers stepping off, coming to roost at the roadside inns, to quench their many thirsts, especially that for life, after their long association with death. A symphony which is the greatest tribute ever paid to masculinity, a monument to men and their glory and the penalty of their calling. A tableau of brilliant uniforms and decorations stained with blood. A battlefield with bucolic reminiscences of love.

"It was not me, it was Beethoven. Where he is, there is no room for anything else. The master, always in full command, the greatest of all showmen and first of the true romantics." He was talking much more calmly now, but still with something of that kidding way of his: "And also insincere, I suspect; playing with his audience like a storyteller plays with the emotions of young listeners—ha—and frightening them. Those short, veiled, ominous passages, letting go and holding back, threatening, preparing, dressing up his victims for the telling blow. Immense! Inexhaustible capacity for presenting any idea in the best possible way. Probably the most successful artist ever, the only one who has been able to express fully everything he wanted as he wanted to express it. And then his unparalleled capacity to top perfection—not gild the lily, but to go beyond one's wildest hopes of completeness and fulfillment. That is the true mark of genius: to transcend the strict limits of perfection and emerge into the boundless reaches of greatness. There is nothing much a musician can do with him except let him take over." He paused a moment: "Yes, it was not me. It was him."

The critics had acclaimed his conducting as their greatest discovery. His reputation spread like wildfire. Everything pointed to a brilliant career in serious music and then, the accident.

There are several conflicting stories and rumors concerning the accident, most of them, no doubt, started by the Moor in order to confuse the issue and surround it with an aura of mystery ranging from the sadly romantic through the droll and heroic sacrifice, to the downright fantastic, but from more sober and reliable sources I have learned that he was the undisputed champion brat of the nineteenth century and his game leg the consequence of an early prank. Be this as it may, the Moor had thrown a smoke screen of whimsicality around his lameness, capitalized on it and parlayed a common bum leg into a lifetime career.

This day he did not dwell or elaborate on the accident itself and only brought it up with but a hint of reminiscent melancholy and a repressed sigh as the turning point in his life. While he was laid up for months, some books on mathematics fell into his hands. They must have been well written or his condition may have made him susceptible to their contents, because for the first time in his life he became feverishly interested. It proved a revelation. He had considered himself fairly intelligent until then, but he felt now like a child in arms as compared with the men who had thought up these things or when considering what they could do with them. The satisfying generalizations, the logical conclusions and unexpected demonstrations which, once understood, appeared so simple as to make one feel like a fool; the embracing concept of function and the formidable tool of transformation. All these things reaching conclusions that transcended the very minds which had discovered or perhaps created them. That was the slightly maddening thing about it. Were these things discoveries or creations? Or could one not settle by concluding that they were the system of discovering the workings of one's own mind?

He remembered his delight when analyzing the general solutions of equations. The practical quadratic was a sonnet with two possible endings; the cubic was an ode to ingenuity and perhaps a monument to the controversial perfidy of an unscrupulous mathematician, its irreducible case a hint of irritating suggestiveness; the quartic, a drama in which three unknown victims are enlisted, two of them liquidated to zero only to be exhumed later to yield the solution with their identity; the quintic, the pillars of Hercules, a stimulus to generalizations and conquests which far surpassed the original problem and a profound humanistic lesson which tells us that we should always question whether the solutions we seek to our problems really exist.

During his university days he had swum in a small part of this ocean, or rather, had floated like something impermeable and stationary, without understanding, or venturing to see what lay beyond the horizon, or sinking to find what was in the depths, or even considering whether it might be at times a reflection of the sky. Perhaps it had been his youth, more concerned with immediate and mundane things, perhaps his teachers or the books he read had not been inspiring. The fact remains that while he lay in bed he had been visited by this revelation that changed his attitude about life. Forgotten were all thoughts of serious music, changed completely his sense of values. These were the boundless perspectives to explore, the great game of the mind. He did not regret at all his protracted confinement to bed, but would have prolonged it, nor did he regret being lame for life and thus having lost the fickle love of that wonderful girl who sat in a box the memorable night of *Faust*, basking vicariously in his glory, and whose corsage he still treasured, withered and disintegrated, in a beautifully inlaid coffer carved like a miniature mosque.

When he finished, he was playing something very sentimental and put on a comically contrite look which came unexpectedly to life with his characteristic laugh. I realized that he had been amusing himself at our expense. What a character!

I still held his notes in my hand and turned my attention to them again. For the first time I noticed that many of them were written in the style he talked. There were several dashes in between phrases which probably stood for his derisive laughter:

Those who attack relativity perhaps have never understood it fully, but those who disregard Euclid perhaps have never understood him as simply as schoolchildren do. But possibly this comes from boredom at confronting the same thing over and over again or from a desire to save the profession or put it on a paying basis. Cast doubts, create new things, and your customers come flocking back. Give them something so solid that it lasts forever and soon you have no more customers— The system of the guild. Stand together and protect it at all costs. Nothing as decisive as this final step of higher dimensionalities—and they have on their side the average man. Who can believe such a radical assumption that denies all evidence of our senses, our intuition of flowing time, of real motion? Who indeed? So, one must propagandize the collapse of reason and flood the market with startling revelations. It is a carnival with fireworks and all. Take a group of sightseers who don't know what it's all about, disguise them brilliantly through an ingenious transformation and make them dance on tensors over nets of matrices to the syncopation of covariants and contravariants and they are at your mercy. When they hear that the addition of velocities has a limit and that infinity has been clocked at three hundred thousand kilometers per second, they don't realize that while they have been stood up with the intuition-cuddling assertion of the reality of time and motion, their reason has been knocked down with the absurdity of a limiting velocity, so long as it is considered a velocity to which nothing can be added and from which nothing can be subtracted, and they have been swindled out of the very ground from which they were contemplating the mental pyrotechnic display. They are all yours. The implied flattery has won them over, and you are back in business again.

Yet, this concept of a limiting velocity becomes simple when considered as an extension where all inclinations which appear as velocities from zero to infinity take place within a quadrant beyond which they only appear as motion in the opposite direction with less than ninety degrees as the difference between an explosion and something that stands still and endures, for the conversion of static mass into energy, or more properly speaking, for an observer to experience mass as energy or vice versa—curiously enough, a multiplication by the square root of minus one. It is by viciously interpreting this graphic representation that a sophistic proof of a contraction, instead of an elongation, is spuriously obtained, thus contradicting the very premises of the argument. Anything in order to explain the inescapable negative results of an experiment which was doomed to failure because it was no experiment at all.

In the light of our concept, we have a type of infinity to which something can be added and from which something can be subtracted, contrary to the relativistic viewpoint. The fundamental concepts are the same, but the conclusions are very different. These conclusions appear in both cases as paradoxical, but while in one system they become understandable, in the other they defy reason.

I should have known better, but I allowed myself to be dragged into the discussion. Not being at all sure of my ground, I tried to advance behind a shield of generalizations and demagogy. This was, I said, being iconoclastic and unfair to the great men of science—and the world does not applaud or sanction people for nothing—who had achieved such remarkable conclusions and contributed so many things to our modern world. I did not go into what conclusions or what things, because even if I did not know them well, I felt certain that I must be speaking the truth, but the Moor turned the tables on me and said that I had chosen the wrong word when I said "iconoclastic" because modern science was certainly a specialist at laying low idols and old tried and respected truths. He was sponsoring the movement of back to neo-Euclidianism and the tautological neo-Newtonism and I think I caught something of his perennial phrase "don't know what it's all about."

I contented myself with saying that even a dumb clock is right once every twelve hours, but he looked at me with the eyes of a hypnotizing fakir and emitted in a stage whisper:

"Right every moment while stretched out, taking a nap, on the fourth perpendicular, but don't tell anybody." He held his pose pointing his fingers at me and then went: "Boo!"

This time I gave up.

He pursued his line of reasoning as if there had been no interruption and, temporizing with Dr. de los Rios, who had argued some of his implications, he conceded that perhaps modern science is only endeavoring to avoid boredom at the repetition of the same old postulates and redundant formulas, perhaps scared by a frightful suggestion of futility once tossed off by Poincaré, by creating a novel mental game whose price lies outside an imaginary vicious circle and befuddles the main issue with the razzle-dazzle of surprising apparent contradictions: "To take the decisive step, to lift the frame of the little machine, would be exhibiting paradisiac innocence. The oversimplification would be intolerable—anybody could understand it. No more inner sanctum or chosen few."

I was still slightly irritated at him and both revenge and prudence dictated to ignore the conversation. I read the notes instead:

. . . with the decisive step, all these things could be expressed in terms of a time including classical relativity, elementary geometry and reciprocally equivalent Galilei transformations, without resorting to any devious calibration curves, principles of indeterminacy and all the usual rigamarole. Newtonian mechanics remain valid. As an example, the square of the radius is implied in anything isotropic, such as gravitation and also time, but the fact that accelerations like that produced by gravitation involve time as a function, that scientists have been squaring time as the most natural thing in the world, constitutes a tacit acceptance of the validity of this theory and makes it self-evident.

All problems and phenomena which appear incapable of explanation or understanding because we insist on considering them as isolated and disconnected become simple in a universe which is connected and immobile and they resolve into the shape of things, the pattern. Problems of action at a distance evaporate because the universe is one, continuous, solid, rigid, and there is no action. Force and acceleration reduce to the difference between sets of coordinates. Laws of physics become platitudinous to the point of idiocy when thus stated. The laws of motion appear self-evident; the first law is tantamount to saying that a line is straight until it bends; the second law, that the rate of separation between a certain curve and any of its tangents increases as both are produced; the third law is equivalent to the division of an angle by the fourth perpendicular.

It all boils down to the statement of a structure in which the words "fourth coordinate" and the deviations from it are substituted for the words "time and motion." The result is the same, but the intuitive implications of the words commonly used only succeed in rendering the concept more confused and elusive.

I was going to address a remark to the Moor, my irritation having left me during my efforts to concentrate amidst the conversation and music around me, but he was deep in the subject of music, praising the orchestral grand stunts of Strauss and maintaining that his *Till Eulenspiegel* was the most remarkable production of modern times. This led to further discussions of fine points of what one might mean by "modern" and the beginning of an epoch, and he and de los Rios discussed new harmonics and acoustic effects and their validity. He soon linked these things to the same desire to escape the boredom of repetition and accused Beethoven of being as exhaustive as Newton and therefore leaving little if anything for others to do along fundamental lines. The manner in which he jumped from one thing to another was extraordinary and I don't know how de los Rios managed to keep pace with him so easily.

He had been playing the weird number four of the *Kreisleriana* and now played number six. It held us spellbound with its unearthly beauty which became even sadder in the unexpected dance tempo, and then he began to discuss Schumann's artificial fingering and systems of inducing cramped positions of the hands in order to bring out a particular voice, and he played some more of his things as an illustration. It was all highly technical, so I read some more—from the pan into the fire:

. . . they refuse to take the plunge. They who have assumed so many things, who accepted ether so tenuous that everything could move through it without resistance, yet was so rigid as to propagate things at unheard-of speeds; they who accepted so many contradictory hypotheses and maddening conclusions, who have carried open-mindedness to the point where there is nothing more to open, refuse to take the decisive, final plunge, refuse to lift the frame of the little machine. Anything but that. And yet, that would explain so many things, as Lagrange said of the hypothesis of a Creator, except that here the problem would be dissolved, rather than solved. The contradictions of the ether disappear. It can be the most rigid thing imaginable and at the same time offer no resistance to motion, because there is nothing to resist, there is no motion.

I put a question to him which I thought would go unheeded, but he caught it:

"Of course, the darn thing is as rigid as can be—dead and stiff, that's it. The universe is dead but one cannot admit that fact. The Olympian optimism. In decent, cultured, well-to-do society, it is not proper to speak of death, one avoids this word and the verb 'to die' as almost obscene. Nice people only refer to this fact as 'passing on,' or 'away.' Nice people never die. One can die only on the wrong side of town and a man must cross the tracks before he can die simply, in peace. Anything else would be a misdemeanor. Mind you, people may be dying everywhere like flies, but this is considered bad taste. Never mind if people are decimated, the thing is inadmissible, one must be optimistic and suggest other possibilities. One cannot come out and say that someone died, or that something is dead. It is shocking, revolting—and yet the universe is not passing on or away as many well-bred scientists have insisted, because there is no motion and despite our scruples, nothing is passing. The universe has been, or is, dead all its life, to speak like Berlios."

This put us back into music. Out of the vast tracts of records that covered the walls of an adjoining room, he picked unerringly the album he wanted and in no time at all had a record spinning on the phonograph, a tremendous contraption wired to loudspeakers distributed through the walls, with two turntables so perfectly synchronized that one could detect no break between two records. The music took possession of the room with majestic pride. It was the *Leonora* No. 3 overture.

"Nothing much to do with Berlios, but listen to that, Dr. Jesucristo. It comes at you from afar, straight at you and then explodes over your head like a storm of eloquence. Much good music has created the impression of latitude, but this one adds to that the impression of depth, of acoustic perspective. It reminds me of that," he pointed at a reproduction of a picture of Toledo by El Greco which hung on the wall. "It is the empress of overtures, the most dignified and arrogant, the most subjugating and convincing." He stopped the machine when the music had reached the fulfillment of its first section—exploded over our heads as he said. I was now working on a dish of ropa vieja and his Cuban boy filled my glass with a light red wine, whose color tended more to the vermillion and whose taste left an aftermath on the palate, like a dark shadow of ineffable delight. From my bacchic heaven I considered the Chink's dish of rice and concluded that if I lifted "the frame of the little machine," as one might do the cover in an elegant restaurant, I would find that, four dimensionally considered, it was really a dish of spaghetti. Logical but insane.

I set down my dish on the vast moroccan cushion where I was sitting and picked up the Moor's notes:

. . . there is no motion; hence, the impossibility of explaining it—should be evident to anyone who has looked at the graph of a function . . .

. . . all the little things that check, if only one takes notice. Bodies with greater mass are naturally less liable to have bends along their fourth dimension—questions of action and reaction—two interacting bodies—displacement inversely proportional to mass—the body with the lesser mass has the more bend, its fourth dimensional length is greater, its time more rapid—checks with some conclusions about the rate of vibrations in heavier and lighter stars—simplification.

The Moor's phrases reached me disconnectedly, intruding and alternating with his notes:
". . . the same romantic school. Abel and Galois, the Chopin and Schumann of mathematics, but immensely more successful in their medium—utterly ridiculous . . ."

Seen in this light, phenomena reveal a pattern where details fall accurately into place. Cosmology, things of growth, procreation, evolution, questions of heredity, even matters of social movements and trends—the very words give the whole thing away. The following graphs illustrate . . .

"Aside from Day and one or two others, there has been no analytical attack on the question of harmony—the minor key as a composite of old Greek modes. It is to laugh. Obvious to anyone with an ear that the minor is but an accompanying key derived from the old method of accompanying in thirds. Perfectly simple."

... here is something else that checks: orbits sweeping equal areas in equal times. But of course the elliptic orbit is nothing but the projection of a circular orbit inclined into the fourth dimension. Properly speaking, it is a four dimensional helix. Anything that moves represents such an inclination —naturally! Equal areas in equal times as it should happen in any uniform circular motion. A spinning wheel seen at an angle appears as an ellipse whose spokes sweep equal areas in equal times. No need of complicated mechanisms to slow up and accelerate—doesn't know anything about our calculations of its projection, but goes merrily on about its business of a simple harmonic motion— Perfectly natural. What else could it do? As for the eccentricity of the orbit—the center becoming a focus...

Here followed more equations and diagrams which I chose to disregard. Garcia, who had been looking at the notes over my shoulder, had left, and through the big open French doors I could see him pacing back and forth in the Moorish garden, a drink in one hand and a cigarette in the other. Garcia had always entertained the misconception that all sciences, and particularly mathematics, were dull and unimaginative. Now I knew that he felt they were not only that, but also evil with a purpose and intent upon the mocking destruction of everything he held dear. I was sure that he disapproved of all this talk and theories on subjects he knew nothing about and had decided to remove himself in protest, but then he came in, laid his glass down on a taboret by the doors and stood there framed, dramatic. He said:

"But if you eliminate time and motion, you rob life of all its drama, of all romance, of all adventure." He must have been ruminating and worrying about the matter while pacing the garden. "You kill it, you kill everything. It is a dead universe, as you say, changeless, hopeless. Life becomes—" He groped for words and then gave up with a resigned shrug, picked up his glass and resumed his pacing in the garden.

"Nonsense," the Moor was saying. "A picture or a statue is not less beautiful because it is all there to be seen at once. Why is there nothing absurd about my finding a similarity between the *Leonora* overture, which is all sequence in time, and El Greco's *Toledo*, which is all simultaneity in space? Possibly the fourth dimensional structure of the one suggests to me something about the two dimensional structure of the other— Oh! I know," he waved away the objection. "It might suggest something else to you. We Spaniards must always be individualistic, have our very own viewpoint—the national system. But that is beside the point. The fact that the similarity is admissible, that it may be considered, is what makes it significant, and besides, understanding these things would change nothing, at least not for a long time—"

The note I was reading seemed to elaborate the point:

Man will have to change a great deal before he can have the intuition of the fourth dimension spatially. We don't even see three. We see only two and interpret the third from deformations of the others. We can only conceive of three coordinates as interrelated and making any sense of space, of coexistence, of simultaneity. Anything beyond that puzzles us, eludes, bewilders us, makes us dizzy with that feeling of time and motion, of flowing and enduring which we cannot explain, but which is irrevocably bound with our intuition. We see, we feel, but don't know what it's all about. Someday perhaps man will actually see the third dimension, but to see it properly one would have to see all sides of an object at the same time. This could only be done from a fourth dimension which in turn would be interpreted as perspective and no longer as time and motion. Who knows? The more advanced man is, the less motion he will see, the less time he will experience . . .

And the Moor was still talking:

"In the future, a long time distance from here-now, as the relativity publicity agents put it—and you know, it is perfectly safe to consider happenings so far removed that we will never be held responsible— we may be able to see yesterday, today and tomorrow spread out before us. What a panorama of interwoven lines, spirals and helicles and undulating curves—a tangle so thick, leaving no empty room, that in the limiting case it will appear like a solid mass, perfectly homogeneous and continuous and simple— Completely insane; the virtuous circle; from primitive and paradisiac simplicity to the conception of absolute complexity which only leads back to simplicity—and they may even have telescopes which will show beyond yesterday and tomorrow and the confines of our own existence—remarkable telescopes like the one on Cherry Street. Now I know the reason why I baptized that place El Telescopio. There, after a few bottles, one can see the past and the future at the same time without difficulty and it is anything but boring or dead—there I go arguing with myself. Typical castizo. It is the national system. Forestall any possibility of your interlocutor winning a point. Beat him to it—simply divine."

The mention of divinity must have put him in the spirit of the mystic revelations because he was soon talking of the hyperspheres of human lives whose centers are world points and the possibility of escaping from such prisons. The centers represented birth and the surfaces death. Consequently we always reach our end at the same time-distance regardless of the direction we chose. But liberation had something to do with still higher dimensionalities: "Add one more coordinate and you are saved!" he shouted, convulsed with laughter. He was addressing the Señor Olózaga who had come awake again and was punishing the rum bottle. "As an Oriental you should know and appreciate these things, Chink." The Señor Olózaga smiled and the Moor began to talk again more earnestly to de los Rios. I was trying not to listen. Between the tapitas, wine, rice and clams and the notes, there was no point in adding more to the confusion. I ate some more of the ropa vieja, took a moderate swallow and settled again with the notes:

. . . disregarding the postulated interchangeability of dimensions, the fourth should be properly considered the first since nothing can be without it. A point is really a line into the fourth dimension. When it stands still, it is parallel to the fourth coordinate; when it deviates from this, it appears to move, but in reality we are only tracing its length. If it moves rapidly enough, it appears as the line it really is, fading into the fourth dimension, because its inclination approaches more our three dimensional field . . .

I thought this was undisguised pseudology. It disregarded completely the impression left in the retina, but it maintained an apparent consistency. I doubted the seriousness of the Moor but that was his way: to leave one wondering whether he was joking, considering one always as unworthy of his serious controversy. Since that occasion, this unflattering suspicion has only become more of a certainty, but somehow one does not mind where the Moor is concerned. Therefore I did not voice my objections and besides, he did not seem to be in a serious mood for discussion any longer. Instead I turned over some sheets and read further on:

Modern science is disconcerted and desperate and its last hope is the second law of thermodynamics, that most dramatic and also fateful of all laws, but even this must be denied in a system of simplification. They claim that there is always more entropy in the future than in the past, that this is an index to the time vector, as the centrifugal force was the last hope of the absolutists—completely confused. It reduces to the problem of the other side of the street always being where we are not. A simple geometrical construction shows that there are always more things away from us than close by. When one is at the end of a street, one can see more buildings at the other end than close by, but the fellow at the other end sees the same thing in reverse and both conclude that there are more things far than near and decide that they agree and that this is an index to a very clever city planning and prepare letters of congratulation to the mayor for having arranged things so wisely that they find themselves where there is room to move, because considering how crowded the buildings look at a distance, it would have been very inconvenient to have been located there—impossible to get out or even move. Absurd! A result of muddled thinking due to demoralization. The whole question is but a matter of isentropic perspective along the fourth perpendicular. Like a man standing on a sphere (silly as it sounds) who finds its surface curving away from him in the same manner regardless of the point he occupies or the direction in which he looks— No more drama and no more fatefulness.

To allow the question of time and motion to enter the discussion only leads to those paradoxes of the infinitely small and infinitely big which have marred scientific history since time immemorial and continue to embarrass any pedagogue who takes his job seriously. It even placed Newton on the losing end of a theologico-mathematical argument when all the time he knew that he was right, and all this over the thing that is elusive to the vanishing point; the derivative, which can never satisfy the demands of our intuitive reason. Yet, if geometrically considered, the thing satisfies the stiffest requirements of both our intuition and mysticism and even the most hyperdialectic bishop has to recognize a tangent to a curve when he sees it.

Toward the end of the opus, bold type arrested my eyes and then sent them back a few lines:

... once the illusory nature of motion has been detected and exposed, not only do all such embarrassing situations evaporate, but by the above axioms, one can stop making laws about imaginary things, discard unwarranted assumptions and thus, with greater generalization, arrive at the

FUNDAMENTAL POSTULATE
The configurations of any given reference system appear as motion in any different system of reference

Perhaps because it was thus set apart, I read it aloud without thinking. All at once it rebounded scattered in crashing applause, laughter and words from the Moor:

"Wonderful parrot act, my lad! Commit that to memory. You now hold the key. That is my testament and I bequeath its implications to mathematicians and physicists alike, to think them over and argue them." More noisy display.

With withering, unflinching equanimity, I disregarded the clownish outbursts and read what seemed to be written in a more serious vein:

From this fundamental postulate, all the laws of mechanics can be disengaged more naturally by the application of logic. All these reference systems are equivalent and differ only in their position with respect to one another within the general plenum where they coexist. It is their orientation that we refer to as inertia.

Motion varies as the difference between the systems. As this difference diminishes, the apparent motion also decreases until, in the limiting case, it vanishes, the systems coincide, become identical and the motion is zero. Force, acceleration, stress, etc., are but ways of looking at and evaluating this difference between the systems and their mutual impingement.

But since this difference or reciprocal displacement apprehended as motion assumes tacitly an extension not contained in the three dimensions of the space of our common experience and since, by our own definition, motion implies time, we are led inevitably to label time as another dimension. This is a test of the fundamental postulate's strength in guiding us to conclusions which our intuition fails to disclose. One should not accept one's impressions and then derive laws from them. One should formulate postulates epistemologically, in their greater generality, and then allow them to help reach conclusions despite impressions.

I turned the page and read on:

If we conceive of every particle of matter (and this provisionally, as we do not know clearly what we mean by particle and by matter) as determining a reference system, the more of them that coincide, the greater the common system; hence, the greater the mass, the inertia, etc., which are but the quantity of the system. A misunderstanding of this has led to the confused idea that the presence of matter creates space and time.

There is nothing startling about these revelations. It has long been accepted that vibrations of air create the impression of sound—for that matter, a visible wave, the thread of a turning screw pointing perpendicularly to the line of vision and that little machine which I have exhibited at previous lectures are instances showing that, at least, the direction of motion may be illusory and deceptive, and there are many other sensations which are accepted as our own interpretation. The truly perplexing fact is that no one suspected motion in general long ago of belonging to the realm of illusion and of being one of these interpretations. Without doubting its reality and without knowing what it was, they went right ahead and formulated its laws, exactly as later physics, without knowing what light is, went right ahead and measured what appeared as its speed.

The fundamental postulate makes no such assumptions; it is the springboard for the first systematic attack upon a problem that has no right to be as old as it is.

I turned to the last pages and read:

It is easier to imagine all the complications which evaporate when our concept of time is eliminated than to explain these things, and this is the only business of any hypothesis in science. Our language is hopelessly inadequate; it implies time in most of its parts and the moment one tries to explain, one falls into contradictions. Verbs—one of the strongest tools of our expression —are essentially time. The thing is impossible and must be expressed in mathematical language. But whether such ideas may or may not be stated in everyday language is immaterial. Once understood, questions of beginnings and endings become simple questions of structure. We conclude that there is energy of highest availability at one place and its complete degradation or utmost thermodynamical equilibrium at another, within a structure that always shows more entropy away from us, along a fourth coordinate, regardless of the direction in which we measure it. Conflicts between science and religion cease to exist or at least become exceedingly weakened as both views grow considerably stronger. The problems of what was before everything was created or after everything ends dissolve once the concept of time, as we conceive it, is removed and become considerations of what is not or what might have been. Why the Creator did not begin things before, or what he will do after, is meaningless and, having discarded the tenses, which are but ways of looking at the infinitive of our own making, the Creator emerges as the verb in the present indicative.

Garcia had come in and sat down, his head buried in his chest, his legs, one over the other, stretched before him, in one of his characteristic poses. The Moor looked at him and for a fleeting moment his face registered a sad fondness. The Moor could be very warm sometimes, enough to make one forgive him his many faults, and he was sly. He knew that Garcia abhorred his scientific leanings as much as he loved his music, that in his presence he was always in a dilemma, unable to reconcile both activities which he considered as radically opposed. The Moor said to him:

"About the question that worries you, I will try to answer in a moment. Now I want you to hear this from the master of reiteration. Perhaps it will answer you." He was playing the slow movement from a sonata of Schumann: "You can learn more literature from him than from any writer, to reverse his own saying." The music went through a passage of appeal that verged on despair: "This is one of the most concise modulations in musical literature," and through it the music became serene once more. "Now you are in the presence of greatness." The music grew, invading the keyboard, expanded to its natural fulfillment, to end in exhausted finality.

What point had he made? I don't know, but he had fully made it and won Garcia over. The Moor spoke to him:

"Perhaps the reason for not accepting these theories completely, for not taking the decisive step, for not lifting the frame of the little machine, is fear of what they might uncover behind." He laughed again but the sound was not derisive: "The corpse of free will, of the free will they have exercised so well and yet does not let them buck the moralists. That is what the denial of time and motion, as we feel them, implies: no free will, and man will buck anything but that." He paused a moment and swept us all with a blank stare:

"And yet, there is a way out of the difficulty. We can have scientific consistency and at the same time save face and human dignity." The Moor could speak as directly as he played music when he chose to and I wish I could remember his words because, aside from his playing, this was the only thing I would have cared to remember from that depressing day of painful revelations.

He used the analogy of a sculptor working on a block of stone. It contains all possible shapes, all statues, good or bad, inspired or mediocre, and it is the decision of the sculptor which one he wants to carve out of all that infinity by removing and ignoring all the rest, to leave only that one. His statue was there all the time, yet no one can deny his creation, his discovery, his choice. What we remove, what we do not want, is what we call empty space and no time, what has not been and what might have been, and we remove by simply ignoring. We see the shapes in their fourth dimensional extension as moving things, things created, born, growing, becoming old, dying, disappearing, even ourselves, all of it cast as one with the static universe. We are at once good and bad and constructive and destructive and beautiful and ugly. It is what we choose and what we inspire others to choose and be conscious of in us that determines what we appear and the moral code or conduct on which we decide. This permits the concept of free will in a universe which is set and where past, present and future coexist. Our freedom consists of our selection of a shape out of an infinity of possible shapes, even if that shape, once selected, still contains within itself another infinity of possible shapes. In this manner determinism is not opposed to an illusory free will. It is up to us what somewhere or somewhen we conceive in this continuous extension of existence.

"And there are six degrees of freedom: three dimensions of space and three of time, all we need for our complete realization," the Moor proclaimed. "Six coordinates at most are all one requires for a full simplification and understanding of all cosmology, of the whole shebang, including ourselves, because the sixth coordinate, the coordinate of consciousness, of thought, also points to the legend: 'Everything that is possible exists already,' and this is the mysterious field of metanthropy and the stereochronic sense." He spoke like one making astounding revelations. I don't remember his words but in part it went something like this, if I understood him right:

The man of genius is a mutant; he advances ahead of his time, beyond the frontiers of knowledge and common experience, into the blackness of the unknown, but he does not want to be alone and his achievements are his way of illuminating the darkness that envelops the future, and they are also an appeal for understanding which is a call for company and for help, because alone he feels futile and lost. Following his light, others follow hesitantly with painful misgivings, reaching out to him until he finds himself once more surrounded by those he has taught to be his peers. That is what makes the genius do his work: the fear of loneliness. His work is an explanation and an explanation is a call for spiritual company. Then comes the fermenting stagnant period of recapitulation, a relative recoiling recession, and the process is repeated by someone else and thus the race advances to the next stage by discontinuous eruptions. It is a racial syndrome of mutation.

And this is the stereochronic sense of life: to change, to retrace and to advance, to sidestep oneself and join one's other past, present and future selves, and by undergoing this displacement along the axis of possibilities, to raise the curtain of man's next stage and let consciousness flood our total identity which remains invariant under all transformations. This is metanthropy.

Yet, when I left the Moor's house that day, I was not altogether convinced in the broader sense. Perhaps I had not understood him well. I fear that now, or perhaps I hope for it. There is such a thing as preferring to be fooled when it suits our purpose. I think it was Dr. de los Rios who said once: "Reason pursues the truth whether convenient or not. Common sense finds the convenient whether true or false." And that day also, de los Rios had summed things up quite well. He said that whether it was motion or extension, or time or fourth coordinate, it was only a matter of names and what we meant came down to the same thing, as I remember the Moor himself had implied in his notes. Whether we call a certain color a rate of vibrations or

simply red, we mean the same thing; the vibrations strike us as redness
even as the fourth dimension strikes us as time and the inclinations in
it as motion or as all simultaneous universes, existences or identities
appear to us only as possibilities. It is only a matter of nomenclature.
But the Moor replied by accusing de los Rios of temporizing as usual
and said that it was not only a matter of names but of thinking of
things in different terms which made our concept of reality more
clear, and then Dr. de los Rios said: "And what is reality?" and the
Moor looked at him with mocking, glaring eyes and said cryptically:
"Someone asked you a similar question about two thousand years
ago. What was your answer then?"

At any rate, I felt that I was going back to the comfortable reality of
my dreams or illusions and that this idea of no motion and higher
dimensions was, if anything, quite the thing for a lazy world. No effort
required except to condition the mind to realize that one is there
already, that one is everything one can possibly be.

And here I was sitting and drinking at El Telescopio and again listening
to the Moor. I let him ride his own storm and looked around. Sitting
at a table at the entrance to the patio, there was a majestic gentleman
with the air of a priest in mufti, whom I did not know but assumed to
be someone to be reckoned with from the reverence which surrounded
him. I asked Don Pedro who the gentleman was, but he was too busy
talking. I kept insisting and he kept on, and only when he was quite
satisfied that he had finished, he recognized me: "Now, what was it
you wanted to know?"

I changed my question. Another more peremptory one had flashed
into my mind: "What is this party, this gathering about?"

"That is not what you were asking, you know? Well—one is not a
fool—but anyway I'll answer it." The sly Svengali had been listening
all the time and only feigning disattention: "This gathering you ask?
Well, nobody knows. Nobody knows what it's all about, but they all
come simply to increase the total entropy of this vale of tears. Our
nation has contributed more to the entropy of the world than all the
other nations together—had more available energy originally than
anyone else, and this is a typical Spanish situation. It was anonymous,
that's it, typical. I assume, mind you—one can only assume—that they

all received anonymous invitations asking them to come today— The appeal of the mysterious, the unknown which we can never resist. Spaniards are essentially mystic—although I suspect the hand of the Chink making publicity for El Telescopio and intending to ruin it with commercialism and well-needed funds. My own mental child! El Telescopio of my soul—! So I came and asked you to come and . . . here we are, man. What more do you want? Have you been so long away from the land of common sense that you must know the reason for everything? Here we are all in New York, but no one knows why or cares. In Spain we know the sentiment, so we don't have to know the reason. That's only good for the Nordics— And to get away from that delicate topic, because you know, there are those— Well, I'll answer your first question: The portly gentleman you see at the table by the patio is Gines Cáceres in flesh and bone. You have heard me speak about him and, for your information, he is giving a concert this coming Sunday, but don't tell anyone. The whole city knows it already, including you, see?"

"Cáceres? You mean the great guitar player?"

"That's him—the best."

I looked then more carefully and noticed the guitar in its case propped up on a serving table behind him, and my hopes rose. Since I had heard his records on the Moor's machine, I had wanted nothing as much as to hear him play in person and perhaps today—

He was surrounded by some musicians and the Spanish vocalist from Don Pedro's—I mean, Pete Guz's band, and seeing him answering politely, kindly, drinking little, saying less, one felt that one was in the presence of greatness, as the Moor would put it, and one knew that this was no importation of the Señor Olózaga's. This was the man who had elevated the guitar to unsuspected and yet most legitimate heights of dignity, who played the classics and all other composers of the so-called highbrow music with a good taste and responsibility never surpassed if indeed equaled. I am only repeating what Don Pedro had told me.

Dr. de los Rios had joined Cáceres at his table and from the effusive quality of their greetings, I could see that they were good friends. This only started the Moor again:

"And who else would join him but Dr. Jesucristo— It was inevitable."

According to him, Gines Cáceres embodied all the qualities of the Spanish grandee and nobleman, the true Spanish artist. Even now he was saying:

"In Spain there is no aristocracy but only nobility, and there is a great difference, oh, yes! A great difference, if you know what I mean." He waved his glass at Cáceres: "This one is to you, Reverend." He could capture people's attention with extraordinary ease and Cáceres looked over and acknowledged the toast. "Perhaps you will deign to oblige, you know, a little later."

The affable words of Cáceres floated peacefully across: "Always glad to play for you, my friend, and the Doctor here, who also honored me with a request, and also your talented children." He gestured toward the musicians surrounding him and he reached for his guitar. Don Pedro signaled to one of the waiters to shut off the machine but no one, except those at our table, seemed to have noticed until the music of Cáceres began to saturate the room.

This was magic. I was watching him carefully and his hands did not seem to move; yet the music flowed and sprang. It partook of the harpsichord with the vibrato of the violin, of the organ with the crisp color differentiation of the orchestra. Again I am quoting the Moor. I did not notice the deceleration and fading of the voices and it was only after a while that I realized the transfiguration of the audience.

La Colombina was leaning intensely forward, her elbows on the table, her hands clasped, and her great earrings hung motionless. Miguel Pinto had turned around and looked without seeing. The Señor Olózaga's chair was empty, but Pilarte, the wrestler, sat with his arms akimbo and his mouth open and actually appeared to be thinking, or at least making an effort.

The faces of Lunarito and Bejarano glowed with recognition of their national instrument, and La Niña de los Madroños sat transfixed with eyes closed.

But all might as well have had their eyes closed because to see or imagine the things this music suggested or brought back, one needed no eyes. I know that they were all remembering or perhaps imagining that they were remembering, recalling some past inner triumph which towered over present outer success and failure, or only recalling some past hopes which had never been attained. I did not look at the meek man with the thick lenses. I feared what I might see there, but then I looked at Garcia and I have never seen this melancholic Spaniard look so sad, so crushed by nostalgic despair. I could well imagine what went on in his soul; his desire to recapture and relive the past, an imaginary past that might have been; his frustration and feeling of inadequacy which he shared with so many of his countrymen, his racial sadness and national regret, his love for the unattainable and for his own stories, his poetry and his romanticism, the complications of having to express his race and identity in terms of another.

Only the night before he had read to me the last part of his story of the family, a work quite wasted in my opinion, but which showed the tenacity of his Spanish consciousness and refusal to forget old ideas and sentiments. The novel itself meant nothing, but the fact that he had engaged in writing it, his self-deception in not seeing that it was a thankless task, that he was doing it at the wrong time and in the wrong place, the candid impracticability of it all, was a synthesis of his personality.

We were at my place where he had come to show me the anonymous invitation he had received to come to El Telescopio and to ask me whether I had received one also, but this was a pretext and I am sure that his elation was not due to this invitation, as he soon demonstrated.

He produced the well-known sheaf of papers and said that the first draft of his novel was now completed. He looked so happy that this was one of the few times I invited him to read.

He taunted me: "Are you sure you want me to read?" and I said yes, to go ahead, that I had already grown hardened.

Laughing, he made himself comfortable in my soft chair and was on:

Ruin had fallen suddenly upon the Sandoval family. The summer residence outside Madrid had been sold long ago. Then the creditors descended like vultures upon the jewelry shop to tear it apart. It did not even pay one-tenth of what it owed.

The Sandoval family was in utter misery, but not the metaphoric misery of rich people who come to less, but literal misery of no food, of nothing to turn to.

The day when the crisis took visible shape, they were all in a room upstairs, cringing together like victims of a shipwreck, listening to the noise going on in the shop below.

Ledesma was on the sidewalk looking at people behaving inside and outside of the store with vulgar authority. He beheld the shameful sign in the window. He had rendered his last accounts and then had been shoved aside by the creditors as something worthless.

He was old and he had nowhere to go after that. In a week he would be turned out of his pension and he would die of hunger. He would not beg for alms. He had no friends and had he had them, he would not use them.

He went upstairs to tell them that there was no more to be done. He found them all in a group. All except Enrique, who had not been living with them for some time. Jorge had one arm about Lolita and she clung to him like a child. Trini sat straight, stiff. She had grown very thin and her hair was streaked white and lent her an ugly, weird aspect. Fernando sat half asleep in a chair.

"Well," said Ledesma, "this is the end."

Lolita hid her face in her brother's shoulder. Fernando did not move. Trini said without even looking:

"There is no hope, Ledesma." She pointed at Fernando. "That man is finished. His brain is gone."

Fernando looked flatly at Ledesma: "There is nothing I can do about it. No, there is nothing." And he bent his head and closed his eyes again.

"Listen, Ledesma," Trini said. "We must move somewhere. We can't stay here. Even the furniture is going." She took a pin from her dress: "This is my last jewel and it does not even have a story to go with it, not even a memory to make this a last gesture. Go and sell it so that we can go somewhere."

Ledesma took the jewel mechanically and left. He returned an hour or so later and handed Trini a few bills. Fernando had opened his eyes and saw him: "Thank you, Ledesma, my good Ledesma."

Ledesma felt that this was unjust, but why explain? There had been so much injustice! He turned on his heel and left. He knew that he was parting with this family forever and there was no good-bye.

In the street he stopped: "And now what?" he said to himself.

He had dedicated all of his life to them and to the business. There had been no gratitude, only phrases of politeness. The last sentence of Fernando continued to echo in his ear. It had been the only time he had expressed gratitude sincerely, the only time that it had not been deserved. Ledesma was used up. He was but a leftover and he thought that death was inevitable.

"Now I belong to the sewers of the city."

That last thought stayed with him and all the way, as he walked, he looked at the gutter and the manholes along the way.

He stopped at a corner and looked at the hole under the sidewalk, like a gaping mouth of a hideous, abject monster, the dirty water rushing into its perennial thirst. He looked and then laughed, and his laugh sounded strange to him.

He realized that it was years, countless years since he had laughed, and he walked on.

He stopped in front of a jewelry shop and looked and then saw his reflection in the glass.

He realized that he had not looked at himself for a long time.

"Oh! You are old, very old. Nothing but a bag full of years, of rotten, wasted years." And then he saw that he was shabby. "Yes, a bag full of holes too, for the years to run out, for the empty years to run out. You are old, too old to hold your own time."

And he realized that he had not thought of himself for many years, for countless years.

"You are only a piece of dirt for the gutter, to drift through the gutter into the sewers of the city."

And he walked on looking at the gutter all the time.

In his room he felt he wanted to write a note. He did not know to whom he would address it, but he wanted to write a note. He did not know what he was going to say, but he wanted to write a note.

He took a piece of paper and while he thought, he scribbled on it with a pencil. Then he decided not to write at all, and when he looked at the paper, he saw he had written a name on it. Only one name.

He looked at this name and suddenly his head dropped on his arms and he cried for a long time.

The Sandovals moved to a gloomy ground floor apartment at the end of the Calle Mayor. It had bars on the windows and even in a land where gratings can be so cheerful, those were only bars, cold bars that lent the place the sordid air of a prison. It was dark inside also, very dark.

They scarcely had any furniture there and one or two boxes, in which some of their objects had been moved, remained to contribute to the depressing aspect.

And Fernando had chosen to sit on a box and to look into space. He was in the last period of his ailment and in a state of utter idiocy. He begged for food constantly.

Jorge left the house and did not return until night. Trini and Lolita wandered through that empty house quarreling, insulting one another like two creatures possessed, like two specters of a strange fantasy.

One day Jorge came in and dropped in a chair with exhaustion: "You know? Ledesma committed suicide."

There was a long silence during which no one looked at the others and no one knew what the others thought, or perhaps knew it too well. They did not ask how it had happened. Possibly they did not want to hear the details. Possibly they were indifferent.

Fernando did not seem to notice and only began to cry for food. Then Jorge said: "Here are five duros I got from a friend so that you can eat something. I ate with him already."

"Go ahead and get something, Lolita," said Trini, motioning toward Fernando. "This man is sick and starving."

Lolita went out and Jorge went with her. Trini stood there looking at them distractedly and then she caressed Fernando's head.

"I want food, Trini. Just a piece of bread."

"Yes, dear. You will get it soon. Lolita has gone to get it."

"Good Lolita, good Lolita."

Trini scowled and for a moment something indescribable descended upon her.

When Lolita returned, she found Enrique there. He and Trini were talking loudly.

"So you still come and ask for money, when we have been starving. There is Lolita. She has gone to get the first food we will have in thirty-six hours."

"She went to get food? Where is my share of the money?"

Fernando had stood up and dragged himself to Enrique. He thought he was Ledesma. He had not even recognized him: "Ledesma, my good Ledesma. Do me the last favor. Give me a few centimes for a piece of bread." Bread as a symbol of food had gotten a terrible hold on his mind: "I am hungry," and he tried to put his hand in Enrique's pocket.

Enrique was possessed of an insane fury. He lifted his hand and struck Fernando in the face several times, knocking him down to the floor nearly unconscious.

Lolita dropped her bundle and bent over her father. She looked at Enrique and the whole thing was beyond her comprehension.

Trini had remained there like a statue of stone. Then she said: "Enrique, you are mad. You will be hopelessly mad if you continue the life you have lived, and I, your mother, will stop it. I know it is that accursed vice that is destroying you and those women who will kill men for money, men who pay to be slowly murdered, mentally and physically. Enrique, even if I have to fight from woman to woman, I will save you yet. I will recover my son and you will live to repent and to justify my action. You will not leave us again, you will stay with us, and I will not lose sight of you." There was an icy coldness in her manner that was fearful: "You struck your father. Here!" She lifted her hand and slapped his face.

Enrique retreated with eyes strangely alive. Trini slapped him again and he retreated further. She was in a frozen paroxysm and continued to slap him with scorn. His eyes gleamed and he only retreated step by step, without any attempt to defend himself.

Lolita looked at them in amazement, while holding her father's head. She saw them disappear thus into the dark corridor and continued to hear the sound of the slaps and of his panting until the whole thing faded into a back room.

"Did you see, Lolita? How bad Ledesma is! How he treated me!"

Lolita knew that this was a horrible injustice, but why explain?

"Yes, Father. Here." She gave him something out of the package and he began to eat it right on the floor where he was. Lolita looked again into the shadows of the corridor and smiled a wry smile.

But since that day, Enrique remained in the house, and although they all continued to quarrel, he behaved better and was calmer. He and Jorge went out to ask everyone they knew for money. It was all the work they were capable of doing, but what they got they brought home. People began to fear them and avoid them.

People in Madrid were puzzled by the fall of this family and no one knew where they lived. When people passed the site of the jewelry shop, they saw a brand-new pastry shop. They inquired about the Sandovals and then left according to their temperaments, sometimes smiling, sometimes frowning. Only once a very old lady was crying when she left.

Enrique and Jorge continued to ask for money although their field became very reduced. Lolita also left the house and came back with more than her two brothers had been able to collect.

They all regarded her bitterly, especially Jorge, but she had to live.

One night, as they surrounded the dinner table, Jorge said to Lolita: "You might as well stay away and live better."

"No. I wouldn't be happy. I want to do this for all of you as you are all trying to do your best for all of us. Let us feel that there is still something that will make us stand together to the end."

"Yes," Trini said. "The wreck has brought many things to the surface, many unsuspected things—" and they all looked at Fernando, who bent over his food and did not even seem to hear them.

Jorge turned to his sister with an appealing look. He seemed very young and very tired.

"But I can't bear to see you live this life, Lolita; I can't—" He broke down and cried. Lolita went over to Jorge and he embraced her tightly. She led him to the other end of the room where it was darker and sat down with him. It was a gloomy scene as all those people stood there in that flickering candle-light. After a while and right on his sister's shoulder, Jorge fell asleep.

Two days after that, Jorge went out and later they found a note from him containing a little money and saying:

> This is the last money I could get. Do not think I am forsaking you. I am worthless and what is worthless cannot forsake. Some day I may return, when I have outgrown my sorrow.
>
> Although my flesh tells me that I will die, I know that I will come back some day. Now I want to leave and forget this scene, where things have happened that I could not continue to see.

They all saw the note and they all knew that the flesh seldom deceives, but as usual, they were all silent. They were already used to tragedy, they were callous.

Here the story shifted to the farm where Rojelia and Albarran were rudely awakened from their seraphic existence and brought down to earth from their lofty heights by a letter from Lolita telling them of all the calamities which had overtaken the Sandovals. The letter said that her father was at death's door and that in his moments of lucidity he always called for Rojelia.

Albarran, noble, stout fellow that he was, and his incomparable wife decided to forgive such lesser souls and fly to their side—if not to help them, since they were beyond redemption, at least to lend them some comfort in their last hours of struggle against the merciless attacks of Garcia's plot.

Garcia was not very satisfied with this part. The descriptions of the mental and physical activities on the health farm turned out to be reiterations of things which had already been told to the point of exhaustion, and after he had spent considerable time composing the letter for Lolita in the style which he thought a girl like her would use, he discovered that it only repeated what he had already described in his story during the many times it shifted to Madrid. He decided to shelve that part for a while and then went on to the end of his novel, from the moment that Rojelia and Albarran arrived in Madrid:

When they arrived at that house, the impression they received was disastrous. Rojelia leaned on her husband's arm, closing her eyes, and thus he led her in.

Fernando was in bed and looked at them with a long, fixed look. Rojelia said something.

"He cannot hear," Trini said. She was like the picture of madness: very erect, her white hair in disorder. Her whole countenance seemed to cry out: "I am right, I am right!" But for no reason at all.

Rojelia fell embracing her father in an outburst of all the love she had withheld. He had a moment of lucidity and laid a trembling hand upon her head, and against it, it looked very pale, almost greenish:

"Rojelia—my pride—Rojelia!"

Albarran said very loudly as if to reach that lonely mind: "And how are you feeling, Don Fernando?"

Fernando smiled at him: "Yes—!"

Albarran looked down and his jaws tightened. He stepped out into the corridor hurriedly.

Lolita was huddled up in a chair in a corner. Rojelia had slipped to her knees and cried with her head on the bed. Fernando said to no one in particular: "There is nothing I can do about it," and went back to his stupor.

"Where is Enrique?" Rojelia demanded. "Is he still carrying on the same way during these moments?"

"No, Rojelia. He has been different lately. He has changed. He only went out to get some money."

Albarran had reentered the room and his eyes were red. He went close to Trini and put an arm about her: "Mother, when he returns, tell him not to worry. We are here now. He does not have to resort to strangers when he has a family."

That evening Fernando fell into a coma and thus submerged into death. No one could ascertain the exact time.

The family of the deceased assumes an undue importance. They consider sorrow a great honor and will fight for its supremacy and control upon the corpse, like vultures for a prey.

They want to monopolize sadness. All through the night they cry loud and long in mournful and fantastic serenade, so that their tragedy may not pass unnoticed and that everyone may know that they are being consumed by the fires of sorrow which renders them exceptional, superior, unique, which renders them so pure.

When in front of witnesses, they fall upon the corpse and embrace him and kiss him and maul him, so that everyone will see how familiar they are with corpses. And then they praise him shamelessly and tell astounding lies because, as they all know that pride is the last thing to die in a corpse, they are sure that he will not stand up to call them liars. And they promise impossible things, because everyone knows in his heart that death is impotent and that no dead one ever comes back to collect.

The neighbors gather in the street and see the procession emerge, furrowing the mob, disappearing like a snake in a forest of petrified people.

The priest sneaks away from the house like a thief, pressing something he hides against his breast. He grows in importance. He has been nearest the dead one. He has just killed a conscience by delivering it from remorse, the thing that keeps it alive. He knows everything and in exchange for a wafer has robbed death of its own secret.

When the procession has disappeared, people behold the house and the closed windows and the door with a black bow like the negative of a child who has taken his first communion.

Then they all feel unimportant, as unimportant as spectators always feel, and their admiration for the family of the deceased knows no limits.

The house begins to drip serious, pompous people with black gloves and each one knows more than the other and they all distribute among the childish audience the sweetmeats of that which they have seen and that which they have not seen.

And people grow curious and they grow jealous of their neighbor's sorrow and their curiosity and jealousy creep up the walls which defend the pride of the mourners.

Someone says something about the purifying intensity of sorrow and envy creeps faster and it creeps higher and lands on the windowsills, even on the roof, like vultures assaulting a house of death.

The family sits around in a circle with strange dramatic poses, like dethroned kings of a tragedy in a parody of their own sadness, of their own truth. They all sit around a dummy that lies in state.

If they look at one another, their eyes meet in the center and, fearing to discover what they disguise, they descend upon the coffin which tapers like a gloomy street seen in perspective, leading the dead away.

And there lies the cadaver, the pride of the mourners, upon a funeral pile and more proud than all. A fallen emperor among servile kings, who says: "My throne is higher than the others'. I am emptier than you all."

And there is a cast smile upon his features that deepens as death digs in. For death does not kill with one blow. It kills first when it sets the face and casts its veil of pallor, then when it freezes, and then when it rots.

And the cadaver smiles and his smile is superior, almost despotic, because he knows what he arouses:

That the more cynical his gesture, the more interest he awakens; the colder he grows, the more he holds and the more rotten he is, the more he attracts.

Such is the pride of the mourners.

The family comments on the past and memory, the last enemy of the dead, pursues him back to infancy without giving him quarter.

Oh, memory! Scourge of death!

Oh, pride of the mourners! Oh, most outrageous iniquity hurled at a defenseless corpse!

Four days Fernando lay in state and all the time the family roamed about him. In those four days everyone aged. Death is contagious and through proximity with it, they all died a little. Before death had entered that house of disgrace, there was sadness; later, there was morbidity, increasing every day that death spent in their company.

Trini sat constantly in the same position. Her eyes sparkled with two still tears. They seemed to be the same tears that she had borne when Albarran and Rojelia had arrived. They were old, aged tears, tears crystallized like diamonds by the action of time and pain. Lolita moved around her father saying something no one could understand and then went back and perched herself on the corner chair, like a little cat.

Albarran had taken care of all the expenses for the funeral and had even gone beyond his means to secure a decent burial. When the moment came to dress Fernando and place him in the coffin, Rojelia went to a closet and looked for his clothes but could find none.

"Mother, where are his clothes?"

"He didn't have any."

Rojelia spoke to her husband and both left hurriedly. They went to a ready-made clothes establishment. A clerk came to meet them

"In what can I serve you?"

"We want a black suit."

"Step this way, please." He took them where the suits were kept: "What size, please? Is it for you, sir?"

"No, it is not for me. My dear, do you know the size?"

"Sir, perhaps it would be better if the person came, so we could fit him."

"But he cannot come. Can't you understand? He cannot come."

The clerk looked at them both and then understood. Rojelia gave him an approximate size and as the man walked away, said: "How horribly sad this is! Who would have thought that you would be the one to pay for his funeral, his coffin, even his suit, after the way all the family treated you?"

When they had placed Fernando in the coffin and before closing the lid, all except Trini grouped about it. Then the men also arrived to close the coffin and carry it away and they seemed to be in a hurry. For a moment it was tumultuous.

Trini stood at the door as a person turned to stone. She saw them all upon him and her thoughts rushed to her youth and she remembered the scene in that village of South America when they were first married. She heard and saw the vultures again, screeching, demanding the rotten flesh, and she remembered when he had tried to drive them away. And now he could not defend himself. The scene emerged and burst upon her like a thunderbolt that nailed her to the frame of the door:

"Stand away!" She gasped: "Please—leave him in peace!"

Then she approached the coffin and said: "Forgive me, Fernando. I loved you well."

Lolita came next and said in a childish voice: "Forgive me, Father, for all the things you never knew." And she went to her chair and was shaking.

They had already closed the coffin hastily and Enrique stood there looking at the blank top. Sorrow had spread a certain dignity upon his cadaverous countenance. A tremendous sob shook him from head to foot and resounded all over the empty house: "Forgive me!"

The men took the coffin and threw it over their shoulders. Trini was standing at the door: "Stop. Don't carry him away!" And she collapsed like a log. The men stepped over her and went on. The horses waited impatiently outside, shaking the tuft of black feathers on their heads.

Rojelia hid her face in her husband's chest. When the coffin passed through the street in front, something made her look up. She grew tense and then hurled herself against the window. Her arms went out between the bars reaching out in silent appeal.

She stood there motionless and for a moment it seemed that time was arrested and all the light in the world concentrated in her red hair, in her white arms.

When someone dies, he is buried. It is the best thing that can be done. But no matter how bright the day may be, it is always somber for those who loved him. Through their tired eyes, they see the indifferent happiness of others like a sunny day from a dark dungeon.

They will bury him as one hides a treasure in the night, as a plant is sown in an orchard. What else is a cemetery in the restful fragrance of its peace?

He will descend the frondose hill where birds nest in the spring and everything will be silenced a moment, even as it has been silenced wherever he has passed, strange, wrapped in somber elegance, like an unknown artist of weird conceptions.

No one will look at the coffin, suspiciously fearing that it may be empty or that it may not conceal a real corpse, because if the dead one is all there is in it, the coffin is really empty and they all know that in this world of strange ideologies, dead people are only dummies of cardboard.

The procession will advance, the song of birds now crowding his ears, the heavy scent of funeral wreaths and flowers filling his nostrils, the luxurious green carpet of grass underneath. He will pass by facing the clouds and the blue sky, jostling majestically, and enter the great vegetation of the cemetery, its warmth, its coolness, with regiments of trees marching by, their crowns sweeping overhead, and then a halt while they rise, higher and higher as he sinks within a circle of mournful faces emerging over the ascending grassy rim, and their sad chanting voices; everything growing upward and away, pushed by the brown moist walls all around. Then all blotted out by an avalanche of dirt.

The house has remained behind, frightened, hollow, like a freshly dug grave. The tree has been pulled by the roots, leaving a frozen, stupefied wound, like a gaping mouth.

They all sit benumbed in the silent room, empty, palpitating with memories, and all of a sudden they all stand. A broken cry of help has pierced their ears, followed by a deep crunching thud. It is the last appealing cry of one who sinks in the ground forever.

The funeral procession went down the Street of Bailen and then turned to the left. At their right, far below, past the royal palace, stretched the Prado, sprinkled with thirsty, dark green shrubs in a sea of dry ground.

They descended a steep dismantled hill, where the trees growing in all directions and in strange positions seemed to have gone mad, and then they took the dusty, scorching road to the cemetery.

It was for what followed that Garcia had prepared his grand epilogue and apotheosis on the farm, with far-reaching philosophical considerations about Spain and its people in particular, transcending to the world and humanity in general.

I suggested that it was better to leave that out and end his story with that funeral march to the death of a fool. Being in turn inclined to philosophize, I mentioned that it was good to let the reader collaborate and that, as he had once said, the reader often put in all the good things which the author had left out and never thought of implying, that it was better to let the reader make his own generalizations and reach his own conclusions which he would, in the end, credit to the writer: "Who knows, Garcia, but that the reader might have a happier idea than the author could ever conceive? Happier for him at any rate?" And I believe that Garcia was convinced.

That had taken place only last night.

The music of Cáceres inundated my ears. It had been gaining the upper hand over my reveries and now was master and held me in its grip again. It suddenly burst upon my consciousness and woke me up. I found myself standing in a semicircle with all the others. We were all like somnambulists, closing in, suctioned, hypnotized by the presti-digitations of Cáceres as if we were all seeking to be carried through the round hole of the guitar, back to the womb of our mother country.

This was a strange sight. It suggested mass hypnosis and the un-European quality of Spaniards—that man in the center with his musical conjurations, holding this people at his mercy, prisoners in the net that he wove on the loom of his guitar—and he was merciful. He saw their nostalgia and with a quick modulation, he struck a few chords which commonly finish many Spanish tunes.

Before we recovered and could burst into superfluous acclaim, he was speaking in his soothing voice: "Why so solemn, everybody? This is an occasion for gaiety and there are good dancers present." His hand moved as if stirring a vat: "Go ahead; I will play for you." And he took a short sip of manzanilla.

The Moor's voice boomed: "To dance to the music of Cáceres is something for which every dancer should live and then die right after." He swept the glass from Lunarito's hand and gently propelled her into the patio. There Bejarano was already poised, regarding her under converging eyebrows, his back arched, his jaw and lower lip protruding defiantly, ready for her, and he met her like a bullfighter meets a bull.

Much has been said about the sexual implications in dancing, but the Spanish dance implies the bullfight, its stylization and synthesis. One could say that the bullfight is the apotheosis and ultimate, complete realization of Spanish dancing.

Like two confluent spirals, they circled and flowed along the increasing rattling of Lunarito's castanets to a spot in the common center, face to face, as a wave comes to a crest. They froze a moment and then melted and boiled into the dance. It was a furious exhibition of bristling, eloquent, gesticulating motion, of proposition and answer, a complete argument with inevitable conclusions, but self-contained in the world of dancing where the subject was movement and the answer and resolution given in dancing terms.

These two were dancing as I had never seen them dance before any other audience. They were dancing up to the great Cáceres and for their own people and also with rivalry for La Colombina and Miguel Pinto. They whirled and clashed brutally, like two gamecocks in a fight to the finish, their heels hammering like pneumatic drills. I don't know what all this proved, but it certainly was convincing.

Through the pandemonium of enthusiastic comments, music and dancing, I could hear Don Pedro talking to no one in particular, spawning his ego-eccentric philosophy. He was everywhere, tapping shoulders with his stick, calling attention to fine points, a self-appointed arbiter and interpreter extraordinary, conducting the whole performance in his imagination. He sipped Lunarito's drink, which he had appropriated, and juggled it with stick and cigarette, waving his arms and all miraculously without mishap:

"Look, but look, you fools! No one should miss this. Don't you notice? Lunarito and Bejarano are expressive dancers, not interpretive as Pinto and La Colombina, and that is the right thing, the truly racial. Spanish dancing is expressive, not interpretive." He went on without regard for the feelings of anyone, but the Moor's enthusiasm carried him at a clip where he could get away with anything and cause no offense. The impact, if any, was too swift to be apprehended. "But notice now—anyone who is not deaf or blind. Expressive dancers? nothing. Expressive music, that's all. It is the great Cáceres who is expressing himself through them."

He was right. Cáceres was controlling this dance. No one could dance with such violence and fury without scattering himself in pieces. Lunarito and Bejarano moved spasmodically as if shaken by an invisible hand, but the Moor's words had exposed the hand; it was the authoritative, imperious hand of Cáceres that moved them, that made them dance up to a great tradition, like marionettes controlled by the strings of his guitar, making it literally a command performance.

"It is quite simple. With our people the prophecies are always fulfilled. Now you know why we are all here. Could you want a better reason? And remember the ellipse of which I spoke before? Now the two foci, Dr. Jesucristo and myself, have approached and merged into the common center of Cáceres and his guitar. We have disappeared and no longer exist. You think you see us, but you don't. What you see is our reflection mirrored in the center of Cáceres and his guitar and the ellipse is now a circle generating through the perspective of Lunarito and Bejarano, terpsichorean families of confocal conics. The celestial qualities of Dr. Jesucristo and my musical genius, both embodied in Cáceres." The conceit of the man was boundless. "But talking of celestials, where is the Chink? I know that he is here even if we cannot see him. He would not miss this music and dancing, but where does he come in on the equation? Is he an integrating factor, or the constant of integration? Of course, he must have been the one who drew the ellipse in the beginning, or perhaps it was a four-dimensional ellipsoid that he projected and this is but a section of it and he is in the other dimension. However, see? Everybody in a circle. This is a segment, of course, the one that lies on the real plane of El Telescopio. The rest runs outside into the imaginary plane of New York, but the perimeter is a string of pearls and Lunarito and Bejarano are sliding on it. That is what sounds like the rattling of castanets and heels. You don't know what it's all about, but it does not matter because the string is growing tighter and is going to choke all bad Spaniards. Now you know why we are all here— Boo!"

This man was fantastic. He produced an idea, tossed it with extraordinary agility, making it bounce all along the gamut of his absurdity, and when it seemed that it was about to escape him, he turned it into a concept where his imponderable mind libated like a bee on a flower.

Lunarito and Bejarano had finished in the same spot and the same pose where they began and now walked away demanding wine in commercial quantities to replace the liquid contents of their systems, Lunarito fanning herself with her hand in that manner that says: catch me before I collapse. What a dance can do to a woman! The dance itself having assumed the inconsiderate significance of an impetuous lover, exhausting in his demands—Bejarano wiping honest sweat with that delighted resignation to the imposing tasks of a career that says: one does what one can, and: what I wouldn't do to chuck the whole thing and join your ranks, happier mortals who, in your innocence, envy my wretched greatness. Both of them endeavoring to minimize the applause as one does after an informal exhibition for a friend. Why, glad you liked it. Anytime, old fellow. It is nothing and I honestly enjoyed doing it for you because you appreciate it. This time it is not for dollars, for those who don't understand the fine points. Who would put himself out for any but you? It is only a job to be done for money, that's all, but this is for a great cause—in this case our common love for our country. The dollars go hang. You are less talented, though more happy than I and can do nothing about it, but I can and it is all in a day's work. No applause this time, please. Just let me have a little rest and a little wine before resuming the lifelong struggle.

All this their well-trained countenances said in the very short time it took them to blend with the embracing semicircle and attack the proffered bottles, but Don Pedro added words to his actions. By now an established behind-the-scenes commentator and master of ceremonies, he limped grandly about waving his shillelagh and diluting his comments among the fortunate:

"Look at them. Acting more tired than they are and they scarcely ate or slept until the Chink brought them to New York and I gave them their start— Well, it is the national system—these Spaniards— The moment they are out of their element, they coagulate. The Spaniard is not a Spaniard until he leaves Spain. It is Calderonian, that's all. We will never come out of our Calderonianism, thank the devil."

"I understood that about the national system," put in his American vocalist, who was always saying that something was not fair. "And boy! You've got a system! Do Spaniards ever speak of anything but themselves and Spain?"

He looked at her with commiseration: "The poor kid—right on top of a tree. Doesn't know what it's all about— But of course we do. What else is there to talk about? The only things that matter, the things one knows and the things one likes, which are synonymous, with honorable exceptions of course. We Spaniards like to speak of ourselves and explain ourselves to others and even to ourselves, but so do the Anglo-Saxons and other foreigners, except that they pay a psychoanalyst in order to speak of themselves and explain themselves to him and to themselves. It amounts to buying a trained audience, and while the simple solution in this case favors the Anglo-Saxons and the others, one must admit that it is more expensive. Of course, the patient is delighted and the treatment is prolonged indefinitely. He never sees any good reason for quitting his favorite topic. We count on the politeness of our audience or don't give a damn. They count on the business sense of their analyst and don't give a damn." A long swallow of wine while he held his stick poised as a warning to anyone who dared interrupt wound him up to continue:

"We Spaniards are preoccupied with ourselves as individuals and as a race. We know that we are isolated, don't belong to the civilized world. We are in Europe but are not of Europe—half Moor, half Oriental and half I don't know what—we have more halves than make one whole— Paradoxical, you know? That's us. Look at me. Look at the Chink. Look at the shawls. Foreigners call them Spanish shawls—utterly confused. We call them what they are, or what they were originally anyway—let's not overdo our national habit of splitting hairs— We call them shawls of Manila, of the Orient. There you are and that's what we are, because we know how to use them as we know how to use the cloak. That is our country: the cloak and the shawl, the mixture of Occident and Orient, nobility and exoticism, a land of contrasts and organized inconsistency, Don Quixote disguised as Don Juan in a harem in order to deliver the odalisques, Calderón eating angulas with chopsticks because it is more castizo, adaptable and Roman Catholic, conceptualist and brachistological, traditional and cosmopolitan— So we have thirst for understanding. What can we do? We have conquered lands and want to conquer minds now that we have lost the lands and that our spirituality has asserted itself more with age—the devil fed up on flesh. We must talk of ourselves, of the fine points. That is our obsession, points, points of honor, points of view, points, points— All right, we are has-beens and this is our only consolation, the fine point which is all that remains and at any rate a has-been is better than a has-not-been or never-will-be. A good point, see? Points again."

He checked himself and with the shillelagh to his lips signaled for silence. The table where La Niña de los Madroños sat was right in the semicircle of people and she had remained seated, her back to the table. Cáceres had hinted an invitation to her and had begun to play, and she began to sing.

"Now for the cañí," the Moor whispered down his shoulder to those near him.

Her voice rose, hesitated purposely, holding and increasing the suspense, and then rolled down, swaying like scallops of lace, to submerge itself in a sea of olés. She sang with a coolness and absence of gestures that was the more remarkable after witnessing the exhibition of Lunarito and Bejarano.

"Do you notice the flatness of delivery and the richness of the voice?" the Moor was saying now. "Like French horns properly played, like molten gold— And positively liturgical. Like a litany where the 'ora pro nobis' is substituted by the olés—our chulismo and our mysticism rolled into one. That's the point—haa—points again— an infinite system of points that would have delighted the soul of Cantor, but if he had been Spanish he would have kept his equilibrium and would have seen that it is perfectly natural for the part to contain as much as the whole—as much of nothing, that is. Sounds theological, but for that very same reason, it is perfectly clear to any Spaniard. There has always been complete understanding between God and ourselves—"

I felt the pull in my eyes and looked into the thick lenses of Fulano. There it was again, but I could still hear the Moor's voice while I submerged.

"—the pure intonation. It is immaculate, it implies the harmony. Did you notice the passages where Cáceres was not playing? She was on her own then, but the intonation implied the accompanying chord. There would have been a number of chords which might have applied, but by her form of attack, she suggested the one she wanted. She has the perfect voice for flamenco: rich in overtones. With the exception of Dr. Jesucristo and Cáceres, of course, you don't know what I am talking about, but no matter. It must be said—a matter of acoustics. Of all the overtones present in every one of her notes, she knows how to intensify the right ones which make the proper harmony and that is true intonation for you. She acquired that singing in church—the only proper way. That's how she began to sing. Of course, typical, exemplifying the Castitholicism of Spain as well as the phrase of that thinker who said that the essential characteristic of our country was Jesus Christ with castanets."

I could hear no more, I was looking about me in the meek man's mind:

He was back at his exercise of creating grandiose situations of self-denial. In this one he was a very good man, a very virtuous man, but being Spanish, it was not as simple as that. His virtue must be kept secret so that he might not even test that honor. He must study all his good actions with a severe and critical eye, lest he catch himself doing something good to derive self-satisfaction. This would rob goodness of all its purity. He remembered the night when he had met a very old lady on Sixth Avenue lugging a heavy suitcase in the rain. He offered to carry it for her and she let him do so gratefully, and he carried the case for two blocks to her dingy apartment. She thanked him profusely and asked him to step in and have some coffee, but he suddenly felt ashamed of himself. He knew that he had done it in order to derive some satisfaction out of his good deed, to atone, that was it, to atone, but he did not know for what. He felt it was a smug gesture, a contemptible action, and hated himself for it. He declined the invitation and rushed away in blind shame.

All the rest of that night he was beset by confusing thoughts and contradictory emotions. God! Could one not even do one good deed without repentance? This was becoming involved to the point of insanity. What mattered what satisfaction one derived from one's good actions if they benefited someone? Was not that the purpose of virtue? But something told him that this was not so, that virtue must remain purer than this. It was complicated to the utmost and disconcerting and for a dangerous moment almost forced him to the conclusion that the true goodness should be to sin, in order to deprive oneself from what is the greatest joy of the good man: the virtuous deed. Then where was the salvation? In sinning, or in doing good? And salvation could not be the reason for virtue, without destroying its purity.

This was too much. One could consider the matter for an eternity when after all there were but two choices. It reminded him of the game he played as a boy with a friend. It consisted of holding two small pebbles. If the two pebbles were in one hand, this was called odd. If one pebble was held in each hand, it was called even. He held his hands behind and then in front before his friend and if the friend guessed right, it was his turn to hold the pebbles.

Well, assuming he held one in each hand and the other boy said odd, then he would reason something like this: He will think that I think he will call even this time and that I will hold the two pebbles in one hand in order to fool him and so he will call odd again; so, let us carry the reasoning a little further. He will think that I think that he thinks that I think— It was maddening. If the game itself was nothing, its implications of futility were frightening because, after all, there were but two possibilities. This was like the result of Spanish involved thinking that had burned the brains of Don Quixote. It was the super-Calderonianism of which Don Pedro spoke. He recalled the Moor speaking once along similar lines. He had mentioned a mathematical series that ran plus m, minus m, plus m, minus m— Was it converging, or diverging? He did not recall, but what did one get at the end, m or nothing?

These divagations were getting him nowhere and he wanted to enjoy his situation. He went back to the original proposition: that Spanish or not, simple or Calderonian, odds or even, he was a very good and virtuous man who had always managed to hide modestly all his virtues and good deeds and—he was now in a hurry to get away from this rut and on with his business—he died one day and naturally went straight to heaven. And here is where the problem sprang afresh in all its dramatism:

He was in heaven but he was not happy. This could only happen to a Spaniard. He was very unhappy thinking of all the souls in hell. He could not enjoy his eternal glory knowing that so many suffered eternally. His virtue, his love for his fellow men, had not stopped with his death. These were theological problems worth investigating. It had occurred to him that good people, when they died and went to heaven, behaved rather selfishly and that anyone who could enjoy celestial graces with such a disregard for the sufferings of others could not possibly deserve eternal salvation. But then, what was the solution, if other people insisted on being bad? Of course, the answer was that one should not be good in order to go to heaven, in fact, that a truly good man should refuse to stay there after arriving. The lines of the famous mystic poem went through his head:

My Lord, I am not moved to love you by the heaven you have promised,
Nor am I moved to fear you because of the hell by all so dreaded . . .

Only a Spaniard could have written that. It posed the whole theological question with remarkable sentimental clarity. He decided to lay the problem in the lap of his Creator and directly went to Him. Only a Spaniard could thus complicate the existence of God.

"My Lord," he said, "I have a problem which I would discuss with You."

The Lord answered: "Yes, My son. For some time I have noticed you brooding and distracted, going about without taking part in the celestial general happiness, and it grieves Me, because you were brought here to enjoy eternal glory. Unburden your soul, My son, since that is all you have now."

"My Lord, I am not happy here and I will never be happy so long as I know that there are so many other men burning forever in hell. To me, this is the height of hard-faced selfishness, to be enjoying myself here while numberless souls are in eternal torture. To be a noble soul the situation is intolerable." He checked himself respectfully but it seems that the Lord was listening without any intention of interrupting and he proceeded:

"I have a request to make and if You grant it, my gratitude will be greater and more lasting than the one I feel at having been admitted here." This was Spanish and of the Attic culteranismo school, matching infinity with transfinity and recalled something he had heard Don Pedro say about the paradoxes of the infinite. "It is axiomatic that it is better for any number of guilty to go unpunished than for one single innocent to be punished unjustly and my proposition is this: that I be banished to hell and that all those who occupy it now or may go there in the future be moved to heaven, we might say at my expense and in memory of my beloved Spain. Knowing this, I shall be happier in hell than I could ever be in heaven."

The Lord made certain that he had finished and then said: "You know? You have a great deal of arrogance and you are almost trying to give Me a lesson and go the limit of virtue one better. The national system, I suppose— made you that way of course—wanted to have someone capable of understanding and feeling greatness. One is not a fool and One can appreciate a castizo, but you don't know what it's all about. You know? You flatter yourself. Do you think that your soul is worth all the souls in hell, present and future?" The Lord dismissed an interruption: "If you have that great capacity for self-denial, would not this be reaffirming yourself to the utmost, would not this be basking shamelessly in universal acknowledgment and admiration and everlasting gratitude?"

"But I wanted this to remain a secret between us two."

"Never mind. My knowing it is worth more than for the whole world to know it. Where is your modesty? How many condemned souls do you think your soul is worth? One million, one hundred, three, one, or none?"

And then the Lord knew human greatness and did no longer regret having created man, because this one before Him averted his eyes and answered in the best Spanish tradition:

"None."

"I am glad to hear you say that and I am inclined to grant your wish conditionally. For one thing, your original proposition would involve an injustice because if all sinners were rerouted to heaven hereafter, they would go absolutely unpunished and the sinners brought from hell would feel that this was not fair. Remember that you are now outside of Spain and everybody insists on fairness. They would feel this because they had already been punished, if only partially, and you may not know it but I do: that those who deserve to go to hell are very exacting in demanding equal rights and cannot tolerate the thought of anyone getting away with more than they do. I am sure that they would claim some compensation. The fact that this would be eternal glory for both, thus obliterating any differences in the limiting case, would not lessen their irritation before that limit was reached. Every time a scientist has suggested that according to that illusory second law of thermodynamics I started the universe a certain time ago, the first question that pops up in the human mind is: Why not before? But never why not after? There is that quality of the definitive about the past in human terms that carries a tremendous weight and conviction with men, and while there is a general saying that one should not look a gift horse in the mouth, your countrymen have another saying: Once a blow has been delivered, not even God can remove it. No, that would not do, but I will find a solution and, looking at the other aspect of the matter, what a soul is worth must be carefully evaluated. You have quoted yours at nothing and I like you for that. I am going to let that stand because I know that you want your pride to be crushed and I am going to send you to hell at first for nothing. That will make your gesture greater—no reward. However, with your suffering there, the value of your soul may increase and, remaining there an eternity, who knows but I? So go to hell, be happy there forever after your own fashion, and I will find a solution."

As he sank forever, he saw the Almighty smile an inscrutable and wise smile, but what His solution might be is beyond all human understanding. Then his whole universe was flames where he was lost—an endless holocaust where he would burn in eternal glory.

I was saved by the entrance of Tia Mariquita; that is, the wife of the Señor Olózaga. She made her appearance carrying in tow her eternal companion, a poor, tall, lanky, and run-down actor with a face somewhat contorted by his desire to cast it in a dramatic gesture. He was an institution in the Spanish theater and no performance was complete without the Tia Mariquita and him. They moved solicitously from table to table, declaiming and playacting, exchanging bits of dialogue which they had well memorized, and presently they were ministering to Lunarito and Bejarano.

"Look at them, and what a pair!" This was Don Pedro again. "He should be holding up her train, except that it is too short and the sight might frighten him. Look at their teamwork. Probably trying to enlist the services of Lunarito and Bejarano. Hope they don't have the audaciousness of approaching Cáceres for one of their theatrical phantasmagorias— But look at the approach. It is inimitable. The attempt at the grand manner and only succeeding in making everyone feel like a client. And the Chink insists that he has no interest in El Telescopio— But look at them. The eye of the master fattens the horse." The pair had reached our table, but Don Pedro carried on: "How is business, your highness? Not bad? That is the main thing. This one will place El Telescopio on the top of New York's gay spots. I might even move my band here."

The Tia Mariquita clasped her hands, laughed with rolling eyes, extended her arms in delighted reproach: "This Don Pedro, this Don Pedro. He says such things—"

"That's it, that's it, and we are near the Bowery." He sang in English: "The Bowery, they say such things and they do such things in the Bowery, the— Come on everybody. Hey, you," to his English vocalist, "—Bowery . . ." He swung his shillelagh, conducting, and all at the table joined him in chorus: "I'll never go there anymore." His laughter shook the place: "Did you hear that? Tia Mariquita, no one is coming here anymore—no more business."

"Well." The elongated actor had got hold of the backs of two chairs and was leaning over: "This is fine. We were so Spanish a minute ago and now we go into English. Well, I for one do not understand it and have enough with the language of Cervantes. I hope you enjoyed the little Spanish interlude we had a while ago, especially after the very illuminating explanations which probably did not let you hear or see anything."

The actor resented English. He imagined that his ignorance of it had closed the doors of the American stage to him and that while Don

Pedro basked in Anglo-Spanish fame, he had to wait for some bedraggled Spanish play in order to show his wares.

Don Pedro bent forward: "You know?" This in a stage whisper. "This mountebank, this desiccated strip of ham must have been listening all the time and we did not see him because he was hiding behind her skirt as usual, but now he is shooting at me by elevation. He thinks I don't notice it, but I can see every one of his little words. They are ham actor's words, cut out of paper and well chewed, and they dart in a little stream of harmless pellets—their graph is of the form . . ." he gave the equation in x and y, "very elementary, but after all, coming from him— You people think that you are sitting at a table, but you are really standing on an axis like bored ordinates and he and I are at zero values, see? We are nothing and that is what bores you. But I am going to depress the equation and shoot straight at him." His voice came out of the whisper: "You are a fool and like some actors nothing but a wastepaper basket full of discarded roles." Tia Mariquita had moved away with unusual show of discretion. "Now, you mangy lapdog, run along, you know where, and be sure to pull the chain as you jump in."

The actor's face was more contorted than ever and as red as its professional pallor allowed: "Why, you fake, you inconsiderate and insulting fake! You think that you can go about saying what you please with your crazy x's and y's and everyone must bow—" He was incoherent with rage: "Your highness, your highness— Who is the actor now? You wine-drinking devil, you confounded fraud. I am as Spanish as the next one. More Spanish than some Moors who stayed in Spain in disguise, you—"

With deadly calm the Moor let him splutter to a finish: "And I say that you may be Spanish—every country has many things, you know?" The Moor's hand moved in a devastatingly insulting gesture: "But you are a fool and a moocher. Go away or, by the beard of the Prophet—"

"Me a moocher!" the actor screamed as one who has been slapped with the culminating outrage. "*Mee* a moocher!" He moved threateningly and the Moor, still sitting, raised his shillelagh. The two men who were sitting in front of the actor stood up and held him. The green man had jumped to his feet and backed away in alarm, but his two companions looked on with contentment, declining to be surprised by anything that took place there. The actor was bellowing: "He called me a moocher, did you hear? Will somebody please hold me before I lose my head?"

"His head— Let him come, boys. I am ready for him. Let him come and I will wrap this precious stick like a turban about that pumpkin he passes for a head. Perhaps I did not give him enough the last time and he wants more of the same—the little puppet has ambitions. Let him come." But the two who were restraining the actor managed to take him away. He cried over his shoulder: "You are mad and evil. You are Satan," and the Moor, gloating diabolically between swallows of red wine, a veritable reincarnation of Dracula, repeated as a parting shot: "Moocher."

The last remarks of the Moor referred to another altercation he had had some time before with the same actor. It was at a play in the Spanish Theater. Lunarito and Bejarano had been lured to dance during the intermissions, having been given to understand that the performance was for some Spanish charity, and Lunarito had gone even further and acted a part in the play. It was a classical Spanish play in which the part of the gallant is always played by a woman, and Lunarito looked very engaging in her tights.

At the time, our actor had developed an overdramatized crush on Lunarito, opposite whom he had played that night. Incensed by the occasion, the applause, no doubt meant for Lunarito's legs rather than for his acting, and emboldened by the masterful role he had concluded, he went up to Lunarito's dressing room ready for an extra scene, some kind of a rousing encore that would win her favor. There he met the Moor, who had come to fetch Lunarito and Bejarano and take them back to the nightclub where they were appearing with his band in a late show. It was easy to become entangled in words where the Moor was concerned and one word led to another and eventually to a fight in which the Moor cruelly belabored the ill-protected bones of the actor with his proverbial shillelagh.

Again the music of Cáceres came to deliver me from these considerations and Garcia was pulling me out of my seat. I followed him gladly toward the patio, near which everyone was again collecting. There had been general demand for La Colombina and Pinto to dance, with the aroused audience overlooking their well-known rivalry and overruling their objections that they had never danced together. The Moor was cleverer. He taunted and insinuated, conceded, and in the end it was he and not the others who broke down the resistance. Perhaps, too, the presence of Cáceres had to do with it. His invitation and condescension to play was tantamount to a command. He enjoyed unrivaled prestige among his people.

This was not to be missed, these two dancing together in these auspicious and informal circumstances. It was something that had never happened before and would probably never happen again. The arrogant manner in which Pinto yielded and the demure docility of La Colombina. He stood looking into her with his very cold eyes and then his face softened into a crooked and sad and inviting smile that dissipated all professional jealousies, spread to both and lowered her eyes, that ran down like a histrionic mantle of regal magnanimity, welcoming her into its folds and sweeping both into the patio.

It was midafternoon and the sun was red gold on the dance. Garcia and I had squeezed nearest the entrance to the patio where we had a full view. Garcia recited in whispers at my ear:

"The dancers were shadows and their shadows were shadows of shadows—"

And so it was. No rattle of castanets or trigger heels here. No furious contortions or defiant expressions. Where previously the two friends had danced like enemies bent upon mutual destruction, the two rivals danced like friends committed to mutual interpretation. They moved about in silence like ghosts. One had been all flesh and reality; this was all soul and fantasy. It was the height of stylization—nothing to distract from the purity of the music but absolute plasticity to be fashioned by it, not accentuating but becoming a reflection of its rhythm, caught and frozen into the perfect tableau.

Although the dance itself was a typical Spanish dance, which therefore they could perform together for the first time without difficulty, they lifted it to the category of a symbolism undreamed of by anyone without their understanding of movement. Their insight into form, their silent dancing, did not stress the tempo but the phrase, and seeing them sway, diverge and converge in silence, like two shadows abandoning and recapturing their shadows, one realized that this was the ultimate in motion with a meaning: the gesture.

From where I was, I could see on the other side of the semicircle of people the face of Fulano, now and then blotted out by a shoulder or a projecting head and reappearing under somebody's arm. His thoughts, although silent like the dancers and also motivated by the same music, clashed at times in unplanned syncopation. It was disturbing, these short flashes of someone else's mind:

Out of place here and yet he was glad for this opportunity to see all this and it was a good substitute for his frustrated desires to return to Spain, but not the Spain where he had lived in his early youth, but the one he had imagined then and imagined since and which had grown in his mind into a great artificial, international stereotype, fed on the things he knew most foreigners thought of his land. But that Spain, had it existed, he had never known. He came from another section, not from that southern section where all this color and gaiety was supposed to exist, nor from any place with popular history or tradition, but simply from a place which might have been anywhere, and he had come to New York and waited all these years to see the Spain he had imagined. It was a very short substitute and he was out of place—

His face disappeared behind someone. They danced with subhuman indifference to each other and complete dedication to the common task, like two cogwheels, and with the same implacable beauty of precision; not actors but dancers, their faces like masks, their bodies like words building eloquently the syntax of their choreography.

There were his eyes:

The commonplace office near Hanover Square—import and export, but he only an employee, inconsequential in this world of international barter, nothing like that other importer who had brought the shawls. They had met here on equal terms and the other man had assumed that he was something in the business world and there had even been a suggestion about getting together sometime. Was he not here with the celebrities, brought by Don Pedro Guzman, the famous bandleader? Yes; through the careless generosity of Don Pedro, the disorderly and extrasocial Irish Moor who went about like a rushing junk wagon, dropping favors, alms, things for which one might or might not have any use—

And it was gone. The structure of the dance developed. It was like a series of stills in rapid succession from picture to picture, creating the illusion of smooth motion, almost cinematographic, but if it had been recorded on film, one could have considered any one of the pictures as a finished position. No awkward position could have been found in passing from one telling attitude to another. Every intermediary step would have been found completely balanced in form and a thing of beauty. Not only the structure, but the way it was built, was perfect.

The face was between two shoulders that were not his own and he was not torturing himself as usual, but appraising with certain calm:

Why this nostalgia about a country he scarcely remembered? Why not nostalgia about this other country where he had been so long? About his youth in this country? But he did have that at times and even now at this moment and, although in these surroundings Spain had gone to his head, there was a vague desire to slip out, to leave and hurry, run back to his own room where he could be alone with his own memories of his own Spain and not the one he made believe he shared with all these luckier people. They had not been like him, separated from their past, feeding their personality on their own identity. Half of them just arrived, the other half visited the old country frequently. They did not remember his Spain and he did not know theirs, and the ones who might have remembered had their memories obliterated by seeing the place change gradually and grow with them, and why should they pick that one particular epoch more than any other to remember, to see it, to endure the poignant sweetness of its isolated clarity? He resented them. He envied them and they were his brothers, his own more fortunate brothers—

The voice of the Moor between Garcia's and my own head interrupted: "This is a picture, you know? A very good picture symbolizing all dancing that has been and will be, as it should be, but a picture. The others, they were alive, they were an incident, not a generalization. Exactly as I said before: expressive, not interpretive, although one could take it the other way around—of course, the perfect concept may be stated backwards and remain consistent— But no matter, the other two, of course, found dancing in cafetines in Granada or Córdoba, I don't remember, but not these two. Nothing but the stage all their lives. The others: dark, Gypsies, all fire; but these—look at their color—and no spontaneity—dead. This is the dance of death, a race committing suicide at last. The others were a race burning in a final glorious pyre, they were a bonfire. These are a stone monument erected to the death of a people—"

I caught the mind again:

When any countryman was introduced, the usual remarks: "So? The gentleman is a Spaniard? From Spain? Well, yes; I could tell by the face, there is something—"

"—but that is our country: a continuous death. We have been ending since our beginning—"

"—but I thought perhaps Latin American. Your accent, you know? But real Spanish, you say? Well, well; you wouldn't recognize the place anymore. So many years in this country! Practically a lifetime. Must be quite an American by now."

"—of course, it is Góngora with something of the humanism and mockery of Quevedo, culteranismo and conceptismo—the national system. The moment of death held and sustained for an eternity. The identity and assertion of a country; not before dying, certainly not after, but exactly at the moment of dying. Puzzling, irritating point; the same thing that worried Newton when endeavoring to explain his fluxions. He must have known the despair that all of our people know. To conceive of something that cannot be explained. To be convinced of the truth of something which on explaining becomes obscure to the alien mind, absurd, full of contradictions, and will always remain unbelievable but convincing—"

It was true. He had lost much of his native accent and mannerisms, but he was a Spaniard and would continue to be one to his death, perhaps more so than the others. Distance and time made it so. One remained less adulterated living in the past, holding the past. His was a people of nostalgia who became more themselves by separation when parting—

"You think they are dancing, but they are not. They are standing still, cast in rhythmic shape upon the fourth perpendicular—"

I desisted. His thoughts clouded and out of the fog came a clear picture of Pinto and La Colombina dancing. He was no longer thinking but paying attention to the dance and then, no more. His face was there, but it was a blank, soft, doughy face.

The dance ended as it had begun, with cool circumspection, and yet at the very end, there was something difficult to define. It was a motion closing the dance that was above all typical and everyday Spanish, that in one instant suggested and condensed everything that Lunarito and Bejarano had done in a whole dance. More than the masters showing the pupils, it had a quality of personal warmth and the quiet gallantry which Pinto had shown throughout the performance suddenly flared in evidence and was never more engaging. Yet, as they left the patio to mix with the others, there was that distant speculation growing like a chasm between those two, and it was interesting to speculate what might have been—I mean, between them. The ice, however, had been broken and they were in the same group.

The Moor took charge again: "Superlative of course and delightfully artificial, but this is the modern generation of dancers for you, neoclassical and analytic—like comparing some of the modern toreros with Belmonte or Machaco and finding the answer in the old school of Lagartijo to convert safety into the virtue of his half-thrust or the modern adornos and remates. It is the ballet. Too much ballet and too much self-consciousness, but with the capacity to be castizo when one wants to. Did you notice that final step? That was telling the world how it is done; that when they want to, they can be as chulos if not more so than the next one. That was real and cañí. It was the desideratum in alpargatas, but all in all, too artificial and stylized. Even for the modern school, they have gone too far— Wonderful but less and less of Spain, until like the smile of the Cheshire cat—"

Pinto and La Colombina were listening with amusement and the criticism of Don Pedro seemed to bring them closer together, to cast them in the mutual role of misunderstood pioneers who are way ahead of their time and consequently find themselves alone, to enjoy their esotericism, and they began to talk, pleasantly at first and then more intimately. Had it not been for this, they might have parted on that dance floor never to see each other again. I have noticed no decrease with the passing generations in the unyielding pride of the Spaniard and they would have parted with their eloquent figures saying the well-known phrase: "I want and I know that you also want and it would have been wonderful, but it could not be."

I wouldn't be surprised if the sly Moor, always the conductor, had brought this about on purpose.

Cáceres had continued to finger his guitar, half plucking, half tuning it. This correction of tuning went on almost continuously, even while he played. It could not have been a reassuring reflex; he was too much of a purist for that. He must have had a remarkable sensitivity to variations of pitch. He looked around smiling while his hands caressed the instrument and his left flew to the pegs and then he bent a little and began to play in earnest.

Spanish music is singularly extra-European, a quality marked to such a degree that it permits even the most unmusical Spaniard to pick it out from any other music of the white race without hesitation. Possibly the one exception is its superficial similarity to southern Russian music, but clearly this would be more a confirmation of the rule than an exception. The fact that this relationship, if it exists, has bypassed Italy is one of those apparent puzzles intended to encourage research and classed by Don Pedro with the other one about the propinquities of northern and southern peoples in various countries.

It is known, or at least maintained, that in most countries the people from the south are easygoing, while the people from the north are industrious, but it so happens that the south of many countries lies north of the north of many other countries; yet the characteristics are maintained within each. This stratified alternation between indolence and activity parallel to the equator is curious indeed and a challenge to the investigating mind, but to get back to the Spanish music: its singularity makes Spaniards feel that it is more their very own than any other nationality can feel about its music. Music in many other countries is a product of culture. They have produced symphonies, operas, chamber and instrumental music of all types and, while these show national traits, they are not very noticeable to the uninitiated. Although Spain has also produced what is loosely termed serious music, what is known as Spanish music, both in Spain and abroad, is essentially popular, traditional and possibly of unrivaled individuality.

It is not continental, whether one refers to the continents of Europe or Africa, because although it enjoys a good deal of Moorish influence, it is a very conditioned Moorish, well digested and assimilated. It is the one music fully developed on white man's harmony by a European people, which stands apart from all others. Don Pedro claims to entertain the suspicion that this applies not only to music but to the whole of Spain in all other manifestations and that the saying attributed to the French, that Europe ends in the Pyrenees, may be conceded and accepted, but whether as a compliment or otherwise, he has kept a moot point.

It is for this reason very likely that a Spaniard, no matter how musical, cannot listen to his music critically and consider it simply as music. With him it is involved with traditional recollections which transcend the individual and constitute an inherited memory, creating a response which, more than personal, is racial and atavistic. Again I am drawing on the surplus stock of the Moor.

And there are some tunes and compositions, to be specific, that are particularly dear to us because of their felicity in portraying our impressions while we are there and our memories when we are away, which makes them more representative than any national anthem could be. It was one of these that Cáceres was playing, one called "Sevilla."

To play a thing so well known, and a transcription at that, requires someone of the stature of Cáceres, but in this case one could say that the transcription followed the original only by the merest chronological accident and that it is in the guitar that this composition achieves full realization. Much Spanish music implies the guitar and this was never so patent as in this instance. As Don Pedro exclaimed with purple face and yelling himself hoarse when Cáceres was finished, this was written, intentionally or not, for the guitar and it is sacrilegious to play it otherwise and no one has heard it until he has heard it thus played.

"Viva!" and "Bravo!" he groaned with ferocity into his own chest, like a dog shaking a rag doll. Like him, everything had become intensified with that music and even the sun in the yard was more red gold: "This is the culmination of the dance. Alone, with his guitar, without dancers or props, he has given us more dance than La Colombina,

Pinto, Lunarito and Bejarano." He pointed at them with an indelicacy, he felt instinctively, that was excusable in a burst of philharmonic patriotism: "He has fed you soup with a sling, my dears, that's all. This was not this dance or that one, but the dance of a whole country, physically and spiritually, the soul of a nation dancing." He finished with the shameless cliché and with so vehement a manner and suggestion of mockery that it conveyed accurately that he was on the road back and with full authority and complete justification to use the abused logotype.

Again the thick lenses. He was in full view across from me and he looked sad, probably not because of Don Pedro's phrase but on his own:

In the dark chamber of his mind was reflected the sunny yard, but it was a chromo of a legendary patio in Andalucia. Majos dressed in short jacket with calañés and fringed leggings; some in colorful bullfighters' costumes and manolas with shawls and mantillas, high combs and full skirts and guitars and castanets and kegs of manzanilla, flowers on women's heads and in men's teeth and everywhere and bright sun as only it can shine in one's imagination. He had never been to Sevilla.

"Ay Sevilla de mi alma!" came inevitably from Lunarito accompanied by an acquiescent chorus.

Knowing that she had really been there only made him feel worse. He was Spanish also and felt entitled to as much regret as the others. Sevilla was not only a town. It spread out to all of Spain as an invented symbol of a desirable way of life, of a dreamed way of being, but he had never been to the real Sevilla. Even this had been denied him. He would have wanted to say something about Sevilla or Madrid, or anything acknowledged as Spanish, but he would have felt like an imposter. If he had uttered a set phrase, he would have been a traitor to himself. If he had uttered a word with fresh meaning, he would have been a traitor to his people.

But the chromo persisted. It had faded somewhat under the veil of his more abstract considerations, but now it came back as bright and there were a burro erupting with madroños and two more figures added to it. One was a dashing soldier, complete with mustache, sideburns, epaulets and shiny boots. The other a rosy-cheeked and jovial priest inspecting the divertissements, and behind, like diffuse clouds to animate an otherwise limpid blue sky, the colossal inescapable shadows of Don Quixote, Columbus and the Gran Capitán. This was too much. It was grotesque and the very picture pointed out a way to escape the emotional by running into the critical and avoid this foreign infection of his fancy weakened by so many years abroad, by thinking more like a Spaniard, which at least he was by birth and right. He considered that while his countrymen have been depicted as flashingly bemustached, the members of the two most significant callings in Spain, priests and bullfighters, were clean-shaven, with the irrelevant consideration that while one boasts the coleta, the other bears the tonsure— His thoughts scattered.

The Moor was completely carried away. With arms upraised, one hand holding the shillelagh as a scepter giving authority to this raptus patriotic, the other snapping fingers with surprising loudness, he tore off into peteneras contriving to make his lameness an added contribution which made his contortions more flamencas:

"You see?" he rattled. "No need to kick your feet. Everything can be done right on a tile. Spanish dancing is all positional." And he was good. Standing almost on the same spot, he created the impression of the Spanish dance, probably more by leaving something to imagination: "Give me more, Cáceres, more!"

And Cáceres gave. With syncopations and counter-syncopations, with his heel beating like a common tavern guitarist, they put on a rousing show.

"Come on, Cáceres! We are feeding these dancers soup with a sling— And speaking of soup, I want food, I need fuel. Gaudeamus!" and panting, he led the way back to the tables. Like one loaded with armfuls of commentaries, he went back to his seat, dropping many on his way, and fell on a chair exhausted with enthusiasm, dumping the whole load on the table like a cataract, drowning everybody around it.

To observe this man in talk and action was amazing. His constant gestures that blended into one another smoothly like those of a deaf-mute. His manipulation, his prestidigitation with bottle, glass, shillelagh and cigarette, shifting from hand to hand, leaving always one, sometimes both free to mold his speech, to emphasize or subdue the idea. Out came a sentence and a hand or two close on its heels to shove it along or hold it back, to pat it or spank it or roll it between skillful palms until it emerged balanced, rotating or bouncing on fingertips, or to help it float in midair with glass underneath or suction it with hand above to suddenly squash it against tabletop. To spring and catch it on the wing, palm it; now you see it, now you don't, and make it dissolve within his fists so that the hands could be opened with disarming innocence. See? Nothing. It was a performance that would have dwarfed the art of any circus magician.

At times he emitted but one word and then the gestures went on by themselves, building, completing a whole sentence out of it. Other times nothing, only passes and motions dancing in the silence. Many of his answers consisted of nothing more, and his gestures were not confined to his own speech but to that of others as well; approving, condemning or evaporating it until it reappeared incorporated or digested and embodied in his answer, until one was convinced that this was a fantastic metabolism of words and ideas changing into each other cyclically.

Food had already begun its pacific invasion of tables in that nomadic way typical of our gatherings where people never sit to a regular and orderly meal from soup to nuts. Indeed, the garlic soup and, if the place has some Basque leanings like El Telescopio, the purrusalda and also in summer the gazpacho will be found there and also piñónes in some form and other things of the hard-to-crack family and smuggled-in turrón, even if it is not Christmas, with blessings to the canning industry—the refugium pecatorum of so many homesick foreigners— but never in the conventional sequence. This takes casualness by the scruff of the neck and nails it to a chair. It congeals the carefree, happy atmosphere and ruins the occasion.

The Señor Olózaga had ordered calamares for La Colombina and had before him a whole roasted suckling, a specialty of the house which no doubt felt with this like a loyal outpost of the famous Botin of Madrid. Don Pedro was eating angulas and his vocalist asked him what they were.

"Sewer worms, woman. See? They are heavenly worms and those two little black dots at one end are the eyes."

The girl did not push her curiosity any farther, but Garcia, who was eating something with peppers, laid his tools down:

"Please! Do you have to put it that way? Besides, I am not so sure that they are what you say."

"Ah! But they are, my friend. Handpicked by the light of a lantern at night." Garcia bent over his peppers resignedly, a picture of utter desolation. "This national squeamishness, inevitably enhanced by the presence of foreigners." The Moor held some of the angulas in his fork and shoved them toward the vocalist: "Try them. They are wonderful." She averted the threat with agility born from panic: "Even better than calamares, eh! Colombina?" he shouted.

La Colombina engaged him in a short discussion about the comparative virtues of angulas versus calamares. Oh! The calamares in their own black sauce! According to Don Pedro, the only fish that wears mourning for itself at the table. He finally deferred to her gallantly, avowing that nothing could be so good as she, properly or improperly served, and would she submerge in a tub full of black ink and thus be brought to his table?

His attention returned to his companions. He explained that once, unable to procure angulas and in despair, he had tried, and communicated for the benefit of those who collect recipes, broken-up spaghetti with the juice of a can of herrings and plenty of fried garlic, but it had proven a dismal failure as a substitute. His English vocalist was following his every word with fascination and especially a favorite gesture of his which consisted of pulling his lower eyelid with his thumb and following up with extended index finger. His long, strong hands gave this common motion unmatched meaning. His talking mechanics were superior.

"That must be a Spanish gesture. Is it a Spanish gesture? I have seen him do it all the time and have also seen other Spaniards do it. I'll bet it is a Spanish gesture."

"It is more than that, my gambling Trilby. It is an exorcism. It captures the alter ego of the eyeball and makes it roll like this." He picked up an olive and with astonishing skill made it roll back and forth on the curve between thumb and forefinger: "He knows the most amazing table tricks." She applauded: "He is wonderful!"

"You see?" He went on: "The eye that has sighted the idea runs after it in hot pursuit and this offers the best way. The fingers form part of a cycloid—the tautachrone, the brachistochrone; path of swiftest descent and supreme equalizer of all starts, whose invited guests all arrive at the same time— The curve that captivated Galileo, Pascal, and impregnating the minds of the Bernoullis, Euler sired the calculus of variations nurtured by Lagrange, but never mind. That way it catches up with the idea sooner, do you see?" The olive left the curve of his fingers and popped into his mouth: "The desideratum of tobogganic democracy— It would be interesting to speculate on what would happen to a democracy if all immigrants chose such a path. What a convention! The valley of Jehoshaphat." He had left his chair and ranted on while limping about the table, finishing the dish of angulas in his hand. Right in his element. That is what he liked, what most of us really like: to eat and drink in disorder and endlessly in continuous ingestion, alternating a little bite here and a little swallow there, all day long.

Someone mentioned the tapitas in the Spanish taverns and a chorus followed of many other words with diminutive endings and any other endings at the discretion of the speaker. One of the greatest freedoms of the Spanish language is that of endings which can impart to a word any number of shadings and implications. One takes a good part of the word and then ends it to suit the meaning intended as one wishes and the same word assumes all possible aspects: awesome or insignificant, lofty or contemptible, pugnacious, indifferent, benevolent, even back-slapping, caressing, tickling, and the endings used on that occasion for the well-remembered little things to eat were a masterpiece of endearment and reminiscent lip-smacking and tooth-sucking. Possibly it is this alternating of food and drink that makes for the high alcoholic tolerance of the Spaniard.

The Moor had finished his angulas and was in front of the table occupied by the green man and the two ladies who looked like school-teachers. He laid the empty dish in front of one of the ladies: "Smell that garlic, madam. Good for you."

She astonished everyone by agreeing with him and insisting on ordering some. The green man bounced and screamed: "Don't you dare order those horrible things, you bad girl! You ought to be spanked. You should be tied to a post and thrashed with a horse-whip." His voice had risen almost to a pitch that only a dog could hear, and he was congested with ill-concealed and uncalled-for delight.

Don Pedro turned away and called to a waiter to bring the lady's order and then said that Garcia's peppers looked good: "Bring me some, but with the meat cut thick. These Spaniards with meat are unbelievable. Don't know what it's all about. They take a cutlet and go into battle with it, swing it with all their might and slap it down on the chopping block so that when several of them are working at the same time it sounds like an ovation or a battery of guns. Bang! Every time the meat hits, they jump from the force. They treat meat as if it were their worst enemy. After that, they attack it with a special mace, bang! crash! swing it and slap it some more, crush it again: swish, slap, bang, crash! And tough as the meat usually is, they win in the end and attain their sworn purpose which is to make it so thin that it has only one side. A perfect dish for the great Möbius."

The general eating and drinking went on. Most everyone had left his seat and walked about holding a plate or a glass. The conversation hummed and chairs scraped against the floor. The green man and his two ladies, probably thinking that the party was getting a little too fast for their speed, were gathering their belongings and getting ready to leave when the blast of the Moor's laughter hit the fellow flush in the back. He turned around, purple with indignation, nostrils dilated, his fingers curled as if ready to scratch, eyes now flaring, lids now drooping with intolerable disgust, but the Moor pointed significantly at his stick and the fellow hurried behind the two ladies, his back attempting the impossible feat of combining dignity with swift evasion of a possible kick or a well-directed missile. The man did everything with an air of surreptitious guilt, of being caught in flagrante, even of getting away with things which anyone would have felt entitled to. I observed him. Right at the door, on his way out, he adjusted his face, but he did it as someone would adjust his clothes before leaving a washroom.

Besides me, the only ones left at our table were Garcia, munching quietly, and Fulano with his thick lenses focused into space. Someone had turned on the radio and a voice sang in English something about the secret tragedy of a woman of the streets. There were protests and loud commands to turn it off. I heard snatches of the Moor's conversation and then looked into the lenses. He was thinking now of something that had happened and not a dream.

It was a Saturday and he was going to a party at the apartment of some Spanish fellows. They agreed that they should all bring girls, gay ones. He did not have any particular girl but he knew a prostitute uptown whom he visited with some regularity. She was a pleasant blonde girl with whom he felt at ease. Once on an impulse, he had decided to bring her a present in order to make things less businesslike and more personal, and perhaps she might dedicate the rest of the evening to him, go for a walk, sit on a bench in the park, like others did. Not that he wanted to become involved with a girl like that, but at least he could safely try to make it less cold, less clinical. He debated between bringing her flowers or candy and decided on the candy because there were always people at the entrance of her place who would notice flowers and might think him a fool.

She was very grateful that time and he asked her to go out with him to a movie or for a walk, anything, and she said that she could not do it that night because she expected two other men, but that she would be glad to do it any other time and not to forget to ask her again and to give her a rain check. So now that he was going to this party, he called her and asked her to come along with him and she accepted but said that she would have to leave by midnight because she had another business date then, and because his funds were low as usual, he had to check an impulse to tell her to forget business that night and he would make it up to her. However, he felt very elated at their going out together like any two human beings.

So they went to the party and he did not have a very good time there. The men all insisted on talking Spanish and the girl and two other girls there had little to say. Once, one of the fellows walked with one of the girls into one of the other rooms and there was some laughter and Fulano thought of putting his arm around his girl, but he felt that this would be taking advantage between business hours and she might resent it and he felt morose and drank some more instead, and anyway he wanted to show her that he did not like her only for that. Then it was midnight and the girl had to go. He offered to escort her, but she said that she could manage by herself and for him to stay and have a good time with his friends, and one of the men asked for her telephone number and she passed that off with commendable delicacy.

After she had been gone some time, someone who was roaming about from room to room as people sometimes do in such circumstances claimed that an unopened bottle of liquor was missing and that she must have taken it. Fulano came to her defense with drunken truculence and said that if necessary he would pay for the bottle and was told that there was no need to grow so upset and insulting.

In the end the bottle turned up behind a chair where one of the fellows had placed it to save for when they ran out of drinks. After that he felt more out of place than before and he also went home.

He did not see the girl for several days but about a week after this, he had the dream. He was walking with her on a square with a great big house at one end that was all boarded up except for the entrance, and they went in. The corridors were immense, like avenues with other corridors like streets running across them and the whole place was dark and there were many doors that led into pitch-black rooms. They soon were lost in this maze of corridors and then saw a very faint light and walked toward it. Following the light they turned into a side corridor that ended against a wall and there was a small glass dome on the ceiling from which daylight came. Right underneath the light and on the floor there was a bucket of white paint and a pile of discarded telephones, their black dusty surfaces splattered with white specks. A noise was coming from the telephones that was like the cooing of doves, but on listening carefully, one could make out some words: "Hello, honey. Is that you? Hello, hello—" like the cooing of doves: "Will I see you this evening?" — "Hello, honey, hello— Will I see you this evening, darling?" — "Hello, honey, hello, honey—hello—hello—hello—" Like the cooing of doves.

He explained to her with all honesty that these were old conversations trapped in the broken wires and the explanation satisfied them both, and they went out of the house without difficulty.

They came out into another plaza, but this one was oval in shape and was illuminated by street lamps. There were no buildings around, only a wall, but he knew that this was the Puerta del Sol in Madrid and that they had been in Spain all along.

She said: "I know that nobody likes me here. I am going away."

He said: "I will walk with you. It is not your fault. I think you are fine."

They walked out one end of the plaza and came out on a road that passed in front of the entrance. The road ran between masses of trees. The sky was very dark on top, like an enormous awning of black clouds, but it was clear all around the horizon and it was from there that the yellow light came to cast the shadows of the trees across the lonely road. They walked on it a few steps and then stopped. There were two stone pillars on each side of the road hung with black crepe.

Again she spoke: "This is as far as you can go. I must go the rest of the way alone."

He stood there looking at her walk serenely along the road between the walls of trees, under that hostile dark sky, and a breeze that came from the same direction as the light played on her dress and on her hair and on the tree leaves.

The day after he had this dream, he called her up and was told that she had been taken ill to the hospital where she had died soon after. This was the first time that one of his dreams could be considered a premonition, but he thought that it must be only coincidence and that things like that are bound to happen, but life would be more interesting if one could believe more in premonitions.

This experience affected him excessively and depressed him for several days, and for a while he thought that he was in love with the girl.

"—Yes sir," came the voice from the Moor. "The pillars of Latin civilization: garlic, the chamber pot or the bidet. No real civilization without these things." And Garcia, who had moved his plate next to me, protesting: "Please! You are indeed Don Pedro el Cruel. Wait at least until I finish— Please, some other time." And in my ear through clenched teeth: "He does it on purpose. I tell you, he has the strangest type of cruelty. It is the Moor in him."

Past the moving figures I caught a glimpse of La Colombina and the Señor Olózaga, two of the few still sitting at a table. She had found a cordobés and was wearing it. The cordobés is one of the few items of man's apparel which is especially becoming to women, probably because they wear it with their hair done up in a bun at the back of their head, which fully realizes the knotted-up coleta of the bull-fighters who wear it when out of uniform. One could look at that woman for hours without tiring.

I missed the voice of Don Pedro. On the table was his unfinished dish of peppers and meat—in chunks— I looked around but could not see him anywhere. The Señor Olózaga had also left his privileged place and disappeared, but his position had been taken by several people who were talking to La Colombina.

Darkness had filtered gradually and one of the waiters went about with a chair, climbing on it and lighting the farolitos.

There was a rattle on the stairs leading to the cellar and soon there appeared the Señor Olózaga and the Moor carrying large baskets full of bottles. Don Pedro was having a laborious time of it with his lame leg, his shillelagh under his arm and both hands occupied.

"Careful there, Moor," said the Señor Olózaga. "This is a special load."

"One more step, Chink, and excelsior!" They emerged on the top step and Don Pedro declaimed: "Careful, everybody. The gates of hell have opened and the devil is coming out with bottles full of genii." He turned to some waiters that followed with more baskets of bottles: "Place those by the windows. Come on, Chink. Let's place these on our table."

They laid the baskets on the floor and began placing bottles of assorted sizes and contents on a table next to ours, until there was scarcely room for anything else:

"Look at the pretty skyline— Until now El Telescopio was in Manhattan, but now Manhattan is in El Telescopio—the situation reversed, the world inside out. The absurdity typical but the results good. Nothing to it. You know? We had to weed the good from the bad. Most of the stock downstairs is junk, but we managed and I think the Chink knows his rum and he thinks now that I know my wine, but I know little about rum and he knows little about wine, so how can we tell about each other? Of course, the national system—never fails. Talk of things one knows nothing about—the perfect simplification. Well, Chink, ready now?"

They walked to the windows facing the street and some of us followed. A crowd had gathered in front of the restaurant, attracted by the music and noise, and many of them must have been regular customers who were told that the place was not open to the public as there was a private gathering going on. A couple of waiters were uncorking bottles fast and reinserting the corks halfway. The Señor Olózaga and Don Pedro stood at a large window, a bottle in each hand, and saluted the crowd.

"With the compliments of El Telescopio," said the Señor Olózaga loudly, and a bottle sailed across the street. There was no crash.

"What do you mean the compliments of El Telescopio? This Chink always advertising and still he denies— With the compliments of the Chink and the Moor, fellows," and off sailed two more bottles in quick succession. There was a roar of approval from the crowd across the street, and as the barrage of bottles continued and they passed from hand to hand, there were shouts to the health of the Moor and the Chink and even vivas.

Don Pedro kept a running commentary: "Look at them, Chink—

That's it, boys. Drink out of the bottles, that is the national—in this case I mean the colonial system of El Telescopio, the only true advance post of Spain— And now it is overflowing into the street and the epidemic is spreading. Drink up, boys, to the second conquest. Catch!" And another couple of bottles went forth. "Come on, Chink. Let's lay down a good barrage. The Latinamericanization of the continent is proceeding according to schedule. These are from the king of the tango." A bottle: "the sultan of the rumba." Another bottle: "The master of the ay, ay, ay imported from the land of eternal lamentations. These are from the emperor of Latin America appearing at the balcony of his palace, El Telescopio, to greet his faithful subjects." The light from the windows was reflected across the street by a growing array of bottles with bottoms pointing skyward and Don Pedro turned to the audience gathered behind him and the Señor Olózaga: "Look at the convention of astronomers—this is castizo!"

A young voice speaking English came from the crowd: "That's Pete Guz, the bandleader."

"Right you are, my child, and here is my autograph on the label of this one. Leave the Pedro and cross out the other name. It is from Don Pedro el Cruel, but tonight Don Pedro the Just—as many Spaniards still insist he was. Let them go, Chink. Put more English into those bottles—haa—English into Spanish bottles—a hangover from prohibition. Typical. That's Spain for you, and that's El Telescopio in New York. Watch them go, like little airships that sail in the night— See if you can heave one over the buildings into Chinatown for your countrymen. The Chinks are tonight the allies of the Moors in this battle for the aggrandizement of Spain in a campaign for advertising El Telescopio." The last two bottles were swallowed by the crowd which now packed the opposite sidewalk, and with a parting wave of the arm the good samaritans ambled back to their table. They were quite a pair, these two. After having turned the gathering into an open juerga, they knew that things were out of their hands, going their merry way, and they settled down to their serious drinking.

But the juerga had become public property now and it was more like a carnival where friends and strangers mix alike. Every vestige of formal restraint was swept aside and everyone began to enjoy himself freely. Cáceres began to strum parts of tunes from different regions—

ghostly ones from the north and warm ones from the south. Pinto and Bejarano began to show each other steps in time with the music and Lunarito and La Colombina were laughing together. Slowly the crowd from the street invaded the billiard room beyond, many of them still holding bottles in their hands, and then stood there reverently looking upon the celebrities they had never had occasion to see in person and only knew by fame and pictures.

"Look, Chink. They enter the palace as it should be and as it was done in Spain where individualism is what makes all men equal. They come to say: We, each of whom is as good as you and altogether better than you, elect you to be our king, eh, Chink? After this, you and I remain Spanish forever— Viva España!" He bellowed: "Come on, all of you. Put on a good show for the Spanish colony. You could never wish for a better audience."

This is where my memory begins to fail me about that memorable night and from there on until the end, I have only recollections of disconnected scenes. One of these is that, at the words of the Moor, the crowd in the billiard room advanced into the main room, and then that Cáceres was playing for them with a devotion that he could not have surpassed in the concert hall. Then the four dancers dancing in pairs and together with a dedication impossible to understand after what they had eaten and drunk for hours and the crowd cheering, accepting the royal gifts with magnificent appreciation. I caught sight of Dr. de los Rios beaming with cheerful benignity. His eyes swept over the scene and then, almost unseeing, over me and Fulano and for one moment it was as if a very tenuous cloud had passed over the sun. Instinctively, I looked at the thick lenses.

More than once he had caught me looking at him and had looked away, but this did not make any difference. All I needed was to look into his eyes a moment. Once I had entered his mind, I was well established and he could look where he pleased without seeming to be aware of my presence in him. Otherwise, I assume, he would have changed some of his thoughts, although one can never tell and I was ready to believe anything, having witnessed how deceptive external appearances could be.

At this particular moment he was not recalling any dreams or experiences, but indulging in self-flagellation and savoring another of his favorite tragic roles. He enjoyed this game better, but at the same time, the implied responsibility made him restless. So as usual, he chose a good, solid, cast-iron stock situation with most of the well-tried-out and worn trimmings:

He was a beggar in his last moments of despair and shame, a meek panhandler, wanting but not daring to ask for a dime at a beer hall and looking hungrily at the free-lunch counter. The place he had well figured out; the circumstances not so well. At one end was a piano and a cynical, if intellectual-looking fellow, cigarette dangling from his lips, playing with a feeling and understanding that the most select audience would have been honored to hear. He too was a desperate soul, a kindred soul who, casting aside a brilliant career, swept by disillusionment, elected to seek solace in anonymity among the rough and simple folk. But he was there by choice and this made a difference.

Then in came the burly fellow, radiating self-confidence and insolence, surrounded by his henchmen: "Hello, Mozart," he greeted the pianist who did not turn but acknowledged the greeting by a shrug of his shoulders without interrupting his play. "When are you going to play something cheerful?" Then he had bought drinks for everybody and, observing the forlorn beggar, had tossed him a bank note.

Fulano picked up the note avidly and wanted to kiss the fellow's hand, thanking him profusely, but the fellow had pushed him away, telling him to forget it. He had made a killing that day and felt generous.

But Fulano did not intend to forget it. This was the turning point in his life. Having reached the nadir of abjection, when he was contemplating the redemption of suicide, this man had extended a helping hand and saved his life. He skipped over the details that followed, but his gratitude increased as he gradually recovered his self-respect and began to take his rightful position in society, until he reached that point where he was considered a solid citizen.

As the years passed, he never forgot his benefactor and always followed his exploits with solicitous dismay. The man had become an arch-criminal, commanding a vast underworld empire, and all during his rise to that position, he had been the recipient of inexplicable favors, not knowing whom to thank for them. Once when it appeared certain that the law had him at last and all his sinister influence could not help him, he had been presented with an alibi which he and his lawyer had lapped up like manna from heaven.

Out of gratitude Fulano had protected a sinner and obstructed justice.

A moral dilemma but flavorful. The little man could not figure out how to maintain his anonymity all those years, how such an influential gangster had failed to discover his identity and connect him with the former beggar. Fulano had in reserve an ending in which he, having become a distinguished judge, resigned dramatically when having to pass a death sentence upon his protégé, but there was another ending which he thought might be better. All these doubts annoyed him and he decided to skip it and reach unhindered the other grand finale.

The great moment came at last, the situation that would offer the proof of supreme gratitude.

The arch-criminal with his bodyguards was entering a theater, or a music hall or whatever it was, it did not matter which, when the black sedan closed in, its windows bristling with gun barrels.

And then Fulano threw himself in the way, arms outstretched, protecting his former benefactor—

A series of explosions disrupted and blacked out the scene that I was watching in the little man's mind, and for a moment I did not know what to make of it. Then I realized that they were the Moor's words intruding in his thoughts and scattering them:

"Boo, boo!" The extended fingers pointing at him, words shooting out of them, in one of Don Pedro's habitual gestures: "Why so thoughtful and gloomy? Not that I blame you, but one must keep up appearances and, after all—you know—" There followed some more of his motions and incantations.

The little man smiled wanly but managed a quick introspective look to finish the scene in a hurry:

He was lying on the sidewalk, dead, and a crowd was gathering. One of the bodyguards said, and the uncultured words were well memorized: "The little punk must have been one of your admirers, boss. Maybe the guy who done you all them favors."

"Yeah, maybe. Let's get the hell out of here, boys."

And Fulano lay there, still unrecognized, his debt paid in full.

But the Moor had really spoiled it and with satisfaction walked back to the table where the Señor Olozaga was waiting for him, surrounded by bottles. After this I can remember only a blank and a glimpse floating in its midst of El Cogote with a red and yellow cape making veronicas and adornos right in front of the crowd and demanding a bull desperately— Then nothing, and out of that, Lunarito in laughing collapse at her table and drinking manzanilla thirstily while fanning herself, and then I woke up to a clear scene.

A man detached himself from the crowd and staggered forward. He had a fine head of white hair and luxuriant beard and a manner of grandiose and hurt kindliness. The unusual silence which accompanied this, possibly the only complete silence since my arrival at El Telescopio, must have aroused me from my stupor and fixed the scene in my mind.

The patriarchal, godly man stopped before Lunarito's table and stood there swaying drunkenly without uttering a word, only looking down at her with a mixture of regret and compassionate forgiveness. She looked up once startled at him and then lowered her eyes. Bejarano came quickly to her side and stood looking at the man belligerently, his face that maroon color that the rush of blood produces in a very dark complexion. For that type of scene, it lasted long without a word being said. Then one of the waiters approached and, touching the man on the shoulder, inquired whether there was anything he wanted.

"Go back to your chores," Don Pedro commanded. "And don't interrupt the dramatic moment. Don't you know yet that Spaniards cannot get together without a tragic, heart-rending situation appearing like a rabbit out of a hat? Leave them alone, let the scene play itself. This is typical."

There was a ripple of comment ever so slight while the waiter, feeling quite foolish, hesitated and the man looked him over with dignity:

"Nothing, nothing," he said. "I made a mistake." And with that he turned and began to walk away with faltering steps. Royal with solicitude, the Moor rushed over and held his arm to guide him out respectfully and the man then marched erect, with stiff aplomb, his head held aloft from all base, mundane ugliness, with all the heroic bearing of a stubborn invalid. If the old guy had come in, as we say, through the little door, now he was going out through the big one. Everybody made way for them and together they passed on processionally, the Moor holding an arm around the other with defiant solidarity, pouring

words of consolation down his shoulder—one renegade to another—
and thus they walked right through the crowd and out of the place.

The Moor returned and made straight for his table. Once there, he
faced the audience: "Curtain! Bravo! Wake up!" He applauded loudly
and others imitated him with relief: "I propose a toast: To the
Spaniard's love for the elegiac and may situations never fail him." He
drank out of the bottle.

This lessened the tension and all began to act as if nothing had
happened. Lunarito became voluble with forced gaiety and the noise
went on. More wine, more talk and confusion. I don't know how long
after I noticed the crowd of people who had entered the place begin to
withdraw, but it could not have been very long because there were
objections to their going. This was a fiesta for Spaniards and all those
available should share it. Yet all those people, unanimously and politely, with a grateful murmur and a gesture, excused themselves and I
heard Don Pedro praising the innate discretion of his countrymen.

Again more confusion and shouting. Lunarito and Bejarano exchanging steps and fine points with La Colombina and Pinto. The
voice of the Moor: "National system—the fourth perpendicular—
don't know what it's all about." And El Cogote demanding a bull:
"Please, gentlemen, a bull, a bull, even a little bull—" the English
phrase running stupidly through my mind: "My kingdom for a horse.
What kingdom?" — "Please, gentlemen. For God's sake, señores; un
toro, un torito," and the controversial Moor telling him: "Hay que
vaciar. Let me show you how to vaciar." All this against the ample
well-satisfied inspection of the Señor Olózaga and above all Cáceres,
rising majestic in his serenity while all around him broke down, still
standing in the unassailable omnipotence of his art.

Here the pattern of the gathering was lost. The Moor was persistently toasting La Colombina and Lunarito as the two prototypes of
Spanish women: both all fire, but one a smoldering volcano and the
other an open conflagration. This led him to speak of women who
believe their sole duty consists of being beautiful without contributing
anything else, only to accept and nothing more.

"I recall the generation of the chorus girls: women without imagination, without talk, without expression, glorying in their statuesque
stupidity—lifeless statues, posturing corpses, making one wonder

whether one was living in a world of frustrated Pygmalions or necrophiles; women with the same centripetal gluttony of the dead, accepting all homage and giving nothing in return. They could also come under my heading of perfect examples of feminine putritude—"

I felt an almost physical pull in my eyes and found myself looking into the face of Fulano and there was indescribable anguish in it. For a few moments I could see nothing but that face hanging in front of me and then the countenance of Dr. de los Rios floated in and out of cigarette smoke clouds, radiating infinite clemency and understanding, and I could only hear the conversation all around growing dim, as if it were receding and then returning and becoming banal. Garcia had said something about the limerick form not having a counterpart in Spanish and somebody recited a ribald one. Then someone else began to recite another—

The face before me suffered a frightful transfiguration from despair to insane panic and frantic appeal that met me with brutal arresting force. I had not witnessed his emotions in such a tempest until now. Then the thick lenses seemed to expand and spin like two all-powerful maelstroms that swallowed me. As I sank I heard the limerick in the distance:

"There was a young man called Dave—"

He saw her the first time in a window of a second-rate shop where she did not even occupy a prominent position. It was like a short circuit. Even before he looked, he had seen her and the recognition struck him like a blast. She was the composite picture of all the qualities he had wanted most in all the women he had desired and those he had conjured in his daydreams. She was his secret perfection, the undivulged mistress of his innermost self, and what had been irritatingly elusive in his thoughts took in this visible composition a power that swept him like a cyclone.

He stood like a living volcano, the blood rushing hot to his head, then ebbing like crawling sparks through his nerves, turning him into a human anthill.

To avoid attracting attention, he went by, but shaken, dizzy like a drunkard, until very gradually he composed himself. Then he turned to pass the window again and have another look.

She had everything he wanted, including, he thought in confusion, that she was not alive and therefore could live only for him. From her elevated position she averted his eyes with heavy, provocative demureness. She had the confident proud carriage, the ease and yielding assurance that comes from possessing that irresistible carnal attraction of something which is not human flesh: her densely creamy complexion, the thickness that only artificial lashes can possess, the indescribable, exasperating suggestiveness of a final reward that could never be granted. He knew that whoever had fashioned her had his twin soul and must have adored her as he adored her but that she had rebuffed his love as improper, acknowledging all the time that it was inevitable. His thoughts overtook each other tumultuously.

They must have been mad not to place her in the most exalted position, not to know that she was the queen of all mannequins, of all women, real or artificial, dead or alive. Or perhaps they were also ashamed of having their feelings discovered. It would have killed him if anyone had known what his feelings were.

He observed her guardedly. She would be the only one who would ever know it and the fire of his love would break her pride and indifference because with her, he could abandon himself to the limit, and although she would despise whoever loved her, she could never throw his love back in his face, she would have to submit and he would conquer her in the end. His life, despicable as it might be, was a life and would be communicated to her. She would collapse from her superiority and sink to the most degrading depths of passion, then come alive, wake up with shrieks of joy to wallow in subjugation to their common depravity.

He stood at the curb facing the building, to one side of the shop as if waiting for somebody, but her face and body pulled at his eyes. He looked from one person to another with the air of someone whose time is valuable but has a good reason for standing where he stands, frowning with concentration on all those small incidents which constitute an active sidewalk, self-consciousness mounting, crowding, choking him, shame oozing out of him in cold perspiration. All those people must have been as blind to him as he was blind to them. How could they miss his inner agitation, not to see that he worshiped her?

And the phrase continued to burn him. The fire of his love would melt her insulting pride which had brought his desire excruciatingly alive, like the blow of a lash. The fire of his love— What did she want to keep herself for? Not even the worms, but the fire of his love.

Then a man and a woman came into the window and he turned away in horror, not wanting to see. He walked away fast at first and then more slowly and then he became calm and finally the spell was broken.

He must have been momentarily mad and this was a hallucination. No one could fall in love so suddenly—certainly not with a mannequin—but perhaps one could thus fall in love if one had begun to love an ideal since his childhood and had nursed that passion into maturity and then come face to face with the embodiment of his ideal, its perfect realization. He decided to put this out of his mind and cautiously never to come near that window again. Such things could easily become an obsession.

And it did become an obsession which he could not cast off and he returned the next day and the next and stood as he had stood the first time, and in the end he knew that he was lost, that she had won and drawn him with a power he was unable to resist, with that power of her inner emptiness, the power of the vacuum, of nothingness, which is an appeal to all things. It was no more his decision than to say of a falling man that he has decided to hit the ground. He had to get her and she was the type who, contemptuous and mocking of the humble lover, could nevertheless be bought.

Then began the scheming. He had to be as careful as any lover who wants to attain the forbidden object of his love, and he made his plan.

He entered the store with trepidation. He explained apologetically to the same man he had seen entering the window that he was a foreign business-man who had a store in his native country and was here on a pleasure trip but always with an alert eye for profits. He could easily combine business with pleasure. The figure in the window had caught his fancy and not knowing his way about, he was ready to buy it as it was, to dress up his own shop. He knew that his elaboration was stupid but he could not help himself. He remembered that interview with painful lucidity.

The man listened, at first puzzled as one whose routine is subject to an unexpected approach, and then, as he gained comprehension, with that set courtesy which every merchant shows to any other merchant engaged in his or a similar line, and then he explained.

He knew and understood very well that business was conducted in a very different way in other countries and he was very happy to have a window display which deserved the approval of other professionals, but he was afraid that he could not be of much help. The boss, the real boss, was not there and, of course, he could do nothing on his own initiative, but he was sure that they could not spare any of the dummies. Anyway, the logical thing to do was to go to one of the concerns that supplied them. There were some, he was certain, in the upper Thirties on the West Side, where he could find all the mannequins he wanted.

How could he explain to the man that he wanted that particular one, only that one and no other, that there was no substitute for a love such as his? How could he insist without giving himself away, without laying bare for all to laugh or feel revulsion the horror of his mad passion?

The two salesgirls in the store had been looking on, but then a woman customer walked in and caught their attention. That was a relief and even offered a very farfetched point of departure. The man continued politely to be helpful, meanwhile explaining that he could not help. The real boss took care of all such things and, if he cared to return when he was there— He was polite, but still puzzled, possibly even quizzical. Could he help noticing the tenseness, the glow of combined embarrassment and elation at being in the place where she lived, breathing the same— Oh, no! The hopelessness of it! The man had to be blind, incapable of conceiving such things, not to see and understand his despair.

He felt his heart pumping, the blood ascending like the tide, and went out mumbling that he would look up the suppliers, that he would return.

Outside he felt calm once more and walked fast away without one look back at her. His next step was foreordained. He was now committed to this, and there followed the days, long and dreary days, like a tunnel, but with the far light of hope at the end, days of debating with himself before buildings whether to go in and make inquiries from the concern whose name he had seen in the directory.

From the beginning he had suspected the great difficulty of attaining his desire, but now he began to see that this was a formidable task and then the fear that he might not find her and trying to assuage it by repeating to himself that he was bound to find her duplicate somewhere, that the manufacturer must have turned out many alike. But would they be exactly alike? And if they were, if there were so many twin sisters, how could he bear not to have them all? One must be calm and resigned. No love is perfect. It wants to possess completely, leaving nothing for those who have not been made deserving by it. But this can never be, and much less in a love as absurd and doomed to imperfection as the one he now realized would eventually destroy him.

One after another he went into buildings without finding her and endured discussions and persuasion to accept a substitute, an insulting suggestion of disloyalty, an invitation to abominable betrayal. He endured the humiliation of jeering remarks from persistent dealers, disappointed in their hopes for closing a deal, the accusations of not really wanting to buy, the adhesive tenacity rising and then flaring into inquisitorial high pressure, the fear, mind-obscuring fear, of being found out, trapped in the end, and the ultimate total disgrace. He felt that he was living in danger, risking the most vulnerable part of his being.

And at last he found her.

How he lived through the moments of that transaction will always be a monument to self-control. It was not the deal itself. Compared to what had gone before and his gradual adaptation to his quest, this was easy. It was conducting it in her presence, the imagined disdainful mockery of her countenance congealing through imagination into a visual fact, fluctuating in and out of his consciousness like the pulse of a life all her own and like no other's.

The fellow was ease and accommodation personified. He did not show any particular interest in his reasons for wanting her and he would deliver anywhere he wanted that same day. Her clothes were another thing. He would furnish a complete outfit: underwear, shoes, stockings, dress and hat, but of course, that was extra. He did not supply those as a rule and only had them for display purposes, but he could let him have those for an additional consideration. He did not ask the obvious and feared question of why he wanted the clothes if his purpose was to display those of his own shop. He was only interested in making a sale.

When he left, he felt as if all his organs had come loose and were bounding inside of him, colliding among themselves and against the shell of his body. He felt tears gathering in his eyes, the flesh quivering over his skull. He took the subway back home and found the station quite deserted at that hour of the day and, walking to the far end, he waited for the train while his whole frame was shaken brutally by sobs.

When he arrived home, he had the foolish idea of fixing the place up for her arrival and then decided that it could never make any difference to her. It was only for his love that she was coming and nothing else mattered. With her he could be himself, completely, unabashedly himself as no one ever could be with another human being. No matter how intimate we may be with a real lover, there is always a last recess that is closely guarded, and even as the intimacy grows, the recess also grows stronger by the importance which this intimacy lends to that person's opinions of us. If we sometimes open that recess to a chance acquaintance, it is because we feel protected by an anonymity which makes a vaster recess out of the rest of us.

Being able to exercise this self-criticism diminished his fear for his sanity. He thought of going out again to kill time, but the deliveryman might arrive in the meanwhile and he wanted to be there to receive him and make things as quiet as possible lest the neighbors might notice. He was in danger of discovery, when everything he had built would come tumbling down to bury him in disgrace. He noticed a well-known fear creeping up and was filled with sadness and remorse. He thought of abandoning the whole adventure, sending the deliveryman back, but the memory of her set his body on fire and in panic he succumbed to his destiny.

He sat and smoked cigarettes, but he was too tense to sit still and do nothing. In the end he began to fix the place up and do innumerable little things which did not require any concentration of the attention he was incapable of giving but rather distracted it.

Then the bell rang and he was outside his door and heard his name called and the man ascending the stairs laboriously with the great package. He went down and met the man halfway and helped him carefully, gently, to avoid unnecessary noise and because of the nature of the contents.

Up in his room he paid the balance and a good tip, and once alone, turned to his bed where the long bundle had been laid. Patiently at first and then furiously, cutting cord with kitchen knife, he undid the heavy wrapping, endeavoring not to look at her face until he could do so undisturbed. With anticipation already at the flood level, he stuffed all the paper and cord away, made certain that his door was locked, pulled down the window shades and then, with fumbling, trembling hands, shaking from head to foot with desire, he began to undress her.

That was one of two converging ways. The other way was more forthright. The other way was like this:

He had met her while working as a helper for a window dresser in a department store. There he had met her among others in the storeroom and there all his will to resist, strengthened by fear of fateful premonitions, had been brought down to its knees in helpless surrender.

He always managed to get hold of her first if they were using her, but one night—that was the time when they dressed the windows—another fellow beat him to it. He screamed at him not to do that. It was a howl torn from him before he had time to stop it. The fellow inquired what the matter was and he explained that he had thought he was dropping her, and the fellow answered that screaming like that had nearly made him drop her and then, with gross mockery, he asked another helper whether this chap was one of those.

That time he was sure he had given himself away and, after a surge of panic, the realization that the game was up made him feel remarkably calm. She was not appearing in this particular show, and when the others began marching along the corridor that led to the stairs up to the main floor, he lagged behind without even bothering to act up an excuse. Then he wrapped her carelessly in a large piece of canvas and rushed along the same corridor in the opposite direction. Then a door that opened on a short flight of stairs and he was on the street.

The street was empty at that hour but even so he walked cautiously, without undue haste. He met no one, however, until he realized that he had no clothes on and then he began to notice an occasional stroller, but it was dark and by holding her between him and the other person, his nakedness would not be noticed. After thus walking for a while, he used some of the canvas wrapping and held it around himself, holding her with his other arm. She was a precious burden and his love made her feel light. Being thus close to her under the same cover was a delightful foretaste of greater, immeasurable happiness to come. This made him quicken his step. He wanted to reach home soon and he did not want to be long exposed to detection. His lack of clothes might be noticed. He might be suspected, his crime discovered.

He broke into a run and flew swiftly through dark, abandoned streets. He chose a route of unfrequented byways of which he had no recollection, but he seemed to know his way unerringly. He met a few people and once he crossed a vast square swarming with traffic and revealing incandescence, but he went right through it unchallenged, no one taking notice of this strange, ghostly group that swam in the night like a cloud in the sky.

When he entered his room he found everything in great disorder; an overturned lamp was still lit. It was the scene of a desperate battle or a vulgar orgy. He deposited her on his bed, then straightened up the lamp and a few other things. Turning, he regarded her shape under the canvas. They were alone at last and then the boldness which had brought him safely here gave way to the well-known sadness and panic. He knew that panic well, one could never be completely free from it. It haunted you wherever you went. There was no escape. With superhuman efforts you shook it off, you cast it beyond your horizon, and then you heard a muffled rumble in the distance: panic creeping back, up and at you. You knew that you had not cast it off, but that it had broken loose from your control. And then it came like waves, swamping you, crushing you with overpowering centripetal force, like a hurricane of howling wolves, tearing away the ribbons of your scattered soul, drawing you into merciful insensibility.

When it had passed, you still stood there wondering. Why don't the wounds bleed if I am wounded to death? Or, if I am dead, why does the corpse stand?

By now both of them must have been missed. The kidnap, his unmentionable crime must have been discovered and probably this very minute he was being hunted like a dangerous beast, but seeing her shape in his bed under the canvas made the fear-clotted blood in his veins flow in torrents of molten lava, and with the pit of his stomach coiling like a gigantic snake strangling him from within, he approached her and drew back the canvas.

Here is where the two alternatives converged, crashed and fused together into the cry and the leap of an animal pouncing on her.

He woke up with an effort which propelled him from a bottomless shaft. He was exhausted and aching, and all desire except that for sleep had left him. The lamp was still burning. He felt the cold hard body and looked at her. Still the same expression, impassive, unchanged by what had happened. Was she never tired, that she continued to beckon and taunt when there was no life left in her victim? That unyielding, ever-demanding imperviousness revolted him and that strange inhuman smell—

He brought himself up from the bed, grabbed her brutally and shoved her stiff figure onto the large chair. The room was stifling and he gasped for breath. Then still semi-conscious, he staggered to a window and threw it open and went back to bed. Before sinking into sleep, he could see the same fixed expression that nothing could efface.

He walked in no particular direction through places that he did not know. The city had changed completely since he last saw it, with magnificent terraces overlooking immense boulevards. It was a wonderful city, but there was no one about. It seems that everybody was busy and he was the only one who had nothing to do but wrestle with his problem which was to rid himself of her. It was impossible to keep her in his room, always in sight, stiff, mute, accusing, and he was sure to be found out.

He dreaded going back to his room and finding her still there waiting for him, but there was nothing else he could do and night was falling and he must dispose of her body.

When he arrived home it was quite dark, and when he entered his room he could only see her outline from the last light coming through the window. He was careful and shrewd. He tiptoed about and did not turn the light on, so that no one could suspect that he had returned. He sat on the bed almost facing her, waiting for complete darkness, and he spoke to her in halting, disconnected sentences to pass the time, and when he looked out the window, it was night, complete, absolute night.

He crossed the room feeling his way, mindful of the furniture, to avoid making any noise, and peered out the other window which looked on to the backyard. Everything was pitch-black. All windows and shutters closed, but he knew from faint noises that everybody was behind them busy with their own things, their company and conversation, and this time he was also busy.

He opened his door and looked and listened to the silence and emptiness of the stairs and went back in and got hold of her, and with her body under one arm, her hip resting against his, went down swiftly and noiselessly, turned quickly past the hall entrance and made for the cellar.

There by the light of the single bulb, he found the shovel and went to the back stairs and out into the yard. He walked carefully, so carefully, until he was in the center where he was equally far from all who could hear, and with painstaking care began to dig, very cautiously because of the mixed gravel and broken glass in the dirt.

When he thought that the grave was deep enough, he placed her in, but it was not as deep as he had thought and whichever way he tried, either an arm or a leg or the head protruded, so he pulled her out again and dug some more. It was an endless task but he also knew that the night was endless. After a while he placed her in again but one of the legs still did not fit. He leaned on that and forced all his weight on it and it yielded until it was below the level of the ground. His job was nearly finished and hastily he pushed the dirt back around and over her and stole back to his room.

As he entered his room he heard a cackling laugh coming from the yard and knew that it must be the landlady, mocking him without having even recognized him in the darkness, but he did not care. His room was his alone again and he could sleep at last. He threw himself in bed.

A deep reverberating murmur, like the cooing of a tremendous flock of doves, woke him up. The day was well on its way and the murmur was coming from the backyard.

He left the bed and, like a somnambulist, went to the window and looked out, and then total wakefulness and realization froze him where he stood. The yard was alive with hostile, curious, jeering people. Every window open, crowded, as if every stone in the walls had become a face. It was a great well of terrible, condemning, shocked faces, their eyes all converging on the grave he had dug.

His sight slid down the inverted pyramid of all those gazes and then he saw it. Her leg was sticking out, plainly in view, a thin ridge of dirt still clinging along the uppermost side.

He knew then that he was finished. The thing he had feared most had come to pass, his secret discovered, a thing worse than any penalty he must pay for his crime. He realized that it was useless trying to fight anymore. She had won all the way through to a final, crushing victory. He was finished. Even now he could imagine the lynching party marching to his house, gathering reinforcements and fury.

He looked at all those faces, but they were not paying any attention to him. They continued to look down and comment in murmuring giggles, and their sound was like the cooing of a tremendous flock of doves.

Then he heard his own voice say: "My life is a suicide."

Resignedly he turned from the window and adjusted his rumpled attire. Without another look at the yard, he went out to give himself up.

It is sad to walk among people who look away or turn their backs on you, people who stand in small circles, their intimacy and conversation excluding you, stealing quick looks out of the corners of their eyes. It is sad to walk alone among crowds of hostile backs, knowing that your sentence has been pronounced, that you are a man condemned and your hours counted, when the sky is overcast and the light so white, and unbearable despair tears you apart and you walk like a soul in pain.

Why did he not run away if he was free to go where he pleased, if no one seemed to know him or notice him? He had been sentenced and that fact held him in its grip more powerfully than any chains or prison walls could. He knew that there was no hope. The sentence would be carried out.

He walked some more to get away from the smug crowds, the giggling, peering, cooing pharisees, and then reached streets that were empty, gray, forsaken as on a late Sunday afternoon. It was late and it was growing dark when he found himself in a street that was closed at the far end. There were no doors or windows, only a small iron door at the closed end. He walked almost the whole length of the street, feeling more alone than he had ever felt, until the dim rumble far behind made him turn around.

He saw them come toward him, several women all in black, with black veils covering their faces, and they moved down the broad gray alley in a jerky manner, their legs immobile, as if on roller skates. They came zigzagging down at him, careening ominously, their arms extended, their fingers pointing:

"You have killed·our daughter. You have killed our daughter."

He was trapped, at their mercy. He looked about for some escape and they were closing in, like mechanical dummies, their paths interweaving, converging on him. This was the end. The only way out was the little iron door and he could not go through that.

He woke up again, but it was broad daylight. He jumped from bed and fear catapulted into his brain. He saw the open window, the light that had been burning all through the night for all to see that gruesome, immobile figure propped up against the chair, pouring out his secret, his loathsome shame.

Rushing to the window, he pulled it down and then the shade. Then he turned out the light and stood there shivering, endeavoring to gather his thoughts. He avoided looking at her. He must get her out of his sight and he had no place to hide her. He could not let them find her in his room. Must get rid of her. It would be the most damning evidence, and there was a woman who came to clean up and he knew that the landlady also was in the habit of coming in and looking around when he was not there.

His immediate desire was to run away anywhere, far away, but he knew that one could not flee from such things; yet he could not stay there and again, while he was gone, someone would come in and find her. He had to stay and let no one come in, unless his crime had been found and they came to get him. He had to stay there with her in the same room, and if all went well, he could dispose of her that night. But he had to stay there with her all day.

Fighting revulsion, he lifted her from the chair and placed her into his only closet where his hanging clothes shrouded her and then pushed the door closed.

After that it was a question of waiting. He walked the limited space of his room back and forth, and once when passing the mirror, he saw himself and his own reflection terrified him. His face was all ruins, it was an earthquake. He decided to dress and after that he paced again back and forth, his hands going in and out of his pockets, the tenseness increasing, pulling back his scalp. He must do something to pass the time. He could not endure these waves that ran up and down his body any longer. Would God ever have pity on him and bring him peace and quiet, leave him alone?

There was a pot of cold coffee on his small stove. He thought of heating it but he had no patience to do anything inconsequential to the main issue and decided to drink it as it was, right out of the pot. After that he smoked cigarettes and moved about like an animal in a cage, looking for a way out. He did not want to sit on the chair she had occupied all that night but forced himself to do it, and the sensation that spread over his skin made him jump out and stand there wildly. Then he laughed and talked aloud, but his laughter and voice alone in that room was too hideous to bear. He lay back on his bed and tried to make out designs in the cracks in the ceiling, but guilty terror gripped his cranium and literally lifted him up. Thus he stood stock still, and once his eyes darted up and past the ceiling in one final appeal, and then remorse and hopelessness made him crouch and grasp his head as if to ward off the most terrible of all wraths, the wrath of the unknown.

After that he moved about, fear lashing at him, but he kept on moving, knowing that he could no longer defend himself. And at last darkness came. He lit the lamp and this set him into action. He went to the closet and flung the door open.

She came straight at him and into his arms: the same aloof, seductive, demure expression. This was eternal and he must control himself lest he go mad. Must endure anything, everything but go mad. He must save at least his mind.

Avoiding that hateful face, he dragged her to the center of the room and there lay her on the floor. The method was simple. She made too long a bundle to carry without arousing suspicion and he wondered how he had ever taken that risk. She was now heavy and he felt so tired!

His tiredness made him quieter and as such was a blessing. From a drawer he took a cheap saw he kept with other tools for small chores. All these household tools suggested to him a life of lonely masturbatory self-sufficiency culminating in this disaster. He moved with deliberation. He studied her, trying to think of her only as an object that must be disposed of. He considered the neck and discarded that as it would not make the whole much shorter. He decided on the legs, high up, near the hips, and he began.

The saw slipped and it was difficult holding her steady for the operation there on the floor. He looked around endeavoring to discover a better way and then he brought a chair over and, laying her across it, he set one foot upon her and began again carefully endeavoring to keep the saw in line.

After a time which seemed inordinately long, he had made a shallow groove, but in his cramped position, he was perspiring and his arm already tired. He hacked away desperately, his head and face burning, yet the rest of him chill and clammy, but he did not seem to be making any headway. The stuff packed around the teeth of the saw, then gripped it, and the inadequate tool bent.

He stopped and straightened up, gasping for air, and the smell of her dust on the floor, over his shoe, still floating in the air, penetrated and choked him. He decided to try the kitchen knife, and as he walked away, he heard her body fall heavily to the floor. He came back and furiously attacked her with the knife as she lay on the floor, but he soon gave that up and then stabbed away insanely until the blade bent. He cast the knife aside and, sitting astride her, pulled her leg with all his might, trying to break it or bend it, and once again he rose and, in a fit of vesania, jumped on her repeatedly like one possessed.

Finally he stopped and stood in paralyzed indecision, surveying the grisly scene, panting, bathed in perspiration, his lungs bursting, like a beast cornered after a long chase. He could not imagine what was the stuff she was made of —some devilish new invention of incredible permanence, something that would last forever, that would stand long after he had succumbed, something eternal.

She was indestructible, impervious to everything, and her face, her attitude, continued to call him from the floor, relentlessly, bent on pulling him down to her, on destroying him. He looked all around him in an atavistic reflex, and it was then that the fireplace met his intuition flush and burst upon it.

It was a large enough fireplace, and even if it could not accommodate all of her length, he could push her in as she yielded to the flames. Now at last he was her master.

He picked up her clothes and packed them loosely on top of the ashes. Then he laid her on top, head first; only her legs protruded at an angle. That was it: begin at the head and thicker part of the body. And then the same phrase flowed through his mind: The fire of his love—the fire of his love—And this time he laughed and was not frightened, and he was still laughing when he applied the match.

The clothes took the fire easily and then it touched her. It spread suddenly alive, a sheet of blinding flame, too strong to be absorbed by the flue, jumping outside the fireplace. In one instant it ran along her legs, yet without seeming to eat at them, but glowing dazzlingly from her surface. It ran along her dust leading to the chair and then the old rug was also burning. He backed away, slapping the flames from his shoe and the cuff of his trousers. He saw her there all on fire and still whole, maddeningly incandescent in her final decisive triumph. What was she made of, God? What was she made of?

The fire on the rug was spreading to the furniture. He stood a moment petrified by a panic he had never known before and knew that he was doomed. A white, thick, asphyxiating smoke filled the room with her unearthly odor. The flames darted at him, reaching like possessive prolongations of her limbs, and he recoiled beaten and then ran. He ran wildly for his life, threw the door open, and as he scrambled down the stairs, he could hear the room behind roaring like a furnace.

He emerged in the street and gulped large mouthfuls of the cool night air, and as he ran he looked back and up and saw the flames leaping out of his windows, giving away his secret, proclaiming his loathsome crime, damning him and mixing in infernal chorus with the accursed instant response of fire engine sirens and angry red clouds that rose with unchecked fury to make the sky blush in untold shame.

He fled repeating obsessedly: "Is this the fire of my love?" And as he turned the corner, he saw the engine on its way, swallowing up his path, cutting off his escape, bearing down on him to exact retribution and extinguish the fire of his love.

I was brought back to the present surroundings by the roar of laughter which greeted the end of the limerick about the fellow called Dave.

Fulano had fallen forward on the table, his face hidden, his head resting on his arms, and his frame trembled ever so slightly.

"Too much to drink," somebody said indifferently. "Should be the signal to break up the party."

The last group was leaving. Garcia had just gone a short while ago with Cáceres for whom he had developed an admiration verging on superstition. Then followed La Niña de los Madroños and her mother with the Spanish importer who with the aid of some friends had carried his shawls and tapestries to his car parked down the street. The last group contained La Colombina, Pinto, Lunarito and Bejarano and also some others who, probably because of the late hour and the alcoholic consumption, I cannot recall. As they paraded past Dr. de los Rios, Don Pedro, and the Señor Olózaga, I thought that the responsibility for the party had been tacitly bestowed upon them.

Of that last scene I can remember only two things clearly:

Lunarito was in front of Don Pedro. She took a red flower from her hair and threw it at him: "To one of the best and the most castizo."

He caught it deftly: "Thank you, my child, and I will not forget today and your dancing. You know? The memory of some experiences, like this flower—as they say, it perfumes longer than it lasts."

Others said good night and then La Colombina came forward. She stood very symmetrically erect, holding a white flower with both her hands as if it were a prayer book, or as if she were going to kiss it fervently, and she recited:

"Of all the men I knew who then left Spain, you and Dr. de los Rios are the only ones I remember—the Señor Olózaga, I only had the honor today. Over there, they thought you were mad and I am glad that this country has not returned your sanity. I should like to hear your band. They say it is the best."

"I doubt you would like it—you know—" His hand moved with dismay. "But what can one do? Perhaps someday, again in Spain." His usual laughter was missing. "That is what we always say: perhaps someday, and we know the day never comes. We leave in order to think of returning, in order to love more. It is a very old vice and that makes it a virtue, but let us dream, my dear."

With a very neat curtsy, she offered him the white flower. He held it tightly together with the red one and bowed deeply.

After they left we stood about for a while aimlessly. The place denuded of decorations, under garish fluorescent lights and no more farolitos, looked dismal as any place looks after a big party. We decided to go.

"Coming along, Moor?"

"No, I think I'll stay a while yet." He was methodically taking empty bottles from the last table he had occupied by the patio, placing them on the floor, and then replacing them with full or partially full bottles he gathered from nearby tables. His face had the pallor induced by alcohol when it has reached the point of saturation. Then, heaving a deep sigh, he sat down heavily. The bottles were arranged before him like a fence. He poured wine into a glass and placed the two flowers in it.

"Now I am well barricaded for the rest of the night. Don't worry, Chink, I will close the place when I go. I have keys." He spoke tiredly: "You are the material owner, but I am the father, the spiritual owner of El Telescopio. I will take good care of my child."

"Don't you think you would sleep more comfortably on a bed? You have had enough it seems."

"No. I want a bed for my soul and not my body, and this is it. One never has enough, life is short but no one knows what it's all about—little time—the fourth perpendicular shortened by perspective of memory or vision. Who knows? The place is empty now but the recollections of the day still reverberate here and in our memories. We all pass, go home, sleep, but the scene remains here entangled in the corners. The great music of Cáceres echoes and he rises in our minds still omnipotent when all the rest has fallen, making us create recollections of things which perhaps never took place but might have been if life were as we want it, to build up a past that dissipates our feeling of futility. Even I don't know what it's all about and yet it all must be so simple—but I know that the scene still lives here and I want to move along with it into time." His head fell forward and he regarded the two flowers in front of him: "Wine for the pretty Spanish flowers grown in another land."

Then we went, but at the door, Dr. de los Rios turned impulsively and walked back to Don Pedro. He ran his hand through the brush of his hair, pushing back the head, and looked affectionately into the pale face, like one would do with a sullen, spoiled child who has done enough mischief for a day, but there was still that look of indomitable defiance in the Moor's face, tempered with one of approval. His eyes swept slowly, appraisingly, up the figure of his friend and with quiet endorsing pride, as one delivering the final imprimatur: "You are very all right—one of the few real ones left—very good, very good."

As Dr. de los Rios released him to join us, the head fell forward again and that is how we left him: still looking at the flowers.

Outside we stumbled on empty bottles. De los Rios and the Señor Olózaga consulted the time and proposed to go to Brooklyn Bridge to watch the sunrise. Not for me. I wanted to go home. They walked down the street. Someone had started a rubbish fire on a corner and I saw them outlined against the glow. Then I looked back at the café and saw for the first time its real name on the window glass, in chipped black and gold letters. It read: CAFÉ LA DEMOCRACIA.

I must have looked at it many times before but probably always from the inside, and seen that way it had never meant anything.

Then I started for the West Side through the empty streets, the music of Cáceres still assaulting my mind in waves of memory, in bright visions, making the mind a torch in the night. I knew that all those who had lived there that day must feel as I did, because of our common bonds, that the thoughts that had been evoked, whether real or imagined, had proven authoritative, legitimate, and with the music still in my ears I began to understand Don Pedro and possibly my people and even other peoples, within myself.

But then, the present surroundings began to assert themselves, the visions began to fade, the waves to abate, and as I crossed Park Row, another memory insinuated itself: the strains of the dusky, doleful waltz: "The Bowery, the Bowery—I'll never go there anymore."

Was this intuition of fate, a threat of destiny, or an evident conclusion? I lit the last cigarette of the night.

The flame biting into my fingers made me shake off the match and the dark walls closed in on me again. Blindly I rushed out of that room, leaving behind an empty space in a bookcase, like an open mouth, more eloquent than all the volumes around it and, on the floor, exhumed, a book like an open grave.

Outside the Moor was leaning against the iron railing still smoking the cigarette I had given him. A stiff breeze had come up and I saw the sparks fly away like constellations carried by the wind of time.

"You see? Now it is all done and it did not take long. One knows these things—one knows—" He held me when I turned to close the door: "Leave it open, man; that way they can escape more easily, come out into the open, mix with the other Americaniards. Get me?"

We started walking and then heard the door banging in the wind as we went.

A few days later—Sunday afternoon it was—Dr. de los Rios and I walked down to the park, went around the 59th Street Plaza, and then down to Radio City and wandered around there looking at shop windows, the people and the flower displays. We had little to talk about and nothing to do and were, as they say, following our own noses, wondering how to pass the time. Clouds were beginning to obscure the sun and with it drive away the last vestiges of desire to do anything. As we emerged again onto Fifth Avenue, we beheld a well-known figure.

The Moor was leaning on his shillelagh and against the wall. He appeared to be looking at the passing throngs, but his head was cocked to one side and anyone could see that his ear was glued to the radio set of a couple of boys, listening to a tune he had made popular. He saw us and signaled to us not to interrupt and we stood there waiting until the song ended. Only then did he open his arms and limp forward:

"Oh, amiable youths—" he recited. "Walking on Fifth Avenue like the elegants— That's the Spaniard for you. Always adaptable, going where others go, becoming one of them and then, meeting others like themselves. Here we are: three Americaniards." He spoke to me: "You are in very good company, you know?" His hand moved, implying in nice detail how good the company was: "But you both look bored, not mutually complementary, but understandable. You needed a third one. You were lost because two straight lines can enclose no space. Three is the minimum, although some hyper-modern foreign geometers, totally incapable of understanding the obvious, might argue the point."

We admitted that we were at a loss for what to do.

"Well, let's walk down and wonder together. Something will occur—"

"We have walked enough and I was thinking—" With extended arm, Dr. de los Rios swept an invitation across the avenue to Saint Patrick's Cathedral. "What about it? Let's go in and sit awhile. Meditation is good."

"Oh, no! Today is Sunday, a day of rest, and I have meditated enough in my life—"

"But not in the right places, you infidel Moor."

"—besides, if we are going to church, we might as well go to a Spanish church, and I don't know of any in this neighborhood. A church in English has never seemed quite right to me. Catholicism is a heritage with us. We made it famous. We understand it. The others don't know what it's all about— We are living contradictions. I boast Moorish blood and then claim priority to the religion that banished my people from my country."

He went on like that and, still arguing, we crossed Fifth Avenue. The day had become overcast. Ominous darkness hung over the downtown section. We stopped before the cathedral and, with the day suddenly gone dark, the glow that came from within was more noticeable.

"Nonsense! By the same token I maintain that any Catholic church is Spanish in essence. You yourself have insisted that God is from Madrid or Sevilla and a Roman Catholic, and when a Spaniard enters any Catholic church or any country in the Americas, he does so as if it were his own house by divine right. Agreed? Furthermore, this place is named after the patron of the Irish." As he ascended the steps, de los Rios beckoned to us: "Come on in. This is growing complicated."

"No, not today. A Spaniard is a Catholic without having to go into a church to pray. It is of the potence and the essence, but not of the presence. He is that way as his eyes are light or dark, but he does not have to pray in church. His whole life is a prayer and an expiation. He is inevitably a mystic."

Dr. de los Rios looked long at him in his inimitable wide way: "Yes, and we do not have to work at it all the time. Sometimes we can rest at it, sit in there and rest." He indicated the street: "One gets tired of this."

Don Pedro addressed me again: "This Dr. Jesucristo, always trying to save souls painlessly— He is a castizo. Just like him to go in there— and why not, if he wants to? You let him go and come with me. We'll go down and find something to do."

"Not this time. Don't let that infidel Moor tempt you. Let him go alone to his own perdition— Oh, come on, Moor." De los Rios's hat was already in his hand.

"No, not yet. Perhaps some other time—you know—" He turned away: "I am going down there. So long." His somber figure limped down the avenue which was strangely silent and empty, and we heard the syncopated rhythm of his steps and his stick on the pavement as he went down into the darkening distance. Only then did I notice the fateful Hispano-Suiza following slowly.

Dr. de los Rios had turned to enter the church, and I also saw his back outlined against the glow coming from the door and fancied that it formed a more concentrated halo around his head. I stood on the steps undecided, possibly hesitating more between emotions than between thoughts, not knowing what to think and even less knowing what to do, and suddenly I hesitated no more. I almost shouted: "Wait for me!"

Sitting there next to Dr. de los Rios, I felt confidently safe and looked at the surroundings in the candlelight and, considering the other things I had seen from the heights in the light of day and in the lights of night and the other things I had remembered or imagined in the depths by the light of a match turned into an Aladdin's lamp, decided that I could do nothing about it. I had seen only a kaleidoscope of fancies materialized by forgotten chromos, dirty, discolored chromos. This is what the possible visions of greatness suggested by the conquistadores had finally come to: rhapsodic, nomadic incidents with hanging tarnished threads of past splendor out of time and out of place. Chromos in disrepute.

To express this in my own language would be superfluous. To attempt to describe it in another's, impossible. In Spanish I don't have to explain my nation or countrymen. In English, I can't. It is the question of the synthetic method as opposed to the analytical. In Spanish one sees and things remain unquestioned and clear. In English, one studies and uncovers meanings that one does not understand. It is then that, as I said in the beginning, complications set in.

But were those things from other times and other places really as great as they seemed now? Contrary to space, time increases the proportions of such events, but like the enlargment of a picture, what they gain in size, they lose in sharpness until they are so vague as to seem boundless. In either case it was for someone else to bring back their true colors, to integrate and then exhibit them in the primitive and complete equation of their significance, a job for a pen much better than mine, which is rusty, not so much for lack of use but because it is no feather from a soaring wing, work for a pen mightier than the swords of those same conquerors, to span the years and distances, to elucidate the vaster meaning of these things and in the longer view of history, from the heights of the present, to decide whether my ancestors were but immigrants disguised as conquerors, or whether all other aliens are but conquerors disguised as immigrants.

New York, 1948

ABOUT THE AUTHOR

Felipe Alfau was born in 1902 in Barcelona, Spain. He emigrated
during World War I to the United States, where he studied music
and wrote music criticism for a brief period for *La Prensa*, the
Spanish newspaper in New York. Deciding to write in English
because he felt he could not reach a Spanish audience, he completed *Locos* in 1928, which took eight years to find a publisher. In
1929 Doubleday published a children's book of his, *Old Tales from
Spain*. After the publication of *Locos*, Alfau worked in a bank in
New York City as a translator. *Chromos* was written in the 1940s but
never published until 1990. Felipe Alfau now lives in retirement in
New York City.